WALKING
WITH THE
DEAD

Charles Domokos

Black Rose Writing | Texas

ISBN: 978-1-68433-505-3
PUBLISHED BY BLACK ROSE WRITING
www.blackrosewriting.com

Printed in the United States of America
Suggested Retail Price (SRP) $22.95

Walking With The Dead is printed in Baskerville

*As a planet-friendly publisher, Black Rose Writing does its best to eliminate unnecessary waste to reduce paper usage and energy costs, while never compromising the reading experience. As a result, the final word count vs. page count may not meet common expectations.

To my grandmother Giselle, whose life-long work
at the Budapest State Opera House provided for
my father's and aunt's classical music careers
and made writing this story possible.

Special Thanks: Yvonne Bennett, Jeanne Collachia, Robert Grant, Tom
Ray, also to Stella Ong for proofreading the manuscript, and to my two
Pomeranians, Sushi and Wallace who accompanied me on the journey.

WALKING WITH THE DEAD

CHAPTER 1
EMERGENCY HEARING

Charlie Tobias, already in his mid-forties, eager for a more stable calling than singing in suburban music choirs around Los Angeles, was changing careers. Dressed in his only pin-striped suit whose deep blue threads complemented the blue of his eyes, he sat down across from the "G.Q." cover worthy law firm's principal, where Charlie's interview for an "Associate Attorney" position had just started. Earl Guarder, sitting behind a carved mahogany desk, looked the part of a successful attorney and was, at least, successful enough to hire a clueless Associate for his struggling Fairtown law practice.

Earl scanned Charlie's ivory bond paper resume.

"Undergraduate major in classical music? Unusual background to be an attorney."

"It taught me strong discipline, logic, precision – detail."

Earl dropped the resume and locked eyes with Charlie. Charlie knew, this was a make-or-break moment, and it was crucial to look at ease. Earl's thin, handsome face relaxed into a welcoming nod.

"I think we'll get along. Each of us comes to the practice of law in our mid-careers."

"You were an astute legal commentator on Channel Six. 'Earl's Law' was razor sharp and witty."

"Thanks. I need a Probate Associate. The position is yours if you're interested."

Charlie tried to think back on his night law school to remember what "probate" was.

"You mean like 'Trusts and Wills?'"

"Well, not much about 'Trusts.' Our probate practice is everyday disputes among families over who gets what slice of the pie after daddy dies, and mom is in some rest home."

"It sounds intriguing, but I studied business law."

"Probate is so rewarding. You get to make all the difference in people's lives."

Charlie thought for a moment. *I need a job, bad.*

Earl saw the hesitation. "Death is a challenging and legally crucial part of life. Clients expect a mature attorney, not some jacked-up kid, worried about scoring a snow bunny at a ski resort."

Charlie made up his mind, reached his hand across and Earl Guarder reached his.

"It sounds challenging. I'm in."

"Welcome aboard. Let me introduce you around. We're a close knit office. Like a family."

With the miserable working conditions at The Law Offices of Earl Guarder and Associates, the family turn-over was every six months.

Now, six and a half years later, in the fall of 2007, as the downtown Los Angeles signal light at the corner of Temple Street and Grand Avenue turned red, Charlie balanced his frayed legal valise bulging with probate files on the chewing gum pockmarked sidewalk while he paused to catch his breath.

Charlie focused on his destination across the street – Los Angeles' Central Court's probate courtroom. In that courtroom, "Department 17," the subject was always death, and pin-striped attorneys from major law firms showed up to peck at estates of the deceased, morsel by morsel and to lay waste to small legal practitioners like Earl S. Guarder and Associates.

Charlie filed emergency papers two days ago and was assigned this morning for a hearing to solve the "Estate of Barry Beneshan's" newest crisis. David Alex, the wealthy, real estate mogul, the Estate's recently appointed administrator, wasn't able to do his job.

Charlie was about to petition Judge Matthew H. Bittenkopf to relieve Mr. Alex of his duties and appoint Charlie's other client, Angel Sedona instead.

Mr. Alex was found slumped over his desk in his Santa Monica office.

Charlie received the distressing news in a panicked telephone call two days ago, from Alex's business assistant, Gary Frank. The high-strung assistant never called Charlie unless it was an emergency.

Gary Frank's voice trembled as he whispered seeing the slumped body with a knife stuck in the back of the neck. Gary had panicked, screamed for help, ran out of Alex's office into the hallway and dialed the "911" Emergency Dispatcher.

The paramedics and the police arrived in less than ten minutes to Alex's imposing west side Vision Associates penthouse office. Gary was not brave enough to re-enter Alex's office, but he was able to see the cause of death and it was not pretty.

A red Swiss army knife stuck in the victim's neck as the body slumped over a kidney-shaped glass desk covering it with seeping blood. Gary described the gruesome scene to Charlie in that disturbing phone call. The victim's arms extended from the swivel chair, reaching for the contorted fingers' apparent goal, the desk phone. The side of the neck still oozed blood.

The last time Charlie recalled a bloody knife splattering was when he was still performing in a few operas as a choir member seven or eight years ago, and he was dressed in an Italian peasant costume in the North Valley Opera Company's production of *I Pagliacci*, the ever-popular, bloody Sicilian opera by Ruggero Leoncavallo. Charlie's rich baritone voice gasped on cue as the cuckolded clown, Canio's spring-loaded prop knife plunged through his arch-rival Silvio's blousy Neapolitan shirt, and fake blood spurted onto the Valley Community Center's modest stage including on Charlie's costume, all to the delight and claps of the suburban Los Angeles crowd.

This time, Gary's horrified voice on the phone underscored that the knife-thrust blood-letting was real.

Two nights ago, Charlie, shaken by Gary's call, barely put his telephone down, when his other Estate client, Angel Sedona called and also conveyed information about the shocking death. She called right before Charlie, having decided to shelve the crisis until the following day, was set to leave the empty law office and head home, too tired to think through the implications of a client's murder.

Charlie, after calming Angel's panic, took a deep breath, and pondered the best course of action. Charlie made up his mind, texted Earl, "Client David Alex dead. Please send instructions." He received an immediate reply text: "Find another administrator, now!"

Charlie sat at his desk in his law office two nights ago, following Earl's instructions to write a petition for an emergency court hearing.

■   ■   ■   ■   ■

As the downtown Los Angeles traffic light turned green, Charlie dodged the left-turning buses, reached the courthouse side of Temple Street, and passed the gaunt homeless woman who staked her position in the courthouse's marble recess. Charlie noticed the homeless well-groomed woman every morning he came to the court over the course of almost seven years.

In his mind, Charlie had given the woman a name: "Rose." He liked seeing "Rose" at her customary spot. She was an oasis of calm in his chaotic Associate life.

Outside "Department 17" on the courthouse's first floor, Charlie pulled out the engraved "Charlie Tobias, Associate, Law Offices of Earl S. Guarder & Associates" business card, ready to drop it in to the clerk's basket.

He pushed in with the attorneys, grieving relatives, administrators, sundry rascals and peripheral supplicants.

Charlie saw Mark Ashland and sidled next to him but not too close. Counselor Ashland, a certified probate specialist appointed by the court, represented the minor-aged beneficiary of the convoluted Barry Beneshan estate, Gabriella Beneshan. Gabriella was headed for the fifth grade, introverted, smart. She knew she didn't have a dad, and that was that. She lived with her mother Angel Sedona, in a Beneshan estate-owned modest two story craftsman house in the suburbs of Los Angeles.

Angel had been Barry's wife in all but the legal sense. That was a source of problems with this estate, along with her dead boy-friend, Barry Beneshan not having made a will.

Ashland's diminutive stature was buttressed by an expansive ego.

Charlie nodded a polite, whispered "hello."

Ashland was always brusque: "Was it a heart attack?"

Charlie considered how much to reveal, shook his head "no."

"Suicide?"

All Charlie wrote in his "Notice" was that Alex passed suddenly, and a new estate administrator must be appointed.

Charlie knew why Ashland would think "suicide." That was the rumor behind the subject of the estate's death. Charismatic wunderkind entrepreneur, Barry Beneshan, just turned thirty-three years old, was found face up, by the police, hands outstretched, on the bathroom floor of his Venice commune hideaway about a year and some months ago.

Charlie decided it was best to be open. "Alex had a knife through his throat." Ashland pondered.

Angel burst through the courtroom door, headed towards Charlie. Angel Sedona was a beautiful woman in her early thirties, fiery and energetic. She should have been the administrator in charge of the estate, but she had a major fault as far as the court was concerned. She was poor. The bond company declined to insure her for an estate with huge assets and debts.

At first, the court appointed Jones, Sharke, a downtown Los Angeles law firm to deal with the estate's business, but properties foreclosed, businesses failed, until Angel and The Law Offices of Earl Guarder convinced Judge Bittenkopf to fire Jones, Sharke and approve Angel's stand-in nominee, elegant, wealthy builder and developer, David Alex, as administrator. That was some six months ago.

Angel moved next to Charlie. She exuded warmth from her large brown eyes and an endearing smile. Her combed light-brown curls fell around her lovely face. Her modest attire included a grey jacket over her ironed white blouse, not quite a match for her tan skirt and dark brown dress shoes. She looked coordinated enough for a court appearance.

"I'm sorry, I'm late," she whispered, leaning over to give a side-ways hug. Charlie returned her hug. It was always a warm hug, asking for kindness, promising caring.

Ashland nodded in Angel's direction. That's the most he would do for anyone. Charlie whispered to Angel: "We're far down the list."

The well-coifed redheaded court clerk, dressed in a green plaid suit, got up, faced the public. She requested everyone's attention.

As Charlie mumbled the Pledge of Allegiance to the flag of the United States of America and its Constitution, he glanced around the oak paneled courtroom that reeked of generations of aspirations, disappointments, triumphs and defeats.

There was a good turnout of interested creditors for the hearing. The only missing major player was Captain Jack Wonder, U.S.N. Wonder was a decorated Navy Special Operations Officer, before his discharge from the Navy and then becoming Barry's clandestine partner in shady real estate deals.

Neither Charlie nor Angel was surprised at Captain Wonder's absence. He was a ruthless stealth fighter, a Navy SEAL master of clandestine attacks.

Formalities over, the clerk informed the supplicants, court was open. Judge Matthew H. Bittenkopf took the bench. He was energetic, wiry, in his fifties – almost too young to be a judge. He ruled about death more often than Vulkan, the god of Hades.

Part of the advantage of Charlie's probate job, or so he had told himself when he signed up for it, was that estate clients were always dead. However, despite such apparent finality, life would go on about their concerns, desires, assets, and debts – in probate court.

It was almost ten a.m. when the clerk read off: "Calendar number 164, Estate of Barry Beneshan." Charlie and Angel hurried past the swinging wooden gate, to stand in front of the judge's dais in the courtroom's well. The other attorneys also swarmed to the wide oak table that served as a formal resting place for briefs and notes.

"Charlie Tobias of The Law Offices of Earl Guarder. I have next to me, Angel Sedona, mother of the beneficiary to the estate. Mr. Alex, alas, cannot appear."

"Okay, Mr. Tobias," Judge Bittenkopf nodded. "I read your papers. Apparently, the upshot of this is that we need a new administrator."

"Yes, your honor. I move that Ms. Angel Sedona, who is the mother of Gabriella Beneshan, the minor beneficiary of the estate, be appointed, without bond."

Ashland shifted his feet and followed with his low-key distinctive crisp voice: "Your honor, since Ms. Sedona hasn't qualified for a bond, we oppose her appointment. I, on behalf of the beneficiary of the estate, nominate Richard Battle, a professional estate administrator."

A drably dressed, silver haired man stepped next to Ashland. "Good morning, your honor, Richard Battle, estate fiduciary."

"Good morning, Mr. Battle. Thank you for stepping up."

The attorney from the creditor law firm interjected: "Henry Gilliam, your honor, for Jones, Sharke. The estate was ordered to pay our law firm for work we did prior to Mr. Alex's appointment and Mr. Alex never complied."

A whale-sized elegant litigator, with hair falling onto his right temple in the tradition of Clarence Seward Darrow gestured with his arms to all corners of the court with considerable flair, "Richard Soda, your honor representing Eric Dart and Dart Construction Company. We have outstanding claims and an unpaid judgment."

The third major creditor attorney, smooth, lean, affable, chimed in with a mock concerned voice. "Leon Lambert for Blue Orchid Financials, L.L.C., your honor. Ms. Sedona can't be trusted as an officer of the court."

Angel seethed. Charlie caught her eye to calm her, but it was too late.

"Haven't you vultures stolen enough of Barry's money?" Angel spoke up with conviction and defiance. Charlie groaned. Judge Bittenkopf brought down his gavel.

"Ms. Sedona, keep silent or leave this courtroom!"

Angel realized she had not helped her cause. "Yes, your honor. I'm sorry." She looked to Charlie to pick up the dropped lance, bit her nails.

Charlie tried the practical approach: "Your honor, the estate has no funds to pay Mr. Battle's fees."

"Well, then, Mr. Battle will supervise selling off whatever assets need to be sold, won't he?" Judge Bittenkopf apparently made up his mind.

Henry Gilliam interjected into the face-off: "Our law firm is fine with Mr. Battle. He must sell all estate properties, including Ms. Sedona's home to pay our overdue legal bills."

Charlie was about to object.

"That's what we'll do, Mr. Tobias," Judge Bittenkopf's voice became authoritative. "We'll appoint Mr. Richard Battle. Write up the order."

Charlie knew there was no point to argue. Judge Bittenkopf like Solomon, liked to "split the baby" in half.

Whether it would live was the attorney's problem.

CHAPTER 2
AN UNEXPECTED VISITOR

Late that night, Charlie opened the side gate, walked past the trellises and pushed open the tiny door to his Hollywood studio bungalow he used as a launching pad, when he needed to get to far-off early court hearings.

"Working late, aren't you?"

Charlie dropped his satchel. It split open, scattering toiletries and baked rolls across the Berber carpet.

Sitting in front of him at the minuscule round dinette table was a dapper, casual David Alex. Charlie looked closely at the elfish face, the neck. There was no sign of a knife wound.

"What are you doing here – you're dead?"

"Gary left your address on my desk," said the visitor, with a self-satisfied twinkle.

Charlie remembered with chagrin giving Alex's assistant the bungalow address when Charlie needed Alex's original signature on a court document. Charlie never locked the bungalow as his only intruders until now in the quiet Farmdell neighborhood were four legged raccoons and possums.

"I told Judge Bittenkopf you were dead." Charlie flashed on the consequences of having lied to the court.

Alex chuckled, self-confidently, looked at Charlie as if being in Charlie's space was perfectly acceptable. Charlie didn't find Alex's laughter infectious.

"My apologies. It was important that you and Angel didn't know, so you wouldn't intentionally lie to the court."

That Angel wasn't in on the deception offered only slight comfort.

Charlie flashed on the best scenario for the deception: Judge Bittenkopf would lose trust in Charlie and rule against him accordingly. And the worst-case scenario?

"I will lose my law license," Charlie shuddered.

"Well, it'll be our little secret. Besides, it was just luck I wasn't killed. Harry, my brother, was waiting for me at my office. He's only a year older, about my size. It was his body slumped on the desk. He didn't have I.D. on him."

Charlie's look conveyed that he didn't believe Alex.

Alex, seeing Charlie's skepticism, fleshed out the events of the previous Tuesday night.

"Someone's been trying to kill me ever since I was appointed administrator. I'm the proverbial cat with nine lives, losing them – one by one."

Despite his doubts, Charlie was curious. Alex sensed Charlie was hooked.

"After the court appointed me, I thought I'd better check out the estate properties. I drove to Woodfall one weekend. I was trying to see what we could salvage from that drug infested Misty Acres Apartments cesspool, when the tile roof above me, crashed. Lucky for me, that court receiver took the brunt of the tumbling tiles."

Charlie remembered the incident. Dennis Millhouse, the harried court-appointed receiver overseeing the Central California apartment motels that Beneshan and Wonder co-owned, cushioned the falling tiles with his shoulders and left arm. Alex escaped unscathed.

Angel suspected the accident was engineered by Boohau Cyclops, the charismatic, now former Cham apartment manager who was a deity to the ethnic Southeast Asia Cham residents. When Millhouse fired him, Cyclops lost his rent-free status for his Misty Acres apartment and was unhappy.

Millhouse tried to collect the rent as it came due, waving the Woodfall Superior Court Order in front of Boohau's one good eye without success.

"Angel suspected it wasn't an accident," Charlie said.

Charlie's guest placed his feet up, by way of an answer, on the small white ottoman at the side of the daybed that filled in the space next to the table.

As much as he was distraught by being ensnared in the deception, Charlie was also terribly annoyed by Alex's attitude of entitlement to Charlie's personal space as he looked at the soles of Alex's shoes. Alex must have seen the scowl, took his polished brown shoes off the ottoman.

"I flew on to New Orleans to review the two other estate properties. There was another incident I didn't tell you about." Alex paused to let this sink in.

Despite himself, Charlie's scowl disappeared and his eyes opened wider. He cocked his head, appreciating that the brown oxford loafers were definitely Bruno Malle or some other designer brand.

"A rental car waited for me so I could inspect the Mississippi River chateau, that *La Reve du Monde* place. Wow! Well, I'm doing at least sixty and there's a sharp turn up ahead, and I hit the brakes — Nothing! Luckily, I drove onto the marsh and jumped out before the car sank."

"Why didn't you let me know?"

"I had collision coverage."

"I'm glad you're okay."

"Thank you. It was odd, but I didn't have time to stick around. I had a flight to catch."

"You're a hell of an administrator."

"I only agreed to sign on after I found out the value of the properties."

When Charlie courted Alex to become the estate administrator, Charlie was careful to make it clear Alex could not profit from his court-appointed role. Yet, Alex seemed to have an agenda above and beyond serving for the joy of civic pride.

A wave of exhaustion washed over Charlie. "Okay, I get it. Look, I've got to get some sleep. Come to the office tomorrow evening. I'm sorry about your brother."

"Yeah. Thanks. Having a brother isn't always a blessing. He was waiting to squeeze me for some dough."

Charlie nodded in a noncommittal way, too tired to pursue Alex's thought.

Alex pulled a letter from his address book and handed it to Charlie. Charlie unfolded it:

Yu don't became administrator. Quit, or own estate worry.

The handwriting was meticulous, the lettering arching backwards, unusual, except for left-handed people. The note wasn't signed. Charlie handed it back.

"Well, whoever wrote it could use a few English lessons."

Alex nodded. "I want out. I'm resigning."

Charlie thought of all he and Angel had done to persuade Alex to sign on. Like much else with probate practice, it was wasted energy by the living, to clean up the messes of the dead.

The new administrator, Richard Battle — if he remained in place after Alex's non-death was sorted out — would soon realize there was no cash in any estate account. He'd resign, and the estate would collapse into bankruptcy.

Charlie's waning energies focused on an immediate issue. As Angel's representative, he had to act in her best interest. However, he also represented Alex and had a duty to represent Alex's interests with zeal. At the moment, the two interests may be in conflict. Then again, he didn't want to cause a client's murder.

"Call me tomorrow. We'll work it out so you can resign."

"I can't go home. I'm terrified."

"Where are you staying?"

"With you. You're my attorney."

"Gosh." Charlie tried to calm.

"By the way, don't tell Angel. This is all attorney-client privilege."

Charlie nodded. "Right."

"Some of Angel's friends? You never know."

Charlie did a quick mental inventory of Angel's friends — Gary Frank worked for Alex, and was a reputable mortgage broker who could lecture clients on the subtleties between no interest, no down payment loans and negative amortization loans before the sub-prime mortgage business and the national economy tanked. Gary was the original connection to Alex who had asked Alex to consider the administrator position. Charlie recalled it was Gary, who first called about Alex's supposed death.

"Gary doesn't know?"

"He's never met Harry. I was in the bathroom down the hall trying to avoid Harry when all this played out. I heard Gary's panicked call to the cops and skedaddled as the sirens approached."

Charlie catalogued connections: Gary, since his mortgage business collapsed in the spring of 2007, lodged in Angel's attic. Gary was tight with her questionable entourage.

Devlin D'Alessio, Angel's current boyfriend, was definitely a question mark. His willingness to risk others' moneys hid a Machiavellian streak. Charlie wouldn't be surprised to find Devlin was double-crossing Angel, with Jack Wonder or another Beneshan sidekick. But murder?

Charlie agreed with David Alex's caution and nodded. "Okay."

He couldn't miss the pleading look in Alex's eyes.

"Just for a few days. There's the futon."

Alex's eyes softened. "You're a hell of an attorney."

CHAPTER 3
CONTEMPT HEARING

The following morning, Charlie restrained himself from singing practice scales or one of his favorite operatic tunes as he tip-toed around Alex sleeping soundly on the futon, took a shower, threw on a not quite fresh suit, left his sleeping guest, stepped out the door, "clicked" the studio gate shut but not locked, threw his valise stuffed with briefs for his next hearing into the back seat of his car, and raced down the freeway back to court. Even a well-heeled client on the lam, interrupting your routine and snoring most of the night on your futon, wasn't an excuse to show up late in front of any judge.

■　　　■　　　■　　　■　　　■

Charlie jostled into probate Department 17 maneuvered through clumps of attorneys. He had his brown suit coat on, his tie knotted. He saw his client, Alice Mobley, a well-dressed, sociable lady in her mid-80's whose physical support not only included her usual hand-carved dark-wood walking cane, but also the bevy of young and old relatives who accompanied her to each court hearing. Charlie learned that family support in court made a huge difference in the final ruling. Judges respected family ties. Charlie hoped Alice was an unlikely candidate for the slammer, for "contempt of court," but you never knew, until the judge ruled.

In Alice's case, her deceased husband Ozzie Mobley was found permanently expired with one of his ladies, voluptuous Dixie May, still crying her eyes out, in a hotel penthouse suite at the Chacoshan Indian

Reservation Casino Hotel near Palm Springs. The panicked Dixie May, seeing her famous paramour gasping for breath, had called the paramedics during a strenuous day-time amorous interlude that preceded Ozzie's 5 p.m. parlor show in the Casino's lounge. By the time the paramedics got Ozzie out from between the sheets and tried to resuscitate him, legendary rhythm-and-blues warbler Ozzie Mobley was past his final tune.

Alice Mobley, Ozzie's widow, was trying to hang on to their modest home where she lived with her grown daughter Denise, a feminist science fiction writer who was well-respected in the surrounding Leimert Park neighborhood artistic community for her visionary stories about girl bands fighting for freedom in an intergalactic, totalitarian universe.

While Ozzie Mobley was alive, fights escalated between Ozzie and Alice regarding Ozzie's disposal of the family source of livelihood, a popular Crenshaw Avenue Los Angeles sausage eatery. "Pappa's Louisiana Sausage Shack" was the source of Ozzie and Alice Mobley's incomes during the difficult four decades when Ozzie's once-iconic vocal quartet, "The Castaways" had been cast off show business's radar. Ozzie, the sole owner of the eatery, signed over the diner to Dixie May in a contract, in which the benefits that he would receive were not clearly spelled out.

Attorney Sonny Field had seen a lot in his life as a thirty-eight year probate practitioner, but even he was shocked when Alice Mobley found the contract, and brought it to the Mobley family attorney's attention. According to the terms of the agreement, the only way to obtain the return of the sausage company to the Mobley family was if Ozzie would sign a Declaration stating he was no longer happy with Dixie's personal physical services. Alice kept wiping her brow with her linen handkerchief during that excruciating meeting, while Sonny Field explained the legalities to Alice in his tiny office in the Crenshaw mall. "She's a whore. Isn't that illegal? How can Ozzie give away what we worked for decades to a whore?"

Sonny Field calmed Alice down and explained that "happiness" was to be determined by Ozzie's interpretation, which considered a "subjective" standard. Alice cried, and insisted Sonny Field get the sausage factory back.

Sonny Field tried and failed. The court ruled that Dixie May was entitled to the fruit of the agreement as long as Ozzie was happy with her "physical" assistance.

Dixie May ended up keeping the sausage factory, and according to the bitter Mobley family, Ozzie's affections, as well. The court did appoint a conservatorship some eight years back to prevent Ozzie from continuing his largesse.

The court also appointed Attorney Clyvester Kurtz, an elegant barrister, to represent Ozzie and make sure Ozzie, who was going on 80 years old, was in good health to continue to work. At one point, prior to Charlie becoming involved, Kurtz, who served as Ozzie's attorney for some six years without being paid by either Ozzie, nor by Alice, obtained a court order to sell Alice's home and pay himself out of the proceeds.

Counselor Sonny Field forgot to oppose Kurtz's filed Petition for Attorney Fees, and the Order for Payment out of the proceeds of the sale of the Mobley home was signed by some previous judge.

Alice was convinced Counselor Field "forgot" to show up to oppose the Petition on purpose, so he, too, could get paid.

With the family's backing, Alice Mobley fired Sonny Field, and hired Charlie's law firm. That's when Charlie first met Alice Mobley. She must have been about 83 years old at the time. She was feisty and good natured. She refused to leave the small house where she continued to live with Denise.

Prior to his death, Ozzie still performed with the Castaways, and rarely came home from Palm Springs where he mostly stayed at the nearby "Desert Palms" rest home.

Alice Mobley had her own health issues recently.

When the case was called, Charlie helped Alice walk to the petitioner's desk to face Judge Bittenkopf's wrath. Charlie stood next to attorneys Field and Kurtz who pressed for their long-running fees to be paid with interest.

As Charlie laid out his notepad on the bench, his mind was far from the morning's Mobley proceedings. His mind re-played the events of the previous night. Charlie thought Alex was brazen to turn up in Charlie's studio – or absolutely desperate. Alex was like all rich people, considering any attorney's personal affairs and life of no value, to be used and disposed as with a squashed bee.

Charlie wasn't sure what to do as he faced Judge Bittenkopf. He could keep Alex's secret as he had agreed. However, as Charlie looked into Judge Bittenkopf's eyes, he knew that in doing so, he was also deceiving the court, and a fair judge who trusted him. Charlie forgot about his legal quagmire from the night before, as Attorney Kurtz punctuated his shrill demand for payment by pounding the oak bench in front of all three attorneys. Charlie could see the sweat on Alice's brow and the terror in Alice's eyes.

"Your honor, Administrator Mobley owes our law firm over $25,000. She's had plenty of chances to comply by selling her home as Judge Tovalkian ordered several years ago. She must be cited for 'contempt of court' and jailed."

Sonny Field didn't look comfortable as he chimed in on the extreme demand. "Yes, your honor. This is contempt. We're owed our just fees."

Charlie held on to Alice's tiny arm and frail body, as she swayed. He pulled a chair for her to sit facing Judge Bittenkopf and countered the extreme demands.

"Your honor, this is preposterous. Contempt of court is not called for. Ms. Mobley has administered this estate the best she could and complied with all your orders."

Judge Bittenkopf pondered, looked at Alice, looked at Charlie. Charlie knew he couldn't lower his eyes for Alice's sake from the judge's piercing gaze, despite the troubling secret he held from the previous day's court hearing.

CHAPTER 4
THE SIDE JOB

On his way back from the court to the parking lot, Charlie detoured across Grand Avenue into the underground tunnel under the Los Angeles Music Center complex and hurried down the dark corridor. He turned into an innocuous double door, which only Music Center employees knew led to the backstage dressing room of the Music Center Auditorium, the home of grand opera in Los Angeles.

The gray shirted Music Center security guard nodded as Charlie pulled out his "Music Center" I.D. card. Charlie flashed the I.D. with his curly brown hair covered smiling face, and headed down the hallway. Harshly resonating sounds of stagecraft hammering accompanied his hurried steps. No one at the Law Offices other than Earl knew about this other life – as a part time singer in the Los Angeles Lyric Opera's chorus.

Like many others in Los Angeles with an artistic dream, Charlie had one job that related to his real calling, in his case being a classically trained singer, and another job, that related to having a steady source of income – his Probate Associate position.

Charlie's passion had always been classical music and to sing on stage, but little by little, that dream faded. Even to obtain the most boring clerical jobs, you had to feign enthusiasm, and eventually, the artificial enthusiasm suffocated the youthful passion. Charlie enrolled in night law school while working paralegal jobs. He married. His new wife, pretty schoolteacher Tina Olson, who Charlie had known since singing together in the U.C.L.A. college choir, and who was willing to take a chance on him, wanted more out of life than a modest apartment in North Hollywood and a stack of collectible Arturo Toscanini records, not to mention piles of worn choral scores from oratorios and tattered opera scores for baritones.

Charlie worked at major law firms as a legal assistant for years after he and Tina married, and slowly lost his dream of singing for some years as he concentrated on his second career, feeling lucky he didn't have to become an insurance salesman, or a caterer as many of his fellow artists had. When he became a Probate Associate at The Law Offices, the thrill and pressures of his new calling pushed his artistic dreams aside. It was difficult enough to get through each day and rack up enough billable hours to keep the anxiety level that related to getting fired, down. Reckonings came whenever the monthly billing time was reviewed by Earl Guarder, resulting in stressful confrontations, nods of Earl's head, or maybe even praise.

Almost as important to Charlie's psyche was his new easy-to-recognize status in the community. "I'm an Associate at a law firm." It was a simple answer to the question "what do you do?" that acquaintances would politely ask. He no longer had to make excuses about "being between jobs," or state "I'm an opera singer" and have inquiries about where he sang, and if he made enough money to get by, or just have people outright laugh. "Opera singer? No one's an opera singer."

Then, serendipity brought the faded ember of the artistic dream back to a modest glow when a long-forgotten singing friend called him out of the blue during the five minutes he was home alone on a Saturday afternoon and asked him if he could sing part-time in the Bellflower Civic Chorus, one of the many suburban Los Angeles community choral societies. The musical ember in Charlie's heart glowed and urged him to say "yes," and Tina approved of his occasional disappearance for a Saturday with his tattered music scores. He sang at the Bellflower Civic Chorus on weekends for some months before a time-conflict, when Earl insisted he work on a Saturday, forced the issue. He revealed his new part-time job.

"You sing opera? Was that on your resume?"

"Remember? My undergraduate degree at U.C.L.A. was in music."

"Yeah, but *opera?*"

"My dad was a classical musician, played opera when I grew up."

"Jeesh. You got hired to sing? You must have quite a voice."

"I'm a baritone. It's just part-time."

Earl, to Charlie's surprise, approved, and revealed his own truncated dreams.

"I wish I could go back into TV broadcast. I was pushed out by those blonde bimbo News Reporter rejects. They can't analyze court decisions, much less legal precedent. TV audiences liked me. Damn." Earl had a momentary wistful look out over the Fairtown red-tiled rooftops.

With Earl's approval, the Bellflower Chorus led to the Music Center a year ago. Oscar Thornhill, a wire-thin mustached, elegant tenor from the Bellflower Civic Chorus alerted Charlie that the Los Angeles Lyric Opera was looking to fill a few "extras" back-up slots. Being an "alternate," you participated in rehearsals, and might get a shot at getting on stage if a chorus member got sick. So far, it had only been rehearsals, but Charlie was glad to be an "extra" even for rehearsals.

The "extras" job paid little, but so did the probate associate job. Earl was amused at Charlie's new part-time job which required an occasional evening getaway from the Law Offices instead of Charlie's customary late night exit. However, Earl was shrewd enough to understand that acceding to Charlie's newest engagement would keep Charlie in the Law Offices of Earl Guarder fold because no major law firm would allow any Associate to have a second job.

"Keep your clients happy and make sure your billing hours don't fall."

"Thanks, Earl. I will."

"Oh, and keep your mouth shut about this to clients. Understand?"

"Got it. Thanks."

Charlie was happy. Now, Charlie performed in one of the respected choruses in Los Angeles and received a small pay check for doing what he had always wanted to do: sing. With his probate job, he was also making a living, his days were full, productive. Life was sweet.

■   ■   ■   ■   ■

Charlie arrived at the dressing room and in the wardrobe section found his soiled costume from the previous Saturday's final rehearsal of one of the Italian war-horse operas, *Cavalleria Rusticana* by Pietro Mascagni.

He had not had a chance to take the costume to be cleaned. He did not perform in the previous Sunday afternoon's final show. That was that for *Cavalleria* or rustic chivalry. Time to dry clean, re-pack the costume, and turn it in to the wardrobe mistress and hope another opportunity would come. Charlie grabbed the blousy soiled shirts and soiled pantaloons with his name pinned onto a note, wished his cleaning allowance amounted to more than the rock-bottom four dollars a performance, to cover dry cleaning at the "Artistic Discount Cleaners" on Vine Street in Hollywood.

Charlie raced back out of the Music Center Tunnel with the costume and detoured up the Hollywood freeway to Vine Street to drop the costume off at the cleaners on his way back to Fairtown and the afternoon of dealing with anxious clients, taking phone calls, and drafting responses to antagonistic correspondence from opposing counsel.

He considered whether he should tell Earl about Alex's re-appearance from the dead. He decided to hold off the bombshell for a few days.

As far as the ruling on Alice's "Contempt" hearing, Charlie breathed a sigh of relief at the outcome.

Judge Bittenkopf's piercing look into Charlie's unflinching eyes led the judge to conclude that Alice had not crossed the line. Charlie had looked back into the judge's gaze, and not dropped his own eyes. Charlie could hear his heart beat as the judge looked, considered, pondered and ruled.

As Charlie had exhaled relief, and led Alice out of the courtroom well, past the scowling creditor attorneys, to her waiting, anxious family, he repeated to himself, that the Judge's trust in him had to be maintained, no matter what consequence to David Alex or the Estate of Barry Beneshan.

CHAPTER 5
CLIENT STRATEGIES

In the elegant British country squire motif reception area of the Law Offices. Devlin D'Alessio, in his thirties, devilishly handsome, with a chiseled face, leaned possessively over Angel. Charlie stepped off the elevator, greeted the clients with his easy manner, and led Angel and Devlin past the reception counter, nodded a quick thanks to Jamie the receptionist, and headed under the portico that led to the main halls that radiated from the reception area. Charlie turned right down the fluorescent-lit Law Offices hallway, and turned left into his modest office, which had a glass-plated expansive south-facing view overlooking Fairtown's graceful white alabaster dome covered City Hall and little extravagance other than a pull-up wooden armchair for clients such as Angel facing the attorney's desk.

Charlie pulled a rolling office chair in from the hallway's empty paralegal cubicle for Devlin. He didn't like Devlin hovering, pacing. Charlie fell into his chair behind his modest wood desk and turned his computer on. He'd try to read his e-mails while getting through this "strategy" session.

Charlie practiced law long enough to learn that clients rebel against being charged to talk about their cases, no matter how fancy the billing description. This was the time to multi-task, so he'd meet his billing requirements and avoid another fight with Devlin over his billed time.

"I wonder if that rich pansy Alex left a will?" Devlin had no finesse, nor show of concern. Devlin turned to Angel: "Did Alex leave a will?"

Angel shrugged. "He's got a wife and a brother. They'll deal with it."

"Ask Gary if he found a will in Alex's desk."

"Honey, Gary's out of a job! He hasn't come down from his room since poor Mr. Alex's death."

"Well, I'll light a fuse under Gary's ass. He's got to go back to the Vision Office. I bet he'll find a will. You could inherit a bonanza."

"Mr. Alex wouldn't leave a plugged nickel to me. I barely knew him."

"Damn right he would. You gave that weasel developer a respectable position as an administrator. That's worth a bushel of dough."

Charlie understood Devlin's game. Since Gary lodged in Angel's attic but had worked for David Alex, Devlin fantasized slipping a forged will into Alex's office files, which would will the bulk of Alex's estate to Angel. Charlie knew Devlin was too smart to make himself a beneficiary, but he would be in a sweet position with Angel as the beneficiary.

Charlie concentrated on his e-mails.

There were a dozen e-mails from the Korean perfume manufacturer client, Channel Lotus Petal Perfume in its trademark infringement case against a Chinese knock-off product made of a honey and soy bean muck, "Chantel Rumors Petal Perfume." That case was settling. An unhappy situation, as the case was a respite for Charlie from his daily probate disputes.

There were e-mail updates on the Dr. Henry Moon case. Opposing party, Jenny Mak, still had her brilliant father, 80 year old Henry Moon, a Cal Tech Ph.D., hidden away in her South Fairtown home, while The Law Office's client, Jimmy Moon, Jenny's brother, remained stymied from access to his *Time* magazine cover anointed genius father, and to his accustomed monthly five-figure allowance. Charlie knew where this would end: the father would re-write his will excluding Jimmy from his inheritance, leaving the bulk of his multi-billion dollar "MoonStar" internet media empire recently sold to a media conglomerate for a reported six billion dollars to his daughter Jenny and her family.

Earl wanted to get off that case, because Jimmy Moon's biggest asset was his boyish exuberance. Without access to his father's fortune, Jimmy could never pay his legal bills.

Charlie's focus returned to Devlin's twisted scheme. Charlie tried to look nonchalant as Devlin spun his rationale for forging Alex's name on a spurious will that Charlie would witness. In Devlin's fantasy tale, Angel had, after all, given Alex the best career sprint: becoming an estate administrator. The will would just show how grateful Alex was for Angel's trust. Charlie was disheartened to see Angel nod her head, swept along by Devlin's scheme.

Charlie decided it was time to bring an end to this madness. He couldn't tell them Alex wasn't dead, but at least, he could let Devlin know that The Law Offices would not commit fraud.

"Forging a will? It's not a good idea." Charlie leaned forward to sound authoritative, yet neutral in his assessment, as if in some circumstances it may be a "good idea," but just not now.

Charlie learned to sound neutral no matter how outrageous the client's proposal. Ultimately, clients paid the bills.

Devlin was unhappy with the blunt rejection. Angel looked puzzled but had other issues on her mind.

"A police investigator, Detective Phillip Oswilla called me about Mr. Alex. I drove downtown for an interview yesterday to police headquarters. Have they called you?"

It was clear from Angel's matter of fact voice that she hadn't heard about David Alex's real status.

"Detective Phillip Oswilla?" Charlie shook his head and noted the name on his yellow pad. The police had not called Charlie – yet.

"The detective told me they couldn't identify the body for sure. There was no wallet or I.D. They are trying to contact the family back east."

Charlie shuddered. *Would I lie to the police? I'd just have to tell them, I couldn't comment. Otherwise, I'd betray Alex's secret.*

Devlin leaned forward all the better to impress Angel. "Don't let those downtown cops harass my sweet Angel. What would she know about that dick-head's death?"

Charlie nodded. *It was pointless to pick a fight with Devlin.*

"What are you going to do about Richard Battle?" Charlie looked squarely at Devlin. "He'll be gone the moment he finds out there's no cash in the estate bank account."

Devlin leaned into Charlie's face. "You shouldn't have let Bittenkopf appoint that ricky-dick-head Battle. You got to squeeze their balls."

Charlie lived through stressful encounters like this before. Charlie shuddered. Dealing with unleashed aggression wasn't one of Charlie's strengths.

Even so, if it would have been his own law office, Charlie might have told clients like D'Alessio to walk. Here, as a law office employee, he had to go along with Earl's guideline: never talk back to a client. Do it their way. Charlie wished he had a job better than as a short-order cook at a legal fast-food burger joint.

Devlin exploded: "You shouldn't have let that black-robed butt-hole appoint that manikin dick-head. He'll eat up whatever moneys are left."

"Bittenkopf's the judge." Charlie was glad he always had that come-back. Furthermore, it was true. Whatever Charlie's assessments or Charlie's clients' demands, a judge made the decision. And that was absolutely okay by Charlie.

"Well, I would have pushed that black-robed pussy into his own pile of do-do. You got to show 'em there's turds to slip on if they don't play ball."

"I'm looking for another administrator."

"Yeah, well, who?"

"Give me a few days. There are several possibles." Charlie faked it. He had no "possibles" lined up. Nor did he know anyone crazy enough to guarantee personal assets against the nearly bankrupt estate with vultures perched on every picket of the 360 degree circling fence that bottled-up the estate's assets. Multi-millionaire developer Alex was a unique find.

Charlie managed a tentative smile back at Devlin, hoping his cheeks didn't twitch to reveal his terror. "I'll give you a call."

Angel got up, shook Charlie's hand and gave him a quick hug. Charlie didn't have much time to think of what he got himself into, lying to one client, to cover up for another. It was what was termed according to the California Rules of Professional Responsibility, an "actual" conflict. Charlie's main aim in his job was to stay out of trouble. This was becoming a challenge.

As Charlie tried to do his time sheet for the morning and figure out the rest of his schedule, the receptionist transferred a call on the "Beneshan" matter. Charlie assumed it was Alex with some lame excuse for not showing up. He took the call.

"Charlie here."

"Henry Gilliam. How are you?"

Charlie's stomach did a back-flip as he tried to sound calm, talking to the creditor python.

"What's up?"

"We're placing a lien on Angel's house and going forward with a forced sale. You'll get the papers in a few days," said the python.

"I'll oppose," replied Charlie.

"See you in court," each attorney echoed the other.

Charlie clicked the phone and did a quick mental assessment. *Ashland would oppose Gabriella getting kicked out on the street. Bittenkopf was not likely to approve Jones, Sharke's enforcement action. At least not yet. Nothing critical was happening the next day. That meant, for the first time in three days, I can go home.*

So, what if Alex was hiding out in his bungalow? Let him. Charlie would be there soon enough two nights from today preparing for a court appearance in far-away Norfolk Superior Court.

Charlie dialed home.

"Hi, sweetheart. What do you think about some take out Chinese? I'll pick it up on the way."

Between the law office, rehearsals at the Opera and Tina's school schedule, Charlie hadn't seen his wife for a week.

CHAPTER 6
ORDERS AFTER HEARING

Around the media mecca city of Burbank, the Ventura freeway metamorphoses into the "118 Freeway." Charlie wasn't sure exactly where the freeway name change occurs, but, the following morning, as usual, cars accelerated from their crawl into a furious gallop.

Charlie sped up as best as he could, as he did every morning on the way to the Law Offices, passing Glendale, Pasadena, Monterey Park, and several other bedroom communities. As Charlie cruised onto the left lanes leading to Fairtown, maneuvered to the Ferndale Avenue exit lane – a dangerous daily dog-fight, – his cell phone rang. *The call could wait*, Charlie thought. *Better ignore whatever client called, than have an accident.*

Once inside the underground Law Offices' parking garage, Charlie got out of the car and checked the cell phone message while grabbing his valise and bag lunch. No call showed on his "voice mail." He forgot about the phone call as he hurried through the dim parking lot.

When the garage elevator opened onto the ornate historic building's lobby, Charlie, like everyone else, dashed into the second elevator that would take him up to "The Law Offices" on the fourth floor. Everyone crowded in to the ground floor elevator, dazed, strengthening ties and hair in the aluminum mirrored door in which distorted reflected faces attempted to paste on unconvincing smiles.

Charlie got off on the fourth floor, stepped into the 19th century country-gentry lobby that served as the reception area and entry way to the Law Offices. British hunting green wall-coverings and Queen Anne furniture impressed potential clients and spoke of the gravity and heritage of the law office hinting back to pre-Columbian *Magna Carta* Charter ties to King John and British nobility.

In fact, the Law Offices of Earl S. Guarder was a sub-tenant of Hannah, Ashley, Tannenbaum Law Offices which occupied three entire floors. The "Hannah, Ashley" logo graced the portico which led from the elegant waiting room and reception area decorated with crests and heraldry into the business offices down radiating hallways including the hallway that was the Law Offices of Earl S. Guarder's home. Hannah, Ashley was known for its influence in Los Angeles' City Hall. Elegant, well-coiffed clients and immaculately attired attorneys entered and exited under the carved wooden portico, but the confident clients rarely turned to the Earl Guarder sublet section that led off from the main hallway. Among Hannah, Ashley's clients was the Metro Transit Authority, administrator of the Southern California subway and bus system. Even if the historical decoration was a bit of a stretch, Hannah Ashley was an old-line player in the major leagues of L.A. law.

Charlie waved to Jamie Winter, the blond haired, cute-as-a-TV weathergirl receptionist, walked to his office, briefly taking in the spectacular view of the San Gabriel hills through the tinted glass sheathed walls. Earl was in court this morning. No one else had made it in to the office as Charlie turned on his computer.

Charlie prepared the "Order after Hearing" stating the judge's ruling from the previous day's Estate of Ozzie Mobley Contempt hearing. Judge Bittenkopf had been lenient with Charlie's client. He could have placed Alice Mobley in contempt of court for not selling her home as previous judge Tavim Tovalkian had ordered several years ago. That could have meant a huge fine – or worse.

Charlie had argued passionately that Alice Mobley's health issues prevented following through on the long-ago signed court order. Charlie promised that now that she was making a recovery, she was able to function on behalf of the estate. Looking down from behind his dais, Judge Bittenkopf saw Alice Mobley sit in the chair Charlie pulled up for her, leaning with both palms on the oak bench for support, as she nodded and cast pleading eyes up towards the judge.

Charlie knew that the only concern the creditor attorneys had was getting paid. Judge Bittenkopf abided by the unspoken probate court rule:

don't rock the boat unless someone complains. It was touch and go, but Judge Bittenkopf relented and told creditor attorneys, Sonny Field and Clyvester Kurtz to cut Alice some slack. The two creditor attorneys acquiesced. Both attorneys dropped their pleas to jail Alice for contempt.

Charlie was happy with the outcome, as Alice deserved a better life than constant court hassles.

While the Law Offices was relatively quiet, Charlie wrote up the Order after Hearing for the judge to sign, approving Alice applying for a loan, with the condition that payment to the attorneys would come out of the loan before payment for any other expense. Charlie knew Alice was grateful for what he was doing. Now, the critical issue became: who would give a home loan to an 85 year old widow, with no means of support other than a modest social security check?

Alice and her daughter had prayed for a miracle in the court corridor before the hearing began. Charlie echoed their pleas when he joined in the court hallway prayers and bowed his head, saying "Amen."

Earl, in reviewing the case urged Charlie to forget about "hallelujah" and "wrap it up." Earl knew Alice had a limited income and couldn't afford the Law Offices' services much longer.

As an employee of Earl Guarder's law firm for some seven years, Charlie learned what it took to run a law office and came to admire Earl's flamboyance, confidence, optimism and business sense. He also knew he could never pull off having his own law firm.

"Hi Charlie," Aki, the newly hired paralegal came in. "Wow was that freeway bad." Akapour Baudakharma, or "Aki," a trim, muscular young woman with dark, flowing hair, whose family had immigrated recently from Serbia or somewhere in Eastern Europe to Los Angeles, had just completed the U.C.L.A. paralegal program and received her paralegal certificate. She also had a small baby at home. Charlie knew the two "callings" would only co-exist so long.

This was Aki's first job in the real world. Aki was not too happy about the working conditions and pay. Charlie knew in a few months, like almost everyone who came to work for the law firm, she would move on.

Charlie finished the Alice Mobley "Order after Hearing" and filled out the attorney service delivery form to file the form in downtown court.

Charlie turned to update his time-sheet. Two of his conservatorship cases were ending. Clients weren't paying their bills. Earl sent frequent e-mails to Charlie to get The Law Offices off the hook. That was an aspect of the job Charlie hated – getting clients to leave the Law Office, when they refused to substitute out. Earl left it to Charlie to find the way to do it.

Usually, a simple request to a client would not work. Amanda Dorsett Weston, the Law Office's energetic, elegant, and assertive accountant, a former New York fashion model who retired from the fashion industry in time to go to college to study accounting, would remind the recalcitrant client about owed money. If worse came to worse, (and it usually did), Charlie would make a "Motion to Withdraw," which was basically a plea to the court to let The Law Offices off further representation. Courts became finicky about letting law firms withdraw from representing clients. Justice was to be dispensed equally to those who had money, and those who didn't. At least that was the theory. Earl would fume when such a Motion would be denied. "Those judges don't give up any of their taxpayer funded paychecks. Why force us to subsidize those who can't pay?"

Charlie would nod, because he had no answer. Charlie suspected the judges in their lunches and seminars swapped stories about law firms that eagerly courted clients to sign with them, when a retainer fee was available to cash, and then tried to cut and run when clients became insolvent.

On occasions, when Charlie was sent to the court to beg for The Law Offices to be relieved, the most he could say is that "differences" had arisen between the client and the law firm. Saying anything more was not allowed, because it would violate that holy rule of professional responsibility: "attorney-client privilege."

In the old days, some four or five years ago, The Law Offices would just place a lien on the client's pricey home, and that would ensure eventual payment because no one in Southern California was crazy enough to lose the home residence piggy bank over an unpaid legal bill. Now, there was no real estate piggy bank to tap into. Most clients' properties were underwater or in foreclosure. The Law Offices had to stay in tune with the times, so payment reminders were brutally swift as the mortgage crisis worsened in 2007.

Charlie submitted his timesheet into the computer. He was caught up for the first time on the most important part of working for any law office: the billing time requirement.

Despite the somewhat less than ideal circumstances of working at The Law Offices of Earl S. Guarder, there were a few perks. Earl was mostly good natured. His optimism was genuine and gave Charlie a belief that anything was possible.

Earl S. Guarder, Attorney at Law accepted the fact that winning wasn't always possible. Finally, Earl, mostly left Charlie alone.

Earl Guarder was sympathetic to Charlie because he himself had become a law practitioner as a second career. Earl had started out as a TV stand-up news reporter back on the East Coast, and finished his law school studies in New York, before coming to California with his family, passing the California Bar, and becoming a TV legal news analyst on a local station.

Charlie knew Earl wished he could return to broadcast TV.

Charlie didn't know of any other law office that would accept an Associate taking on a secondary night job, such as singing in music choirs. So for all the detriments of working at Earl Guarder's – miniscule pay, no benefits, rotating office staff, the arrangement of Charlie being an Associate of The Law Offices worked, and Charlie was now in his seventh year with the law firm.

Charlie reacted instinctively and picked up the ringing phone that Aki transferred.

"How's it going, man?" Charlie's stomach sank, hearing the aggressive voice. "Find an administrator?"

Charlie was brought back to his major quagmire with Devlin's phone call.

"I'm working on it, Devlin."

"What have you done aside from jerking off?"

"I'm open to suggestions."

"You said you'd 'work on it,' and now you ask me for 'suggestions?' Okay. Here's my 'suggestion:' Get rid of that scum court administrator dick-head, bleeding us dry, or I'll wipe my ass with your face!"

The phone clicked onto dial tone.

Charlie's hand trembled. He knew he shouldn't react to Devlin's threats, but the guy had nothing to lose. Without Angel, he'd be living in his ancient microbus van in the beach parking lot next to the Venice pier.

Charlie thought of possible new administrators. He spent months doing "research," and he had come up with no-one other than Alex. Charlie sadly knew why he hadn't pursued anyone else in the last two days. Alex was the only viable candidate. Charlie reaffirmed his decision: He'd appeal to Alex to tell Judge Bittenkopf what happened. That was the only road back.

CHAPTER 7
A PUTRID SMELL

Charlie left the office late, and decided to stay in town, leaving a message for Tina who was already in bed since she had to be at Centennial Middle School in Zelzah by 7 a.m. It would be close to 11:00 p.m. by the time Charlie collapsed into his pull-out bed in his Hollywood Hills studio bungalow. He had a family-law court appearance the next morning in the City of Norfolk, some 40 miles east from downtown L.A. He hadn't heard from Alex and hoped he would have the studio to himself.

Charlie got off the freeway exit and headed into winding Beachwood Street, into the Hollywood Farmdell Canyon. Charlie pulled up in front of his studio.

The Hollywood Bowl attendees had mostly left and there was parking space. That was a plus arriving at the bungalow so late.

Charlie grabbed his valise, his suit, considered whether his music score was safe in the back seat, and placed it in the trunk, just in case a homeless crazy spent the night in the car and needed toilet paper.

He walked past the manicured hedge, bathed in the gibbous moon that lit the canyon, opened the six-foot high side gate to the bungalow, and brushed past the overgrown bougainvillea. Charlie's stomach growled for a muffin or something to eat from the small refrigerator.

Charlie reached his studio, opened the door. He hoped his unwelcome guest was gone. He flicked on the two interior canvas-covered scone lights.

David Alex was lying, arms stretched into a twisted pretzel, on the Berber carpeted floor, face up. His still-open eyes stared at heaven, or at least at the cob-web laced cracked-plaster studio ceiling.

An ulcer radiated from Charlie's intestines causing him to drop his valise. *Of all the places Alex had to die, why had he picked my floor?*

Charlie, shocked, tiptoed up to Alex's body, leaned down just above Alex's unmoving staring brown eyeballs. *Should I touch the body?* He could see every pore on David Alex's sallow skin around his forehead, cheeks and jaw. Charlie panned his eyes down the blue sport shirt and khaki slack covered torso and fixated on Alex's scuffed light-brown loafers pointed up at the end of wrinkled pant cuffs. Charlie turned his head back to examine Alex's upper torso. The long-sleeve blue sport shirt covered the Lego-like arms and on close examination the shirt was seen to be covered with saliva, bloody drool. Charlie could smell a smell – it was a bad smell, putrid smell, the smell of human death.

Charlie jumped back, hesitated, stared at Alex, taking in the immensity of the apparent dead body lying in front of him, looking at the details that created a frozen Rodin statue made of real flesh. *Did the body just twitch?* Charlie, unsure, sweated a pungent perspiration. He focused on the prone body. It was a large body. Alex was a powerful victim to overcome. Alex's shirt was open, torn. His arms were in a defensive position, with angled palms broken from trying to push something or someone away. The fingers and knuckles dangled above the carpet, having apparently been broken, as they were forced apart by the deadly assailant. Alex's neck was in an unnatural position, off-center, at the extreme flat angle of an Egyptian funeral fresco showing a deceased noble who had crossed over into the underworld. David Alex could have been a children's block toy or a wooden disjointed puppet, missing its strings. From any angle that Charlie could see, Alex appeared to be beyond saving.

Charlie, his heart and his hopes sinking, walked around the body in the center of the room, sat down at the dinette, pondered, and concluded there was only one thing to do. He reached for the phone on the tiny table, where Alex had sat nonchalantly just a few nights ago, dialed "911," ignoring a tear falling on his left cheek. Then, another tear traced the wetness and a third tear fell.

Charlie wasn't sure if the tears were for the corpse lying a few feet away, or for his predicament. *Why do I have a dead pigeon so close to my feet, and even worse, what am I going to do to get out of this sinkhole?* Charlie grabbed his head with both arms, and tightened his grip, hoping his physical hurt would make the pain of his professionally challenging situation vanish. Nevertheless, David Alex's body was still there, on the floor of Charlie's inner sanctum, no matter how hard Charlie pressed against his ears and teary cheeks.

Charlie released his arms and his breath. They didn't teach you how to dispose of dead clients in night law school.

CHAPTER 8
INCIDENT REPORT

Time stretched and metamorphosed into a seeming eternal void as Charlie waited at the driveway for the police cruiser to arrive. He tried to look up at the cloud-covered night sky punctured by the Hollywood Bowl searchlights and occasionally by the almost full moon peeking in and out of dragon-like black clouds that ate the coy moon orb in a slow digestion of its bright surface that disappeared into moving black jaws and snouts. His thoughts couldn't stray far from his predicament.

The "911" Operator Charlie dialed while he was still looking into the staring eyes of the deceased inside the studio, had been brisk, professionally comforting, but aloof. The emotionally neutral voice asked Charlie for the address where Charlie was calling from and asked if this was also the address at which he found the body. Charlie's gaze focused on Alex's lifeless body and the open eyes gazing at the ceiling as he responded to the operator's questions. Charlie was unable to answer the questioning voice while he was still in proximity to the bent and jagged corpse. The "911" Operator alerted the Dispatcher and advised Charlie to leave the studio and meet the police outside. Charlie did not need the urging of the unseen police Operator who instructed him to leave his quarters and walk up the driveway towards the street.

"Do you have a gun?"

"No. I have no weapon."

"Okay. The police cruiser is on its way." She sounded friendlier. "Good luck."

Charlie, after placing the phone receiver back in its cradle, stared at Alex, one last time in privacy, backed away, and hurried outside, hesitated, looked around the side yard, but couldn't see anyone lurking. Charlie walked in the moonlit path to the street to wait, not knowing how police cruisers respond to dead bodies, and not wanting to attract attention from neighbors awakening to blaring sirens of approaching first responders.

Charlie stood, waited, worried, and waited some more. He wished he'd be somewhere else. Anywhere else where he wouldn't have to deal with the consequences of finding a dead body.

It took only five minutes before the police cruiser arrived, turned off its siren and headlights, and stopped near Charlie.

The two police officers got out of their dark police car, but became suspicious when Charlie approached them. Charlie could see their badges reflected in the moon's hazy light, but didn't make out names or badge numbers. One officer was lanky, a veteran, in his '50's. The other officer, a Latino in his '30's was shorter than any policeman should have been. Charlie couldn't see much as the short cop aimed his flashlight at Charlie's eyes, forcing Charlie to blink repeatedly, and feel off-balance. Perhaps that was the point.

The two policemen checked out Charlie's I.D., and seeing the California State Bar card, loosened up. Very few attorneys were known to kill clients. Usually it was the other way around, the short police officer, trying to joke, retorted.

Charlie did not find this observation funny. He didn't find anything funny at midnight, nor did he even think it wise to call home and inform Tina what happened. She was asleep already as on all school days. There was nothing she could do. He had no reason to alarm her.

The two police officers came inside with measured gait. One of the police officers had opened the catch of his holster and balanced his fingers around the gun. They looked around, and as the veteran lanky officer checked out the closet and bathroom, the short police officer stood over the body. The lanky officer joined the circle.

"All clear."

"He appears to be dead."

"Yeah. Dead."

"I didn't touch the body. I came in from my car and found him on the floor."

The short police officer kneeled, took out his flashlight, turned it on, waved the light back and forth above Alex's open eyes. The eyes and eyelids didn't move. Charlie could see the police officer wasn't sure what to do, and turned his face to look at Charlie, while still aiming the flashlight in Alex's unmoving face.

"Did you know this victim?"

"He was a client who turned up here two nights ago."

The police officers glanced at each other, non-committal. They took notes on their Incident Report and asked Charlie particulars of the meeting two nights ago.

While the short police officer interviewed Charlie, the other officer called the Coroner's office and asked for a coroner's wagon to come take the victim's corpse away. Charlie told the officer on the phone to make sure the coroners come up the driveway to the bungalow.

"Is anything missing?"

Charlie tried to concentrate, gingerly walked around the studio, avoiding stepping near Alex's body. It was a feat, tiptoeing, stepping around, looking around the sofa bed, looking in the closet. The TV, the dvd player, the piles of opera scores, the bed coverings, a few opera posters, and the Navaho wall hangings seemed to be in place. He remembered when Alex took off his jacket and got ready to sleep, he pulled a pair of pajamas and an overnight kit from a rolling black leather airplane-sized valise.

"I think he had a small overnight rolling valise. It's gone."

"Anything distinctive about it?" The tall L.A.P.D. officer jotted on the Incident Report that covered his clipboard.

"Typical, black, business valise. The kind that fits under an airplane seat. Every business man has one. Oh, that's where he put the note that he showed me."

"What kind of note?"

Charlie explained about the threatening note as best as he could between yawns. The tall police officer jotted, without seeming too interested.

"Anything else?"

Charlie shook his head, walked outside. He didn't want to be near the corpse. The tall officer followed to the edge of the door and kept writing.

The short officer stayed behind, writing the specifics of the victim's size, and measuring the position of the victim from each wall with his tape ruler.

．　　．　　．　　．　　．

The coroner's team came about two a.m. Charlie had come back in to the bungalow, fatigued. He was sitting in his chair, hands around his face, semi-dazed, knowing he could not fall asleep, even if the two police officers would let him.

Two young techs from the Coroner's office walked in, unannounced, dressed in light-blue scrubs with the emblazoned title of the "Los Angeles Coroner's Office" above their shirt pockets. The logo was also stamped in large black lettering across the light-blue uniforms' backs. One was a handsome Afro-American man in his late twenties. The other death *meister* was an older Latino veteran, whose face revealed years of seeing corpses and mutilated humans. Alex's corpse had not been moved, and his open eyes kept staring at the ceiling.

The Coroner's Assistants leaned over the body, for what seemed to be an eternity. One opened the remaining buttons of Alex's shirt, and reached expertly with his latex gloved hand, placing two fingers on a tissue over David Alex' neck's carotid artery. After looking at his stopwatch for what seemed to be a very long time, the Coroner's Assistant pronounced Alex officially "dead."

The short police officer with the notepad noted "Death pronounced at 2:17 a.m. by the Los Angeles Coroner's office." on his Incident Report.

At least, if Alex had been killed face-down. Charlie wouldn't have to look into those deep brown eyes, which projected a vacant expression, staring fearfully upwards. Alex must have been terrified as he confronted his ugly grim reaper. Charlie shuddered.

The second Coroner's Assistant put on his latex rubber gloves, moved in and touched parts of Alex's body. The L.A. County death masters were methodical, noted findings on charts on two separate clipboards. Charlie couldn't help himself, yawning repeatedly. Even murder can only keep you up for so long.

After a few palpations, one death *meister* told the other "No visible cause of death, guys."

"Yeah. Ditto. Possible strangulation. A few bruises and lacerations around the neck. If that's the cause, it was an expert assailant, a pro."

"Yo, officers. Ask for an autopsy."

"Thanks, guys." The short police officer wrote the finding into his Incident Report.

The kneeling Coroner's Assistant, the younger Afro-American man with features that could grace a movie star, closed Alex's eyes gently, took out a large white chalk from his kit, and marked Alex's body's position on the carpet into a crude body outline.

.   .   .   .   .

As the two Coroner Assistants pushed the gurney supporting Alex's corpse out of the studio and stood back respectfully, Charlie blurted the question that concerned him the most:

"Officers, do you think, they'll be back? The killers?"

"Could be just one pro."

"Am I safe staying here?"

"Gosh, Sir. That's not for us to say," the tall veteran police officer stated.

"If it were me, I'd deadbolt lock the doors and windows," the short police officer added.

With that, the tall police officer came up to Charlie and asked Charlie to sign the two Incident Reports. The short officer with the camera, stepped away.

Charlie, being used to obey instructions, complied with the lanky Officer's request, without reading what he was signing. The officer handed a copy of the report to Charlie. "This just documents what you told us, and our observations. Here's my card, if you have any questions."

Charlie took L.A.P.D. Sr. Investigative Officer Nixon Tracker's business card.

"That's my partner, Officer Carlos Mendoza."

The short police officer, holding his camera, nodded an acknowledgment.

"What's next?"

"We'll hand the matter over to the homicide detectives. They'll call you in to sign a Statement. You might want to jot some notes now, so your memory stays clear. Incident Reports are hard to read. Eventually, if there's a suspect, you might be called to testify in court."

"Is someone coming to take fingerprints?"

Officer Tracker considered. "I doubt there'll be any prints that can be lifted."

"But it's a murder." Charlie was visibly upset.

Officer Tracker considered. "Okay, I'll put in a request. A tech will contact you in a few days and come out to dust."

Charlie nodded, too tired to think about the fact that he would be needed to let the tech in to the studio.

Charlie looked at the clock. It was 3:30 a.m. In two and a half hours, he had to leave for his next court hearing in far off Norfolk.

"Thanks, Officer Tracker."

"If it's any consolation, we get a lot of attorney clients who end up in the morgue."

"It's a first for me."

Charlie sank onto the day bed, scanned the Incident Report. Most of the officers' printing on the document was in acronyms. He could make out that the Coroner's Assistant had placed the estimated actual time of death as opposed to the "official" time of death in the early evening. Charlie shuddered, thankful he had arrived late. Otherwise, he would be on the way to the morgue, too, as collateral damage.

Charlie's hands trembled as he clutched the Incident Report.

One Coroner's Assistant popped his head back into the studio.

"Are you guys going to do an autopsy?"

"I doubt it. Straight-on homicide. Nothing kinky."

Charlie shuddered to think what the Coroner's eyes had seen at other murder sites.

"What's the cause of death?"

"Asphyxiation. Simple, straightforward. No need to waste taxpayers' dough."

"So, that's it?"

"Yeah. Don't sweat it. We see it all the time."

"I don't."

"Take it easy."

"Like I can."

"See ya."

Charlie hoped not.

With that matter-of-fact salutation, the Police Officers, the death *meisters* were out of the studio, and so was David Alex, but not as Charlie had hoped, leaving of his own free will. Charlie sat for a moment. It was almost 4:00 a.m.

Charlie glanced at the chalk outline on his Berber rug, and lifted his eyes to the small Navajo rug with the three protective Navajo Eie square faced spirits that hung on the far wall. He bought that rug in Arizona where he vacationed with Tina the previous year. It had been an extravagance, but the Navajo spirits had done their job – saving Charlie's life.

Charlie reached for the light switch. He realized the door wasn't locked, got up, locked it and fell onto the bed, exhausted. His senses were torn between terror and fatigue. He may have fallen asleep for an hour at most before the alarm woke him with its shrill unrelenting buzz.

CHAPTER 9
BAGELS AND CREAM CHEESE

Charlie remembered little about the following morning's court hearing in Norfolk Civil Court's Superior Court Department 7.

As he drove back on the eighteen-wheeler truck convoy filled San Bernardino Freeway through the industrial bowels of L.A. to the more genteel Fairtown environs and tried to stay out of the trucks' behemoth paths, Charlie's goal was just to make it through the day.

He got off the Ferndale Avenue exit, exhausted, depressed, and pulled into the Law Office's parking lot. All he recalled was he had looked around in terror as he left his studio, his heart beating fast, locked everything for the first time, including the side gate, and struggled to stay awake to get to the courthouse in time for his 8:30 a.m. hearing.

Charlie couldn't recall much other than grabbing several cups of coffee in the Norfolk first floor coffee kiosk before the hearing started. In court, Charlie stood next to Micky Minsky, wishing his bearded, long blond-haired client had worn a suit. Charlie nodded a lot as the judge admonished Charlie and his client with being six months late on child-support payments. Charlie took notes with trembling handwriting on points the judge, who was well beyond retirement age, articulated in a disgusted hoarse voice.

Norfolk Superior Court was an outlying Los Angeles County court, where a lot of disputes happened over child-custody and such sundry divorce matters. His client had been a highly-paid aerospace engineer who had lost his job after the divorce decree had come through awarding his estranged wife the house, child support payments of several thousand dollars a month, and generous spousal support payments for five years while the ex-wife retrained and became self-supporting. Altogether, with interest and penalties, his client was in the hole, and the hole was caving in.

"Man, I ain't got the dough. I ain't got a job. I'm living in a dump. I ain't got shit! What is that judge going to do? Jail me?"

Charlie shrugged, didn't want to mention that jail was a possibility if things kept going south.

"You'll have to ask Mr. Guarder. Officially, he's your attorney. I'm just making a 'special appearance' for him." Charlie was using his reserve energy to even respond to Micky.

"So, I'm going to get a huge bill and you can't even give me advice?"

Charlie was too tired to tell the client that there was no solution for his problem, short of skipping out on his family, moving to another state, or getting wasted in Juarez, Mexico or Key West, Florida on tequila or rum. He'd let Earl Guarder come up with the legal strategy this client was paying for.

Earl sent Charlie to make such "special appearances" because someone just had to show up. Earl also sent Charlie, because judges knew that an Associate making a special appearance couldn't exactly be completely blamed for the client's misdeeds. It brought some time for the client to figure a way out of his legal and financial sinkhole. At least, Charlie managed to show up in court.

Charlie got off the elevator, stepped into the Law Office building's ornate marble ground floor. Standing squarely in front of him was Devlin D'Alessio.

"Don't screw with me, dude. I know Alex is dead."

Charlie nodded, not sure which death Devlin referred to.

"He called me yesterday afternoon, to whisk him out of town. They got to him by the time I reached your place. I was so angry I could have killed him myself for croaking."

Charlie groaned. Even if Devlin didn't end Alex's life, Devlin now knew the whereabouts of Charlie's hideaway.

Charlie was suspicious of Devlin since The Law Offices took on the "Barry Beneshan" case eight months ago. Angel was mesmerized by Devlin's confidence, and totally subservient to his every manipulation. Devlin also pushed Gary to do his bidding. Devlin, on his own, did not have money to replace his worn out Nike shoelaces, but in his role as Angel's boy-friend, he was not to be trifled with.

"Come here, dude. We need a serious talk. We'll grab a bagel."

Charlie, exhausted, found it difficult to object.

"Sure. I need some coffee, too," Charlie rationalized.

He followed Devlin into the ground floor café, fancifully called "The Howdy Do" whose meager attempts at a cowboy décor consisted of maple chairs and tables, and a red-and-white checkerboard bandana around each server's neck. Devlin ordered two bagels with cream cheese.

"He'll pay," Devlin nodded to the cashier. The cashier gave Charlie the bill. Charlie knew enough not to object, fished for cash, and put a ten dollar bill on the counter.

"Keep the change," Devlin added. Devlin was always generous with others' money.

"They weren't after Alex. The scumbags wanted me dead. They don't like me trying to give Angel back her dough from that Beneshan madman."

Charlie pondered. Devlin would be the sort who'd make people want to kill him. He was a meddler, living off Angel's largesse. How many other pigeons had he caged before her?

"Why would they look for you at my studio?"

"The goons tried to squeeze info out of Alex about me and he balked."

Charlie didn't want to argue with Devlin's megalomania.

"So, who would 'the goons' be?"

"It's one of the estate creditors. Which butt-hole? I'm no private dick. But I know there's millions of dollars hidden somewhere. I will find it because it's Angel's."

"…and she'll be generous with you, won't she?"

"It's my vision that drives this gravy train. Without my whip on your ass, you wouldn't do shit. Do what I say, and you won't be sorry."

Charlie wasn't sure if this was a bribe or a threat. He had deeper concerns than worrying about Devlin's schemes.

"We'll get Angel appointed as administrator. It's the only way."

Charlie thought back on the imprecisely lettered death threat Alex had shown him two nights ago. The cops and the coroner techs hadn't mentioned finding the note, nor was it in the studio. Whoever killed Alex had taken it, along with Alex's valise. Charlie couldn't help notice Devlin pick up the half-bagel and cram it into his mouth with his left hand.

"I tried to get her appointed."

"You were a pussy. When I say 'do it,' do it. Don't' be a pussy."

Devlin grabbed the rest of his bagel and left the café. Charlie let out a sigh. Every quiet moment was precious.

CHAPTER 10
A NON-PAYING CLIENT

Earl Guarder was in a good mood, just getting off the phone when Charlie dragged himself into the office and plopped into the leather chair facing Earl's oversized carved desk.

Earl glanced at the full length "Big Ben" wall clock behind Charlie. Earl had a habit of doing that, whether from instinct, or to check whether Charlie's billing time would match the actual time he spent on the morning's hearing.

"How'd it go?"

"The Judge gave Minsky a strong lecture on catching up with his payments."

"Did you make it clear to the judge there's no way he can pay that obscene back bill?"

"Sure. I explained to Judge Garza that Minsky was laid off, scraping by on unemployment."

"'Explained?'" Earl had a habit of exploding, hearing about realities that didn't fit optimistic scenarios he spun to clients and even believed in, more or less. "You don't 'explain.' Judge Garza read my papers which laid out the case. Did you *fight* for our client?"

"Of course, I did."

"How come the judge didn't change the payment terms?"

"The judge stuck to his tentative ruling and that's the final decision."

"You got to fight! Clients expect you push it past what a judge allows. That's what they're paying us for."

Charlie was becoming depressed. In his heart, Charlie knew that becoming histrionic at a family law judge's ruling was professional suicide, only done for show, to impress clients and certain to antagonize the judge. Judges based their rulings on well written submissions of briefs and supporting evidence. Family Law was blood-sport, just slightly short of Roman gladiators who at least had the decency to bow to each other before slashing, stabbing, and slaying their opponent to death. In his court appearances, Earl expanded the dramatic range he had developed in his TV persona. Clients loved Earl's bellicosity – and were eager for more show-time, but even the angriest clients would get to the point where they couldn't keep writing the ticket-price checks.

Charlie put his arms up, half acknowledging Earl Guarder's oft-repeated wisdom, half to protect himself from further verbal confrontation.

"Best I could do, was to get Judge Garza to agree to a further hearing two months out, to see if a change of circumstances is warranted."

"Oh. Why didn't you say so? Sorry. You did fine." Earl calmed, hearing that there was a tangible positive outcome for the fickle client.

"Thanks."

"Was Denise Lapka there?"

"Yeah, she sat in court and watched Mickey squirm. Her attorney was pushing for contempt, but it didn't happen."

"Excellent."

"Mickey wanted to discuss the next move? I told him to talk to you."

"You did terrific. Next time, give me the good news first." Earl was back to his upbeat mood.

"Thanks. I will."

"That unfortunate David Alex death? Can we get off the Beneshan case? It's nothing but headaches."

Charlie was about to update Earl the most recent dismal news, but avoided the new gory headache details of the previous night's murder and its aftermath for the moment and tried to deal with Earl's anxiety about getting financially shafted.

"Not for a while. With this new administrator, Judge Bittenkopf won't let us say 'adios' very soon."

Earl acquiesced. "What a shame. Never lost an administrator to foul play. Well, Alex was a non-paying client."

Charlie knew Angel had not been happy paying David Alex's bills, but that was a condition Alex demanded. Alex had agreed to become administrator and sign and pay for the necessary bond, but would not be responsible for any other estate costs.

Angel had an insurance policy that paid out after Barry Beneshan's death. The moneys from the insurance policy were almost gone, spent entirely on estate expenses. More and more, it was credit card time, on every occasion when Earl asked her to pay the estate's ever-rising bills.

Earl's main focus was how to distribute billing times Charlie would spend on the estate matter to the timesheets to have Angel acquiesce and pay.

"She's the one who came up with David Alex. Just because he's dead, it's still estate business. Any other time you put in, like, if the police want to interview you? Bill it to Angel."

Charlie nodded, glad he was a staff employee. Earl's phone rang and Earl's attention turned to another matter as he responded to an upset client's venom. Charlie didn't have the energy to wait out Earl's telephone conference. Charlie saw Earl's attention shift, retreated out of Earl's office, and made it back to his own office, dead tired, but hoping he was getting past the worst night of his life.

As he turned his attention to preparing a civil restraining order in another family law case Earl had dumped on his desk, trying not to think of Alex's open eyes staring into his studio's ceiling, an outside call came in on his line. Charlie, on automatic pilot, took the call.

"Attorney Charlie Tobias, here."

"This is Detective Phillip Oswilla of the Los Angeles Police Department Homicide Investigative Unit. I'm assigned to the David Alex murder. Are you the attorney where his body was found?"

"Yes. I found the body."

"I need to ask you to come down to my office in the downtown police headquarters and answer a few questions."

Charlie knew this was billable time.

"Sure, when?"

"How about now?" Charlie didn't like the idea of driving back downtown, but it beat the restraining order assignment.

Charlie called out to Earl as he was leaving: "Going downtown to police headquarters for an interview. Back after lunch."

"Bill your time."

CHAPTER 11
DETECTIVE PHILLIP OSWILLA

Charlie thought back on the ugly night as he drove in a daze downtown, feeling like one of the swaying zombies in the *Halloween* movies. Charlie struggled through Chinatown, and parked in a multi-level low-cost decaying concrete parking lot north of the new bland police headquarters, on Spring Street where urine smells of the skid row homeless competed with the urine stains of well-groomed French poodles led by hipster dog-walkers.

Charlie found the antiseptic entrance to Police Headquarters on Spring Street, showed his I.D., and was led down a bland hall to a small office where he was introduced to a large swarthy olive-skinned and pockmarked complexioned man sitting behind a metal desk.

Detective Phillip Oswilla, broad at the shoulders, wearing a colorful silk tie that contrasted with the plain white, long-sleeved shirt, didn't stand, but shook Charlie's hand with his oversized palm and fingers, and seemed friendly as he grabbed a clipboard and a notepad, and pulled files marked with "Homicide – David Alex – Central Division" tabs.

"Charlie Tobias? I'm Detective Phillip Oswilla, Homicide Unit."

Charlie, exhausted, nodded, didn't hear any words leave his mouth and waited as Detective Oswilla reviewed the files and looked up.

"Thanks for coming down. I'll make this short." Detective Oswilla started writing on the pad.

Charlie nodded. "Sorry. I've been up all night."

"Nothing to be sorry about. Murders will do that to you."

Both men exchanged a hint of understanding.

Detective Phillip Oswilla's chocolate dark skin suggested a Mid-Eastern background. He chewed gum incessantly. Charlie considered who could play him in a TV series. Morgan Freeman seemed a possible choice, earnest, no-nonsense. After a few minutes, Charlie figured out why Detective Oswilla stayed seated. He was in a wheelchair. Charlie thought best not to ask why.

Detective Oswilla broke the ice. "I guess you don't do criminal law."

"I don't know the first thing about it."

"All you need to know? Whoever is brought in? He's guilty. Only question is: can we prove it?"

Charlie nodded, accepted the detective's wisdom, hoped he wasn't being "brought in."

The detective handed the clipboard with a Police Report Statement Form across. It was titled: "Homicide Witness Statement."

"Write down how this all happened. How you found the body."

"I was interviewed by Officer Tracker from the L.A.P.D."

"I have a copy of the Incident Report, right here." Detective Oswilla waved some papers in the "David Alex" file. "That's just the official stats, the 'who, what, where, and when.' Focus on a narrative. Write from your point of view. What happened when you came back to your place?"

Charlie looked puzzled.

Detective Oswilla leaned forward. "Pretend you're a camera and jot down what you saw."

"Okay."

Charlie picked up the clipboard, and the pen, wrote about the previous night. He was exhausted beyond any experience he ever had. Charlie took out the scribbled notes he had brought with him. Looking at the notes was upsetting, but Charlie knew it would help avoid blanking on critical facts.

"Is it okay to refer to notes? Officer Tracker thought it was best to write something down."

"Officer Tracker? Sure. He's detail oriented."

Despite having the notes to refer to, Charlie could barely remember anything other than Alex's eyes staring at the ceiling in a chilling final prayer to an unresponsive Deity. Charlie placed the details of finding Alex's prone body onto the formal Police Homicide report, and looked up. Half the sheet was still blank.

"Nothing else?"

"No."

"Sign it and you're done."

Charlie meticulously wrote his name. "I haven't heard from the tech about fingerprints. Officer Tracker said they'd dust for prints."

Oswilla didn't appear too concerned. "They'll get to you when they can."

"Don't prints smudge?"

"Depends. Not if they're oily. Most bad guys eat tons of greasy food. Keeps the fingerprints fresh for a long time. Avoid washing the place down."

Charlie was impressed with this bit of homicide wisdom.

"Do you have any suspicions who had a motive to strangle your client?"

Charlie saw Detective Oswilla take a yellow pad, and pen, and start to write.

"I was only in Alex's office twice." Charlie thought back. Both times Charlie had gone to Alex's penthouse office, there was no hint of any unsavory or ominous danger. "I met with him to discuss becoming an estate administrator." At the initial meeting, Charlie remembered meeting Gary Frank, the Assistant at the reception area. Gary Frank looked cool, hip, high-strung. Gary escorted Charlie to Alex's office.

Gary sat in on the meeting. When the meeting ended, Gary escorted Charlie on a quick tour of the Vision Associates offices and showed Charlie his own cubicle.

Gary confided he was lucky to have this job since the sub-prime mortgage crash decimated his previous business. Now, he arranged mortgages and construction loans for Alex's commercial projects.

Charlie remembered David Alex was charming. He was sophisticated without appearing to be slick. Charlie was surprised that Devlin D'Alessio also had his own desk, near Gary's. When Charlie's eye caught Gary's, Gary laughed and shrugged.

Alex ascribed a lot of his success as a developer to luck, and to the turn-around in the Los Angeles real estate market in the early '80's. Alex's company, Vision Associates became a major urban contractor when it became eligible to contract for "Metro" building projects around Los Angeles at all the newly built subway and rail stations.

Not everyone was pleased at Alex's success. Charlie, in doing his homework, prior to the initial meeting, researched the court rolls and found a lot of suppliers and co-venturers had lawsuits against Alex's company. Alex was stubborn and quite the autocrat. He'd fly over his developments in a helicopter, land, and accost his building sub-contractors if he saw anything amiss. The eccentricities had not deterred Charlie from making his presentation to Alex at that first meeting about becoming the "Estate of Barry Beneshan Administrator."

Alex responded favorably to Charlie's presentation, especially, after learning about the estate properties. Charlie, with Angel's help, put an analysis together of the possible estate value. Despite the estate's setbacks, there were still major rental properties co-owned in Woodfall, California, and properties in and around New Orleans, Louisiana.

Alex asked for a week to think about the offer, but responded to Charlie at that first meeting he was "interested in doing his civic duty." He acknowledged that payment for his services as administrator would be delayed until the estate's court life was closed.

Charlie, wanting to lay out all the cards, pointed out that all the estate properties were in title both as to Barry Beneshan and Jack Wonder, who was nowhere to be found. Charlie also pointed out the numerous other liabilities of Barry's dwindling empire.

Alex took notes. Charlie left the spreadsheet. They planned to meet again in a few weeks. Gary escorted Charlie out of the office. Things seemed promising.

Detective Oswilla scanned Charlie's Statement and jotted notes. At one point, the wheelchair bound detective wheeled himself to some ice water and a pencil sharpener.

"Any unusual telephone calls while you were with him?"

Charlie thought back. The second meeting with David Alex had been postponed several times. It had been almost a month later when he returned to Alex's office. He wasn't quite sure why the postponement occurred, but assumed Alex was assessing the estate's assets to see if being an administrator was worth the risk of paying for a huge bond and depending on an earned fee in the future from a shaky estate.

That second meeting lasted all day. Angel had been very upset by the five hour billed time Charlie typed into the billing software.

One telephone call Charlie remembered seemed unusual. Charlie overheard Alex talk about an exclusive development called "Isis" that Vision Associates was building.

Alex apologized for the distraction and explained that his silent partner was one of the ten wealthiest families in Southern California. The family was making plans with Alex for its next generation to survive. Alex pointed to some architectural renderings and a precise balsa-wood model of the proposed city laid out on a display table in the adjacent room.

"We're building a utopian development complete with a protective dome to seal off the residences and common buildings."

Alex, Charlie recalled, became serious.

"We are all in danger of man's eco-fuck-up of mother nature. Spewing a cess pool into the oceans, the air, the earth."

Alex's intensity disturbed Charlie.

Alex leaned forward, hissed: "We must get ready, if we want to survive."

Charlie shivered in the face of the apocalyptic pronouncement.

"My colony, called Isis will be a domed self-contained city in the arctic on the west coast of Greenland near the Ilulissat Icefjord. I deal with people who think ahead. Ten years from now, with global warming, the temperatures in these frozen tundras will be pleasant. Rich people are buying places to escape with their families from the coming eco-calamity."

"Isis?"

"The Egyptian goddess of fertility and life," Alex whispered.

Alex got up, led Charlie to the long work-table filled with sketches, architectural renderings and the model of the Isis colony. Charlie was impressed with the colored renderings and models of domed shaped igloo-like structures that echoed Buckminster Fuller geodesic futuristic designs he saw long ago.

Charlie thanked Alex for showing him the model of Isis and raced out of the office. Looking at architectural renderings, models, and blueprints was definitely not billable time.

Detective Oswilla considered the information from the second meeting, kept chewing on his gum, and wheeled behind his computer.

"Why did Alex come to your place?"

Charlie was surprised by the question. Didn't Oswilla hear about David Alex's earlier reported death?

"I received a hysterical call about five days ago from Alex's business assistant, Gary Frank."

Oswilla jotted.

"The assistant, Gary Frank told me Alex was lying dead in his office with a knife stuck in his neck. My other client Angel Sedona, confirmed his murder, and my boss told me to go to court, have an emergency hearing to relieve Alex of his duties and keep the estate functioning."

Oswilla took out his gum, and wrapped it in a piece of yellow-pad sheet of paper and threw it into the trash.

"Angel Sedona. That clean-up guy Beneshan's girlfriend?

"Right."

"Go on."

"Two days after getting the call about Alex's supposed death, I told the court we need a new administrator without going into details. Then, Alex turned up at my place and said it was his brother, Harry who was mistakenly murdered and he needed a place to hide out."

Oswilla picked a new stick of gum from his pack and started to chew. He offered Charlie a stick, which Charlie declined.

"I hadn't heard about Harry Alex. I'll check into it."

Charlie chilled. Had he been set up? The chill became feverish sweaty discomfort. His pale demeanor did not escape the detective's observation.

"I told the court David Alex was dead."

"Well, he seems to be."

"Oh, a final thing. Alex showed me a note with a threat."

"What kind of threat?"

"Vague, but the upshot was to quit as the administrator."

"Did the police pick up the note?"

"It was gone when I found his body. Also, his overnight valise was gone."

Oswilla kept writing. Charlie considered mentioning that the note was written by a lefty.

"Anything else?"

Charlie, too exhausted to continue, shook his head.

"Okay. I guess we're done."

Charlie sighed, relieved to be past the interview.

"Here's my card. I have a capable investigator, Tammy McCormack. She's the best. I'll put her on the case. Don't worry."

Charlie took the card, saw that Detective Oswilla's title was "Senior Homicide Investigator, Phillip Farquan Oswilla, Homicide Division, Major Crimes, Los Angeles Police Department." Oswilla was about as big-time in the police department hierarchy as you can get.

"Thanks."

Detective Oswilla wheeled around and let Charlie out of his office.

Charlie left the police building in a daze.

Charlie knew from his own training, that if a professional in any field said "Don't worry," that was the time to be scared.

CHAPTER 12
CLIENT CONFERENCE

Having steeled himself with a quick sandwich on Spring Street as he walked on autopilot to the parking lot, Charlie made it to his office and prepared for his first meeting. The conference room where Devlin and Angel had been placed by Aki was a flesh-eating Venus fly-trap, waiting for Charlie to enter to clamp its poisonous petals shut and stab him with its deadly stingers. Charlie, wary, entered with his files. Devlin paced, eager to lash out and suck out the vestige of Charlie's confidence.

"Well vegan eagle, what's the plan?"

Charlie winced. He should never have let on he was a vegetarian. It was just one more wound Devlin could inflict.

Charlie, seeing Devlin glare, thought it best to keep quiet, especially since Devlin knew the whereabouts of Charlie's bungalow and revealed to Charlie he had been there the night of the murder. Charlie might be hauled in for further questioning by the homicide detective if Devlin's fingerprints would be picked up in the bungalow. Charlie could not reveal to the police that Devlin had been at his studio since Charlie had no independent knowledge about it, and Devlin's confidence, acting as Angel's agent, was protected by "Attorney-Client privilege." Besides, it was an unwritten attorney rule not taught in law school: let clients vent, and then come up with a plan.

Charlie knew what motivated Devlin was fear – that after a year of living as Angel's bully-boy, this good life was crashing.

"I've had a telephone meeting with Richard Battle after I sent him the estate accountings. He was discouraged to learn the estate account was upside down. He'll resign. Then, we'll get Angel appointed without posting a bond. Ashland will go along and Judge Bittenkopf will appoint her."

Devlin looked into Angel's beautiful, questioning brown eyes, lifted her chin delicately. "It's all right, sweetie. It's a rock-n-roll wild ride. You'll be the administrator - "

Devlin's face turned steely as he focused on Charlie " - or I'll saw your balls off."

Charlie forced an embarrassed chuckle across his face, opting for pretend levity.

"Ashland could have saved us all this grief. He's such a button-down – lawyer." Angel couldn't think of any worse pejorative.

Charlie was used to this. Clients' anger against the legal profession was to be expected, especially when the outlook was dismal. The fact that it was expensive to fight for justice made clients unhappy with their messengers, the members of the California State Bar. When things weren't going their way, and the bills kept mounting, the most well-meaning clients lashed out.

Charlie explained his plan: "I already received a call from Ashland who was concerned that Richard Battle underestimated the estate's problems. Ashland's writing a motion so Richard Battle can step down."

Getting that call from Counselor Ashland had taken Charlie a lot of leg work in the last few days. Charlie had given Richard Battle the accountings from the two Woodfall, California apartments. The sheaves of accounting ledgers had not made for light reading. The Woodfall court-appointed receiver, Dennis Millhouse hadn't been paid in three months and was petitioning Fresno Superior Court, the local court, to be relieved of his duties. That made an impression on Richard Battle, underscoring the difficulty of any fiduciary getting paid.

Battle also learned of Millhouse's arm fracture from the falling roof tiles. That, combined with the circumstances of the previous administrator's demise may have done the trick, kind of like a sledge hammer crashing on Battle's beating pulse.

Counselor Ashland called Charlie within the morning after the accountings had been messengered to Battle. "I'll have Battle resign, and support Angel as special administrator without bond."

Charlie was confident that, with Ashland's backing, Angel Sedona would be appointed administrator. His pulse raced as he thanked Ashland and knew he had the news that Angel and Devlin wanted.

Devlin's visage was becoming smug as he heard the update. It didn't take much to buoy his confidence.

Earl popped his head into the conference. "Hello, Angel, Devlin. I'm so sorry to hear about Mr. Alex. He was a fine, fine gentleman."

"Thank you. We're trying to come up with a plan." Angel hugged Earl.

"Charlie told me about you becoming administrator. I think that's the only solution. We'll get you appointed."

Angel and Earl liked each other, but Earl's support was fleeting. Charlie knew that if push came to shove, Earl would buzz on to other clients, equally sympathetic to their plight, just as positive about their potential outcome as long as they had pollen to feed the Law Office's bank account.

"You should never have let that court nebbish Richard Battle waste our time. What's being looted?" Devlin sneered.

Charlie thought about the vanished Clean Co. truck fleet. Earl was beaming and positive.

"Once you're appointed administrator, you can gather all the assets. The estate has some fine properties. Then, we'll put in a Motion to get our attorney fees. Right?"

"Aren't you guys supposed to get the fees at the end of the probate when the estate closes?" Devlin was suspicious.

"That's for the regular estate administration matters. Here, most of what we're doing is 'extraordinary' work, namely litigation. That's billed hourly. We need some moneys to keep going, too."

Earl was brilliant at slipping in the bottom line.

Charlie knew that Earl was in business to stay in business, not to go broke, and his own job rested on Earl's financial success.

Angel was cooperative. "Earl, I'll pay you what I can."

"Of course. Do you have a credit card on you? More court filings are coming."

Angel opened her purse and sifted through a dozen credit cards. It was either a poker game, or she was baking a complicated recipe out of many colorful plastic chips.

"Here. Try this."

Earl took the card. "I'll just put $5,000 on it. Is that okay? We'll have a lot of costs getting you appointed."

"Get her appointed first. Then charge us." Devlin's hand moved in, reached for the credit card, but Earl had already taken the card and moved away. Charlie looked on, in unstated admiration at Earl's finesse. They didn't teach that in law school.

"It'll be fine. After, all, what other choice does Judge Bittenkopf have?"

What Earl said was true. Charlie also knew, the pressure would be on him to deliver. Earl disappeared to swipe the card. Charlie smiled at Angel and Devlin in a self-conscious waiting kind of way. Earl was back in a moment, with the swiped credit card and a pen in front of Angel to sign. She did.

Charlie knew they were back in business, at least for a while. He also knew, even if his strength held up, he would never make it in time to his rehearsal downtown.

CHAPTER 13
TAMMY MCCORMACK, P.I.

Tammy McCormack, like many progressive young women, started as a college activist, organizing and promoting women's issues and became an investigator for the Los Angeles County Public Defender's Office after finishing college. The trim and talented investigator put her people skills to good use, working on allegations of family battering and alibis of criminal indigents who fell into the Public Defender's bulging case files.

When the County cut back the Public Defender's investigative staff, she switched to the general pool as a "Freelance Private Investigator," to avoid a lay-off. She found herself assigned to the L.A.P.D. Robbery and Homicide Division. Tammy liked working for the homicide detectives, especially for Detective Philip Oswilla who signed off quickly on her invoices. Detective Oswilla was thoughtful and took her recommendations seriously, but the David Alex case, like many murder investigations that formed her caseload, required putting in a lot of overtime for which she received no compensation. As the economy lurched into the Great Recession, Tammy accepted that, at least she was employed and able to continue to pay off her student loan.

After the body of the well-known builder David Alex was found in the attorney's tiny Hollywood Hills bungalow, Tammy knocked on each door up and down the charming canyon street. The streets in that Farmdell area were full of actors, writers, and other Hollywood film riff-raff. She was conscientious enough to not be put off by their flippant dismissal of the murder on their street because the circumstances had no show-biz sizzle.

One of the homeowners, a Mr. Dylan Cowling point-blank told her "Me being a witness? Get me a Tate-La Bianca type murder case, not some nobody."

Her first bonanza was when the door of the modest Spanish-style home down the street from Charlie Tobias's bungalow opened, and she met Carrie Baxter. Carrie must have been in her late '50's, attractive, with ashen hair and sturdy, unshaven legs. She was shy and at first did not want to talk to Tammy, but Tammy's finesse developed a rapport between them. Tammy had done her research and learned Carrie was the daughter of Alvina Baxter, an Irish-American nurse who locked her daughter in the house during the girl's adolescence, and home-schooled the child through high school. Only after Alvina passed away did Carrie explore the outside world with an innocent enthusiasm that reflected her new-found freedom from being kept imprisoned in the pleasant Hollywood Farmdell home.

Other neighborhood residents had mentioned that Carrie Baxter was the eyes and ears of the neighborhood.

Tammy did not push at the first meeting, only established rapport, and talked of the grim murder up the street. Carrie was shocked to hear about a gruesome crime so close to her home she hadn't heard about. Tammy left her business card, but never heard from Carrie.

Two weeks later, Tammy returned for a follow-up interview. When the door opened, she could see in the middle-aged woman's eyes that Carrie wanted to unburden.

Carrie blurted out that she had seen a confrontation on the sidewalk the afternoon of the murder. She didn't know who David Alex was, but saw an elegant, well-groomed gentleman fitting Alex's description confront a neighborhood couple, Benton and Sandy, as they pushed their newly-adopted daughter in a blue stroller down the street.

Carrie could identify with Darlene, the infant in the stroller, and her newly adopted same-sex parents, Benton Wayne and Sandy Trayle. She did not want to believe that the two well-liked TV comedy stars would have any role in that poor man's death, but wanted to tell Tammy she had seen the altercation. There had been a lot of shouting and the gentleman looked upset when he turned and retreated up the driveway of that attorney's bungalow.

Tammy thanked Carrie for the information and filed her report with Detective Oswilla along with a modest invoice for her services. She received a note back from the detective thanking her, and asking her to follow up. He authorized a generous number of hours with a scribbled note that explained "I've gotten a call from Jim."

Tammy knew Captain Jim Abraham's signature okayed her invoices before the county sent her the crisp L.A. County checks. This was important news for her.

"Jim wants this case solved!"

CHAPTER 14
WEST NILE

Like many extras, Charlie did not like modern operas, much less a symbolic minimalist pessimistic piece like the new L.A. Lyric Opera offering, *West Nile*.

The traffic picked up past Chavez Ravine. The downtown skyscrapers appeared around the freeway bend. Charlie's stress level diminished. There was nothing he could do, but flow with the traffic, sort of like the ups and downs of the Barry Beneshan Estate case. First the case seemed hopeless, then, David Alex had signed on, and the case looked promising, and now? Charlie concentrated on getting to the rehearsal without crashing. The cars in front halted and started, and slowed in an algorithm of chaotic non-order as Charlie gulped the last of his coffee. He didn't even remember how he survived the rehearsal the day after Alex's murder. He only knew he had made it and made it back to his home in the San Fernando Valley and crashed into a fitful sleep.

Charlie's opera buddy, Oscar Thornhill had filled Charlie in on how the *West Nile* show became part of the current season. The society matrons who made up the Opera Board, decided that Los Angeles Lyric Opera, being part of a movie town, would invite enigmatic Italian film director, Michelangelo Tantonini, and let him select a contemporary opera to direct.

The Opera's Executive Director, Giuseppe Ferraro was surprised when the famed director of Cannes' award winning films, *Ennui* and *Empty Landscapes*, selected the Gus Gas' penned *West Nile* story.

The chorus was not pleased about the selection of the Gus Gas opera, especially since they would have to suit up in cumbersome paper-mache mosquito costumes before dress rehearsals, and make sure the microphones inside the bulky life-like insect headpieces functioned properly, but there was always the modest paycheck to think of.

Oscar confided that *West Nile* was a hard sell for a Los Angeles opera audience. The music was shrill. The sets were replicas of San Fernando Valley tract houses that could be seen from any Ventura Freeway off-ramp, the eco-twist on the "Romeo and Juliet" story-line was symbolic, and the atonal music disturbed Oscar's inner sense of well-being. Charlie agreed with Oscar, and found his own sensibilities growing gloomier, but it wasn't from trying to memorize the downbeat lyrics, but from the repercussions of Alex's murder in his studio.

Early on the first Saturday morning after the night of the murder, Officer Tracker called Charlie at home to alert him to go to the bungalow and wait for the tech to come dust for fingerprints. Charlie threw on clothes and left before Tina woke. He drove to the bungalow, opened the front gate, and walked to the front door. Feeling very vulnerable, he didn't dare touch a thing, and decided to wait outside for the tech. She came by in an unmarked car, gathered her brushes, greeted him, walked in, and proceeded to dust with her carbon talcum. She found prints in a number of places – on the Formica kitchen counter, the refrigerator door. She attached a clear adhesive tape and lifted the tapes and took notes.

"We'll run the prints through the data base to see if there's a match."

Charlie nodded "Anything else you need?"

"No. Think I got them all. Your place is done. It's all yours."

"The chalk marks?'

"You can clean them up. We've got everything we need."

Charlie thanked her for coming and walked her out the door.

He came back, took in the sad spectacle of a place that has just had a murder committed a few days before and vacuumed up the chalk marks. He had no more energy to clean up the place. He'd do that later.

▪   ▪   ▪   ▪   ▪

Now, a week later from that terrifying night, Charlie angled downhill into Chinatown past the Asian bakeries and Chinese family restaurants.

Charlie made a quick turn and headed into the Music Center's underground parking lot.

Charlie signed in with security, raced through the dressing room, grabbed his radio mike and placed it around his neck. At least, tonight was only a blocking rehearsal, designed to place the chorus members in their proper stage spots. Charlie didn't have to get in costume. He just had to hurry out to the stage. Although he was late, the Assistant Director had not noticed.

Charlie raced to the side of the curtain, just in time, took his position on stage, holding his score and clicking his microphone "on." A few other extras also had their scores as crutches. Charlie was relieved. He wouldn't stand out, as the lone straggler who had not memorized his lines.

Oscar saw Charlie come in, gave him a "V" victory sign with two fingers, and winked. Charlie nodded, raised his two claw-covered arms in acknowledgment. The Conductor gave the signal to the lone piano player who hit the piano keys with force and precision. One-two-three-four, the baton came down again. Charlie joined in with his rich baritone voice.

Chorus
It's a millennium
Since we visited our hosts
Brought cholera
To infest humans,
Turn them into ghosts.

Now, we return,
To attack,
Those who least suspect
The coming – of
The second coming.

Charlie's voice blended with the other chorus members. It was a difficult assignment. Charlie might have even foregone the chance of being in the show if it weren't for the cardinal rule of all working free-lance artists that still guided Charlie consciousness: never say 'no' to any job.

CHAPTER 15
ANGEL BECOMES ADMINISTRATOR

A few days later, at the hearing in front of Judge Bittenkopf, Angel Sedona looked proper in a two-piece grey-blue suit fitted close to her neck with modest, elegant buttons. She whispered proudly to Charlie she picked up the suit at a second-hand store on Melrose Avenue for under twenty dollars. Hardly any opposing attorneys showed up for the hearing to appoint her as Administrator without bond. She was also on time and whispered to Charlie that Devlin dropped her off at the courthouse entrance while he foraged for a cheap parking space.

Mark Ashland and Richard Battle weren't especially friendly as they walked past the swinging wooden gate of the courtroom well to the courtroom bench when "Estate of Barry Beneshan; Request for Resignation of Fiduciary Richard Battle and Appointment of Special Administrator Angel Sedona" was read aloud by the clerk.

Charlie wrote the pleading, faxed it to Ashland's office and Ashland counter-signed it. Ashland acquiesced to Charlie's suggestion that Angel be the new administrator.

Judge Bittenkopf looked up from reading the Petition.

"Now, Ms. Sedona, I know you have your daughter's welfare as your foremost goal, but if you are appointed as Estate Administrator, you become a Court Officer. You must be fair to the claimants and creditors. Some may have legitimate claims against the deceased. Is that clear?"

"Yes, your honor. Thank you," Charlie answered for his client. "I've given Ms. Sedona the *Administrator's Duties and Responsibilities' Handbook* and reviewed the rules with her."

He was telling the truth. However, Charlie didn't add that Angel's retort when she accepted the weighty illustrated paperback written by the court for lay administrators was that the "vultures and hyenas have already stolen almost all of Barry's money. I'm not going to let them steal anymore."

Charlie had nothing against Angel's salty combative language, but in the courtroom, such a retort would not be helpful. Charlie held Angel's arm to keep her from interjecting inappropriate remarks into the proceedings.

Ashland, luckily, filled the momentary silence as Angel was distracted by Charlie's squeeze on her arm.

"Your honor, we have reviewed the estate status. We concur that Ms. Sedona is the only one who has a chance to sort things out. Mr. Richard Battle asks for permission to resign."

There was a moment of silence while Judge Matthew Bittenkopf thought through the alternatives. Charlie looked straight at Judge Bittenkopf, saw the discomfort and hesitation in the judge's eyes. Judge Bittenkopf looked directly at Charlie, moved his eyes over to Richard Battle.

"Mr. Battle, the court thanks you for your service. Your resignation is accepted. Ms. Sedona, you are appointed as Special Administrator without bond. Any encumbrances or changes in the properties or expenses above $10,000 must be brought to the court's attention and approved by the court. I'm also asking you, Mr. Tobias, to have Mr. Ashland counter-sign any Order you submit to the attention of this court. So done. You may prepare the Order, Mr. Tobias. Congratulations, Ms. Sedona."

Angel beamed. Richard Battle sighed a breath of relief, and Ashland stared in his usual enigmatic manner.

Charlie nodded. "Thank you, your Honor."

Charlie's heart pounded as he and Angel left the podium. He was now in the middle of the mess and he had dragged Angel in to a dangerous position. He couldn't shake the image of his last administrator out of his mind's eye, lying in his studio, on the dirty Berber carpet, eyes pleading to an impersonal, uncaring plaster ceiling.

If anything happened to Angel? Charlie tried to put the thought out of his mind. He realized that Angel Sedona's warmth meant a lot to him.

CHAPTER 16
A GLOBAL SETTLEMENT?

In the hallway outside the courtroom entrance, Angel confidently stepped into the center of the circle, no longer a minor player shunted to the side. Richard Battle was glad to see her in the spotlight.

"Gosh, Ms. Sedona, congratulations. If there's anything I can do to help, gosh, let me know."

Richard Battle was in a good mood, undoubtedly sincere, relieved he had been "relieved" of his herculean task.

"We're here to help you make this work." Counselor Ashland was effusive.

"Thanks." She glowed, stepped sideways to avoid a throng as Department 17's courtroom door swung open and another group of supplicants exited, talking loudly among themselves. The bailiff stuck his head out, gave an arm-waving plea for people to step away from the doorway as he pulled the massive oak door shut with a "thud."

"Yeah, yeah." Devlin showed up, just in time to be a thorn, confronted the closed courtroom door, like a toreador.

Charlie and Angel complied with the bailiff's instructions, and pulled Ashland and Battle away from the doorway to continue their conference. Devlin reluctantly followed, still looking at the closed courtroom door, wishing he would have told the bailiff off to his face.

Angel took command: "I think the first thing I need to do is to look at the estate assets. Barry told me he kept a lot of cash in that New Orleans safe. I've also got to track down those looted trucks. They could be sold to raise cash. Plus, I've got to check out all the properties."

Charlie and Ashland locked eyes as Angel formulated her plan. Charlie worried Ashland would ask him about any Alex updates. Ashland didn't. Charlie tried to rationalize. What did it matter, anyway? Alex was dead. Charlie told the truth to the court as best as he knew it at the time. Where the murder happened wasn't relevant – except to Charlie's level of anxiety about the intruder who had brought death close to his personal life.

Ashland offered a fleeting glance to Charlie, turned back to Angel, nodded. "A good plan. Sounds like an inspection trip."

Devlin stepped up protectively next to Angel. "Angel and I are going to figure this out like it should have been, see where we can raise some cash," he said.

Ashland nodded assent. "She can do it solo. If you go, that's not an estate expense."

Devlin seethed. "Of course, I'll pay my way." Charlie knew that meant Angel would pay for Devlin from her remaining insurance money.

"We've got to get rid of that dick-head receiver in Woodfall." Battle laughed self-consciously at Devlin's juicy description knowing full well, Devlin labeled him with the same lack of courtesy. Ashland was used to Devlin's crudities and had no reaction.

Angel added "Barry made the Woodfall apartment buildings profitable, with the Cham manager who spoke their language. Barry told me they revere him as a god. Since the court appointed Millhouse, no money comes in."

Ashland didn't disagree: "That property is beyond saving. Sell it. Jack Wonder is on title. Offer him something to make it work."

"Offer him the property. Get some dough." Devlin could be shrewd.

"I don't have a clue how to find Jack," Angel said.

"If money's on the table, he'll show." Ashland's suggestion was a good one.

"Jack Wonder's on title everywhere," Charlie added. "We'll have to get a global settlement with him to take his name off every estate property."

"Give him all the properties. Get the dough." Devlin was all about cash.

Ashland turned to Charlie: "A global settlement?"

"It's a long-shot."

"It's the only solution. Negotiate it with Jack Wonder. We can make this work. First, check out the properties."

Charlie couldn't help but notice, that Ashland was doing the ordering, but wasn't offering to do any work. Charlie knew it was a waste of time to try to enlist Ashland to do any more than countersign the upcoming documents as Judge Bittenkopf demanded. Charlie knew that like General Eisenhower, or Julius Caesar, Ashland would never soil his hand with more than a signature above the typed line of a document below which his name and title were printed as "Court-appointed Attorney for the Minor Beneficiary of the Estate." Getting that signature was an essential part of Charlie's job.

Ashland nodded and walked away with Richard Battle.

"Why don't you come with us, Charlie?" Angel took Charlie's arm in a gesture of request.

Charlie's heart sank. He knew Earl wouldn't advance the costs of going out of town, even if it was a few hundred dollars. Charlie also had his rehearsal schedule to consider.

"I'm only open for one weekend this month."

Angel's face broke into a wide smile. "We'll go then. I'm so glad you're coming."

Devlin didn't want to seem opposed to Ashland's plan: "Gabriella should come, too. It's her future."

Angel thought for a moment, "As long as she doesn't miss school."

Charlie was sinking into the quicksand, and didn't see any branch to grab.

CHAPTER 17
INSPECTION TOUR

The road to Woodfall south of Fresno, California is not on the list of California historical treasures. Charlie sat in the back seat of Angel's aging sedan with Gabriella. Angel was in the front passenger seat. Gabriella, a self-sufficient, intelligent girl around nine or ten years old, dressed for a comfortable outing, looked at the passing countryside, ignoring Charlie. She tuned in to music on her iPod as Charlie surmised, noticing Gabriella's rhythmic nods of her head. Charlie knew it would be a long ride.

The Mercedes flew down into the California farm belt San Joaquin valley, past the truck stops, the exits marked with fast-food chains and gas stations huddled near overpasses. Gabriella took the ear buds out of her ears and mentioned being hungry to no one in particular. Devlin responded, stopped at a fast food joint. Then, he stopped at a filling station. Angel still had Barry's gas credit cards.

They continued their trip all the way to the first Woodfall exit, where they turned onto the Main Street off-ramp and passed motley big-box stores.

Angel got on her cell phone and dialed. "Hi, Dennis? Yes, it's Angel. We're just about here. Meet you at 'Misty Acres?' Sure. Fifteen minutes. Okay we'll meet you there."

"Mom, I'm hungry."

"Later, honey. Afterwards. We'll get a pizza."

"Why can't we stop now?'

"Mr. Millhouse is waiting for us. We don't want to upset him. He's been very nice."

Devlin, sneered. "Why shouldn't he be nice? This has been a cash cow for him!"

Angel was exasperated. "His arm's in a sling."

Devlin looked at her sideways. "That jerk."

"Watch your language."

Charlie closed his eyes and wished he had ear buds.

Devlin concentrated on the pot-hole covered road. "Oh, my back. Wish Izzie would come give me massages."

"Izzy gives Mr. Millhouse massages because I can't afford another lawsuit."

"What a racket."

To Devlin, everything was a racket. Admittedly, Dennis Millhouse hadn't done a good job, but then, again, he hadn't been paid for six months. The Cham tenants stopped paying rent about then and showed their disdain for Millhouse's threats to evict them. They adored Barry Beneshan as their savior. Boohau Cyclops still was pastor, godfather, and living god to the Southeast Asia immigrant tenants even though he was fired as the apartment manager. When the first estate Administrator and his law firm, Jones, Sharke appointed a court receiver, a guy in a suit, Angel didn't need a crystal ball to know that the tenants would stop paying rent.

"What a cool place." Gabriella liked the old historical section of Woodfall, oozing with 19th century dilapidated buildings, including a red brick courthouse missing a side wall.

Angel took notice. "Here, the streets are starting to be numbered." Indeed, after West Street, the car came to a stop at the 1st Street traffic light. It was just as well the car wasn't moving. A grizzled man ran out from a laundromat, shirtless, stepped into the road, pants barely hanging to his anorexic body. Angel took charge.

"Lock the doors."

The wild-eyed man approached. "I need money. Money. I want a dollar. Give me a dollar."

"Go, go." Angel panicked.

"Mom, the light's red."

"Yeah, honey. I can't go through a red light," Devlin sounded sensible under the circumstances.

The man glared inside, implored. He put his hands together, prayed, dropped to his knees. Screamed. "Please? A dime?"

"Mom, let's get out of here," Gabriella pleaded.

The light turned green, just in time, as the sunburned shirtless crazy pounded the car.

Devlin sped across the intersection.

Angel tried to be cheery and positive. "I think we're getting near the apartments."

Devlin wheeled the car off Main Street.

Gabriella slunk into her seat.

Charlie noticed that this section of Woodfall had no sidewalks, and aside from the block-length two story apartments marked with charming names like "Pleasant Oaks," "Fairview," and "Country Row," the local visible population consisted of grizzled men working on cars, dudes, shuffling on street corners, and smiling, sweating women, standing in door-ways, smoking, while looking sultry and inviting.

Gabriella let out a growl or some similar sound of disgust. "Why are we coming to this yucky place?"

"Honey, this is California gold. The gold that will make you a wealthy young woman, whose future will be assured at Princeton or Stanford. They're very expensive schools."

"Mom, this place is creepy and gross."

They saw their destination, the row upon row of buildings taking up the entire block. "Misty Acres" was straight ahead.

"In here, pull in here."

Devlin followed Angel's gestures, pulled into an unpaved driveway headed into the weed-infested parking area.

"It's like a prison." Gabriella didn't seem impressed.

Charlie, in the back seat, pressed against the driver's side door, didn't make any observation.

CHAPTER 18
BOOHAU CYCLOPS

Devlin pulled the car onto the Misty Acres asphalt yard and bumped along. A pudgy, balding middle-aged man with his right arm in a sling waved with his free left hand. Devlin drove up, came to a stop.

Around the periphery of the asphalt courtyard that served both as a parking lot, and the apartments' recreation area, families bar b-q-ued, children played soccer, men hunched around mai jong and card games. At least Misty Acres was user-friendly.

Dennis Millhouse, in dusty grey slacks and sweat-smeared white dress shirt, limped up to Angel, pulling his valise as Angel opened the passenger door and exited the car.

"It's such a pleasure to meet you."

"How's your arm?'

"Better. That Izzy? His hands are magic."

"Izzy'll come as long as you need him."

"His fingers are – a gift."

Charlie knew Angel sent Izzy Isaacs, her masseur up once a week to give Millhouse the full massage therapy treatment that he provided for top Hollywood stars. Each time he drove up, Izzy provided a two hour session, to make the drive worthwhile and to keep Millhouse happy.

Millhouse moved over to say "hello" to Gabriella who exited the rear passenger side of the car, and introduced himself to her with grace, respect, and a grown-up handshake. Gabriella was, in effect, why he had a job.

Charlie spoke to Millhouse on the telephone whenever Millhouse was unsure how to proceed and Charlie tried to provide guidance. Technically,

Charlie and The Law Offices did not represent Millhouse, but the last thing Charlie wanted was for Dennis Millhouse to hire his own attorney.

"I was so sorry to hear about Mr. Alex. What a shame."

Charlie moved around the car and shook hands. "Yes. His passing was totally unexpected."

"From what I heard, it wasn't an accident?" Millhouse tried not to sound too nosy.

"It was just one of those things." Charlie looked away, tried to ignore Millhouse.

"He was a charming guy and a genius from what I heard."

"It's a shame, and a shame for the estate," Charlie tried to end the conversation.

"He nearly had a mishap when he first visited here." Millhouse pointed to his arm in a sling.

"You were both lucky."

Millhouse massaged his arm, "Well, not exactly lucky."

"Your arm? Looks like it's healed?" Devlin's acerbic observation did not get the desired acquiescence.

"It's better. Slowly, it's getting better. Anyway, let's go over the apartments' status."

Millhouse led the visitors to the nearest patio, brushed off the grime from the plastic table, reached into his scoffed black valise with his good arm, and laid out his accountings. Devlin grabbed the sheaf of papers and examined the documents as if he knew what he was doing.

Charlie knew that the accounting ledger rows and columns of numbers would mean nothing to any of them. Only a Certified Public Accounting professional could make sense of the property income and expenses' bottom line.

Angel and Charlie listened to Millhouse, to be polite.

Gabriella wasn't interested. "Can I go play?"

"As long as I see you from here."

Gabriella headed towards a group of girls about her age in an outdoor gym area.

Charlie comprehended the basics of what Millhouse explained: Less than ten of the tenants in the fifty-five unit complex still paid rent. The city's Building and Safety officers had inspected the units, and informed

Millhouse that the apartments were not up to Woodfall City codes. The huge cost to make them pass the city inspection was not even worth calculating, because it was impossible for the estate to pay. In effect, "Misty Acres" was insolvent, with huge liabilities if anyone got injured on its non-compliant, dangerous premises.

"Would Jack Wonder want to buy out the estate?" Angel threw out the idea.

Millhouse shrugged. "How do I contact Captain Wonder?"

Charlie sighed. "Does Jack Wonder even exist?"

"I've gotten e-mails and texts from him about one thing or another," Millhouse assured them. "I send a copy of the monthly accountings to his New Orleans attorney, that du Chevalier guy."

Charlie paid attention. "Antoine du Chevalier?"

"Yeah. Him."

"Sounds like a fruit," Devlin sneered.

"He's French," Angel chimed in.

Devlin would not change his analysis. "They're fruits and pansies."

Charlie tried to redirect the conversation. "Have you tried talking to du Chevalier?"

Millhouse nodded. "He says, he is not authorized to talk to anyone about Captain Wonder."

Angel was optimistic. "I can try to charm du Chevalier to tell us where Jack's hiding. I took high school French. '*Oui?*' '*Non?*'"

Charlie shook his head. "I've already called du Chevalier. He hasn't gotten back to me."

"Jack used to come here with Barry. They had friends among the tenants," Angel interjected. "Jack's still in contact with some of them."

"Are any of those tenants still here?"

"Well, there's Mr. Cyclops. He's still in unit forty-seven. He hasn't paid rent ever since Mr. Beneshan passed. Of course, he didn't pay rent before, either. The only difference since he's been fired is that he gives me the evil eye."

"Evict that scumbag!" Devlin hated hearing about freeloaders.

"Mr. Cyclops is revered by the other Cham and speaks the lingo."

"Well, where's the frickin' rent? You stealing it?" Millhouse was angered by Devlin's crude accusation.

"I'm a court-appointed receiver. I'm accountable to the court."

"You're accountable to Angel, and that young lady. You're bleeding this place," Devlin countered.

"I haven't been paid for six months. Do you understand? I'm resigning."

"Let's focus on moving forward." Charlie tried to quiet the two men.

Charlie was no real estate expert, but it was clear there was no solution. Charlie summed up the situation: "It's time to chuck this property."

Charlie looked around the dilapidated structures. It was a shame. Barry Beneshan sank a lot of his profits into this property. It was on the verge of foreclosure.

A dark-skinned heroic looking, middle aged man, with wavy dreadlock curls, a double for "the Hulk," or a clone of Hulk Hogan, came over and extended his hand.

Millhouse was glad to shift away from the accounting's depressing conclusion. "This is Mr. Boohau Cyclops. He's in unit forty-seven and helps translate for the Cham."

"I speak little English. My Cham name is Trengh Dao. It's Boohau Cyclops because of my accident."

Charlie saw Boohau lift his right hand to the glass eye in his left eye-socket. The two middle fingers on the right hand were missing. Charlie shuddered to think of the circumstances that caused the fingers to be chopped off or the eye to be lost.

"Hey, Boohau, I hear you're some sort of a god. Well, what are you doing to earn your free rent around here?" Devlin refocused his aggression.

Boohau motioned around at the many Asian families in the quad. "I help my people live in the United States. We are political refugees. Mr. Beneshan brought us here. Promised us this is always our home."

Millhouse explained. "Mr. Cyclops is a Hmong leader from the old country. The tenants worship him."

Devlin wasn't satisfied with Millhouse's explanation. "How did these jerk-offs take over this shit-hole?" Boohau Cyclops ignored Devlin. Millhouse didn't.

Millhouse sought to give Devlin a quick background, with a pleasant narrative. "While he was in the Navy, stationed in Southeast Asia, Mr. Beneshan met Mr. Trengh Dao. The Hmong and Cham tribes sided with the United States against North Vietnam. When the Cham fled, Captain Wonder, who was the senior Navy commander, saw their safety as a personal responsibility. Once they became U.S. political refugees, they qualified for government aid, which meant the rents were paid by the feds. Now, with all the city citations, the government has stopped sending checks. They're – a liability."

Boohau faced Angel. "Welcome, Madonna Angel."

Devlin wasn't pleased with Boohau Cyclops' physical charisma and modest charming greeting. Boohau Cyclops was a prototype hero, a modern day Achilles, or Theseus with a face chiseled by Michaelangelo who gave the over-sized inquisitive eyes a graceful resting place much like an owl's. Boohau's nose was thin and rested above delicately angled lips, and a crisp, well-proportioned mouth. Charlie noticed Boohau was missing two fingers in his left hand. His left eye, upon a closer look, was not a good glass replica of a human eye. Charlie was impressed that Angel smiled and reached for Boohoo's deformed right hand.

Devlin had to take center stage. "You have a duty. Get these leeches to pay. Understand? Pay! That's your god job for Madonna Angel."

"Honey, shut up."

Boohau half understood Devlin was unhappy, but instinctively knew Devlin had no say, and kept bowing to Angel.

"We are grateful for Madonna Angel and loved Mr. Beneshan. Mr. Beneshan was sent by our Buddha to lead us to freedom."

"Mom, look what the kids gave me." Gabriella ran back to join the group and gape at Boohau.

Gabriella showed off the hookah pipe. Angel was shocked.

"Where did you get that?"

"I traded my bracelet with one of the kids. Isn't it cool?"

Angel grabbed the drug accessory away from Gabriella. "What the 'he – ck' is going on?" She threw it into the overflowing trash can. Boohau looked puzzled, walked over and retrieved the pipe.

Millhouse was thrown for a moment, then regained his composure. "Some tenants use opiates. It's a Hmong religious tradition."

Devlin was livid. "You squirmy little jerk. You don't deserve anything but a prison sentence for letting these vermin live here rent-free and deal drugs."

Devlin turned to confront Cyclops. Charlie was afraid of a fist fight. "Let's move on."

Angel grabbed Gabriella's hand and followed after Charlie.

"Hey, I want to see my new friend. At least say 'good-bye.'"

"She's not your friend. She's a dope-ster junkie. Let's go."

Gabriella cried as she acquiesced.

Devlin's face was frozen in piercing looks of aggression. He pondered as Boohau returned, towered over Devlin, unafraid, holding his sacred pipe. Boohau's gaze was solid, commanding, a born leader's stance. Devlin considered his options, and wisely decided not to attack a warrior deity.

"Let's look at the other property – 'Fair Oaks.'"

Dennis Millhouse was unfazed. Charlie, on good terms with Millhouse, nodded. He tried to defuse the confrontation between Devlin and Boohau by reaching in and offering his hand. Boohau turned away from Devlin, shook hands with Charlie, still holding the hookah pipe. Charlie felt the missing finger-stubs, but appreciated Boohau's three-fingered firm grip.

Boohau bowed "good-bye." Devlin backed down. "So, your dudes smoke dope as a religion?"

"It is how we pray to the Dao gods."

"Listen, Boohau, I will make you into real Americans. Not welfare slobs. Boohau, I'm going to get you and your tenants real jobs."

Boohau bowed to Devlin. "Thank you."

"America is the land of opportunity – and big bucks." Devlin backed to the car. "We'll talk again, amigo, keemo-sabe, brujo. You're the man."

Boohau's face beamed good feelings.

Millhouse was already getting into his SUV. Charlie followed Angel back to the car.

Devlin gave Boohau the "thumbs up," but realized that might be misunderstood. "You and me we make money. Big, crispy Franklins and Jeffersons. I'll call."

"Honey, let's go."

Charlie slumped into the passenger seat, not daring to ask about Devlin's latest 'get rich' scheme. Gabriella got in from the other side.

Millhouse leaned out of the driver's side window as his SUV moved past the Mercedes.

"Follow me."

CHAPTER 19
A FLY COVERED ARM

The sun was in Charlie's eyes as the Mercedes approached "Fair Oaks." The street looked quieter than the Misty Acres neighborhood. Fewer rusted hoods were raised on junk cars and fewer home-spun mechanics leaned over carburetors and batteries.

As Devlin swung in behind Millhouse's SUV, Charlie looked at the back side of "Fair Oaks." He could see no oaks, nor any trees or bushes on the property. Two story non-descript paint-chipped buildings were enclosed on the fourth side by covered outdoor parking. The sedan pulled in.

Everyone got out of the car and followed Millhouse across the barren parking area, as Millhouse hurried to the center of the inner back yard where a kidney shaped walkway outlined the complex's former swimming pool now completely covered with concrete.

"There was a crack in the pool, and the water seeped all through the back yard, creating sink holes." Angel explained. "I couldn't afford a new pool so I had it filled with concrete."

Gabriella was not impressed as she walked around her domain. Millhouse came over, showed off the "Fair Oaks" property.

"This property's a winner. With a few improvements, we'll be in the black." Millhouse's news was welcome, even if Charlie guessed it was optimistic.

Gabriella approached the swimming pool area. Her eyes focused on the edge of the concrete.

Gabriella screamed a piercing scream, placed one hand to cover her mouth and pointed. Charlie, Angel, Devlin and Millhouse rushed over.

Charlie's eyes followed Gabriella's index finger. Inside the concrete pool, not far from the edge was what appeared to be a fleshy, hairy, blue-gray arm jutting out of the concrete, with a ragged hand, fingers pointing, flies buzzing around, a few landing, forming speckles on the decaying digits.

Charlie felt nauseous, concentrated on avoiding throwing up. *Images of De Chirico and Salvador Dali surrealistic landscapes flashed by.* However, this was no museum tour.

"Gaby, Gaby, get away. Get back to the car, right now." Angel pulled her daughter away.

"Who the hell is that?" Devlin took the lead and stepped onto the concrete from the pool's walkway. He started to sink. Devlin jumped back to the edge.

"Be careful. The concrete hasn't cured." Millhouse tried to remain calm.

"The hell about a 'cure,' he's dead," protested Devlin.

"I mean the concrete," Millhouse reiterated.

"What kind of a professional are you?" Devlin yelled. "You've got a stiff on our damn property?"

"Honey, zip your mouth." Angel put her hands over Gabriella's ears.

Charlie, for once, did not blame Devlin for swearing, but didn't fail to notice that Devlin always included himself as an owner of any estate property.

"I inspected the place last Thursday," Millhouse apologized.

"Let's cover that arm before the tenants see it." Angel retreated. "Stay here, darling. Devlin? Go get the blanket!"

"Right." Devlin gaped, failed to move. Angel seethed.

Charlie was impressed with Angel's acumen and practical sense. She'd make a good administrator.

Millhouse blubbered: "I'm so sorry. I've never managed a property where this happened."

Charlie thought of the implications. There wouldn't be an arm without a body attached underneath the concrete.

Millhouse was ashen. "I'd better call '911.'"

"Damn, and this is the good property." Devlin was agitated beyond his normal high-strung self and just stood, gaping at the arm.

"Get the blanket!"

Devlin threw an invective at Millhouse. "I guess it's up to me to get the friggin' blanket."

"Watch your language."

Devlin stalked to the Mercedes.

Millhouse stepped apart from the group as he pressed the phone to his ear.

"Yes, dispatcher? We need help. I'm Dennis Millhouse, the Fresno court receiver for the 'Fair Oaks' apartments at 243 Shady Glen Lane. This is an emergency. We found a corpse in the swimming pool. No, we can't see the body, just the arm that extends above the concrete. The concrete covers the pool. Dennis Millhouse."

Millhouse got off the phone. "They're on their way."

"Who?" Devlin confronted Millhouse.

"Well, I imagine, the police. I don't think we need first responders. Do you?"

"Damn cesspool." Devlin hissed. No-one disagreed.

CHAPTER 20
DEATH ROW

The two Woodfall police officers got out of their aging grey police cruiser, met briefly with Millhouse, and sauntered to the swimming pool. Charlie and Angel stood to one side, waiting their turn to speak after the formality of observing the shadowy shape in the concrete. One officer reached from the edge of the pool and pulled the blanket off the protruding hand. The veteran police officer turned to Charlie, introduced himself as Sergeant Gene MacDaniels, got his report form and calmly interviewed each witness. Afterwards, Officer MacDaniels interviewed Gabriella as she sat in the Mercedes's back seat, pale. She could hardly respond in any other way than head shakes.

"She won't have to testify, will she? She's in school in L.A." Angel hovered over Gabriella.

"Don't worry. There's no inquest. This is it," Sergeant MacDaniels assured Angel.

Neither officer seemed particularly shocked. Charlie gave the young officer, the very earnest Patrolman Tom Tenny, his business card as Charlie described how they found the protruding hand. Both officers filled out "Incident Reports" and requested signatures from Angel, Charlie and Devlin. As Charlie signed and printed his name at the bottom, on the form, he could see the other officer offer the clip-board with Devlin's interview for Devlin to review and sign.

Devlin signed his signature with his left hand, a large scrawl with a flourish. He complied with Officer MacDaniel's request to print his name on the form. Charlie had a clear view of Devlin's penmanship, and recalled

Alex's death-threat note and tried to make out Devlin's printing. There was an uncanny similarity.

Charlie, handed his own signed form back to Patrolman Tenny and unobtrusively turned and focused on Devlin's printed handwriting on Officer MacDaniels' clipboard Incident Report. *The back-slanted graphic lettering matched the neat handwriting on the threatening note Alex showed Charlie two nights before Alex's gruesome death!*

Charlie wasn't sure what to do. Confronting Devlin at any point could be lethal. Now, in front of two police-men would be the opportunity to get Devlin to confess.

"Devlin, you've got good penmanship."

Devlin's head turned like a threatened viper towards Charlie. "Are you a faggot or what?"

Charlie was flustered. He could almost see Devlin's fangs sink into his flesh. He couldn't get the gumption to blurt out the question he was getting at: *"Did you kill David Alex?"*

Devlin sounded outraged as he turned away, knowing Charlie had been paralyzed into submission, and handed his signed Incident Report back to the Officer. "Where's your crime scene unit? This is a damn homicide." Devlin sounded authoritative.

"Well, they're kind of busy. This is an active area for field investigations."

"What are you going to do about the stiff in the concrete? Just leave him there?"

"We don't have a recovery unit. It's up to the property owner to dispose the body."

Angel gave back her signed form. "I don't shovel corpses out of concrete crypts."

"Yes, ma'am. But what are we supposed to do? We're just a small town."

Millhouse saw his chance to make a positive impression. "I'll take care of it, Ms. Sedona. I have contacts at the mortuary." Millhouse acted as if disposing bodies was an everyday chore.

Charlie, knowing his moment to confront Devlin about Alex's murder passed, peered into the concrete. He wasn't sure if he could see the shadow of a body underneath the gray textured solid mass. Charlie rationalized: he couldn't accuse one client's agent of killing another client in front of the police. Maybe, a better opportunity would present itself.

Officer MacDaniels hovered on the pool's edge, snapped pictures, leaned out, smattered a few fly-covered fingers with powder, and copied quick fingerprints on clear celluloid patches from his kit.

Charlie was relieved, happy to leave Woodfall immediately. He knew confronting Devlin on the way back was pointless, yet he was curious. Did Devlin write the threatening note to Alex? More important: Did Devlin kill David Alex? The handwriting on the anonymous threatening note matched Devlin's printed name on the Incident Report. Devlin had admitted he was in Charlie's studio the night Alex was strangled, and the note and Alex's valise were gone. Charlie was clear in his mind: at the very least, Devlin was a suspect.

．　　　．　　　．　　　．　　　．

The only breaks in the silence on the drive back to L.A. were emergency requests to upchuck at filling station rest rooms. Everyone including Charlie took turns racing to bathrooms. No one else in the Mercedes questioned the reason for the panicked pleas to stop. Even Devlin got sick several times, luckily, near roadside California rest stops where he could pull in, and run into the public toilets. Charlie was grateful, that the state had not shuttered these essential facilities in its budget cutbacks.

At the last rest-stop before climbing the hills into Los Angeles County, as Devlin raced into the restroom, Charlie followed. He waited for the right moment over the putrid sinks, and as they washed hands, looked into the bent metal mirror on the wall at Devlin.

"Alex showed me a note threatening his life if he didn't resign. It's your handwriting."

Devlin was caught off guard for a moment, but just for a moment, laughed aggressively, kept lathering his hands, rinsed them off, faced Charlie, flicked water on Charlie's face from his fingers.

"You're some crazy bugger. Where's this note?"

"You took it from my studio the night Alex was killed."

"The sun must have baked your brains. I'll pretend you never said this, you punk. Stay with the program, or Angel gets another attorney."

Charlie wasn't sure whether Devlin was lying, but it didn't matter. The note was gone and he had no proof to throw back at Devlin. Charlie dropped his eyes. Devlin saw Charlie back down, flicked the remaining dripping water from his fingers in Charlie's eyes.

"I didn't kill that Alex."

"You wrote the note."

"I wanted the administrator job for Angel. Yes, I wrote the note to get Alex to resign, but I didn't kill him. He was dead when I got to your studio." Devlin sneered, poked Charlie in the side so it hurt.

"You can't tell the cops anything. I'm your client's agent. So, lay off. I got miles to drive."

The two men walked back to the car, side by side, without a further word. Devlin jumped behind the wheel.

"Next stop: home, baby."

While Charlie half-believed Devlin and crossed him off the list of suspects for the moment, Devlin's callousness and the fact Devlin knew the location of Charlie's bungalow didn't sit well. He recalled the chalk marks on his studio Berber rug which still indented the rug's naps. Some shampoo service was necessary to fix the rug and not remind Charlie what happened. Maybe that would make him feel safe.

The Mercedes zoomed past southbound trucks. Devlin was driving too fast. Angel cautioned him to slow down.

Charlie put the note and Alex's death out of his mind. He thought back on his earlier days.

There was a time in his life, when he knew no one who died. There had been the funeral of the distant cousin when Charlie was still in night law school. That's what started it. In those days, Charlie worked at an entertainment law firm as his day job, and the legal crises and issues were mostly centered on which trendy lunch place to set up for celebrity clients. Charlie's role was ephemeral, yet, proximity to movie star legends gave Charlie a certain panache. It made Charlie upbeat, exuberant, positive about his own future.

Charlie couldn't remember when all that hope extinguished. At the entertainment law firm Crainbach-Weinbottom, there was a probate department, with elegant attorneys who managed trusts and estates of major players in town. Charlie had been fascinated, but he, like everyone else who worked for Crainbach-Weinbottom, stayed away from the probate section of the law firm. That was "death row." No one wanted to be a part of it. Now, this is where Charlie ended up, and he couldn't understand the trick fate played to make him the sole "death row" for Earl Guarder's law firm. Was this the way he would come to accept, that he, like everyone else, was mortal?

The lights of the first Los Angeles suburb, Santa Clarita glimmered in the valley below. At least, for the moment, Charlie was headed home.

CHAPTER 21
A VERY PRIVATE INVESTIGATOR

Following up her David Alex assignment, Tammy McCormack focused her investigation on the sidewalk spat between Alex and the two actors who lived a block away from the attorney's bungalow. Tammy researched the actors in her *TV Star Find* data base. The comedians were typical Hollywood Farmdell residents: in the arts, well-off, living in a long-term committed same-sex relationship. They had met while on tour back East and moved to Los Angeles twelve years ago. One of them was already a Headliner but their big break came when their TV pilot for *My Momma* was picked up by one of the networks and the show, starring both, became a huge hit. Tammy knew she would have to be careful not to offend local progressive sentiments. She needed to be sensitive to the married same-sex parents' status. One of the actors, she forgot which one, was the neighborhood watch person. He seemed to have quite a temper, but was also connected with the Hollywood Police Division's patrolmen, including the neighborhood watch liaison, Officer Nixon Tracker.

Tammy walked up the steps of the stately home, about a block north of the attorney's tiny bungalow, and knocked on the Italian bronze renaissance door knocker. After a wait, a crisp housekeeper opened the door a tiny slit, and curtly informed Tammy that neither Benton Wayne nor Sandy Trayle was at home, The door slammed shut as Tammy tried to hand her business card through the opening.

The following day, Tammy came back. Sandy Trayle, a lanky, balding man, with dark eyebrows, and pudgy cherubic face, in his early '50's was at home, and called out at her through the door's peep hole that this was his first day off work in months and he wanted to be left alone. Tammy was used to being lucky in that way.

"This will only take a minute. I'm trying to follow up on a homicide investigation for the L.A.P.D."

He opened the door, and apologized for his sour temper.

Sandy invited Tammy into the Spanish style living room restored to its historical beauty from the silent film era. Tammy had read that this house was built for the silent film star, Rudolph Valentino, but she was sharp enough to deduce that such facts might be embellishments equivalent to "George Washington slept here" claims back East.

"Sit down. I'm sorry I haven't called you back. I've been crazed with our show."

"Your show is very funny."

"Thanks. *My Momma* is based on my mom and what happened when Benton and I were on a cold streak and had to move in with her. All the worries I created for her because I was different."

Tammy sat on a leather upholstered chair that was ornate enough for Bourbon royalty. She took out her notebook and pen.

"It's a great show with a lot to say about acceptance. I'm sure your mom is proud of you."

"Thanks." Sandy wiped away a tear. "I wish she were still here. At least, she saw me when I was on *Mod TV*. That was a crazy, fun time."

"I love *Mod TV*."

"Thanks."

The housekeeper walked out from the shadows with the infant girl, and Sandy turned to dote on his ashen haired adopted daughter.

"This is Darlene. She's the joy of our lives."

"How old is she?"

"She just turned two. We adopted her last year. It was the best thing we've ever done."

Darlene laughed with pleasure at Tammy, who was smitten by the lovely tiny princess. She wondered if she'd ever have any little princesses of her own.

"She is a beautiful girl."

The two-year old gazed at her adopted father's smile, and gurgled laughter amidst occasional bouts of infant age-appropriate tears. Tammy turned to the business at hand and proceeded to take notes.

"Do you know about the recent homicide down the street?"

"Well, I heard rumors of something from a neighbor."

"The victim was a big-shot builder and developer, a Mr. David Alex?"

Tammy saw Sandy blanch. Tammy's gaze shifted to the housekeeper who came and took Darlene from Sandy. Sandy motioned for the housekeeper to take Darlene from the room.

Once Darlene was out of the room, Sandy leaned forward.

"Darlene's birth mother is David Alex's daughter, Chloe Alex. She had asked us to be the godparents after the baby was born."

Tammy was caught off guard.

"David Alex was strangled down the street."

Sandy hesitated, showed both delicate hands to her. I'm an actor, not a fighter."

Tammy shrugged apologetically. "The police are investigating. You understand, we must follow every lead."

Sandy considered, nodded, loosened up. "I'm here to help. What do you want to know?"

Upon listening to Tammy's carefully worded questions, and confirming Chloe Alex and David Alex were estranged, Sandy explained the circumstances of the adoption. Chloe had called from Tom Bradley International Terminal at Los Angeles International Airport, just as she was about to fly off to Nepal on a one-way ticket. Chloe blurted over the phone that she had placed Darlene in the L.A. County Foster Care system because she did not want the eight-month old infant to be with her own dad, the baby's grandfather. As far as the father, he was not in the picture. David Alex had been furious at Chloe for having the baby and Chloe was escaping his rage.

Sandy pleaded with Chloe to let the godparents adopt the infant. Chloe called the County Services while the China Central Airlines plane was still on the tarmac, and obtained permission for Benton and Sandy to take the infant out of the County's foster care system. The County was happy to oblige the birth mother's instructions and save tax money. David Alex opposed the adoption, so, the process took almost a year in the court system. As of two months ago, the adoption was finalized.

Tammy finished the interview with a tour of the fabulous mansion that Sandy learned had been built for silent film movie stunt legend Rama Lewis, best remembered for his classic "Never Safe" scene, hanging from the clock hands eight stories above downtown L.A. Sandy sidestepped whether he had run into David Alex on the street, but agreed Tammy could come back to interview his life partner, Benton, in a few days after the current *My Momma* script was taped.

.　　.　　.　　.　　.

A few days later, Tammy returned and met Benton Wayne, stocky, curly headed, in his early fifties, dressed in faded Tommy Tube blue jeans and faded azure blue T- shirt. Both parents were in the front garden of the home when Tammy walked up, in a good mood as she breathed in the beautiful Southern California day. Darlene happily picked geraniums from the flower-bed that framed the manicured grass landscaped front yard. Benton Wayne appeared frazzled when Tammy walked up and introduced herself.

"So you're a private dick," he blurted and laughed.

"Not 'private,' Mr. Wayne, I work for the L.A.P.D.," she countered.

"But a real 'dick,'" Benton chortled.

Sandy interceded: "Honey, you're not on the set. Calm down."

Sandy shrugged to Tammy in apology.

"Sorry, punch, punch." Benton did a faux fist to his cheek. "Let's get this done."

Benton was forthcoming to Tammy's questions. The two parents acknowledged they had run into David Alex the day in question, some two months ago, but denied that there had been anything more than the sidewalk spat when Alex recognized them on the street. The whole episode was unsettling, but nothing more. The nanny stood behind the two actors during the interview, never breaking a smile.

■   ■   ■   ■   ■

Tammy took notes at the second interview, wrote up a report, and handed her findings to Detective Oswilla.

Detective Oswilla was impressed, but needed more evidence to make a move. Detective Oswilla asked for and received the Forensics Report from Officer Tracker's samples in Charlie Tobias's bungalow. The report found no traces of fingerprints or DNA inside the attorney's studio other than that of the attorney and the vic. You would think the assailant would leave something behind – fingerprints, something. Detective Oswilla wasn't fond of Hollywood types and for the moment, Sandy Trayle and Benton Wayne were his only suspects, but Oswilla didn't have enough evidence to arrest the sitcom stars – yet.

CHAPTER 22
BURIAL COSTS

Tuesday morning after the rocky weekend Woodfall inspection trip, Judge Matthew Bittenkopf's courtroom was unusually sparse. The judge, in one of his lighter moods, pondered Charlie's most recent emergency request while holding the graceful polished aluminum urn containing the remains of the corpse attached to the putrid protruding arm. The judge moved the metal vessel to the side of the dais with one hand for the bailiff to return to its owner, reviewed the death certificate, and looked directly at Charlie.

"You're asking me for an Order for ten thousand dollars from estate funds to reimburse Miss Sedona for the cost of pulling the deceased's corpse from the Fair Oaks apartment's swimming pool?"

"There was no time to inform the court. Ms. Sedona had to pay the mortuary and the workmen immediately from her personal funds."

"Yes, I see the police report."

The bailiff took the urn from Judge Bittenkopf's dais and walked it back to Charlie.

"Our request includes costs for re-surfacing the concrete in the swimming pool," Charlie added. "We had the body cremated at the local mortuary over the weekend and the urn messengered to our office yesterday. That was the most cost-effective way to deal with the unfortunate tragedy."

Charlie reached for the urn and placed Will Wonder's ashes into his valise, having made his point with the somewhat unusual "show and tell."

The bailiff returned to his post next to the judge.

"We didn't learn the corpse was Jack Wonder's son, until we were notified yesterday from the City of Woodfall Police Department that the victim's fingerprints matched Will Wonder's."

"Does Captain Jack Wonder know his son's no longer with us?"

"We telefaxed his New Orleans' attorney's office to give notice to Captain Wonder of this morning's hearing."

"Did he contact you?"

"No, your honor. We also contacted the mother, Captain Wonder's ex-wife, Janet Wonder."

Judge Bittenkopf pondered, shook his head as he passed the death certificate to the bailiff who walked the document back to Charlie.

"Mr. Tobias, the estate is out of cash. Even if I sign such an Order, where will the money for reimbursement come from?"

"From the Fair Oaks property rents. Without taking care of this challenge, the tenants would move out and the Woodfall City Building and Safety Department would shut down the complex."

Judge Bittenkopf pondered and was glad to give Counselor Henry Gilliam a chance to interject objections.

"Your honor, if Ms. Sedona chose to pay for the excavation and cremation of an unknown corpse, and expects reimbursement, that's unconscionable. She owes us over two-hundred thousand dollars by court order, and she ignores paying us."

Jones Sharke always objected to any payment Angel made. Under California probate law, costs of administering an estate had first priority. However, Charlie also knew Judge Bittenkopf depended on Angel's work on behalf of the estate. Without Angel advancing moneys for emergencies, such as taking care of this newest dead body, the estate would collapse.

"Was the deceased connected in any way with the estate or serving it in any way?" Henry Gilliam interjected the question to drive home the point that young Will Wonder should not have an estate paid funeral.

Judge Bittenkopf turned to Ashland. "What say ye, Mr. Ashland? Is this a reimbursable emergency?"

Charlie knew when the judge turned to using old English terms, he wanted support for whatever way he leaned in his opinion.

Ashland cleared his throat. "Well, of course it is. The expense is totally justified. However, I would like your Honor to ask Ms. Sedona to leave my client at home in the future, and not have the minor beneficiary of the estate exposed to this kind of danger."

"Are you paying for a baby sitter?" Angel blurted at Ashland.

"Ms. Sedona. That will be all." Judge Bittenkopf tried to sound stern. If Judge Bittenkopf had forgotten, Charlie reminded him in the submitted petition that Angel Sedona and her daughter were owed family allowance support.

Judge Bittenkopf decided.

"All right, I'll sign the order. Ms. Sedona can be reimbursed the $10,000 from tenants' rent out of the 'Fair Oaks' property at the rate of $1,000 a month."

"$1,500 a month?" Charlie countered.

"$1,250 a month. Submit your Order and give notice."

"Thank you, your honor." Charlie knew he pushed it as far as he could.

Henry Gilliam glared at Charlie, hurried out of the court.

Charlie gathered his papers off the attorneys' bench, whispered to Angel to wait outside in the hallway, walked to the clerk with his Proposed Order and jotted "$1,250 a month" on the document line he left blank for the handwritten insertion.

Terry, the red-headed clerk took the two page Order after Hearing.

"Where's your self-addressed envelope?

Charlie whispered "I'll wait."

CHAPTER 23
FIND JACK WONDER

In the court hallway, Devlin strutted over from the coffee shop with a fresh cup of coffee, pushed next to Angel as she exited the courtroom's doorway.

"What happened, babe?" He held onto his java.

"The judge gave us the okay."

"See?" Devlin sneered, slurped a mouthful of the hot liquid.

Charlie holding his signed Order, hurried into the circle, afraid of leaving Angel alone with Devlin. Luckily, no creditor attorneys impinged the conference. Ashland stepped into the group.

"Thanks," Charlie nodded to Ashland, trying to look into Ashland's recessed eyes, not at Ashland's polished head with the silver hair follicles rimming the reflective pate.

Ashland expected the courtesy for coming to court and supporting the petition on a day's notice. He nodded approval for Charlie's polite deference and turned to strategy.

Ashland expressed concern about Jack Wonder's well-being. "Will Wonder's execution means Captain Wonder's life is in danger. If Jack Wonder dies, all properties which have the 'Wonder' name on title are subject to a new estate in another court."

Charlie knew what Ashland was getting at. Dealing with legal requirements for one court in one state was a herculean task. Complying with court requirements in two courts, possibly in two sovereign states meant that the estate, effectively, was illiquid.

"I liked that kid. He had a good heart, but he never found himself, floated in and out of dead-end jobs. Being the son of a decorated Navy SEAL is a tough act to follow." Angel's eulogy was poignant and momentarily silenced the group.

"Well, if we could track down Captain Wonder and cut a deal, we could get out of this mess." Charlie tried to force optimism he knew Earl felt. Charlie had prepared the petition the previous day after getting the call from Woodfall confirming the victim's identity based on fingerprint identification from the F.B.I. database into which Will Wonder's prints landed from several forged check convictions. Earl approved spending a morning in downtown court and Charlie came to the court early to make the 8:00 a.m. emergency time slot primarily to appease Devlin's demand to "get the money back."

"The only way out of this quagmire is to get to Jack Wonder and cut a deal. Now that his kid's ashes are in an urn, Jack may mellow." Ashland offered no specifics on how to do this. Charlie was always impressed with Ashland's analysis. Ashland's mind cut to the chase, but the details of solving the puzzle were left to Charlie to execute.

Charlie shook hands with Ashland. "Thanks again for coming down, and for your support."

Charlie headed down the marbled hallway alongside Angel and Devlin.

"You got to push the scumbags harder," Devlin hissed. "The ex-wife, Janet Wonder? She'll know where the son-of-a-bitch is at."

"She hasn't gotten child support for over three years," Angel retorted. "If she knew Jack's whereabouts, she'd lasso his wallet!"

Charlie wasn't optimistic. On Angel's advice, he had "served" documents on Jack Wonder at his ex-wife's Silver Lake address for one of the hearings. The envelope was returned with a scrawled obscenity: "Don't contact me about the deadbeat fuck s.o.b."

Charlie had been relieved not to receive a visit from the postal inspectors about sending obscenities through the mail.

"Let's stop at her place. It's not far from here." Devlin had audacity.

"I've got to get back to the office."

"Charlie? It's not far out of your way."

CHAPTER 24
CONDOLENCES IN AN URN

Angel's sedan approached the small overgrown clapboard house on Vendome Avenue. It was one of those transition areas of the Silver Lake neighborhood. A number of properties were fixed up, trendy, attractive. Then, there were the others like Janet Wonder's house with its frayed roof, weed and garbage strewn front lawn, cracked asphalt driveway and an angled garage door that reminded Charlie of one of the geometric angles of Pythagorean harmony, whether obtuse, or acute, he didn't recall.

Devlin pulled Angel's car to a stop on the cul-de-sac, which was shaded by the freeway concrete wall. He sat in the car, egging Angel on.

"You're doing her a favor."

Devlin pulled out a breakfast roll from the small bag sitting next to him on the front seat and chomped on the bear-claw he picked up at the courthouse coffee kiosk.

Charlie pulled Angel out of the car. "I've got to get back to the office."

Angel got out, looked back at Devlin, disgusted. Devlin blew her a kiss, pushed the remaining bear claw into his muscular lips and chomped. Charlie looked back, noticed Devlin's protruding jaw was a direct descendent of early Cro-Magnon Man's facial bone structure. He turned and followed Angel to Janet Wonder's house.

Angel knocked on the dilapidated door whose multicolored coats of paint spoke of decades of neglect. The door swung open, its squeaky hinges needing a lube. Janet Wonder appeared to have just stepped out of a Dust Bowl photo opportunity with her rumpled hair pulled under a kerchief, bellowing in her vintage full-figured skirt and wrinkled off-center blouse.

"What the hell do you want?" She glanced from Angel to Charlie. "Who's he?"

"I'm Charlie Tobias, Attorney at Law."

"Oh, you're the putz who tries to use me as a forwarding service for my ex. I don't know where that dead-beat is."

"Who the hell's at the door?" The graveled voice echoed from some inner sanctum of the lair.

"Shut up, honey. I'll deal with it."

"We found your son, Will."

"Yeah? Under what rock?"

"He was face down and buried in concrete up in Woodfall." Angel handed the small, shiny urn to Janet.

Janet took the urn, didn't seem surprised. She stared for a moment, making her peace with her dead son, or perhaps lost in a senior moment stupor.

"I'm sorry for your loss." Charlie tried to sound as sympathetic as he could. He was sorry. Sorry for her, sorry for finding the body, sorry for getting mixed into this migraine causing estate dispute, being mapped by dead bodies up and down California.

"Get out! Get the hell out of here!" Janet seemed to rebound into an aggressive stance.

Janet grasped the concave metal neck and raised the urn into a battering position. Charlie and Angel stepped back, as Janet assumed a slugger's stance. Charlie was grateful, the urn was sealed tight. Angel had gotten the top of the line model, complete with a screw top, which at the moment wasn't just an indulgence. He pulled Angel away from the doorway. Janet slammed the door.

"What a crazy bitch. No wonder Jack's on the lam."

"Let's just go."

They retreated to the car and got in. Devlin was licking off the almond slices from his fingers.

"Well, she tell you anything?"

"Just drive."

Devlin reached into his bag of goodies, picked out the last blueberry muffin, took a sharp bite, baring deformed teeth. Charlie was glad Devlin had the breakfast baked goods to bite into. Charlie held tight to his valise as Devlin pushed on the accelerator and Charlie's head bounced on the back of the sedan's leather seat.

Charlie knew if he was to find Captain Jack Wonder, it would have to be on his own.

CHAPTER 25
FITTED AND HUNG TO DRY

Devlin pulled in to the Ferndale Avenue loading zone and dropped Charlie off in front of the Law Offices, with no further admonishment or threat. Angel reached out from the passenger seat's window and took Charlie's hand as he stepped onto the sidewalk.

"Thank you. I'm grateful you pulled it off. All those attorneys care about is money. They don't care about my little girl. I'm glad you do."

"Talk soon." Charlie nodded, turned and waved good-bye, raced to the stately building entrance and pushed through into the lobby.

Devlin pulled out of the drop-off zone. Charlie was glad Judge Bittenkopf had approved the payback to Angel, but knew it may be an academic exercise. Where would the extra twelve hundred fifty dollars a month come from? Millhouse would demand being paid before Angel could get her cash. At least the effort had quieted Devlin, and germinated the plan to contact Jack Wonder.

Charlie, lugging his bulging briefcase, headed through the lobby and scooted into the crowded elevator. Alone in the midst of the crowd, he thought about the young man who had been so callously murdered and left as a back-yard display. Was this murder connected to David Alex's death? Charlie shuddered thinking about the deadly game in which he had become an unwitting pawn. He got out on the fourth floor and headed into the Law Offices.

Charlie waved as he passed Earl who was on the telephone in his office, not paying attention to Charlie nor much else, said "hello" to Aki at her thin slice of a desk on which she was assembling new documents that had to be filed in court. Charlie received a hurried smile for his effort to be friendly, and zipped by Amanda Weston's open door. She was punching numbers on her calculator, with perfect posture, dressed in a white linen skirt and matching jacket. It was pointless to even waste a casual "hi" her way.

He turned into his office and slid behind his desk, opened his computer, billed his time from the morning's hearing, prepared the Notice about Angel's signed Order to all interested parties. While the document printed, he raced back into the hall, grabbed the mail from Aki, who was now on the phone advising some caller from the Lawyer's Referral Service about getting a divorce. Charlie winced, hearing her off-the-top-of-her-head legal advice, turned and scanned the incoming mail. Luckily, there were no hostile demands from opposing attorneys. Whoops. There was one: a demand letter from some new attorney representing contractor Eric Dart in the Beneshan case.

Charlie didn't recognize the letterhead as being from any major law firm, so he wasn't too worried. "Legitamate" was misspelled. This attorney was barely legitimate. Charlie didn't remember getting a Notice of Substitution of Attorney from Dart's attorney, that suave Richard Soda guy with the two-hundred dollar Ernie Molar extra-wide Italian silk ties hiding his bloated belly. Eric Dart must be unable to afford Attorney Richard Soda's outrageous Century City billing rates. No matter. Charlie tossed the new attorney's threatening letter demanding one million dollars into the "in" pile.

He'd reply with a measured response telling Attorney Floyd Nobody to jump in the lake. Charlie prepared his own Notice of Substitution of Attorney form for Jimmy Moon in the Henry Moon case, as Earl had instructed.

Just as Charlie finished the form, Jimmy Moon, in his usual long sleeved drip-dry cowboy shirt and jeans, appeared in Charlie's doorway, forced a discouraged smile on his face.

Charlie gestured to Jimmy to take a seat. Jimmy ambled in with the same sweaty fear cows show as they're forced through chutes to slaughter. Charlie tried to look upbeat, but couldn't dissociate from Jimmy's pain. He turned the Substitution of Attorney form around and handed his elegant maroon pen for Jimmy to sign, pointing out the proper two lines that would turn Jimmy from a formidable represented client with a legitimate claim to at least millions of dollars into the dreaded, naked *in pro per* self-represented claimant.

The reality of being *in pro per* was that Jenny Mak, the sister's conservatorship, would prevail in court over Jimmy Moon, *in pro per*. She had been bankrolled by her well-heeled businessman husband, and was represented by two Certified Probate Specialists. There was nothing Charlie could do since Earl had pulled the plug on the non-paying client.

Jimmy took the pen.

"Thanks for all you've done."

Charlie nodded. "I'm sorry, we can't keep representing you." He had done his best. He had recommended Jimmy take the terrible deal offered at the Now We Settle private mediation which ran up a huge bill, half of which Jimmy was forced to pay. Jimmy had balked at agreeing to the Now We Settle mediator's proposal that Jimmy's visitations with his father occur only in public places, such as a restaurant, to allow Henry Moon to see Jimmy's eleven year old daughter Terry on Terry's birthday each August 27th and once every other Christmas holiday, plus, agree to sign off on the sister's conservatorship that Jimmy and Charlie knew in their hearts was nothing more than a velvet kidnap.

"It is wrong," Jimmy had balked to Charlie.

Charlie didn't disagree, but urged Jimmy to compromise. Jimmy refused.

Paying for the Century City private mediation in the plush colonial-themed Thomas Jefferson Conference Room had broken Jimmy financially and led Earl to accede to Amanda's harsh but realistic demand to bring Jimmy Moon's days as a represented client to an end.

Charlie watched Jimmy sign the Substitution of Attorney document, his mind half on Jimmy's acceptance of his future pauper status in life, and half on getting out of the office in the next few minutes.

Jimmy seemed several inches shorter as he stood, shook hands, turned and left.

"Thanks for coming in, Jimmy." Charlie was. Some clients refused to go the easy way. That meant a lot more work for Charlie to get them swept out the door, sometimes with bristles of the legal broom.

A moment later, Charlie was saying "good-bye" to Aki, headed out the door, racing to be on time for his rehearsal fitting. Luckily, Earl was still on the same phone call. Charlie wondered if Earl would insist on going after Jimmy in court for the unpaid four month balance owed.

．　　　．　　　．　　　．　　　．

Charlie made the rehearsal in time. He raced into the men's dressing room, signed in, and ran towards the costume fitting area in front of lit mirrors where the pretty, energetic costume mistress looked at him with a scowl, waiting for him to take his position next to the wardrobe racks. She pulled his costume off the rack.

Charlie was still out of breath, breathing rapidly as he squeezed into his skin-tight mosquito suit. She pulled the scaly sleeves over each arm, brushing her springy brunette curls against Charlie's cheeks as she leaned close, and pinned the arm coverings onto the costume's shoulders using pins from the leather accessory pouch straddling her waist. Veronica Lane was at an age where most women seemed to become unconvincing blondes with dark roots revealing the facade. Charlie appreciated that she hadn't given in to a false attempt to appear youthful.

She eyed his difficult breathing with concern.

"Charlie, are you okay? You're not allergic to any of these rubbery costume materials, are you?"

"Nah. Just racing here from my day job to avoid holding up the line."

"Understood. Seeing your cute eyes and hard breathing? Well, I kind of thought there might be another explanation."

Charlie and Veronica laughed as she defused the stress with her flirty observation. Charlie liked her voice. It was husky, straightforward, very feminine.

"Sure, there's another explanation. But I'm just glad I made it in time to get outfitted."

"I thought so. I'll put a zipper down there. Then, you can unzip yourself."

"I can't unzip anything with these gross rubbery claws."

Charlie gestured to show Veronica his claw-like mitten-covered fingers were non-functional.

"Well, sweetheart, I guess you'll just have to put up with one of the stage managers unzipping your fly."

"You're too much, Veronica."

"You flatterer. Give me more."

"Later, Veronica. Go squish a few other bugs."

"Charlie, you care."

"Well, I have to care about my costume lady, or I'll be in trouble."

"Is that the only reason, Charlie?"

Charlie laughed self-consciously as the seamstress moved her chalk marker and measuring tape expertly to where adjustments were needed – in the shoulder, underarm, in the crotch.

"Thanks, Veronica. You're the best."

"'Flora.' Call me 'Flora.'"

Charlie noticed Veronica's outfit was very old fashioned. Patterned red flowers with graceful petals bloomed on the black background of her blouse. He pulled the paper mache head covering over his head. The fit was acceptable, providing Charlie eye slits, and an opening for his mouth.

"Flora?"

Veronica made her adjustment, took her notepad.

"Like a rose."

"Flora."

"Leave your costume on the rack after the rehearsal."

"Thanks, Flora."

Veronica offered an intimate smile, moved to fit the next chorus member.

Assistant Stage Director, Gerald Schwartz walked by, nodded approval.

"Flare your nostrils, Charlie. Raise your schnoz."

Charlie did as told. The proboscis underneath the nostril opening in the costume uncurled, and curled back again into its French-horn curled position of rest.

"Love it. Keep the proboscis going as you flutter on stage."

Charlie nodded. This "extra" job was becoming too high-tech.

Charlie joined other mosquitoes headed to the edge of the cavernous stage.

"Hey, Charlie. Good to see you."

"Hi, Oscar. Wow, – you look...different."

Thin, elegant, mustachioed Oscar Thornhill did.

While Charlie's costume was somber, anatomically accurate to a mosquito's monotone chameleon coloring, Oscar, as a featured background singer, had colorful red and green stripes on his chest and polka dots around his back. Even his raised headpiece was multi-colored with yellow and red brushstrokes. Charlie thought it would be a step up to be a background singer, instead of an extra. The pay was not only better, but the chance to sing the chorus lines – not just be on stage, buzzing and humming in harmony – would be thrilling. Nevertheless, there was a down side, in that there'd be many lines to memorize, and more rehearsals to attend. There was only so much Charlie could master.

Both men showed off their mosquito bodies and arms as they ambled to the stage, lowered their headpieces, and headed for their first dress rehearsal, knowing it would be a long evening.

CHAPTER 26
DARK PASSAGES

It was 11:01 p.m. when Charlie, back in his street clothes, signed out from the dressing room. He hurried to his car in the underground Music Center parking lot when he heard footsteps echo his own. Charlie knew that the security guard clocked out promptly at 10:00 p.m. He picked up his stride. The footsteps repeated faster, then echoed louder, closer.

Charlie reached his car, took out his key, beeped the car door open and almost slid into the driver seat as a firm hand gripping his left shoulder stopped him. Charlie whirled to face his stalker across the opened car door.

"Charlie Tobias?"

Charlie looked up at a very tall, stocky balding muscular man in his early sixties in sport shirt and khakis and an out-of-place silk cravat protecting and covering his neck. The man had deep-set eyes, the kind of eyes that had grown used to staring down death.

"I'm Captain Jack Wonder."

Charlie, hearing the military designation by the muscular, lanky, coiled adversary inches from his head, knew it was important to maintain a professional attitude. His heart beat in double time.

"Yes, I'm Charlie Tobias. Attorney Charlie Tobias," Charlie tried to disguise his terror, and instinctively knew his best chance for survival was to pretend to be the rumored Navy Special Operations assassin's physical and social equal. "I'm so sorry about your son. I tried to contact you."

Charlie's eyes did not drop from Jack Wonder's. Charlie instinctively knew not to flinch, kind of like when you're face to face with a ferocious pit bull or a momma grizzly bear whose cub has been torn apart. Any sign of weakness or fear meant death. Besides, Captain Jack Wonder had intrigued Charlie, and now he was face to face.

Every sensory minutia processed in Charlie's brain could mean the difference between life and death. The Captain's shirt was starched, and so were the khakis. That reflected the meticulousness that Charlie assumed would be the essence of this ex-military commander's persona. The face was icy, revealing no hint of emotion. The eyes were those of a carnivore, showing no fear.

He had a few cards to play. Jack Wonder would want to learn details about his son's death. As long as Charlie had information that Jack couldn't get elsewhere, Charlie had a good chance to escape alive. Not that Jack Wonder was threatening as he removed his grip from Charlie's shoulder, but Charlie knew Wonder had been a clandestine military officer rumored to have done unconscionable acts in Southeast Asia. He had a reputation as a master of extreme measures who learned to destroy human life not just from the U.S. Navy's Special Ops playbook, but from his Khmer Rouge adversaries. Becoming Beneshan's silent real estate partner was only a recent fallback position.

Wonder dropped his eyes first. "I know you didn't kill Will. I'll dismember the son of a bitch who did."

Charlie nodded in appreciation for the acknowledgment of his own innocence, debated whether he should continue to talk. Jack Wonder had keys to solve estate problems, like getting the "Wonder" name taken off various co-owned estate properties, so the properties could be sold. However, it was getting close to midnight.

Charlie considered he might be better off not knowing anything. Being a probate attorney at Earl Guarder's should not be a ticket to martyrdom. Still, this could be his only chance to find out how Will Wonder came to be in Woodfall, and learn the background to the corpse who had littered his studio hideaway and wrecked his peace of mind forever.

"Dennie's in Hollywood is still open. How 'bout a cup of java?"

Jack Wonder sized Charlie up.

Charlie knew Jack Wonder was hungry to learn every detail about his son's death. He wasn't surprised when Jack Wonder nodded.

"Okay."

CHAPTER 27
THE MIDNIGHT DENNIE'S DEAL

The next day at the Law Offices brought other surprises that sidelined Charlie's meeting Jack Wonder. A high-strung, thin, junior attorney, Larry Diaz, who had worked his butt off past even the late night times when Charlie would leave, was - gone. That left only one Associate other than Charlie, amiable Terry Ketchum, a red headed junior attorney with the unenviable assignment of being the family law specialist. Charlie knew the way layoffs worked around The Law Offices from experience. Employees were given fifteen minutes to gather personal belongings and that was that.

Charlie entered his office and glanced at his desk. Sure enough, it was stacked with a number of new files, Larry Diaz's cases bequeathed to Charlie.

.   .   .   .   .

The first time a layoff happened to Charlie, he had just returned to the Law Offices from a court hearing in far off Rancho Cayumanga Superior Court.

Earl Guarder came into Charlie's office, closed the door, told him to gather his things, turn in his keys and parking pass because he was no longer with the firm. "I'm sorry. You have fifteen minutes to leave." That's all Earl stated in a bland, authoritative voice. It was the day before Christmas, 2006. Charlie, trooper he was, gathered his things, handed over his keys, and said "Happy Holidays" back to Earl as he left. Charlie drove out of the building, headed home to give Tina the holiday cheer.

.   .   .   .   .

Three and a half months later in the spring of 2007, Charlie got an unexpected call on his cell phone from Earl while updating his untouched resume and suddenly, he was back at The Law Offices, as if nothing had happened. Charlie gained some wisdom during those months: things that occurred were rarely under one's control.

.   .   .   .   .

The phone on Charlie's desk rang. The receptionist informed Charlie that Angel was waiting in the lobby.

Charlie exited to the lobby to bring her in, and saw Devlin wasn't with her. Charlie considered how much of what he had learned about Jack Wonder the night before he should share with Angel.

Angel would not be happy with some of the news. Captain Wonder had offered to cooperate, and instruct his New Orleans attorney, Antoine du Chevalier, to work with Charlie to write up a global settlement that would take Wonder's name off all the estate co-owned properties in California. In return Wonder asked for a favor: a Catholic burial for his son, for which Jack Wonder left a substantial check for Angel. The burial would not be that difficult to pull off, even missing Will Wonder's corpse, as Charlie doubted Millhouse was all that careful with religious niceties up in Woodfall. So what if there was no body? Charlie hadn't let on to Jack Wonder that Will Wonder's cremated remains were at Jack's ex-wife's home.

Before Charlie could tell Angel about his meeting with Jack Wonder, Angel blurted out: "I broke up with Devlin." Charlie shrugged, tried to stay visibly neutral.

"He may contact you," she added, uncertain where she stood with Charlie.

"You're the client." Charlie didn't want to put too much stock in relying on a "romantic break up" to develop estate strategy. Angel and Devlin could make up and then what?

"Thanks. Yes, I guess I am."

"I saw Jack Wonder last night."

Angel forgot her discomfort, moved to the edge of her seat.

Charlie described the meeting and Jack Wonder's distress over the death of his son, Will.

"If we could ensure a Catholic burial in Woodfall, he'd work out the global settlement with the estate."

"But we don't have a body."

"He can still have a mass."

Angel thought about this. "I'll get a body. One of the Woodfall tenants is a medical tech who works at the Fresno County morgue. Jack and Janet never talk. You in?"

Charlie begged off. "It's not exactly billable time."

"Could be creepy." She got up, came over, gave him a hug.

Having some qualms about grave robbery, Charlie held onto Jack Wonder's check.

"I'll take care of it." Angel looked into Charlie's eyes. He knew he couldn't keep the check from her, handed it across. Angel's visage became very pleased, held it tightly in her fingers.

Charlie encouraged Angel to meet Captain Wonder's settlement demands. Jack Wonder's willing signature on a settlement agreement could take the Wonder name off all the co-owned California estate properties, even bring in cash for the co-owned properties in Louisiana. Charlie was clear that letting a few properties go would allow the estate to finance itself out of its hole.

Angel had hit a home run with her strategy to negotiate Jack Wonder away. Or had that been Devlin's idea? No matter. Now, there was the execution. Wonder had given a personal telefax number to Charlie to which to send the proposed settlement proposal. Angel recognized the prefix as New Orleans.

"So that's where Jack Wonder set up shop. No surprise to me."

Charlie had already drafted a settlement agreement in meetings with David Alex, Angel and Devlin. Now, Alex was dead, Devlin was banished, and Charlie had the means to get the settlement agreement in front of Wonder and finalize it through the New Orleans Attorney du Chevalier. The negotiated settlement would provide a million dollars to come into the Beneshan estate's treasury - enough to pay creditors and free Angel from the court's shackles. A million dollars!

．　　　．　　　．　　　．　　　．

At the coffee shop, when Jack Wonder heard the huge cash payment Charlie demanded on behalf of the estate, he made his own counter-demand: the two co-owned Louisiana properties' titles would be signed over solely to him.

Charlie agreed to the demands, adding the caveat he had to get Angel and the Los Angeles judge to agree.

Maybe there was hope. Charlie was sure Judge Bittenkopf would sign off on the deal, no matter what the creditor attorneys would say.

Charlie asked Wonder who was behind his son's murder. Wonder looked into Charlie's eyes:

"I'll take care of the sons of bitches."

Charlie shivered and knew he shouldn't nod agreement, but half did.

Wonder asked for a refill. He opened up, talked about meeting and serving with Barry Beneshan in an elite Navy special operations unit tagged "The Wonder Boys." Wonder painted a far different picture of Corporal Barry Beneshan than Charlie heard from Angel.

Wonder talked very softly, but the substance of his story gave Charlie a new perception of Barry Beneshan's adventurous life.

"Corporal Barry Beneshan was an unwilling recruit into the Naval Special Operations forces. The Navy Special Operations unit of which I, a Navy SEAL Lieutenant was in charge, was on a covert mission in the 1990's in Southeast Asia with Hwong and Cham tribal militias, who supported the United States and consequently, suffered deeply after the Communists took control of Southeast Asia in the 1970's."

Charlie was fascinated. "I thought we were out of Southeast Asia in the mid 1970's."

Jack Wonder confided his top secret mission was dubbed "Velvet Underground." The "V.U." mission was in response to ongoing grievous torture and mass murders.

"I was a young police rookie in Denver, Colorado, considered to be an excellent sharpshooter, who joined the Navy in the 1990's, thinking the Vietnam War was a paragraph in the college history books. After completing boot camp in Camp Pendleton, California, I was sent to Navy

Special Operations Officer School in Bethesda, Maryland, and graduated as a Navy Lieutenant, number one in my class. I was technically adept, and took all the engineering courses offered. I signed up to become a Navy SEAL, and survived boot camp in Coronado, just outside San Diego. They gave each of the eight recruits a bowie knife and dropped us off in the Mojave desert. Seven of us made it back. I used my knife to behead snakes for my meals, and cut cactus for water. That's how six days later, I made it back to the town of Kelso, near the Mexican border."

"That must have been something." Charlie shuddered, wondered what happened to the eight recruit. Being a Navy SEAL was only for the crème de la crème of warriors.

"I could tell you stories."

Charlie nodded. "I bet you could."

Over his second cup of coffee, about 12:50 a.m., Charlie learned that in the late 1990's Lieutenant Wonder was assigned to lead a rag-tag trio of "V.U. Volunteers," Corporal Beneshan, and two other young Corporals, Corporal Dylan Vincent and Corporal Coombs Kroft in a near-suicide mission inside Cambodia.

"Corporal Beneshan was the only "V.U. Vol." who had committed a white collar crime. He was adept at languages, picked up the local Lao and Cambodian dialects, and used his people skills, and a substantial government bankroll, to get us out of dangerous jams."

Molly, the friendly Dennie's waitress, who was used to Charlie keeping odd hours, kept the refills coming, in between serving Hollywood producer types and dealing with homeless denizens, who made the Sunset Blvd. eatery extra-special with their growling demands and paranoid complaints.

Why would a pretty young girl like Molly take on such a job? Charlie thought.

Captain Wonder continued: "Corporal Dylan Vincent, a computer geek, had been only sixteen when he hacked into the U.S. National Security Top Secret Intranet Communications System and published a few of the U.S.'s deepest secrets on a foreign internet blog. His attorney advised the genius geek to take the "V.U. Vol." military assignment rather than test the limits of U.S. juvenile legal protection."

Charlie nodded. Molly came by. "How about a banana milkshake?"

"No thanks, Molly. It's fine. Just some more coffee." Molly filled the cups.

Captain Wonder was satisfied that Charlie was eager to hear more. "Corporal Coombs Kroft had been active in the sub-rosa munitions field. The government attorney was not sure that it could convict the misled M.I.T. trained chemical engineer of assembling bombs for Montana paramilitary neo-Nazi cells for quick cash. Kroft was offered a place on my squad and decided to channel his ordinance skills into the Southeast Asia jungles."

Captain Wonder took a breather and drank a third, or was it fourth cup of coffee and continued.

Charlie learned that Corporal Beneshan "volunteered" for the clandestine government assignment, rather than risk a federal Securities and Exchange fraud trial and face lengthy prison time on the grand jury federal indictment for his misplaced acumen to expand his Clean Co. empire with an unlicensed Big Board stock offering.

The four naval special ops called themselves "The Wonder Boys." They parachuted into the Cambodian jungles with maps, inflatable rubber dinghies and wads of dollars. The platoon made its way to one of the most notorious re-education camps in the Cambodian highlands.

The platoon's mission was to free the legendary Cham tribal leader Trengh Dao, who had led sabotage missions against the communists for over a decade after the Vietnam War ended. Even the genocidal Cambodian communist rulers were afraid to execute Trengh Dao, because of his religious hold on the Cambodian Cham population and his acknowledged aristocratic French roots rumored to go back to the French Bonaparte family.

Lt. Jack Wonder's Wonder Boys, surviving water moccasins, malaria, and cannibal head hunters, penetrated the re-location camp in a beautiful isolated tropical valley near the Lao border.

Trengh Dao, under house arrest in an ancient secluded Buddhist pagoda, spoke a bit of English he picked up from American G.I.'s. It hadn't taken much prodding to get Trengh Dao to agree to escape once Jack Wonder's platoon eliminated the guards with bribes, or if necessary, with ASP's, the Navy's acronym not for the slithering tiny snakes whose toxic bites meant instant death, but "Advanced Strangulation Procedures," which had the same silent deadly outcome for the victim. Mass killings were going on all over Cambodia by the communist fanatics. Wonder, Beneshan, Vincent, and Kroft led Trengh Dao through jungles, and crossed the border into Thailand, where Trengh Dao was welcomed as the Cham and French royalty he claimed to be.

Lt. Wonder was promoted to become Captain Jack Wonder and received a bronze star. The other three "volunteer" platoon members, Beneshan, Vincent, and Kroft were allowed to return to their civilian lives. Charges against Beneshan were dropped by the grateful U.S. government. The federal indictment for Security and Exchange fraud against Beneshan was sealed.

Trengh Dao resettled in Woodfall. The "V. U." Mission was altered to enable Cham villagers from the Laotian highlands to escape through Vietnam War era underground tunnels dug a hundred fifty feet deep beneath mountains, and join Trengh Dao in central California.

The Cham received U.S. political asylum. Trengh Dao had taken the English translation of his name as his legal name when he received his political asylum status. His official surname was "Cyclops." "Boohau," his adopted forename, meant "great warrior." He continued to be the Cham tribal spiritual leader in Woodfall, California, ministering to an expanding flock of Cham immigrants and refugees.

At the coffee shop, Charlie, tired but energized, listened raptly to Wonder's story. It did not surprise him that Wonder and Beneshan became owners of the properties that the Cham refugees called home. He had thought it better not to pry how that happened.

Jack looked Charlie in the eye, sensing Charlie's discretion. He excused himself to go to the restroom.

Jack never came back to the table. Charlie paid the waitress and left a ten-dollar tip. They had been at the coffee shop until 2:00 a.m.

■　　■　　■　　■　　■

Angel was inspired as she unfolded and stared at Jack Wonder's $10,000 check for Will Wonder's make-believe funeral costs.

"Sign over what Jack wants, get cash. I'll get a body for the funeral. We have a chance to make this work."

Charlie was squeamish. "What about the urn?"

"Angel laughed. "Those two rattlesnakes never hiss at each other. They hate each other more than I hate attorneys. Whoops, sorry. Not you, of course."

Charlie nodded, happy he was the exception. "We must get the Louisiana judge to approve the settlement, as well."

"I represent Gabriella in Louisiana. I'm called the 'tutor' – kind of like the administrator here. The State of Louisiana? It's Napoleonic Code. I had an attorney who got me appointed. Her name's Colette St. Pierre. I'll give you her number."

Charlie had heard of the fluke. Unlike in the rest of the United States, Louisiana used the French Napoleonic legal system. No need for Certified Probate Specialist Ashland to get involved and muck things up with additional demands to stick to too rigid rules.

Angel looked at Charlie: "Maybe, you could come to New Orleans?"

Charlie looked into her eyes. "Maybe."

Angel got up, gave Charlie a hug. She was out the door with her check pushed into her light brown purse.

CHAPTER 28
NEW ORLEANS

Charlie felt awkward thinking of going to New Orleans with Angel, and had difficulty in getting Tina's reluctant approval almost as much as Earl's "okay," but his discomfort was quashed by Angel's phone call two nights before the scheduled trip. Angel sounded embarrassed letting Charlie know that she made up with Devlin and Devlin was coming. It would be the three of them.

Charlie was relieved. He recalled he tried to smooth the make up with Devlin. "These things happen." He had not expected her response before she hung up the phone: "I'm happy you're coming. I'd miss you if you didn't."

.   .   .   .   .

What Charlie was not expecting even more was to turn the corner into the New Orleans' airport's dated waiting room, after exiting the Southern Air flight from Los Angeles, catch up to Devlin and Angel pulling their respective luggage behind them, and be face to face with Jack Wonder, dressed in civvies, sweating profusely, sporting a Fedora and khaki shorts.

Angel leaped ahead, draped her arms around Jack Wonder's wooden totem pole-like body, burst into tears. "I'm sorry. I'm so sorry about Will. He was so wonderful. I loved him. We all did."

Jack Wonder might as well have been flinty-eyed Clint Eastwood as he nodded his head, looked down on Angel from his six foot, four inch height and said with compassion and sorrow. "Thank you for taking care of the funeral."

Angel wiped away her tear, nodded, reached into her pastel green purse. "I brought pictures. We had Father Daugherty, a Catholic priest, say the mass and offer final absolution. Several of Will's friends from Woodfall came to pay their respects."

Jack Wonder acknowledged Charlie and Devlin's presence as he shuffled the pictures of Will Wonder's modest funeral ceremony in Woodfall, and the burial in the small Catholic cemetery behind the modest church. Charlie kept silent. Apparently, the fact that the actual body of the son was in an urn with Janet Wonder in Silver Lake had gone unmentioned. Charlie never inquired about the body Angel substituted, nor about what happened to Jack Wonder's ten grand, nor who the four attendees were in the pews, who looked the part of mourner friends.

"We'll get the bastards that killed your son." Devlin put on a convincing show of determination and valor. Jack Wonder didn't have revenge in his eyes, only sadness. Angel wiped away tears. Jack Wonder, with a far-away look, nodded in appreciation.

．　　　．　　　．　　　．　　　．

The drive into New Orleans on the raised curved freeway that encircled and eventually deposited travelers downtown was uneventful. The passing city seemed like any other from a distance, and much smaller than a world class city had a right to be.

Jack saw the disappointment in Charlie's face in the rear view mirror as Charlie looked at the city façade of dated skyscrapers intermixed with commercial buildings.

"The precincts that were underwater are on the other side of the French Quarter where we're headed. Some neighborhoods are still deserted, except for rats in rotting collapsed houses."

Charlie was reminded of the swampy foundation for Barry's fortune, and reminded of the death and destruction that Hurricane Katrina and its aftermath caused in this fabled city. Charlie understood his job was to keep as much of the Beneshan estate for his client and her daughter as he could. As he recalled what happened to David Alex and Will Wonder, Charlie reminded himself, *it was also crucial to keep from getting killed.*

The car pulled off the freeway at the downtown exit, crossed historic Canal Street, made several right turns onto one way streets, and pulled into a tight garage next to a two story red brick commercial building on the corner, covered with ivy and signs advertising bail bonds, and pawn shop loans. Cars hurried through the narrow streets, dangerously close to pedestrians. These were "walking" streets, part of the unique French Quarter. Charlie could make out the faded plaque next to the garage entrance that identified the "Edwards Commercial Building" as a historical landmark. The sign's embossed lettering was barely legible, covered in soot and dirt.

.   .   .   .   .

Jack led the way up the creaking narrow wood stairs to the rooms on the second floor. Charlie followed with his overnight bag. Devlin, feeling the call of French chivalry, carried both his and Angel's luggage as Angel spurted up the stairs.

"You've got the best room of all. It's next to the toilet." Charlie's eyes followed Jack's nod towards the tiny bathroom with a pedestal sink and stand-alone tub.

"Thanks."

"It's all charm," Angel observed, stopping for a moment on the carpeted landing below to give Devlin time to catch up.

"Didn't the playwright Tennessee Williams write 'Streetcar Named Desire' around here?" Charlie asked Jack.

"He lived in a small apartment across the street." Jack nodded at the two story building directly across St. Paul Street.

Angel and Devlin reached the second floor.

"We should have stayed in the Hilton." Devlin groused.

Angel responded sharply to Devlin. "Are you paying?"

"I love you, honey. No matter who pays."

Charlie and Jack ignored the spat. Charlie had had his own money spat with Earl who insisted that Angel should cover Charlie's traveling costs as Charlie was on an estate trip. Charlie resolved the problem by bringing $200 of his own money with him. At the least, it was a way to get out of the office for two days. Besides, this was the French Quarter, one of the few sections of New Orleans that escaped Katrina's ravages because it was above-sea level. What could be better?

"We'll meet downstairs in an hour. We'll go have a bite to eat." Jack took charge, barked orders as if this were a boot camp with green recruits. This was, after all, Jack's town, the town in which he and his partner, Barry Beneshan, amassed their last fortune.

■   ■   ■   ■   ■

Charlie entered his wall-papered room, looked around. The room was decorated in nostalgia, with knick-knacks on doily covered side tables and a bare wooden dresser, a simple narrow bed and a wooden desk and chair. The style was depression-era modest for monks.

Charlie put down his overnight bag, and looked over the narrow street. There was a tiny faux balcony in front of the full-length French window, complete with metal art-nouveau swirling grill and vigilant plaster gargoyles standing guard on the peeling window frame sides. At least there was something French in the French quarter.

Charlie lay down for a brief nap, looked at the cracked grey plaster ceiling and relaxed.

Charlie heard a saxophone player on the street, playing a soulful tune. He listened more closely.

Charlie adjusted his sweater, dozed off.

A cell phone ring brought Charlie back to consciousness. He picked up the phone. "Hello?"

It was Tina calling. Charlie was happy to hear Tina's voice and to hear that, at least at home, everything was fine.

CHAPTER 29
ATTORNEY COLETTE ST. PIERRE

The following morning, Charlie met the others in the modest lobby. Angel looked elegant in her trim blue suit. Even Devlin sported a suit and tie for the New Orleans court hearing. Charlie greeted them, and saw Jack Wonder wave from his SUV, which pulled next to the Commercial Building. Charlie followed Angel and Devlin outside to greet Jack.

As Charlie and Jack shook hands, Devlin led Angel to the building's facade, to examine its condition.

Jack's attention was diverted by Devlin's rude behavior. "She sure picks winners."

Charlie shrugged. The last thing he wanted to do was express opinions on Devlin.

Devlin and Angel walked over to the SUV after surveying the ivy covered building fallen on tough times with its commercial tenants keeping marginal shops going, with home-made signs advertising a Salvadorian Café with *Pupusas*, *Empenadas*, and *Pasteles*.

Devlin's business vision was not dampened by the modest tenants.

"These could be writer's offices. The Hemingway connection would make these offices cool rentals."

"You mean Tennessee Williams?"

"Whatever! It's big bucks for the estate." Devlin looked into Jack Wonder's eyes.

"Why let you get this prime French Quarter property?"

Charlie's heart sank. It had all gone too smoothly. If only Angel would have stayed away from Devlin for a while longer. It was that $10,000 check from Wonder that had brought Devlin back to the fold.

Jack Wonder didn't flinch. Jack knew he had to reiterate the down side and emphasize the benefit to Angel in having come to an agreement.

"The offices are not up to New Orleans building and safety codes. I figure I'll have to spend about $10,000 per office to get them to pass the inspections. More than that on each storefront."

Angel was caught between Devlin's spider web of pushback and Wonder's blunt realism.

Luckily, the whine of a silver Porsche Boxster prevented Angel from being squeezed between the squared off men.

A leggy dark haired woman with pinned back hair, in her mid-30's, gracefully swung her flashy legs out of the Boxster leather seat, adjusted her tight, classic business suit with its elegant sheen, and walked up, with confidence and flair. Her looks were classic, her voice was vintage sultry.

"I'm so glad you're here. I have a good feeling about today."

She exchanged two cheek kisses with Angel, and Jack Wonder, French style.

"You must be Charlie Tobias, Angel's attorney in Los Angeles. I'm Attorney Colette St. Pierre."

Charlie shook hands. She had a firm grip and a piercing gaze. Charlie had spoken to Colette St. Pierre several times from Los Angeles. Her throaty voice echoed classic French sophistication. The curvaceous body fit into the snug sedate maroon suit and did not disappoint. Charlie was glad he was dressed in his good blue pin-striped suit and looked presentable, if not dashing.

Angel introduced Devlin as her "associate." She shook hands.

"I'm charmed, Mr. D'Alessio."

"Me, too, honey."

Colette backed away from Devlin's hungry stare.

"You can ride with me, Mr. Tobias. We have a lot to talk about – this case is very complex."

Angel was getting anxious. "Meet you inside the court."

Charlie followed Attorney St. Pierre to her car like a puppy and couldn't help but watch her graceful slide under the Porsche steering wheel. He fell on top of the low passenger seat with a thud, holding onto his black leather briefcase in his lap. She laughed.

"It's not comfortable, but my little car has some advantages."

As Charlie shut the door, the Porsche screeched away, raced through the narrow street. Charlie was thrown back into the headrest, even as he fastened his seat-belt.

"Wow!"

"I like to go fast."

Colette, driving close to sixty in the narrow street, accelerated into a razor-thin opening between two speeding cars. Charlie's mouth became very dry as she squeezed the car into the middle lane, veered back to the right, did a quick right turn onto the intersecting boulevard, and sped in and out of traffic.

"We must not be late for court," she cooed above the wind. Charlie tried to appear nonchalant, but his hands froze on his briefcase handle.

"I was very impressed you got Jack to agree to a deal, although it's a pity the estate will lose the Commercial Building. It has so much history."

"The estate needs the cash."

"Yes, Jack will pay the estate a million dollars…"

"…and take his name off all estate properties other than this French Quarter building and the mansion up river, both of which properties he'll own outright."

Charlie picked up the thread. "…The estate can pay off its creditors, and close its court proceedings."

Colette finished the thought. "Our client, Angel and her daughter can move on."

The two laughed in unison as they reviewed the rationale for the "deal" Charlie engineered with Jack Wonder's New Orleans' based attorney Antoine du Chevalier, via telephone and telefax, and gotten approved by Judge Bittenkopf.

Charlie focused on Colette's angular cheekbones and gaunt neckline decorated with a modest string of pearls. Real or not, the pearls enhanced her beauty to a Vermeer level of classic subtlety.

"Have you seen the chateau?"

"No, just the deed to the property with Beneshan and Wonder on title as owners."

"*Mais, oui*. That Monsieur Beneshan was quite the - " She took one hand off the steering wheel, gesturing to find the right word. Charlie was getting more nervous. " - the rascal."

The Boxster screeched, swerved to avoid a car in front. Charlie catapulted into her right hand whose graceful fingers cushioned him, and left his chest inflamed from its touch.

"I'd better concentrate on getting us there."

She moved her right hand back on the steering wheel. Charlie laughed, but felt the residual tingle.

"I've heard the – 'chateau' is magnificent."

"It will be – with a few million dollars to fix it. By the way, what can you tell me about Will Wonder's death?"

"Bad news travels fast."

"Jack's been a friend for years. He recommended me to Angel to be Angel and her daughter's Louisiana attorney. Since I represent Angel, Jack had to hire a certain pompous idiot to represent him. You'll soon meet Monsieur Antoine du Chevalier."

"Will may not have been the son Jack wished for, but Angel said he was a good kid. Definitely not deserving the end he got from Jack's enemies. Jack looks devastated by Will's murder."

"It crushed him."

She looked into Charlie's eyes. The honk of the horn behind her turned her head back onto the traffic.

"*Merde*, these drivers!"

They turned onto the street that led to the civic center. Colette maneuvered towards the parking garage.

"Who's that handsome Devlin? I hear he's nuts."

Charlie glanced at Colette, hoping she'd refrain from demanding Charlie's opinion on Devlin's mental health.

"My other client, Devlin's boss, is dead. You heard about David Alex?"

"He was murdered. No?"

She spun towards the civic center straight ahead and spoke knowingly.

"That's right. He was murdered." Charlie thought it best to leave out the additional fact that Alex was murdered in Charlie's studio.

"Be careful of our common client, Angel, that she doesn't meet the same fate."

Charlie nodded, thought about Angel's vulnerability, pondered whether he had been wise to let her become administrator.

Charlie followed Colette's finger, pointing to the four story modern glass and concrete New Orleans Parish Civil District Courthouse – the destination. He tried to think Colette's warning through: If Angel died? Charlie's heart sank. He tried to focus on what was suddenly a very crucial issue, now that the settlement was within grasp. Angel was trusting. He couldn't let anything happen to her.

The Porsche Boxster pulled into the parking garage. Charlie was momentarily brought back to the present by Colette's reassuring hand covering his wrist. He looked at her smile, and returned it, without guilt.

"You're right. She's sweet, trusting, in over her head."

"Our client."

"Yes."

Colette moved her hand back to the steering wheel, sharply turned into a parking space, and stopped.

They slid out of the car seats and bolted next to each other. Charlie adjusted his jacket and tie. As they hurried to the elevator, Charlie's mind raced. *Whoever killed David Alex was loose, waiting to kill again.*

Charlie, for the first time acknowledged that Angel was in grave danger.

CHAPTER 30
SETTLEMENT AGREEMENT, 12TH DRAFT

Angel and Devlin walked into the court vestibule that opened onto a grand hall and approached as Charlie and Colette grabbed a seat at the teak wood bench.

"Where's Jack?"

"He's outside with his attorney. They'll be right in."

Colette nodded. "Monsieur Antoine du Chevalier is a distinguished colleague."

Charlie savored her emphatic pronunciation of "distinguished" that hinted of sarcasm.

The portico was painted in belle nouveau pastels. Judges and supplicants on the dark toned walls were painted in frescoes that shadowed standard Christian themes. There might as well have been a "Twelve Stations" of the lawsuit.

Charlie looked up to see Jack Wonder approach alongside an elegant white-haired bamboo-shoot thin gentleman with ruffled cuffs and frilly collar.

"Hello, everyone. Antoine du Chevalier, at your service." Attorney Du Chevalier bowed to everyone in turn. Business cards were passed around. Colette moved next to Charlie. "*Enchante.*" Charlie handed across his *Charlie Tobias, Associate Attorney* business card.

Colette pulled out three sheaves of documents with colored tabbies on the last pages indicating the signature lines. "We can sign the 'Estate Global Settlement Agreement' now, or inside the courtroom."

"We reviewed the documents last night," Charlie added.

.   .   .   .   .

The night before, Jack Wonder handed over the final draft of the Settlement Agreement to Charlie, and left. Devlin insisted on going out to a jazz club, giving Charlie time to review the Attorney Du Chevalier revised 12th draft of the documents thoroughly in his room. After the twelfth draft, there were no changes. The global settlement agreement was done.

The important part of the Settlement Agreement was in paragraphs 19-21. In those paragraphs on pages 12-14, the estate agreed to sign over any ownership claims it had to the two Louisiana properties, the Edwards Commercial Building and the mansion upriver near Baton Rouge called *La Reve du Monde*.

Attorney Colette St. Pierre obtained an appraisal that those two properties were valued at two million four hundred thousand dollars. In return for obtaining the estate's half-ownership of the two properties, Wonder agreed to obtain a loan on the properties and pay the estate its share of the value of one million dollars.

The speakeasy in the French Quarter a few blocks away on Bourbon Street, was pleasant. Charlie walked over to join Angel and Devlin at a jazz club after reviewing the "Settlement Agreement" documents thoroughly in his room.

Charlie ordered ginger ale.

Charlie had noted in his log: "One hour; review final estate settlement agreement received today from Jack Wonder, okayed by his attorney, Antoine du Chevalier, and also reviewed and okayed by Angel Sedona's Louisiana co-counsel Colette St. Pierre." Earl insisted every billing be precisely written, so clients had no excuse to not pay.

Devlin got drunk at the jazz club, about the time *St Louis Blues* was played by a New Orleans jazz combo. "We're in the money, honey. No more day-to-day worries."

"It's not my money, you gorgeous jerk. This is for Gabriella."

"I'm talking about the estate. Of course, it's for her."

Charlie wished he could ooze out of sight under the table.'

"Sign it, honey. Sign it now," Devlin insisted.

Angel was a bit tipsy herself, but luckily looked to Charlie for direction. Charlie knew signing a probate document and a real estate contract in a jazz club while the client was tipsy was not a good idea. He placed his hand over the last page's signature line.

"We'll sign it tomorrow in court." Charlie folded the document and placed it in his briefcase. The jazz quartet played a classic blues tune, *Stormy Weather,* with moody grace and intimate pleasure.

■　　■　　■　　■　　■

The court cases were being called at a rapid pace.

"I guess we'd better go in to the courtroom."

"Do you have the check?" Devlin stepped in Jack Wonder's path.

"My attorney deposited it with the court clerk several days ago."

Charlie could almost see Devlin salivate. Charlie thought Devlin was foolish to confront a trained Navy Special Operations Captain. Then again, Devlin was not the sharpest blade in the rack.

The courtroom's doors opened. Charlie turned to Angel.

"Let's go."

CHAPTER 31
THE BIG CHECK

Blue-robed, bleach-blonde, bubble-coiffed Judge Aurora d'Arc scanned the attorneys and their clients.

"Welcome. It's a pleasure to have you in our modest New Orleans court."

"Thank you for having us in your historic court, your honor," Charlie replied. The judge glanced a silent look which meant it was time to deal.

"Well, I read the "Estate Global Settlement Agreement" between the Estate of Barry Beneshan and Mr. Jack Wonder. Ms. Sedona. I see you are the tutor of your daughter in this jurisdiction, and two of these properties are also within Louisiana jurisdiction. Although I see these properties as being valuable to your daughter, I understand the issues that make you want to resolve this matter. So, it is your sense this settlement agreement with Mr. Jack Wonder is in the best interest of the minor beneficiary, Gabriella Beneshan?"

Attorney St. Pierre, standing next to Angel answered perfunctorily. "Yes, your honor."

"And, Mr. Wonder, you are about to obtain sole possession of two historical buildings. You understand that as the sole owner, and as owner of the former du Beauvier chateau called *La Reve du Monde*, you will be governed by the Louisiana historical society's rules?"

Antoine du Chevalier answered in equally perfunctory tones: "Yes, your honor."

"Very well. Then, each of the parties can sign the documents. Madame Clerk, you will pass out the check for $1,000,000 which this court has been holding in trust from Mr. Wonder's attorney for the benefit of the estate."

Jack Wonder and Angel signed each of the documents, and the attorneys proceeded to counter-sign. The formality was well under way when the courtroom door swung open and a rumpled badly dressed middle-age woman with a sunburnt face walked forward.

"Your honor, I object to this agreement."

All eyes including the Judge's turned to the woman walking to the front whose arms trembled as she leaned her body against the bench at an angle that made the Tower of Pisa look absolutely vertical.

Judge d'Arc addressed the woman in a neutral tone. "Will you state your name and your interest in the matter?"

"I'm Candace Rollins. I run the Louisiana Clean Co. business that I took over, once Mr. Beneshan died. I was his Administrative Assistant while he was alive and helped run the company in Louisiana."

"Well, Ms. Rollins, what is the nature of your objection?" Judge d'Arc was matter-of fact. If she was annoyed by this intrusion, she did not show it.

"I am a Louisiana resident, and have been left to deal with the company. I am desperately trying to keep it going, because Mr. Beneshan gave me this job five years ago. It's the only real job I've ever had. If the properties in Louisiana are no longer in the estate, I lose my job."

"Do you have an attorney, Ms. Rollins?"

The woman shook her head. "I don't have the money."

Angel leaned between Charlie and Colette. "She stole Barry's trucks."

"Ms. Rollins, I'm sorry. You must consult an attorney and file written objections."

"I don't have any money. I worked for Mr. Beneshan."

Charlie could see the judge was not certain what to do. Angel tensed. A court "continuance" for some months would unravel the agreement.

"Ms. Rollins, that will be all. Please consult an attorney and then you may file your objections, even if you're not represented and appear *in pro per.*"

Charlie bit his lips, tried to seem at ease with a quick glance to Angel.

Candace Rollins cried. The bailiff stepped forward - a serious presence - showing off a side-arm, stepping to the side of Rollins, just within her line of sight. She dabbed at her handkerchief as she walked backwards.

"He promised me a new life. He promised me."

The judge waited until the objector cleared the front of the chambers and sat in a back row. Judge d'Arc's gaze panned the crowd to quiet any whispers. "You may proceed, Mr. du Chevalier."

"Thank you, your honor." Antoine du Chevalier collected the signed documents, handed one to Charlie, one to Attorney St. Pierre, and gave one original to the bailiff who took it, still half-watching as Rollins got up from her seat and exited the courtroom. The bailiff, turned his attention to the bench, and approached the clerk with a signed original. The clerk stamped the document, deposited it into the court files, and gave the bailiff a large manila envelope.

"Is that the check, Madame Clerk?"

"Yes, your honor. A certified check to the "Estate of Barry Beneshan for one million dollars."

"Give the check to the tutor on behalf of the estate."

"Yes, your honor." The bailiff walked the check to Attorney St. Pierre, handed the money over. She, in turn handed the check to Angel, who took it, placed it in her purse. It could have been change from a store purchase.

Charlie's heart leapt. For the first time, since he started this assignment well over a year ago, the estate was solvent. He glanced at the courtroom door.

Charlie knew he hadn't seen the last of Candace Rollins.

CHAPTER 32
ATTORNEY DU CHEVALIER'S MISHAP

All court hearing participants exited together to the parking lot, the two parties walked almost side by side. Du Chevalier accompanied Jack Wonder in front. Charlie walked behind with the other group – Colette, Devlin and Angel, to the back, quietly excited. As an attorney, you master who you can walk next to, and who you can't, - even when the other party is reconciled with your client as seemed to be.

Charlie had plenty to worry about. The newly obtained money that the estate controlled would escalate greed. Angel had a happy look on her face. That meant something. Devlin was exultant. He'd become more of a thorn. Colette looked back at Charlie, and didn't look away. That meant something, too.

Charlie heard the screeching tires of the careening jeep pull in front of them, saw it block them from a direct view of Wonder and du Chevalier. He pulled Angel and Colette away. Devlin shrank into the background as the jeep revved its fuselage at du Chevalier.

Charlie saw Jack Wonder scurry away behind du Chevalier and scamper down the parking lot stairs.

Charlie wasn't quite sure what happened next. It was over instantly. Charlie remembered a cursing woman's voice screaming about "scum attorney pigs." He remembered the blur of a small bottle of liquid being thrown on the far side of the jeep, and du Chevalier's scream "Help. Help. I can't see."

The jeep sped away, screeched around the corner, headed down ramp towards the parking lot exit.

When Charlie looked back at the flailing attorney reaching for his eyes with his frilly shirt sleeves, Jack Wonder was gone.

Charlie and Devlin raced to the stricken du Chevalier who was kneeling on the concrete, clutching at his face, rubbing liquid out of his eyes. Angel and Colette ran up. The four of them did what they could to calm du Chevalier.

"Get water. We must put water on his face," Colette blurted.

"Water could make it worse. It's some kind of acid." Angel countered.

Angel reached down and picked up a small vial from the garage floor. "It's nail polish remover. She must have thrown her nail polish remover in his face."

Colette took charge. "We've got to get him to a hospital, right now. No time for '911.'"

Devlin faded from the pained, screaming attorney. "I'll get the SUV." Devlin raced towards the SUV in the corner of the parking lot.

"Help me take him to my car." Colette braced du Chevalier's left arm around her shoulder and pulled him forward.

Charlie took the other arm. The two led the screaming, crying du Chevalier to Colette's nearby Porsche. Du Chevalier's shirt ruffles were a nuisance and smelled of the nail polish remover he had rubbed out of his face. Charlie opened the passenger side of the Porsche and helped du Chevalier in, as Colette raced around to the driver's side.

"Here, take this with you." Angel dropped the empty "Ms. Lovely Nail Polish Remover" bottle onto du Chevalier's lap. Charlie picked it up, read the warning label. "Caution. For external use on nails only. Contains acetone and other chemicals that may be harmful if swallowed or splashed on skin."

"Here." He handed the bottle to Colette.

"St. Mary of Mercy Emergency. Meet you there," she called to Charlie, taking the empty bottle with her free hand.

Charlie nodded as the car growled to life. Charlie stepped next to Angel, as the Porsche backed out of the parking space and screeched away with its flailing passenger screaming his lungs out.

Devlin pulled alongside in the SUV. Angel and Charlie piled in. The Porsche was already gone.

"St Mary of Mercy. She's taking him to the E.R." Angel got the GPS to work on her Blackberry phone.

"Come on, babe. Let's catch up, make sure he doesn't fake his injury."

Angel nodded. "Candy was always such a little revengeful bitch."

Devlin was agitated. "That could have been me."

Charlie didn't say anything, but he picked up on Devlin's fear. *For once, Devlin called it like it was.*

CHAPTER 33
DETOUR

Colette ushered Charlie, Angel, and Devlin to a red molded plastic bench in St. Mary of Mercy E.R. waiting room, where they sat and waited.

Charlie's eyes locked on Colette's. Charlie could feel himself drawn into her oversized blue liquid orbs that were as deep as the swirling fogs of Jupiter or its uncharted mysterious moons.

A bald, white coat clad doctor stepped around the reception desk, cradling a clipboard supported chart, looking like he had just stepped out of a commercial for some unnecessary TV prescription ad with deadly side effects downplayed by the commercial's jingles and happy faces.

"Are you the party with Attorney Antoine du Chevalier?"

All four jumped and faced the composed physician.

"I'm Doctor Mohammed Ahkbar. We triaged Mr. du Chevalier. Luckily, his eyes were splashed with only a minute dose of acetone. That over-the-counter acetone is too diluted to do permanent damage. He'll be fine."

"Can we see him?"

"Are you family members?'

"We're both attorneys (nodding at Colette) – his business colleagues." Charlie spoke up with the right amount of confidence and politesse.

"Just for a minute."

"Good deal, Charlie." Devlin's hissed compliment was a first.

Doctor Ahkbar led Charlie, Colette, Angel, and Devlin past the security door that was hidden behind the reception counter and turned down the antiseptic hallway. There, in a small holding room, Attorney Antoine du Chevalier was lying in a white gown customized with red and blue flower patterns, with oversized taped white gauze pads covering both eyes, and a white sheet pulled up to his neck. He had an IV fluid drip secured into his left arm. Dr. Ahkbar entered first.

"You have some visitors. It's…"

"Charlie Tobias, and the others from this morning's court hearing."

"Jack? Is Jack Wonder here?"

"No. He ran off when you were attacked."

"That bastard. I hate that bastard." Du Chevalier became agitated.

"Please don't upset the patient. His condition is delicate."

"Dr. Ahkbar told us the good news."

"Good news? I'm in a fuckin' hospital bed, practically in a coma, can't even make it to the john without buzzing some aide who can't speak English nor French. That's good news? I'll sue the shit out of your fuckin' estate. It was that Beneshan mold cunt from this morning. I'll sue the lot of you."

"Hey dude, what makes you so special? It could have been any of us!" Devlin wasn't intimidated.

Dr. Akhbar pushed forward. "Visiting time's up."

Charlie led the group out of the room away from du Chevalier's rant. But du Chevalier's voice echoed down the hall:

"I wish Jack never signed the settlement and given you the money, Charlie."

"Shut your yap before I piss down your throat," Devlin retorted over his shoulder. "Come on, babe. Don't listen to that scum face."

Devlin put his arm protectively around Angel's shoulders and led her out the security door. Colette shrugged to Charlie, took his arm as they left.

"*Merde.*"

"We'll keep him overnight for observation and release him tomorrow morning if everything is okay. Check with me then."

"We'll call in the morning, Dr. Ahkbar. Thanks."

Colette pressed next to Charlie through the security door.

Angel and Devlin pushed through right behind. "Candy stole all the equipment from the warehouse. Did you see her saggy tits? I'm sure Barry wasn't balling her." Angel was upset, discouraged.

"Thievin' scumbag loser." Devlin was in a foul mood.

"Will we ever see Jack Wonder?" Colette tried to focus on practical matters.

"He'll show when it suits him," Angel hissed.

Charlie thought back on his work on the Beneshan case. Added to the list of the dead or injured was one frilly Louisiana attorney, who at best would present a huge E.R. bill.

"Let's drive to the mansion. It's isolated. It's got a huge carriage house. I bet we'll find the stolen trucks."

Angel was braver than Charlie, or maybe just foolhardy. "You can bill the time."

"Billing" issues were not what concerned Charlie. *Will we get back to Los Angeles in one piece?* was what was on Charlie's mind.

CHAPTER 34
LA REVE DU MONDE

The trip along the Mississippi River wound through the rural, lush countryside. On the right side of the car, the Mississippi river waterfront multi-story antebellum mansions periodically appeared through dense low-swaying tree branches. Shuttered windows of the stately sentinels stood guard at the end of curving entry roads as the SUV sped past on the winding blacktop two-lane highway that led north from New Orleans to Baton Rouge.

In the St. Mary E.R. parking lot, Colette had looked at Charlie, and shrugged with disappointment. Both attorneys weighed the need for someone to stay in New Orleans and make sure that du Chevalier would not exaggerate his injuries. Colette volunteered, saying she could witness du Chevalier's recovery on behalf of the estate.

Charlie agreed with her plan to stay behind, while he knew he was giving up the thrill of riding alongside in her convertible through the fern and magnolia canopy. He should have insisted she come along, even if du Chevalier's injury became another estate issue.

Besides, in his heart, Charlie didn't want to oppose or deny du Chevalier's injury claim. Du Chevalier, like Charlie, was just a hired hand. Injury to the hired hand's eye-sight was serious, even if du Chevalier was hired by Jack Wonder.

Angel relaxed in the passenger seat, feeling confident, and bold, clutching her purse.

Devlin's erratic driving style was giving Charlie in the back seat, a different type of goose-bumps than he had experienced in Colette's Porsche.

Angel peered out the passenger seat window. "Slow down. I remember that cross-road. We just passed the turn-off. Go back. Go back."

Devlin grudgingly obliged.

Soon, the estates were further apart, surrounded by satellite buildings and lots of land. Small huts dotted the Mississippi river-side. Those had been the slave quarters before the civil war – and had become the home of sharecroppers and itinerant farmers living there, ever since, doing the same backbreaking cotton fields toil.

The Delta soil was perfect for growing cotton: hot, humid, and fertile. The Louisiana Mississippi River delta was still the source of wealth and status for the current crop of agri-business owners.

The mansions became more and more expansive – former homes of barons and baronesses of Southern society competing for power, prestige and honors.

Charlie recalled the names of a secretive fraternal order of his youth. *La Reve du Monde* was just a children's game in St. Louis, Missouri, Charlie's childhood home, a game in which children mimicked French Versailles court society and vowed allegiance to the heirs to the French Bourbon throne.

Charlie had been excluded from these games because his father, Dr. Frank Tobias, a music professor at the St. Louis Conservatory of Music, didn't have the French pedigree that served as tie-in to the aristocratic sub-strata of St. Louis high society.

Charlie's French language instruction started in the fourth grade with Monsieur Claude Prohier's daily appearance in his classroom. Monsieur Prohier solely spoke in French to the fourth grade scholars. His lectures included historical references to the ignominy of the anti-christ Napoleon who sold the Louisiana areas that included St. Louis to the fledgling United States in the time of Thomas Jefferson.

Emilie, the pretty girl in the next seat, let everyone in class know that her grandparents were court painters to the Bourbons, and had painted the frescoes in the royal Versailles court before losing their position with the beheading of their patrons, King Louis XVI and his wife, Marie Antoinette. Emilie's parents, like many French nobility and courtiers escaped to the new world with their lives and nothing more.

Monsieur Prohier had been placed in the embarrassing position of having to ask her the goal of *La Reve du Monde* society that Emilie talked about in class.

Monsieur Prohier's ancestors were not members of French nobility.

"La societe devait restituer le territoire de la Louisiane aux Bourbons qui sont les vrais souverains de France." ["To restore the Louisiana territories to their rightful rulers, the Bourbon Kings."] She replied to Monsieur Prohier in her excellent French.

Monsieur tried to make light of her response. *"Mais oui? C'est vous est une Bourbonnes?"* ["So you are a member of the Royal Bourbon family?"] Charlie recalled how Emilie proudly and confidently replied: *"Mais oui."* ["Of course."]

Monsieur Prohier dropped his challenge and proceeded to segue into the words for "colors." Charlie thought back long ago on the confident enigmatic look on Emilie's delicate face.

"Look. That's it." Angel was excited as she pointed through the ferns at the dark edifice that appeared around the road's bend. "Slow down. Turn right. Now."

"That's a classy pad." Devlin veered onto the dirt road and brushed through low-lying branches of unkempt alluvial magnolia trees. The SUV approached the two story faded relic, that Barry Beneshan made into his far-flung Clean Co. empire's headquarters, but whose gothic facade was better type-cast as a setting for a horror film.

CHAPTER 35
STOLEN GOODS

The SUV pulled up to the two-story faded white mansion with a stately front portico, set off with Greco-Roman columns. Gabled shutters framed dust covered double-hung windows on each side of the arched entryway. The landscaping screamed "abandoned."

Devlin followed tire tracks leading past the main residence towards a carriage house.

Charlie peered up at the gothic edifice and saw the dusty lettering etched above the mansion's main entrance, still half-readable despite spider webs and obstructing tree branches and debris.

Charlie couldn't help but mouth the words he saw, "*La Reve du Monde.*"

Charlie stared. Seeing the letters imprinted on the abandoned building changed the importance of the name.

Angel noticed Charlie's stare. "What's wrong, Charlie?"

Charlie looked at Angel. Now may not be the best time to educate her about what he had learned many years ago in grade school from that golden-locked girl in the next seat during French language class.

The SUV crawled forward, approached the carriage house about a hundred feet behind the mansion. The SUV was bumping and rolling like a Palisades fun house car ride.

"Let's walk." Devlin pulled to a stop and jumped out. Charlie and Angel exited, stepped into marsh cottonwood, and stumbled forward.

Angel and Charlie followed Devlin as he forced his way past the obstructing foliage to the carriage house entrance. The carriage house had stalls for at least six vehicles. The building was larger than most houses were in the outlying Los Angeles suburbs where plain folks moved to enjoy McMansion faux luxury.

All three intruders peered into the dusty garage door windows. Inside the carriage house, they could see three dust-covered Clean Co. trucks with oversized wrapped suction tubes that could be synthetic pythons squeezing out rust from the dirty truck carriages.

"Bonanza, sweetheart." Devlin turned, hugged Angel.

Charlie was quietly pleased. Recovering these trucks would provide some assets, and protect the estate in case Candace Rollins returned to court to claim moneys owed from the newly gained funds. Charlie was cautiously elated.

Devlin tried to open the door. It rattled, but didn't give.

"Stuck door. Damn." Devlin didn't like any form of rejection.

Devlin had to demonstrate his moxie, mojo, and muscle. He elbowed the window and shattered the glass. Charlie's heart sank. Devlin reached inside the carriage house, and after some fumbling and reaching around, managed to unlatch the door. Angel sidled up to the edge of the door, pulled at it, then pushed, then pulled with all her might.

"Candy stole this. It's the estate's property. I'm the administrator."

Charlie became uncomfortable. "Technically, this is Jack Wonder's property, since we just signed and filed the settlement agreement with the court."

"There was nothing in it about handing over stolen equipment." Angel shot back.

Devlin moved next to Angel and pushed with his shoulder. The door creaked open, then stopped just inches in. It wouldn't budge further despite Devlin's repeated jolts.

"I bet there's other stolen stuff." Devlin winked, as he backed off, having failed to dislodge the door.

Devlin retreated to the SUV, reached under the carpet and pulled out the tire iron.

"I love you," Angel goaded Devlin. Charlie winced. Devlin ran to the side of the carriage house and disappeared around back.

"Devlin will get us in." Angel was mesmerized by Devlin's heroics.

Charlie could see how Devlin captured Angel's heart with his bravado. He had aristocratic Italian features. In a moment of candor, Angel confided she met Devlin on the Venice boardwalk on a balmy Southern California afternoon.

Angel had stopped for a drink at the public fountain by Muscle Beach, and she and Devlin exchanged glances.

Charlie never found out what happened next, but there was no doubt Devlin did not suffer from a lack of confidence – nor smooth pick-up lines.

And here they were.

Devlin had Angel's heart and Charlie knew Angel would never deny Devlin.

Several minutes passed. Charlie was getting apprehensive.

"We'd better see what's happening."

Angel nodded, puzzled. They heard noises from behind the main house.

They could see Devlin jam the rear door open to the mansion some hundred feet away. Charlie panicked, hoped he wouldn't be charged as accessory to "breaking and entry."

Charlie pulled Angel, hurried to head off Devlin from forcing open the door.

A blast of flame, flash, and strewn objects catapulted out of the mansion's rear doorway, pushed the side walls of the building out, cracking and breaking the wooden sidings, splintering them into deadly projectiles that flew in all directions including at Charlie and Angel who were still some fifty feet away.

Charlie grabbed Angel, pushed her to the ground and kept his head down next to hers as the force of the blast strew falling debris around their prone bodies.

Devlin's screams could be heard as the force of the blast echoed and diminished. Angel looked up from the ground, got up and sprinted towards the burning building. Charlie knew it was useless to stop her. He forced himself up, followed.

Devlin fell out of the doorway, clutching at flames that ate at his clothes, flashed from his skin.

Devlin's face was cindered. Angel ran up, tore her sweater off, and doused the flames sizzling his face.

"Baby, baby. On the ground. Get in the grass!"

Angel pushed Devlin onto the patio entrance, covered and smothered him with her sweater as he rolled in agony. Charlie reached Devlin, jerked him out of his jacket and smothered the remaining flames licking Devlin's torso and legs.

Charlie pulled each shoe off Devlin's feet, feeling his own hand burn from airborne oily hot liquid as he threw the charred shoe's remains away.

The flames inside the house spread, licking around windows in the kitchen and under other back portions of the house, escaping through cracks and enveloping the shutters outside before cindering the siding.

Devlin forced himself to sit up.

The house had been a decrepit tinder box waiting for any spark to disintegrate, or whoever set the incendiary trap had rigged the rear entrance to destroy the entire structure. Charlie could smell whiffs of burnt oil and chemical smells. He wasn't about to investigate whether the fire was the work of a mad doomsday craftsman.

"Let's split. Now." Charlie turned, focused on the need to escape, reached under Devlin's other arm.

Despite Devlin's screams, Charlie and Angel lifted him onto his legs. Devlin whimpered, cried, and cursed as they led and half-carried him back to the SUV.

Charlie braced his body to balance himself not to fall, crushed by Devlin's weight. However, Charlie's real concern wasn't with getting Devlin to the car. Charlie shuddered, anticipating another lawsuit against the estate was hatched.

"I just crapped. Fuck. I can't believe this shit," Devlin bawled. Charlie looked past Devlin's hideous, crying face at Angel for help.

"We'll stop at a gas station, honey." She might as well be talking to a two year old. "We'll clean you up nice and fine."

Devlin's reply was to grit his teeth, and only emit four-letter curses every now and again from his excruciating pain.

They hobbled towards the car with the silhouette of the burning structure behind them. The reddish sky was getting dark, and with the fading light, Charlie's optimism from the court hearing in New Orleans was also extinguished into the dark of night.

CHAPTER 36
ANGEL'S DISCREET FRIEND

Night fell as Charlie drove the SUV through the unending bayous on the small deserted country blacktop dissected by blurred yellow center lines. Angel comforted Devlin in the back seat as she blurted directions. Charlie's overnight bag came in handy when they stopped at the isolated no-brand filling station a few miles back. The tiny grocery store gas station combo had two ancient gas pumps under its ramshackle building portico with the hand-lettered banner lit by a naked bulb that promised "Gas."

The gas station attendant didn't look too closely as Charlie walked in to the tiny store and asked for the key to the men's room.

The craggy striped-overall clad attendant noticed Angel pull Devlin out of the SUV, lead him towards the outside rest rooms.

"You buying any gas?"

Charlie nodded. "Sure."

The attendant handed the rest room key across, observing Angel pull Devlin's "Penta-Oilers" baseball cap lower over his eyes.

Charlie took the rest-room keys from the taciturn gas station attendant, and backed out of the small office to help Angel maneuver Devlin.

Thankfully, in these parts of Louisiana, the rule was not to inquire too much about goings on. That had been an hour ago.

The SUV bumped along the darkening road. The width of the road diminished to the point where it didn't make any difference that there was no center line. Charlie turned the headlights on high beam.

"That was it. Go back."

Charlie screeched to a stop, turned around on the country blacktop with difficulty on the narrow road. He wished they had a GPS device. Nevertheless, he wasn't sure how reliable electronic direction finding devices would be to find unlicensed doctors in the Louisiana swamps. The tree branches cast shadows, darker than the sky night, over hidden tiny dirt roads just above lapping bayou brush.

Charlie knew they were somewhere near Lafayette, the cradle of creole food and voodoo.

Back at the vintage gas station with its ancient pump's mechanical counter that Charlie watched race past $100 and for which he paid with his cash while Angel was in the restroom with Devlin, Charlie became dejected about his spiraling prospects. However, the attendant's conspiratorial grin and nod of appreciation when Charlie handed his five twenty-dollar bills across, gave Charlie hope.

With a cleaned-up Devlin safely in the back seat, Charlie had interjected a suggestion to go to an E.R. back in New Orleans, but Angel insisted on driving to the doctor who was "a friend." Charlie acceded to the plan, hoping Angel knew a real doctor. Devlin's pain turned into rhythmic muted sobs. Angel gave Devlin enough pain killers to euthanize a horse. At least he no longer screamed. Devlin fell asleep, cradled in Angel's arms.

They had left the excrement-covered pants in the rest room waste container. The SUV cabin smelled of fresh air. Charlie was grateful for the smallest positive change.

"Right there, turn right there."

Charlie screeched to a stop and turned onto the small dirt road. The willow branches sweeping onto the car's roof and the brushing foliage scratching the SUV's windshield slowed his progress up the road. The bayou smelled wet and mysterious even with the windows closed.

"That's it. Pull up near the entrance."

Charlie did as told, pulling to a stop near a small gabled wooden frame house with inviting lights. Angel dialed her cell phone, announced their arrival. Barking dogs prefaced lights going on over the porch. Two shadowy figures emerged and walked towards the SUV as Charlie stopped in front of the house, exited and helped Angel pull Devlin to his feet.

"Que 'est qui c'est passé? [What happened?]" The woman in the homespun dress must have been in her forties. She recognized Angel, and moved to help Devlin up the creaky stairs.

"*Une accident. Il a sange sur tous son corps.* [An accident. He's burned over his entire body]." Charlie was impressed that Angel spoke some French.

"*Angel? Ma petit. Laisse moi prende votre ami.* [My little Angel, let me take your friend.]" The husky bearded man moved in, took Angel's place and guided Devlin into the house, towards an examination table in the side room. From the man's demeanor, and focus on Devlin's injuries, Charlie deduced this was Angel's doctor friend.

"This is my friend Charlie Tobias, Doctor Danny."

Charlie and Doctor Danny exchanged quick nods. Charlie instinctively understood, it was not a good idea to mention he was an attorney.

Devlin cried as he was helped onto his back on the examination table.

"Damn fireworks are dangerous. Just blew up?" The doctor repeated the story Angel had muttered over the cell-phone as to the cause of the injury and the need for immediate treatment. Angel nodded. Indeed, Doctor Danny was a good friend. The doctor's stout wife, Madame was not happy.

"*Angel, tu as beaucoup de mal chance.* [Angel, you have a lot of bad luck]." Madame was an efficient nurse, swabbing and cutting burnt skin off Devlin's face as he twitched and writhed in pain despite all the sedation.

Apparently, this was not the first emergency Doctor Danny had treated for Angel.

"*Mettre du baume sur notre pauvre victim.* [Put salves on our poor victim]." The doctor was kind but firm. Madame turned, reached into the medicine cabinet. It was that type of medical clinic. No paperwork. Strictly cash. Charlie acceded to Angel's request, and handed his remaining five twenties across to Madame. He winced as he saw his wallet was empty. Then again, he still had credit cards.

Charlie knew he was losing perspective. Instead of being scared out of his wits to be in the Louisiana bayou with a burn victim of an explosion in a historic mansion that by now had burned to a crisp, he was relieved there was an actual "salve" and western medicine at hand, and it only cost a hundred dollars. *At least, the doctor wasn't a voodoo shaman.*

CHAPTER 37
BACK TO THE CITY OF ANGELS

As the plane angled and rose to the sky, heading west to Los Angeles, Angel stared out the port window at the receding Gulf of Mexico which appeared colorless in the harsh morning sunlight, and she dabbed tears into her crumpled handkerchief. Charlie empathized with her concern for Devlin.

"Devlin's a fighter. He'll be fine."

"He does so much for me. I could have been the one to walk in that door."

Charlie didn't want to mention that Angel was brighter than breaking in to a locked door of an abandoned mansion after she conveyed the property in court to a government trained opponent who specialized in life-ending physical acts. As an attorney, you learn the art of nodding at the right time to support your client, no matter the issue. Charlie proceeded to nod just as the plane hit turbulence, and his bobbing head and grip on the seat's arm-rest brought a smile to Angel's lips and she followed his caution with her own grip next to his braced arm.

She clutched her handkerchief, held on. The plane's engines roared into turbo drive.

Charlie complied with the red overhead lights that asked passengers to fasten their seat belts and braced as the airplane climbed quickly to avoid the electrical storm over western Texas. Charlie knew that airplane turbulence was just a minor inconvenience and recapped the incidents of the past few days as his mantra to the god of Zen. Charlie had last seen Attorney du Chevalier in a New Orleans E.R., left the ghoulishly injured Devlin D'Alessio at Doctor Danny's home-clinic in the bayous around Lafayette, and had been present at a breaking and entering, that resulted in a historical chateau burning to the ground. Charlie wasn't sure how much longer he would skirt disaster.

On a more positive note, Charlie met his Louisiana counterpart, Colette St. Pierre, and she scooted him around New Orleans in her Porsche Boxster. After Charlie and Angel made it back to the city, leaving Devlin in the care of the discreet Dr. Danny, Colette came to the Commercial Building to report on Attorney du Chevalier's recuperation. Du Chevalier had been released the following afternoon, a few hours after Charlie and Angel returned from Lafayette. Colette presented a St. Mary of Mercy hospital bill from du Chevalier, to Angel. Angel glanced at the unmerciful bill, shrugged, and dropped it in her purse with disdain — the same maroon purse into which Angel had stashed her million dollar certified check.

"Do you want to go see the town? Your plane doesn't leave till the morning."

Angel declined. She muttered something about looking after Devlin, because he had been feeling "out of sorts." Charlie looked Angel in the eye when she made that bald-face lie to Colette. Angel looked at him sternly. He understood this was their secret.

Charlie accepted Colette's offer to paint the town. Why not? Everything that could go wrong already had. Hadn't it? When Charlie got in her car, Colette brought up the trip up-river: "How was your trip?"

Charlie shrugged, and replied "Old man river puts on quite a show."

.   .   .   .   .

Charlie looked through the plane's port window, past Angel's closed eyes as she pressed into her seat. He fixated on the brackish, churning storm clouds and occasional lightning bolts below the plane. He thought back on the evening he spent with Colette. She whisked him to Saint Tammany Parish, hard hit by Hurricane Katrina. Colette stopped the car, they got out. Even at night, the shattered remains of house foundations were visible in the car headlights, interspersed among hurricane debris yet to be cleared.

They walked to nearby St. Louis Street into an old fashioned restaurant, "Antoine's." Michel, the tuxedo-jacketed, curly-haired Maître'd was on his game.

"Hello, Colette. Table for two?"

"Yes. This is my colleague, Charlie Tobias from Los Angeles. Let's show him some real New Orleans hospitality."

"Absolutely. This way."

The Maitre'd moved deftly and escorted Charlie and Colette to a small candle-lit linen-draped table with a view of the narrow historic street outside the curtain-covered window. Charlie saw the silhouettes of other guests, huddled over their own smallish tables. He didn't remember what he ordered. The restaurant was a 17th century museum with its dark age-worn wood, sconce lights and dimly flickering crystal chandeliers. Charlie had stepped back in time.

Colette told Charlie about her law practice. Colette's other clients in her small practice were mostly the dispossessed who lost their homes to Katrina's wrath, and sought compensation from some federal agency or another. Colette bluntly stated that getting funds from the government was a long, drawn out affair. Most clients lost all identification when they escaped the hurricane's ravages with nothing more than their suitcases and lives in 2005. At some point in the conversation, Colette brought up the status of Clean Co. It had not been the only flood remediation company sensing a gold-rush boom town bonanza in post-Hurricane Katrina New Orleans. Clean Co. came to town and set up shop at the up-river chateau. They scored big as long as Barry Beneshan was alive.

"I don't know about that woman who showed up in court, nor about that Clean Co. business." Colette shrugged. After a moment of silence, she continued.

"So, Mister Charlie, what made you decide to practice law?"

"At the time I went to night law school, I was just looking for a job. The practice of law wasn't my first choice, nor much of an emotional commitment. I needed a way to pay bills. My wife was getting tired of living in an apartment."

"Ah, you're married. I'm not surprised."

"Why?"

Colette laughed. "Probate law? It doesn't quite suit you."

"Well, I studied business law. I had worked for a business law firm for a number of years as a legal assistant, but by the time I passed the Bar exam, the dot-com crash ended the gold-rush on jobs writing contracts."

"The start of the new century was difficult here in New Orleans as well."

"And you? What led you to a career in law?"

"My family has been in the law business for generations. We fight for justice, in whatever legal way we can."

"Well, of course, it is a 'legal' profession."

"It's a profession to create justice. The measure of justice is how you achieve a fair outcome for an average or downtrodden person. Not some millionaire or some giant corporation. You should remember that, Charlie."

"Thanks. I try."

Colette formed an enigmatic smile. "It's about finding justice."

"I'm a hired hand. I wish that weren't the case."

Colette took a sip of tea. Charlie knew that the rest of her background was off-limits. Nor did he want to tell Colette about his own artistic background that had led to his present second career as a probate attorney.

Colette buttered a slice of the oval French baguette, returning to the subject that brought them together. She asked Charlie if he found anything at the chateau. Charlie sipped his tea and shrugged an apology that answered her curiosity.

■   ■   ■   ■   ■

Charlie looked past the airplane's wings. Angel was asleep, the turbulence ended and the sky changed from angry, dark, lightning illuminated bulging masses of rain to sun-pierced cumulus clouds. The seat-belt sign turned off, accompanied with a pleasant bell ring. The airplane was flying very high. Charlie leaned forward, looked into the sky as the sun broke through, and he saw the earth below cloud openings, the red sands around Albuquerque, New Mexico pass underneath the plane. Everything looked clean and orderly as the pilot announced they leveled off at thirty-nine thousand feet.

■   ■   ■   ■   ■

Charlie had deflected Colette's question about the chateau by asking Colette what she knew about *La Reve du Monde*. Colette's beautiful eyes opened wider. She sipped her pomegranate tea. Charlie caught her discomfort.

"It's the name of the chateau you visited. It's Jack Wonder's new toy."

Charlie recalled what angry children do to those who break their favorite toys.

"Isn't it also a secret society to restore the French monarchy?" Charlie was bold, confident. What had he to lose?

Colette put her cup down on its swirled saucer.

"How do you know?"

Charlie's mind ratcheted back to that grade school classmate Emilie. "It's a French secret society like the Masons. Its mission is to restore the Bourbons to rule the French empire, including the lost French colonies in the Americas. I grew up in St. Louis, a very French kind of town."

Colette's gaze pierced his soul, trying to figure him out. "You must be tired. I'll take you back to your room."

Colette nodded to the shadowing waiter, pushed Charlie's credit card away, paid the bill, and led him out of the café, back to the car.

Each sat down into the Boxster and looked straight ahead. Colette started the car and pulled out. Neither said anything as the Boxster made its way around the tiny streets of the French Quarter back to the Commercial Building. He knew he had said something that made her withdraw. He was sure, this would be his last ride in her Porsche.

.　　.　　.　　.　　.

Charlie leaned back in his airplane seat, dozed off. When he opened his eyes, he saw the snaking reflection of a river that rivaled the Mississippi's power, pass by underneath the airplane. Charlie knew this was the Colorado River, the other mighty flow of water that sustained North America's life and commerce. They were passing somewhere over the Hoover Dam, headed into California, back home.

Angel reached for Charlie's' hand as the plane descended over the checkerboard suburbs of Los Angeles.

"Thank you for coming."

Charlie forgot about the disasters, the injured Antoine du Chevalier, the sizzled Devlin D'Alessio, the destroyed chateau, as he looked into Angel's glowing brown eyes.

"I'm glad I came."

CHAPTER 38
THE LAW OFFICE SHRANK

The Law Office shrank in the few days Charlie was away. Aki gave Charlie the news as he stepped next to her cubicle to ask if he had any messages. She lifted her dark eyelids. They were always expressive, even if she conveyed bad news in monotone. Terry Ketchum, the remaining junior attorney, was gone. Charlie sighed. There'd be more Family Law assignments from Earl Guarder. That was not a good sign.

Charlie took several hours to update notes about the three day trip to New Orleans. He transferred billing time per day into the billing software program. He debated how to enter the time spent at the chateau and in Lafayette. All billing was public information. He decided to make his entry less specific. The less said about the mishaps that transpired in New Orleans, the better.

Charlie was amused as he read the incoming mail piled on his desk. Attorney Richard Soda's belated "Substitution of Attorney" form to The Law Offices confirmed the Century City Whale, as he was known to colleagues, no longer represented Eric Dart. Dart was now represented by Attorney Floyd Quinn, in the low rent outskirts of Palmdale. Charlie still hadn't answered Quinn's demand letter.

Earl raced in, not bothering with a "hello," or "welcome back."

"Did you turn in your time? Do it now. Do it now." Earl was on automatic pilot, cutting to the chase. "When are we going to be paid?"

"I'm preparing an Emergency Order now. I'll go to court to ask the judge to sign it Wednesday morning."

Charlie knew Earl would demand a progress payment immediately.

"Did Angel bring back the check?"

"Yes. As soon as the judge approves it, we'll open the blocked account, and deposit it."

"Is it payable to us?

"No, it's payable to the 'Administrator of the Estate of Barry Beneshan.'"

Earl was shaken. "What if she runs off with the money?"

"No way. I was appearing *pro hac vice*." Charlie threw out the legal Latin jargon to shut down Earl's attack. "*Pro hac vice*" is the right of an attorney from another jurisdiction to appear one time in front of a judge in a different state.

Earl appeared to be mollified by the explanation. "Get the money, right away."

Charlie tried to change the conversation. "There were a couple of mishaps."

Earl stepped back, took a confrontational stance.

Charlie blurted: "Antoine du Chevalier, Jack Wonder's attorney had nail polish acid thrown in his face by the Clean Co. employee, Candace Rollins. She came to court to block the settlement agreement, and the judge refused to hear her."

"The judge dismissed her? That's terrific."

"The mansion we deeded to Jack Wonder burned down when Devlin broke in and set off a blast."

"Was Devlin hurt?"

"Burns on his face and body. We left him at a private clinic."

"Sign him up for a personal injury suit. He has a case against Jack Wonder for injuries. That mansion was a menace."

Charlie always felt better after telling problems to Earl that Charlie fretted over. Earl would see the same problems as opportunities to sign new clients.

"Is that it?"

"That's it."

"Make sure the blocked account is opened immediately, and she writes us our check."

Charlie thought it best not to bring up the personal funds he spent on the trip.

At least, Earl didn't seem too interested in the calamities. The only facts that mattered to Earl related to money coming in to keep the Law Offices going. Charlie didn't dispute the emphasis.

"Now, listen, you're taking over some new cases."

Charlie nodded. He knew the "new cases" he was being assigned were Terry Ketchum's. Charlie got out his note pad.

"This *Williams v. Straight-Up Construction?* It's a construction defect case. It's coming to trial. Settle it. Tony Williams isn't paying. Get us off."

He took extensive notes as Earl reviewed Terry Ketchum's portfolio. The cases had one common thread: clients weren't paying. Charlie saw the scowl form on Earl's forehead. Charlie understood the law firm needed cash flow – fast.

"How much are you asking for our progress payment?"

"About half of what we're owed."

"Ask for all of it. Settle for half."

Charlie nodded.

Amanda sashayed in, with her oversized designer handbag, as Earl raced out. She greeted Charlie and politely asked about the trip. Charlie responded with the answer he knew she wanted. "We got the check."

Amanda's face changed from apprehension to relief. Amanda, aside from her responsibilities as the Law Office's C.P.A., was also its bill collector, whose calls to clients were constant, trying to get them to pay owed bills. The current year had become a time of collapse in every business, in every corner of the sinking economy.

"When do we get our check?"

Charlie didn't want to lie, but he also didn't want to tell her he suspected the process would be lengthy.

"I'm going in on Wednesday to ask Judge Bittenkopf to approve our payment."

Amanda sighed a deep sigh.

Amanda pointed to the new files that Earl piled onto Charlie's desk.

"None of these clients are paying. They're taking advantage. Get the money."

Charlie nodded, crossed his fingers below his desk. He like almost everyone else, was intimidated by Amanda's confidence, and style.

"I have to go for an errand. Could I forward you my calls, Charlie?" Amanda gathered her purse and designer bag, and was hurrying out.

"Sure. What time will you be back?"

"Just tell them to leave a message. I'll call them back first thing tomorrow."

Charlie, conscious of her ever-increasing errands that she ran, called after her, "Bye."

"Thanks, Charlie." She was already down the hall, headed towards the elevators.

CHAPTER 39
THE SECOND JOB

Charlie hurried into the Opera Company men's dressing room, signed the time sheet in a quick scrawl.

"I've almost given up on you, Charlie. You're forty-five minutes late."

"Gerry, don't be an A.D. shmuck. Let me fit him." Veronica pulled Charlie away from the Assistant Director's wrath.

"The freeway was a crawl," Charlie said with proper contrition.

"Tell me about it." Gerry relented, signed off on Charlie's time sheet.

Veronica pulled Charlie over to the wardrobe rack.

"How's it going, stranger?"

"Barely."

"Well, I'll fit you out nice and snug. Glad to see you."

Charlie responded. "Me, too. Glad I'm here."

Charlie was, not only glad, but grateful, that he made it past his New Orleans assignment. While he hoped the disasters were just a bad side-step in the Beneshan case, he suspected more side-steps ahead.

Veronica picked out Charlie's fitted costume. She grabbed pins and held them in her mouth. She mumbled something that passed for a scolding about not having time to do a proper fit.

"I'm sorry, I'm late." Charlie replied, seeing her scowl.

The irritated mumble in Veronica's throat subsided. Veronica lifted the mosquito torso costume over Charlie's head and helped him slither in. One by one, she took pins out of her lips, pinned the arms and torso for final alterations. With all pins in place, her lips forced a smile.

"I understand why other extras do this gig, Charlie. But why you? You have some full-time big-shot job, don't you? Doesn't your wife mind you staying out at nights?"

Charlie laughed, wiggled into the costume.

"I need to do this."

"How so, Charlie?"

"I studied choral singing. This is what I do."

"Well, I hate to stick you with reality, but all you get to do is 'buzz.'"

"I'm still a part of the show."

"Still hanging on to your dream?"

"Trying to. I gave up on it for a while, but it tracked me down. So, here I am."

"Me, too. FYI, I'm sending my wardrobe portfolio to the San Francisco Opera. I'm tired of this part-time freelance bull-shit. San Francisco is a full time job for a full season. With benefits."

"Wow. Good luck."

"Thanks. One day, San Francisco or, even better the 'Met?'"

"Dreams. Yeah. We got to hold on to them."

"A full time job working at my art? That's my dream."

"I need to hear that."

"Yeah?"

"It's easy to lose focus."

Veronica finished adjusting the costume. "You make for an awesome mosquito."

Charlie grinned. "Thanks, Flora."

Charlie, in costume, placed his headpiece over his head. Veronica clamped the head-piece onto the body suit, attached sleeves to the arms, and mosquito claws to each hand.

"Go bite those suburban brats." She slapped him affectionately.

Charlie hopped on his overlong claws down the hall. He made it to the holding pen in time. Gerry pushed Charlie into position in the mosquito line.

Charlie looked through the eye-slits to follow the extra in front of him as the Assistant Director herded the featured singers out to the stage.

The curtain rose on the main stage. The San Fernando Valley back yard patio and swimming pool set was framed by the San Gabriel Mountains rear-projected image on the back of the stage. Gathered around the patio were the everyman heroes, Maria and Rudolph Starlight with their daughter, Chelsee, a pig-tailed teen-ager, in the Judy Garland, Natalie Wood tradition. Rudolph, the dad, bar-b-que-ed, while Maria, the mother, relaxed in a chaise lounge.

From the other side of the stage, the other ten chorus extras from holding Area B, merged into one circle around the main performers. Charlie moved on cue with his group of extras onto the stage in counterpoint.

Charlie circled Chelsee, the young bikini-clad human prey who lounged on the edge of the swimming pool. Charlie swooped in, hopped, touched his face mask to Chelsee's shoulder.

Charlie forgot who the actress was selected for this skin-baring risqué role. There had been talk of Lindsey Low playing the part, but the rumor was when she tried out for visiting Artistic Director Michelangelo Tantonini, he held both ears, walked up the aisle and left the theater without a word.

The opera then tried to enlist Grammy award-winning songstress Taylor Maid for the "Chelsee" role, but had no way to pay her hefty fee. In the end, they chose a new singer, Cindy See, a wire-thin pubescent model, who had a nice coloratura voice, and was eager to please. Up to this point in her career, Cindy See's claim to fame was as a model in national TV ads singing jingles to advertise acne cover skin creams.

Casting diva, Sequoia Burgogne who had become an international celebrity through her sensational *Carmen* debut in Milan, not to mention her appearances at gala functions on the arm of Italian prime minister and media baron, Giovanni Septadolci, seemed wrong. Being a laid-back valley mom was not part of Sequoia's repertoire. Then again, her notoriety would bring in an audience, eager to see Italy's greatest diva.

The stage lights dimmed to bloody red. Maria, beautiful in her Vera Wing bikini, broke into her first aria, *My Back Yard*, thanked the supreme power for the family's bounty. Her English enunciation was charmingly Mediterranean. She punctuated the aria, with slaps and scratches at the shoulder that the mosquitoes pecked.

Rudolph, her husband, flipped the bar-b-que prop-meat over, closed the grill, walked to the front of the stage, joined Maria. Both stars broke into the opera's first duet, *We are so Blessed*, a rhapsody about their idyllic existence in the plush Calabanana suburb of Los Angeles.

Rudolph congratulates himself on being a mortgage broker at Country Financial in Thousand Acres, helping Country Financial explode to become the largest mortgage lender in the United States. Rudolph's job allows for all the perks of suburban life. He confides to the audience that he serves the greater good, articulated so well by United States President Jimmy Brush – helping all young couples buy homes in which to raise their families.

In the second stanza of his duet, Rudolph puzzles over the financial intricacies of the loans he sells to the eager young couples.

In the third and final stanza, Rudolph brushes his qualms aside. He believes before higher payments come due which the young couples can't afford, the young couples will re-sell their homes at a huge profit and buy bigger homes. That's the essence of the American way.

Charlie started his "buzz" in his baritone voice in unison as he and other mosquitoes sway around the back-yard prey on stage.

Chorus
Flying across backyards,
We see humans bask below
In swimming pools cooling
Afternoon desire.

Chorus
We live our lives, to
Be worthy of our winged kind -

Chorus
To live the American dream, of
Everything becoming better,
Forever.

Gerry leaned from the side of the stage, mouthing lyrics for the mosquito chorus. Rehearsal was going well. Charlie discerned Oscar's bright orange and brown mosquito personage being fitted into the stunt hooks that would hoist Oscar above the stage on barely visible wires.

Charlie, seeing Oscar's doddering and fumbling as he was clasped to the guy wires and Oscar's gyrations as he lifted off the stage and slowly rose fifteen feet above the other extras, couldn't take his eyes off the compelling dance of the colorful, unsteady mosquito. *That sure looks scary.*

CHAPTER 40
THE COURT HEARING

The court hearing to deposit the million dollar check into the estate account was a sold-out affair. His Honor had not yet come out to take the bench. Angel pushed in late, leaned over, whispered: "Sorry, no money for a parking place."

Charlie whispered back, "They wouldn't give change for your million dollars?"

Angel shoved Charlie playfully.

Charlie glanced around. The crowd included the interested parties for the Beneshan estate matter, or their attorneys, salivating at the moneys about to become available to pay off debts.

A cowboy hat and western booted attorney came up to Charlie, introduced himself.

"Howdy. I'm Floyd Quinn, Eric Dart's new counsel. Pleased to meet you."

Charlie returned the handshake. Eric Dart's newest attorney looked the part of a Palmdale strip-mall legal eagle.

"Nothing in this hearing concerns your client."

Floyd gave Charlie a wink. "Thought we might still work something out."

"Did you hear?" Angel interjected. "The estate doesn't owe you. Beat it."

Floyd, flustered, shrugged. "I was in the next courtroom. I thought I'd come by to say 'hi.' I wrote you a demand letter."

Charlie nodded. "I'll respond. I haven't had a chance."

"Scram." Angel was getting angry.

Floyd tipped his hat, scowled, left.

Charlie turned to Angel. "Better hold on to that check real tight."

"Jeez."

Judge Bittenkopf came out. Everyone stood up, raised their right hand as ordered by the clerk, and recited the oath to tell the truth and support the U.S. Constitution.

Although whether they hindered anyone other than truth-tellers from deceiving the court was open to question, Charlie liked these rituals. At least there was an attempt to unearth the truth, and take the blinders off the statute of blind justice. Also, having taken the oath, any deceit was punishable as perjury. Perjury was a serious offense against the court.

Charlie recalled the incident about two months ago, when His Honor had been on the telephone to downtown jail, examining a recalcitrant supplicant, who had apparently been shunted off to the slammer. Nobody in the court-room had an inkling of what the incarcerated man's action had been that crossed the line. Judge Bittenkopf kept asking the man on the telephone speaker if he would agree to tell the court what he knew. The man on the other end of the line was not forthcoming. Judge Bittenkopf refused to budge from his ruling, that until the man disclosed what he knew about some matter, he would not be freed from jail.

"I need my medicines from home. They won't get me my meds," the jailed unseen voice pleaded.

"You can be home as soon as you answer the question before the court."

"I need my meds. I've got asthma."

"Sir, it's your choice. We'll talk again in two days. Same time. Good-bye."

And with that the next case was called.

Charlie shuddered. The public phone conversation had been sobering for everyone in the hushed courtroom, reminding them of judges' powers to compel in ways that hurt badly.

The clerk read off the numbers of the approved petitions, as well as the numbers of the petitions that were requested to be continued.

Charlie's anxiety increased as the numbers got closer to his "Beneshan Estate" matter.

Occasionally, an attorney would speak up, to oppose granting a petition, and the clerk would schedule the matter to be heard after the "calendar" was finished. Reading the morning "calendar" happened in a few rapid-fire minutes. Often, as today, it lasted less than ten minutes. Occasionally, if a matter could be adjudicated quickly, Judge Bittenkopf would call it immediately and rule.

Case numbers 154 was such a simple, yet twisted matter for which the attorneys and clients raced to the well of the court to get a quick decision from the judge. Charlie found himself spun along by the strange facts. The case had been filed by Denise Millet, the sister of the presumed deceased represented by Attorney Lee Timmons. Ms. Millet wanted to take over administration of her brother Joshua Green's estate. Annie Green, the wife, possibly the widow, represented by probate specialist Felicia Tinkerborn, opposed Ms. Millet's petition. Annie Green claimed her husband, Joshua Green wasn't deceased, but was merely "missing." Attorney Tinkerborn placed into evidence a handwritten scrawled personal note from Joshua to Annie with a recent date, "I love you, sweetheart. Josh." There was no return address on the stained envelope the bailiff passed to the judge.

The Judge reiterated to Lee Timmons, the sister's attorney, that the submitted opposition paper-work by Felicia Tinkerborn including the letter was at least some evidence that the missing internet founder of the popular web site, "www.wegottogetwed.com" was alive.

Lee Timmons objected that the letter had not been properly authenticated and thus, should be disallowed as evidence.

Judge Bittenkopf, in his attempt to find a fair solution, ruled to deny the sister's petition "without prejudice." Denise Millet, the sister, was able to re-file the petition when there was additional evidence that Joshua Green, the eccentric multi-millionaire head of the foremost internet gay wedding site, had actually died.

Charlie pondered, as the Joshua Green case attorneys stepped back. At least Charlie was sure that Barry Beneshan was dead.

Charlie was surprised to hear "Estate of Barry Beneshan" read off next – among the approved petitions. No-one spoke up to oppose it, so the hearing was over. It was anti-climatic. Charlie got up, pushed towards the exit as Angel followed.

"Let's go deposit the check into the bank's account."

.　　.　　.　　.　　.

The hallway pow-wow was more congenial than usual. After all, Angel and Charlie had come up with something substantial, a million dollar check which might pay off creditors whose attorneys gathered into a tight group in the center of the hallway. Aside from Ashland, Henry Gilliam formed the circle, smooth as always. Attorney Leon Lambert, III, repping creditor "Blue Orchid," sashayed over, elegant in his light colored business attorney suit and cool as frozen carrot sticks.

Floyd Quinn pressed in, passed his card around to introduce himself as Eric Dart's champion, but knew he was at Ashland's mercy. Unlike the other creditor attorneys, Quinn had no clear claim on the moneys that had come in, as Dart's judgment was against Clean Co., not against Barry Beneshan. Charlie knew Angel was contemptuous of all the creditor attorneys.

Floyd pushed into the circle. "I didn't object to the pay-outs, Ms. Sedona. Doesn't that count for some cash?"

"Go after Clean Co. The Estate is not on the hook to you!"

"We're appealing the judge's grievous error."

"Go – " Luckily, Charlie grabbed Angel's arm before she uttered an unprofessional remark.

"Have a good day, gentlemen – and ladies." Floyd Quinn emphasized "ladies," but luckily had turned his back, and was headed off before Angel countered with a zippy rejoinder.

Angel flashed a silent victory smile. Ashland congratulated Charlie and Angel on having done "good work" ending the estate's dispute with Jack Wonder and getting the cash.

Charlie squeezed Angel's wrist hard when she tried to speak up to chastise Ashland for not being more proactive in obtaining the funds.

Ashland outlined the legal procedure to distribute the funds. Charlie would write up the Orders to disburse to each claimant, Ashland would countersign, Charlie would get Judge Bittenkopf's signature, and take the signed Orders to the bank officer to distribute the checks to the two major creditors, Blue Orchid and Jones, Sharke. As an afterthought Ashland mentioned "And to The Law Offices of Earl Guarder."

Charlie sighed. *Even when things are going well, I'm stuck with the work.*

"Take the lien off Angel's home." Charlie confronted Gilliam.

"After you send us our owed moneys," Gilliam countered.

"Now, or the check's going to be real late." Charlie felt butterflies, but knew he had the ace in the hole that Gilliam and the others wanted: money.

"The judge ordered you getting paid. He never approved a lien or house sale." Ashland lined up with Charlie.

"Henry, don't be a button-downed ass. We want our dough." Lambert, a business-like attorney, well-respected around town, chimed in, pressuring Gilliam.

Gilliam glanced around the tight circle, saw the other attorneys were united in their opposition to Jones, Sharke's hard-ball tactic to sell off Angel's home.

"You got it. I'll file the documents today."

Charlie saw Angel beam. The roof above her and Gabriella's heads was safe, for now.

In the petition which Charlie submitted, and which Judge Bittenkopf approved, Charlie said very little. He attached the signed New Orleans Settlement Agreement and court Orders signed in Judge Aurora D'Arc's courtroom.

Charlie included the petition for the Law Offices to obtain a "progress" payment.

Now, with the approval of the petition without a hearing, he wouldn't have to skirt sordid details in open court, or attempt to withhold unsavory facts that had led to this point in the estate's life: the blast at the chateau, the fact that *La Reve du Monde* burned to a crisp, that Devlin was left behind in some Cajun voodoo doctor's care, or that Counselor Antoine du Chevalier had nail polish remover acid thrown in his eyes.

Charlie was learning the art of being a lawyer. If such disasters became issues, he'd deal with them then. Right now, all that mattered was that the estate was afloat.

Charlie nodded "good bye," and hurried Angel down the hall.

"Where's your car?"

"Way up over the freeway, at Central Jail's visitor's lot. It's free parking."

Charlie winced, hoped she wouldn't be towed.

"Mine's in the lot behind the Music Center. Wait for me there. I need to get the signed Order from the clerk."

Angel took Charlie's car keys. Charlie headed back into the courtroom.

The courtroom cleared for the morning break. Charlie stepped up to the clerk, and she handed him the signed Order. Charlie had become a known quantity, an attorney the judge trusted.

CHAPTER 41
BLINDSIDED

As Charlie exited the courthouse through the lower level side door that faced Temple Street, he saw Angel cross at the light on the green signal and meet up with Blue Orchid Attorney Lambert who seemed to want to start a conversation.

Charlie hurried outside, concerned Lambert was waiting to pressure Angel for some concession, but Charlie's progress was stymied by being stuck at the red traffic light. Charlie looked across Temple Street, as he heard Angel's scream, saw Lambert grab his face, fall on his knees to the sidewalk, painfully yelling for "help."

A frumpy anorexic middle-age woman in jeans and a blue checkered blouse raced away.

Charlie dodged traffic, crossed to the fallen attorney and to his own hysterical client who knelt next to Lambert. Angel tried to blot the liquid off Lambert's face. Charlie dialed "911" on his cell. Lambert crumpled from his knees to the sidewalk as he lost his balance, holding his eyes, then steadying himself on the concrete sidewalk.

"I can't see."

"Don't touch your eyes," Charlie blurted as he placed his emergency call.

"The bitch threw something gooey into his eyes," Angel said, catching Charlie's glance. Neither of them wanted to state the obvious — Candace Rollins had come to town!

Charlie, called in the attack and gave the location to the "911" dispatcher, left Angel to care for the stricken Lambert and chased after the fleeing woman who had crossed Temple street with the light, and was headed to the handicapped zone where cars pulled in to pick up and drop off disabled citizens who had court business. The assailant disappeared into the swirl of people and cars that pushed in and departed the handicapped zone.

Charlie raced up to the bag lady sitting on her usual perch outside the southwest courtroom entrance. She saw Charlie and for the first time spoke: "Return of the Kingdom is at hand. Return of the Kingdom is at hand."

Charlie didn't have time for an introduction.

"The woman who ran by? Which way did she run?"

The bag lady pointed at a black Escalade SUV that veered away from the handicapped passenger loading zone, headed north on Grand Avenue towards the freeway entrance. Charlie couldn't make out the license plate. It would be futile to run after the fleet SUV.

The bag lady stared at Charlie. "Hello."

Charlie looked into her eyes. "Hello. Thanks. I see you all the time."

"I think its license plate was California 2ZAB742."

Charlie was surprised. "You're sure?"

Charlie grabbed a pen from his pocket and scribbled "2ZAB742."

"I have eidetic memory. I'm Rose."

Charlie, shocked at hearing her real name match his fantasy name for her, smiled.

"Thanks, Rose."

"You're welcome, Charlie."

Charlie was uncertain. *Had he ever told Rose his name? How did she - ?*

The Fire Department Medic Ambulance's siren interrupted Charlie's interaction with Rose. Charlie raced back across Temple St. to Angel.

Charlie pushed through the small crowd that gathered around the kneeling Angel and stricken Lambert and the arriving paramedics.

One paramedic squatted and touched a q-tip to Lambert's cheek, dabbed it, and smelled the liquid he swabbed.

"It's lye. Don't touch him. Smother his face."

The paramedics, protected by heat-resistant industrial gloves, covered Lambert's face with towels, as Lambert continued to tremble and cry. One of the paramedics held Lambert upright from the back and encouraged him.

"Crying is good. Tears will help push out the lye."

The second paramedic turned to Angel. "Did you touch him ma'am?"

Angel shook her head "no." She showed the small hand-towel she used. The paramedic took it from her with his industrial gloved hand.

"Let's get him to E.R., immediately! Industrial lye can burn his skin off in a half hour!"

The second paramedic was on his phone calling the emergency in. He handed Angel a wash cloth and indicated she should clean her hands with it. Angel complied.

Charlie shuddered, grabbed Angel.

"You've got the check?"

Angel nodded.

Lambert started screaming. "I can't see. I'm blind!"

A medic under each arm raised Lambert and led him into the Fire Department City ambulance. Charlie grabbed Lambert's briefcase and placed it into the ambulance on the front seat.

"Ma'am, are you related?"

"No, we were in court."

Charlie responded to Angel's look for guidance. "I'm her attorney, officer."

"Let me just take some information for the police follow-up."

"Here's my business card." Charlie handed his business card across, grabbed Angel's arm and led her away.

"Let's get that check into the bank, now!"

CHAPTER 42
MONEY IN THE BANK

Several major banks somewhere back east had collapsed into insolvency. Bankers were eager for new moneys. Angel, with her million dollar check was every bank's dream.

Amir, Greater First Trust Bank's slick-back wavy haired Assistant Director whose cheeks and face were thinner than a wooden walking cane, appeared next to the customer sign-in sheet Charlie filled out in the plasticized waiting area. Amir's eyes popped to twice their size when he heard the new account was to be for a million dollars. Amir escorted Angel and Charlie to the Supervising Manager, who heard the good news about the million dollar check, got up from his swivel chair, warmly shook hands, and assured Charlie that moneys wouldn't be disbursed without signed court orders, specifying the payee, and the amount.

After they deposited the million dollars and returned to the Greater First Trust Bank's parking lot on Portola Street just off Ferndale Avenue, a few blocks south of The Law Offices, Charlie and Angel paused next to their cars.

"Well, we got this far. We might make it all the way."

Angel, having heard about the Escalade, wasn't as upbeat. "That bitch isn't throwing lye by herself."

"Whoever put her up to it, isn't on the receiving end of the checks we're sending out."

"That Dart guy isn't getting a dime."

"Did Dart know Rollins?"

"She ran the L.A. Clean Co. office while Barry and Dart were pals."

Charlie sighed. He knew he was going to get another call from that downtown detective about Leon Lambert's injuries.

"I'll have to tell the cops about Lambert when they call."

"I hate attorneys – but I love you…" Angel looked at Charlie.

"I always knew I was different."

"Seriously. You care about me, about Gabriella. You want it to work out."

"Of course."

"Other attorneys? They don't care unless you write big checks."

"Well, it depends on what you mean by 'big?'"

"I can't afford all this crap. My credit cards are tilting below zero."

"The court approved the Law Offices' progress payment, we'll be fine."

Angel became self-conscious that she may have overstepped the line. "I get it that Mr. Guarder needs the money." She shrugged. "So, what's the next move?"

"Write some checks, and we'll send them out."

She looked around cautiously. "And you stay clear of that Rollins bitch."

"Yeah. You be careful, too."

She gave him a quick hug, a warm hug, a thankful hug. Charlie tried to put the image of that screaming, flailing blinded attorney on the downtown sidewalk out of his mental imagery but somehow, he had a feeling he was in Candace Rollins' line of sight.

.   .   .   .   .

On his route from the bank up Ferndale Avenue to The Law Offices, Charlie had a new consciousness about his role as an attorney: he was making a difference, and he felt good. He had to make sure Angel's life worked out, and Gabriella's future – and they would not be crushed by some vengeful cataclysm unleashed by revengeful or jealous legal opponents.

Charlie exited the elevator on the fourth floor, and headed to the Law Offices.

Jamie greeted Charlie. "How did things go in court?" Charlie's smiling, nodding response brought a sharp pain in his stomach.

He headed down the bland hallway towards his office. All he thought of was whether there was someone waiting to hurt him. He reassured himself that it wouldn't be easy to find his office down these halls since he no longer had his shiny metal embossed nameplate plaque on his solemn dark wooden office door.

There was a time when Charlie was proud of having his bronze name plaque, "Charlie Tobias, Associate Attorney" on the office door in its slightly rusted aluminum nameplate holder. After he was dismissed from the Law Offices the first time, he was upset with being "walked out" of the building, but maintained his decorum.

When Charlie was re-hired four months later in April, 2007 with no explanation as to the reason for his pre-Christmas dismissal in 2006, Charlie was happy to find his nameplate still inside his desk drawer. Charlie took it out, slid it back into the door's slightly more rusted aluminum nameplate holder, happy to resume his "Associate" life, full of stress, racing every day to put out legal fires for clients. Charlie only brought a small box of personal items back for his second stint at The Law Offices. A bright desk light was essential for night work. He wasn't completely convinced about the length of his second Law Offices term.

During Charlie's first stint at the Law Offices which lasted almost six years, Charlie learned the essentials of litigation practice and probate law.

The second time Charlie was re-hired at The Law Offices of Earl S. Guarder, the stint lasted most of another year, and ended the following mid-December.

Earl came in to Charlie's office, closed the office door and told Charlie he was laid off. Charlie was too exhausted to react. He had just finished writing a judgment for a trial. Luckily, The Law Offices client prevailed. However, Charlie's own life teetered. It was December, 2007.

While Charlie argued in court on behalf of the client on a construction defect case, the crash of the world's financial order was escalating into a spin to oblivion.

Average people, such as The Law Offices' clients were going under financially. On the list of essentials, legal bills were not high priority.

The two week trial had been intense, exhausting, terrifying. Charlie put every ounce of energy into presenting his client's case to Judge Adrian Stevenson, an old-fashioned Fairtown Superior Court Barrister, who had apprenticed his way onto the bench. At night Charlie barely fell asleep after consulting with expert witnesses, preparing questions for percipient witnesses, so called because those witnesses knew of the facts at issue, and he also copied documents to place into evidence for the next day's trial hearing.

The client became outraged at the Law Office's demands for further cash payments. The trial had become a torture chamber – at least for Charlie. Charlie wanted nothing more than to "get out." He had no time to worry about the financial collapse of the world. He noticed that across the street from the Law Offices, Indie-World Mac Bank, a major mortgage bank, collapsed over a weekend. Desperate account holders pushed in long lines, trying to withdraw their moneys, or what were left of them. The U.S. government F.D.I.C. insurance agency announced there were not enough funds in the federal bank insurance trust fund to pay off account holders. The lines to get moneys by panicked depositors formed earlier and earlier in the morning. More and more security guards and police appeared, to keep order.

Charlie was physically above the street-side desperation in his cocooned fourth floor office. Charlie concentrated on his intense legal challenge: getting through the trial.

On the day of the court's decision after the seven day trial spread out over several weeks, Charlie, standing in open court, next to his client, heard Judge Stevenson politely order Charlie to write the judgment – a sign Charlie's client prevailed on his construction defect claim. Charlie drove back to the office with the good news, wrote the judgment meticulously. Earl came in, shut the door, laid him off, and that was that.

It was only after Charlie drove home that day in December, 2007, and told Tina about losing his job – again, that he fell in front of the TV and took in the enormity of the economic collapse that had imploded the country's landfill foundation.

Charlie still had his part-time job as an extra in the opera. It was ironic that what had seemed to be the safe-bet job wasn't, and what seemed ephemeral, paid some bills.

CHAPTER 43
ONLY A QUARTER

The desk phone rang as Charlie turned into his office. He picked up the receiver as he slid into his office chair.

"Law Offices of Earl Guarder."

"What's the difference between an attorney and a maggot?"

The female voice sounded distraught. Charlie had a good idea of the voice's identity.

"Candace Rollins?"

"A maggot leaves clean bones and an attorney even scavenges the bones."

"What do you want?"

"Let me keep the bones." The voice quivered. "I deserve something – at least a quarter."

"Did you throw lye in the attorney's eyes?"

"Attorneys don't need eyes. They smell your fear."

"It doesn't give you the right to maim them."

"I want the bones. Something. A frickin' quarter. You took it all from me."

"I haven't hurt you, Candace."

"Angel has. Barry promised me a job. I don't deserve to be shafted!"

"Candace, I'll give you a quarter. But I can't give you what Barry promised. Don't hurt anyone else."

Candace Rollins' voice broke. "Barry promised me I'd have a job at Clean Co. Always!"

"Barry lied to you."

"Barry loved me."

"He didn't own Clean Co. He borrowed all the money to run it. The money wasn't his to give you."

Charlie heard Candace cry. Charlie took the moment of opportunity to half-sit on the desk.

"He took all the money he promised me. That lying scum fucker. Are you going to get my money back?"

"I can't, Candace. I'll do something to help. You've got Clean Co. You still have the job."

"I tried to keep Clean Co going after the money was gone. Even after the trucks were burnt. Some son-of-a-bitch burnt the trucks. All of them."

Charlie answered convincingly. "I didn't."

"Was it Angel?"

"Why would she?"

"She was a jealous fool who hurt me."

"She wouldn't do that."

"Why should I trust you?"

"Candace, you hurt two attorneys very badly."

"Three."

"Who else?"

"I paid that Clean Co. maggot, Harry Swat, a visit. He wouldn't even talk to me."

Charlie shook with fear.

"Candace, we're sworn to uphold the law. It's a legal process, not the jungle."

"I fight back how I can."

"Am I on your list?"

"Not if you make things right."

"I'll get you something."

"Make the pain go away."

"Where are you?"

"Look out your window."

Charlie looked onto the street below and saw the frumpy woman on a cell phone.

"I followed you and Angel to the bank. I didn't mess you up in the parking lot. Do what's right. Give me something. That's all I want."

"I'll see what I can do."

"I'll call in a day."

As the call disconnected, Charlie saw the figure disappear around the corner. Charlie's hand trembled as he replaced the phone into its Taiwan-flimsy plastic cradle, recalling the creepy feeling he had in the bank's parking lot that he and Angel were being watched.

When Charlie and Angel opened the blocked bank account, Charlie had brought up the attack on Attorney Lambert.

"She could have attacked you, but didn't. I think she's taking out the creditors, one attorney at a time."

"We'll get a call from the bitch. It's blackmail."

Charlie had gotten the call Angel predicted. In the parking lot, Angel had shrugged off Charlie's concerns about their own safety.

"We'll get out of this in one piece. Trust me, Charlie. I'll make sure." Charlie recalled her convincing assurance, after the almost-too-long hug. Charlie liked Angel's confidence, but wasn't sure how strong Angel's powers to protect were. She hadn't been able to shield Antoine du Chevalier, Leon Lambert, nor David Alex, nor for that matter, Barry Beneshan, whom she claimed had been killed for his cash.

Two hours before Barry's body was found in his Venice cottage, Barry called Angel as he gathered his luggage off the Southern Air conveyer at Los Angeles International Airport's Terminal Two.

"Hey, babe. This is it. I've got the cash from the Big Easy, and we're getting out of this cesspool. You, me and our daughter. I've got a cute townhouse picked out in Corfu. That's some hip island in the Mediterranean. Far away. I love you. Get Gabriella's stuff packed. We leave tomorrow!"

Angel had been so shocked by that call from out of the blue, that she didn't protest to Barry about his having disappeared to New Orleans without contacting her for almost a year, nor his push to take Gabriella out of school and leave the country on a day's notice.

That call from the airport was the last Angel heard from Barry. Two hours later, he was dead.

"I didn't even wish him a happy birthday," Angel cried as they sat at the waiting area at the Greater First Bank of Trust.

■   ■   ■   ■   ■

Charlie looked through the office window. Candace Rollins was gone, for the moment, but not for good. Charlie shuddered, knowing the Estate of Barry Beneshan had a raging acid-thrower looking for the next attorney to cut down to size.

Charlie opened his computer, tried to focus on other matters, but he couldn't dismiss Candace Rollins' despondent, threatening voice. He needed to make a police report. While she called on the main phone line, her cell phone could be traced.

Charlie picked up the scrap of paper with the license plate number the homeless woman gave him. Charlie didn't have any other leads. He dialed the number on the detective's business card.

"Detective Phillip Oswilla? Okay. Please leave him a message. This is attorney Charlie Tobias calling on the David Alex case. I'd like to have him run down a license number. There was an attack on an attorney downtown. I was just called, threatened. It's the David Alex case."

Charlie gave the information about the SUV and the thrown lye attack to Detective Oswilla's secretary. He debated whether he should mention the threat to the Clean Co.'s attorney, Henry Swat.

Charlie's decision was forced by Earl's entrance. Charlie hung up the phone.

Earl stood by Charlie, very close. "Where's our check?"

"We deposited the estate check in the bank. I have to get a court order countersigned by Ashland for each payee, including the Law Offices. It will take a couple of weeks."

"Do it, do it." Lately, Earl was sounding more upset as fewer clients paid bills.

Earl retreated out of Charlie's office, into his own office at the end of the hall.

Charlie followed him in.

"I just got a call from the woman in the Beneshan case, who is the acid thrower. She hurt another attorney after court. He's in the hospital."

"What does she want?"

"A piece of the Beneshan action."

"Did you report the attack on the attorney to the police?"

"I just called it in."

"Did she threaten you or our client?" Charlie thought for a moment.

"She wants a pay off."

Earl got the message. "We're not giving in to extortion. We're a law office. Forget it. If she calls again, call the cops."

CHAPTER 44
RESEARCH IN THE FILES

The following night, after everyone left the Law Offices, Charlie stepped into the hallway where The Law Offices stored overflow files. The hallway file cabinet row was part of the Hannah, Ashley, Tannenbaum Law Offices, but Earl had files of archived cases stored in the grey metal cabinets among the Hannah, Ashley archived files.

Eighteen months ago, the Eagle Messenger Service wheeled the fourteen boxes of "Estate of Beneshan" files in from Jones, Sharke's downtown office. Charlie never had time to review them, and only kept the two most recent boxes of files in his crammed office. Now, he was digging into the past.

He flipped up the two lowest metal cabinet doors and scanned the rows of "Estate of Beneshan" boxes. One by one, he pulled the twelve heavy boxes, carried them into his office, and stacked them between his desk and the printing station.

He returned to the open cabinets and flipped down the metal cover doors, and noticed another series of boxes labeled "Dart Construction." He didn't think too much about these pristine files. He wasn't sure that they were part of the "Estate of Beneshan" archives, yet the name "Dart" stuck in Charlie's mind.

In the quiet of the late evening, Charlie flipped page after page of the table of contents for the Beneshan file contents. In the first box, he scanned the summary of Estate properties, assets and debts. Nothing to be gleaned from a summary. Charlie had to go through the breakdown files.

These five files in the first box encompassed the Jones, Sharke documentation of assets presented to the court a few months after Barry

Beneshan died. Charlie's eyes scanned the pages of creditors. No new names jumped out as likely murder suspects. Presumably, no beneficiary of the current distribution plan would have a motive to kill.

Dart. Who was Dart? Charlie's nerve cells clicked. It was the silent partner in Clean Co., veteran California licensed contractor, Eric Dart. The contractor who was now represented by that Floyd Nobody. Charlie made a mental note to answer the demand letter.

Charlie found the file on Eric Dart in box four. Charlie thumbed through the multi-volume litigation files that Angel's corporate attorney, Henry Swat handled.

Charlie wondered if Henry Swat was in some E.R. intensive care unit, the latest victim of Candace Rollins' rage.

Eric Dart had been the hot-headed building contractor who had been the front guy for Barry's water and pest remediation business since the early 1990's when Barry Beneshan was still a teen-age wunderkind gaining notoriety in Los Angeles business circles. Dart had a California contractor's license and had "lent" it to Barry's fledgling Clean Co. to do government agency clean-ups in the mid 1990's. Then, Beneshan, barely twenty-two years of age, tried to take Clean Co. public on the New York Stock Exchange, ran afoul of federal Security and Exchange regulators and was indicted for Securities fraud. Beneshan never made good on his agreement with Eric Dart, and claimed in his defense, that he wasn't old enough to sign a valid contract when the agreement was made.

Dart hired Century City litigator Richard Soda, sued Clean Co. in civil court and obtained a judgment against Clean Co. for half a million dollars when Barry, now older and even more savvy, returned from his Southeast Asia tour and had his fraud indictment sealed. Barry Beneshan ignored the judgment as Clean Co. moved its offices to Louisiana.

Judge Bittenkopf's ruling that the judgment was not against Barry Beneshan's personal assets but solely against Clean Co. would be a strong motive for Eric Dart's revenge.

Candace Rollins had worked at Clean Co. She knew Eric Dart. However, Charlie doubted that a big-time contractor like Dart would partner with an unstable junkie like Rollins to do his dirty deeds. She certainly was not a candidate to suffocate Alex. Did Dart hire a pro to kill Alex? Charlie shuddered, reminding himself that Alex had died in Charlie's bungalow.

It was approaching 10 p.m. Way past time to go home. The phone rang. Charlie hesitated, picked it up.

The voice on the phone sounded familiar. "This is Detective Phillip Oswilla from the Los Angeles Police Department. I'm returning your call."

"Attorney Charlie Tobias here. I called you yesterday. Were you able to run that license plate?"

"It was an airport rental from Pegasus Cars. I'm sending my investigator to get the paperwork. I hear you were attacked."

"Well, I lucked out. Another attorney named Leon Lambert got lye thrown in his face outside downtown courthouse. That license plate I left might be the getaway SUV."

"Thanks. Something has come up. Can you come down?"

Charlie hesitated. "I was headed home."

"I need your help to identify a victim."

Charlie's mind focused on Harry Swat. *Charlie didn't want to let on, that he had an inkling who the victim was.* "Tomorrow?"

"Now, while the body's warm."

CHAPTER 45
OUT OF THE LOS ANGELES RIVER

About an hour later, Detective Phillip Oswilla wheeled himself into the tiny, fluorescent-lit conference room in the new Los Angeles Police Headquarters, shook Charlie's hand. Oswilla pulled himself behind the oval shaped white laminate conference table. Charlie had not noticed the detective's powerful upper torso in the previous meeting.

Detective Oswilla pulled out chewing gum, offered Charlie a stick. Upon Charlie's polite "decline," Oswilla rolled a stick, popped it. His face flickered from the unsteady fluorescents, reminding Charlie of criss-crossing venetian blind shadows in old fashioned movie detectives' offices.

"Thanks for coming right down. I'm working the David Alex case. Haven't let it slide off the table. But, I was responding to your court incident you called about."

"What's up?"

"We have a body for you to I.D."

"What about David Alex?"

"My P.I. was pounding the sidewalk around your bungalow and may have come up with a strong lead."

"Are you going to tell me? Might make me sleep better – or rent another place."

"Do you know a couple of TV actors up your street in the canyon?"

Charlie thought for a moment.

"The guys who live in that silent star's mansion?"

"Yeah. Benton Wayne and Sandy Trayle recently adopted a baby. Darlene, a cute year-and-a-half old girl. No. She's about two years old, according to my P.I.'s notes."

Charlie didn't know the neighbors' last names till now, nor what show they acted in. Although the actors had plenty of parties, Charlie did not run in their circle.

"David Alex was that baby's grandfather."

Charlie breathed deeply in and out, taking in this information. His heart raced. He leaned forward, eager to hear Oswilla's scoop.

"David Alex had a daughter, Chloe Alex who got knocked up by Goose Morgan, some ex-con she was trying to turn around in a Newport Beach drug rehab ten-step program, where she was also a patient. She had the baby over her father's objections. He disowned her."

"You think the dad...?"

Oswilla grunted a laugh. "When Alex was killed, Goose was back in Corcoran Prison for killing a flower vendor. He's in solitary for seventeen years."

"A flower vendor?"

"Yeah, one of those illegal Joses next to freeway exits selling daisy bouquets for a couple of bucks. Goose grabbed the bouquet and shot the poor guy in the face."

"Can't blame Alex for objecting to Goose as a son-in-law." Charlie leaned back in his chair. "What's the connection to the actors?"

"Chloe gave up her baby to an L.A. city fire station and flew off to Nepal to find herself. It took a while for the infant to make it through the Dependency Court's bureaucracy for adoption. The adoptive parents had Chloe's blessings. Darlene Alex was adopted through a private adoption agency about five months ago over David Alex's objections. She was about one year and some months old at the time. The adoption became final a month ago."

Charlie's mind spun to new diasporas of consciousness. The last thing he'd think of as motive for murder related to an adoption of a child by Farmdell residents.

"My investigator has been doing some great work to get to the bottom of this."

"Actors? Coming in to my studio to kill Alex? I don't know." Charlie shook his head, considered. *At least if they were mystery writers? That would be more believable.*

"Another neighbor saw the two parents walking on the street, pushing Darlene in a stroller just as they ran into Alex about seven o'clock the evening before Alex's death. As the two dads walked the infant, Alex accosted them, tried to grab her away. That may have been why Alex hid out at your place."

A heavy burden lifted in Charlie's heart like clouds rising above ground level, revealing a low clear sky. The fluorescents stabilized, ceased to strobe, calming Charlie's anxiety.

"Are you going to arrest them?"

"I need more, especially with a same-sex couple and an adoption? I'd better have my ducks in a row. I don't want anyone crying foul."

Charlie's nervousness returned from its momentary exile. *Would Benton Whoever and Sandy What's his Name hold David Alex being in the bungalow against Charlie?*

"What about Harry Alex? The brother? The guy murdered in the Visions office?"

"There is no Harry Alex. Never was a brother."

Charlie turned pale. "Was that Gary Frank guy lying?" Charlie's anxiety escalated, as the clouds crushed the hopeful ground level beams of light.

"I interviewed Gary Frank. He came down willingly to file a witness statement. That guy's a patsy. He found a body, all right, in Alex's office."

"Who says it wasn't Alex's brother?"

"The vic's half-burned off fingerprints. That guy was some loan shark punk after Alex."

"Alex had me fooled."

"My investigator went to the morgue, talked to the Assistant Coroner who signed off on the pick-up of the vic from St. Denis Hospital E.R. where he was taken after the stabbing. Dr. Juibank, the Assistant Coroner and Medical Examiner in the case, while preparing the body, found the vic's motel card key in the morgue locker, about to get tossed, along with the vic's crumpled clothes. Dr. Juibank, being one of our more conscientious city employees, put the card key in an evidence baggie, kept it on her desk, and handed it over to Tammy. Tammy took the card key and headed to the 'Lucky 7.' The motel is a flophouse over near Alvarado and 7th Street."

"Why would Alex lie to me?"

"The investigator talked to the "Lucky 7" manager, with the dude's abandoned luggage, still waiting. The vic was an Armenian, Yevgeny Shukarian. No legal status in this country, nor cell phone. Nothing. Nada. This Yevgeny apparently visited Alex in Alex's office. We know Mr. Alex expected his visit because my P.I. tracked phone calls from Alex's office to the Motel. Alex took advantage of the resemblance to dispose him from the land of the living."

"Alex killed him?"

"That's what the investigator figures."

"Alex wasn't the type to kill."

"Well, he was a slight man, physically. But someone may have helped him, or did the stabbing. Alex may not even have been there."

Charlie thought for a moment. "Why?"

"There was a strong resemblance between the two men, Alex and this Shukarian victim. That may have given Alex the idea to dispose a threatening two-bit creditor and get off other creditors' radars. It fooled his assistant. It fooled you. If my investigator wouldn't have looked into it? It might have fooled me. There was no reason to take prints off an identified vic."

Oswilla reached for a photo of the dead Shukarian and placed it in front of Charlie. While Shukarian's body was prone on a metal table somewhere in the bowels of the county morgue, the face, the hair, the build looked like Charlie's memory of Alex lying in his studio floor. Charlie couldn't look at the photo, turned away, looked back at Oswilla.

"Might be a good way to disappear with his grand-daughter, one step ahead of serious debt collector goons."

Charlie's armpits filled with sweat, despite having used deodorant. He thought back on Alex in his studio. He thought back on Alex, confident, showing off his office and his vision for his new utopian colony, Isis. Charlie knew Alex was not a murderer, no matter how desperate he may have been to avoid creditors. He didn't want to argue with Detective Oswilla, his host. It was getting late. Charlie also recalled Alex's pained dead eyes as they stared up to his ceiling.

"I'll sleep better now, I guess. Thanks."

"You're welcome. That's not why I called you down."

"How the hell did I get mixed up in all this?"

"I can't answer existential dilemmas, but I need your help identifying a body that turned up. Might relate to your courthouse incident."

Charlie realized he was not out of the woods, yet. He was deeper into the alluvial forest.

"I almost feel like one of the homicide team."

"We're in the same racket."

"My clients are supposed to be dead, when I get involved. Usually from old age."

"When big money's at stake? That boatman is eager to ferry another customer across that river to the kingdom of eternal darkness."

"Don't like the idea of crossing the river myself before my time."

"Your time is – when it happens. That's the beauty of it. I've seen everything in this job. And I've only been at it some twelve years."

"Sounds like you had a career before the L.A.P.D.?"

"Didn't you? No-one starts out to be a probate attorney."

"On occasion, I am an extra in the L.A. Opera choir."

Detective Oswilla chuckled. "An artist, huh?"

"For a few years. But couldn't make it pay."

"Hard to make your dream come true."

"Still clutching to a tiny bit of mine."

"Yeah. Well, this vic's lost hers. Some kids saw the body float by in that cesspool, L.A. River. They snapped a photo on their iPhone, texted '911', and scrambled."

Charlie looked at Detective Oswilla's iPad photo. It was a water-logged dark-dress covered body, hands outstretched, face down in the muck of the L.A. river, a crucified victim of someone's anger, or the woman's despondency.

"Let's take a walk." Detective Phillip Oswilla flashed an ironic raised eyebrow at his choice of words. He wheeled himself into the corridor. Charlie followed.

Detective Oswilla led Charlie through the barren hallways to the police department's downtown cold room.

Oswilla knocked on the metal door. When it didn't open, he punched in a code.

"The police examiners are med student interns who specialize in long coffee breaks."

"I would, too," Charlie added.

The smell of putrid death inside the cold room intensified from the air conditioning system's freon blown frigid air. Detective Oswilla wheeled and led Charlie into the room's center, towards a green plasticized drape covered body lying on what looked like an operating table, surrounded by swinging metal reflective lights.

Detective Oswilla signed the "sign in sheet," moved alongside the once living body, maneuvering his wheelchair at table height with his left arm in a forced show of respect. With his free right arm Oswilla pulled the drape off the torso revealing a gray faced, dirt covered, long-haired woman with bruises on her cheeks and forehead.

Charlie grabbed the edge of the rigid metal table. The shiny metal was uncaring. He slumped onto the attached stool, tried to stay upright.

Charlie forced himself to look at the woman on the metal table. The arms were crossed. A blue pallor reflected the spot lights from forehead to cheeks, shoulders, and arms. The fingers were too taut to interlace.

Charlie focused on the woman's stone-cold face with closed eyelids and swept back frizzy hair, falling behind the edge of the morgue table's metal edge.

Oswilla reached for another stick of gum, started to chew. "Ever see her before?" Oswilla pulled thin latex gloves on both hands.

Charlie concentrated on Oswilla's expert fingers pointing at the woman's neck, at bruising near the carotid artery. Oswilla continued chewing gum. Charlie was more and more dizzy. *There was something sacrosanct about death. Even in a cold room. But not if you smacked your lips as you chewed gum.*

Oswilla expertly pointed at indentations in her neck, blue blotches and a blue marked line around the front of her neck and upper chest cavity – Oswilla glanced at Charlie. He caught Charlie's disgust.

"Sorry." Detective Oswilla took out the gum, wrapped and pocketed it. "I need to chew gum when I'm face to face with death."

Charlie nodded, feeling himself about to retch.

"This is a classic military ops style assassination." Oswilla pointed around the blue blotches in the neck's front cavity. "The technique was developed by ORAF, the French counterintelligence agency during the

Algerian War in the 1950's. They taught the U.S. counterintelligence agents during the cold war."

The room spun in Charlie's scrambled mind. Oswilla saw Charlie turn sheet white.

"There's the john."

Charlie raced to the small bathroom in the corner and made it in time to throw up into the tiny metal sink. Everything about his life seeped out of his heart. He gasped for breath, and looked into the tiny mirror – it had graffiti etched into the glass. The only word Charlie could make out was "fuck-u."

Charlie cleaned his mouth with the warm water and tried to control sweating.

Charlie didn't remember what happened next.

CHAPTER 46
CORPSES AND CLUES

Charlie came to, slouched on the armchair in the L.A.P.D. waiting room outside Oswilla's office. He was still disoriented, checked his watch. It was 11:45 p.m.

Charlie flinched as he looked at the shiny coroner's metal gurney next to him.

Detective Oswilla looked at Charlie's puzzled face, chortled. "I disinfected the gurney before pulling you over it and dragging you here."

"Glad you didn't wheel me to the morgue."

Detective Oswilla, in his wheelchair, sitting behind the secretary's desk, leaned back, put down his copy of *Men's Workout*.

"You're just shaky. The formaldehyde doesn't get to me. Then again, I worked on cadavers in medical school."

"Glad I'm in the hands of a specialist."

"I was a medic with the U.S. armed forces in Iraq." Detective Oswilla gestured at his useless legs on the wheelchair platform. "Not my best career move. But med school and brownie points for having served in a combat zone leapfrogged my career with the L.A.P.D." Oswilla chuckled.

"Can I go home?"

"Can you drive?"

Charlie checked his limbs and faculties. He nodded, suppressed the pain from his left calves and hips onto which he had fallen.

"Did you recognize the vic?"

"Looks like the woman who threw lye at the downtown attorney. Did you check out the car rental company?

"It's a phony. Some internet website in Malaysia. You sign your car up and they mail a phony rental license plate for whatever state you want. Then, they charge you a taxi license fee by the month. She worked for a pro."

Charlie knew he had to blurt out. "We had a similar attack in New Orleans last week."

"Hmm. The vic's purse found in the L.A. River had a driver's license from New Orleans."

Detective Oswilla looked down at his notepad.

"'Candace Rollins.' Recognize the name?"

"That's her. She called me yesterday. That's when I tried to call you."

Oswilla popped a curled chewing gum. "What did she want?"

"A quarter."

"A quarter?"

"She rambled about being shafted by this estate dead guy, Beneshan. She claimed he promised her a job."

"Beneshan? The case with David Alex?"

"Yes."

"Jeez. Bad karma. Everyone around him winds up dead."

"I'm still kicking." Charlie got up to demonstrate he could, despite a pain cramping his left leg, and shooting up to zap his back. "Ouch."

"You want to get an X-ray exam? We've got our own E.R. facility."

"I'm fine."

"You were still holding onto the sink when I reached you. At worst you twisted something."

"Under the circumstances, I have no complaint." Charlie resumed a few tap dance beats, but as a nerve in his lower back pinched, he froze his dance number bringing a sudden end to the show.

Oswilla laughed at Charlie's tap dance routine, stretched his latex gloves over his right hand, reached into the large plastic zip bag on his desk, pulled out a yellowed sheet of paper, unfolded it.

Charlie saw the waterlogged list of names in the cursive slanted, jagged handwriting. The water had made some names illegible.

"We found this in the vic's wallet. I compared the handwriting with notes in the vic's soggy check book. Not her writing."

Charlie looked at the list. He couldn't make out the names.

"So, who wrote the list?"

Oswilla placed the yellowed list under a strong table light.

"I was hoping you'd tell me."

Charlie shrugged.

Oswilla's fingers underscored the first name: "'Leon Lambert?'"

"The attorney attacked yesterday, downtown."

Detective Oswilla's fingers passed a name that was illegible, and pointed to the two names at the list's end. The two names were recognizable in their faint blue lettering: "An-el S—d—," and "C—ie T-b–s."

"'Angel Sedona.' Your client. Right?"

"Yeah."

"I don't need to fill in the last name's blanks. That's why I called you in."

Charlie groaned, recognizing his name. "I'm just a hired employee."

"Croaked gang members say the same thing. You're better than that. You're an attorney, even if you didn't set out to be one."

Charlie thought about the detective's insight.

"Thanks for the clue. So, what's the next step?"

"We're doing a handwriting analysis, and a DNA swab on the paper. If we're lucky, we may get some residue of whoever wrote the list. Any ideas?"

"There's a very hungry creditor out there. Last on the list would be the previous law offices, Jones, Sharke. I'm sending them a huge check."

"Okay. Who else?"

"Attorney Leon Lambert, the attorney attacked downtown, reps one of the Beneshan estate's major creditors. Some hush-hush silent backer itching for his dough."

"What's his handle?"

"Angel's been trying to find out. She had two P.I.'s on it who ran up quite a tab. All we know is the name of the private investment firm: 'Blue Orchid.'"

Oswilla took notes. "I'll check it out."

"They're not a listed California corporation. Must be some private investor."

"My investigator is good. I'll send Tammy to interview this Lambert dude."

"I'd give it up if it were me in the E.R. with bandage on my eyes."

"Yeah, jettison that attorney-client privilege bullshit, if you're going blind."

Charlie shuddered. Lyle was a huge step up from nail polish remover.

"It all goes back to Barry Beneshan, doesn't it?"

"Yeah."

"I remember when he croaked. My office got the dossier. He died in some Venice pad about two years ago."

"Yeah, summer, 2006."

"I waited till I got the medic report, and the Inquest from the medical examiner. The death looked routine. Filed it in archives. Had it retrieved when Ms. Sedona came to complain about three weeks later. I reviewed the file with her input, but the drugs they found in his body during the Inquest closed the investigation for me. I thought his death was straight up drug overdose."

"Did she tell you about the missing two hundred grand in his vest?"

"Yeah, but she had no proof. What am I supposed to do?"

"She talks about it constantly. It was her freedom money from all this garbage."

"She filed a police report on the missing moneys. The facts sounded iffy. I bet she put in an insurance claim."

Charlie thought back. Oswilla's suspicions echoed his own. The public records of the missing money would be evidence that would force an insurance company to pay up or risk a sizeable lawsuit.

"Reopen the case and have an autopsy done on Beneshan!"

"I got to have some serious evidence to dig up a two year old corpse."

Charlie filled Oswilla in on Will Wonder's untimely end.

"Woodfall's out of my jurisdiction."

"Bet you all the deaths and attacks lead back to Beneshan."

Oswilla thought about it, shrugged. "I'm an easy mark. I'll put in a request to the Coroner to exhume the body." Oswilla looked into Charlie's eyes. "You plan to stay alive? Tell me your instinct."

"The estate picked up a substantial cash flow from New Orleans. I'm sending checks out to the biggest vultures. A contractor named Eric Dart didn't make the list."

"Eric Dart, a California contractor? He does prison construction jobs?"

Charlie nodded. "What do you know about him?"

"Eric Dart's name has come up."

"Excuse me?"

"Alex and Dart bid on contracts around town. It's some joint transit and city low cost housing project. They were ruthless rivals."

"Dart claims he was owed."

"Hhmm."

Charlie didn't dare interrupt the detective's searching nerve cells, trying to make neural connections.

"Dart is worth a close look. What about the Blue Orchid money guy? Any leads?"

Charlie thought for a moment: "Lambert's in Good Sam, recuperating from Candace's attack. Maybe, he'll spill to your investigator."

Oswilla noted the names on his yellow pad. "A great bunch of pals this Beneshan had."

"I'm stuck with them."

"Time to unstick the glue?"

CHAPTER 47
IMPENDING CALAMITIES

The thing about any impending calamity is that life races on the tracks of routine tasks until the train wreck. Charlie's fear for his and Angel's safety receded as daily problems demanded their due turn.

It was close to 12:30 a.m. when Charlie made it home from L.A.P.D. headquarters. His mind was on auto-pilot as his car raced through the open late night freeway lane ribbon to the valley. Tina was asleep, so he avoided waking her. He watched the midnight local news rerun. There was no mention of a woman's body pulled out of the L.A. River. Charlie was too tired to ponder why. He had enough stamina to lock all the doors. Exhausted, Charlie, tip-toed up the carpeted stairs, fell asleep.

The alarm woke Charlie early. He stumbled to the bathroom, showered, threw on passable work clothes, grabbed his rehearsal kit holding "*West Nile,* Extra – Baritone" transcribed music scores for the evening.

■　　　■　　　■　　　■　　　■

At the office, Charlie caught up on paper work and pretended all was well. He kept looking at the clock to make sure he'd race out in time to get to rehearsal. At one point, Angel called: "Hi, I just wanted to hear your voice. Make sure you're okay." Charlie appreciated the call. "I was down at police headquarters last night, identifying a body."

"Do I need to hear this?"

"Yes. The body was Rollins. They fished her out of the L.A. River."

There was a moment of silence on the other end.

"What happened to the bitch loser?"

Charlie told her. There was one fact Angel latched onto. "Detective Phillip Oswilla? When he interviewed me about Mr. Alex? I reminded him about Barry's death. I made a point of trying to get an autopsy after Barry died. He brushed me off."

"Oswilla promised to re-visit Barry's cause of death."

"That's fantastic!"

"He remembered you."

"I don't want to get my hopes up. So what happened to Candy?"

"The detective thinks Rollins was drugged, and physically thrown over a downtown bridge into the L.A. River."

"She had it coming."

"Well, I don't know about that."

Charlie wasn't sure he liked Angel's lack of compassion – even for Candace Rollins.

"Cops found a list in her bag. Lambert's name was on the list." Charlie hesitated, blurted out: "So were ours."

"She's dead. Doesn't that mean we'll be okay?"

"Oswilla said the list is not her handwriting."

There was a moment of silence.

"I've got to run, pick up my daughter."

"I can ask the P.I.'s to look into it."

"I don't have the money. Do you understand? I can't pay."

Charlie looked at the clock. It was just about 4:30 p.m.

"Talk later."

Earl detoured from the hallway into Charlie's office as Charlie gathered his files to put away.

"Who was that?"

"Angel Sedona."

"Put down your time. 'Teleconference with client re estate update.' Did you do that?"

Luckily, Charlie had noted the call on his notepad, but hadn't entered it into his computer, which was already turned off. He flipped the notepad in front of Earl to confirm that he had entered the call on his personal log.

"Now. Enter it." Earl flipped the computer back on, and clicked on the accounting software program. "You'll forget. Enter it now." As Charlie complied, Earl focused on the boxes of Beneshan files next to Charlie's desk.

"Why are all the Beneshan files out?"

"I'm reviewing the outstanding creditors. Make sure they get paid."

"The only creditor to worry about is us."

Charlie entered the meeting time with Oswilla the previous night into the computer software, as well as the day's "teleconference" with "estate administrator Sedona." Earl stood over Charlie.

"Another police interview? What was that about?"

"They found the acid thrower's body. I 'i.d.'d it."

"We should bill the detective."

"I'm billing it to the estate."

"Okay."

Charlie closed the computer down again, worried he'd be late.

"Make sure our check gets sent out first. Without money in, we can't serve anyone."

"Sure, Earl. Got to run."

Charlie headed out the door. "Put those boxes away. And bill for that time."

"Right. Goodbye."

CHAPTER 48
PRIVATE ITCHES

Many opera chorus members were retirees who sang to make a few extra dollars to supplement meager social security checks. Slipping on the heavy, coarse costumes was time-consuming. The Opera Company, forced to make do with declining donations as the economy shuddered and stalled, refused to pay for preparation time. The extras complained among themselves, but no one dared confront Gerry. Besides, the taciturn A.D. had no say in the company's policies. His telephone receiver, always curved around the side of his balding head, was a one way communicator – barking orders to extras, who were eager for the opportunity to work.

Charlie squirmed into the brown paper mache costume. Sweat dribbled. There was no way to relieve the uncomfortable wetness that seeped into the most private body parts followed by bursts of itching. Charlie squirmed and looked around for Oscar. Gerry loomed behind Charlie.

"Hurry up, Charlie."

"Have you seen Oscar?"

"Your pal's out. He had a mishap at the stunt rehearsal."

"What happened?"

"He had to be taken to the hospital. Want to do some stunts, Charlie?"

"I'll pass. I want to know what happened to Oscar!"

"One of the guy wires snapped while Oscar was in the air. Then, the other wire got tangled and he had a bad fall."

Charlie was disturbed to hear about Oscar's mishap. The one person who had stuck up for Charlie and kept his dream alive, now needed help.

"Which hospital is he in?"

"I don't know, Charlie. Get your butt on stage."

As Charlie was about to cover his face with the headpiece, another extra stepped up, holding his blue emerald colored headpiece in the crook of his arm.

"You're Charlie Tobias, aren't you?"

This wiry extra, in his late fifties, very elegant, was one of the two praying mantis insects interspersed among the mosquitoes for visual serendipity.

Charlie nodded.

"I'm Oscar's younger brother, Desmond Thornhill."

Charlie thought back on his friend, an elegant man who always showed up in his blue blazer, neatly pressed gray flannels, and red-and-blue striped tie. Truth be told, Charlie knew very little about Oscar Thornhill or why Oscar recommended Charlie for the L.A. Lyric Opera extra job opening, but Charlie saw the facial feature resemblance in the energetic, intense younger man he faced.

"I heard about his fall. Is he okay?"

"No. He was injured badly."

"I'm so sorry."

"Oscar told me you are a probate attorney. I need to talk to you."

Both men finished placing their headpieces on in the backstage hallway, and headed towards the offstage chorus holding room. It was about 7:00 p.m., the night of the first full dress rehearsal for Act I.

Despite his efforts to keep his two lives separate, Charlie understood his cover for his day job was blown.

"Oscar can't function. He's in a rest home. Can you get me appointed as his conservator?"

Charlie's sheer nylon leggings stretched on his feet as he hopped. He slapped at the discomfort as he focused on this unexpected legal request. He almost lost his balance and steadied himself by placing his claws on Desmond Thornhill's left shoulder.

"Sorry."

"Son-of-a-bitch costumes. I didn't sign up to be in an underwear ad." Charlie knew Desmond referred to the colorful fruit costumed iconic spokespeople for the well-known underwear line, "Wane's." He joined in Desmond's chuckle.

Charlie had no idea how Desmond found out about his other life. Charlie recalled mentioning his legal career as an excuse for being late to Veronica on a day when he had raced from court to a costume fitting, and she was particularly irate.

"I just work at a Law Office," he said to Desmond with a shrug.

"We need your help. You are a member of the State Bar. I looked you up."

They followed the other insects into the rehearsal room.

"Gosh, I'm sorry. I have a full-time job at the Law Offices, not to mention this side job."

"We'd pay well. Think of it as another 'extra's' job."

The wetness seeped along the side of Charlie's belly and much lower. Charlie tried to ignore the spreading itch in his most private crevices as he hopped behind the stage curtain unable to distance himself from Desmond Thornhill.

CHAPTER 49
A PRIVATE PROPOSITION

Rubbing his legs together discreetly, Charlie felt relief. He had memorized a few lines in the score, practiced his harmonies and could concentrate on the rehearsal. Desmond Thornhill was next to him but focused on his stage choreography and featured part. The few rehearsal musicians in street clothes took their place in the orchestra pit. The lights dimmed.

Chelsee Starlight's family entered from stage right and moved to center stage, around the swimming pool deck, stage left. Chelsee's father and mother were played by the understudies. Danny Starlight, the precocious twelve year old younger brother took his place on stage to a few whistles and scattered applause among well-wishers in the audience. Danny Starlight was played by Kenny Patch, a star on the TV sitcom hit *The Beverly Hills Misfit.*

The brief overture set the tone of the performance: dangerous, ominous. The stage lights came up, as the stunt extras launched from the side of the stage on their circular flight. Charlie's voice rang out with the other mosquitos:

Chorus
You who come to this land –
And seek stardom,
Wealth and fame,
For your lives,
Beware!
The beat of your heart,
Tears your dreams apart.

Chelsee Starlight
Momma, momma. I'll
Be a star.
I'll shine so bright.
The whole world will feel
My blinding light.

Maria Starlight
The sun is hazy, and the pool
Reflects dark clouds…

Danny Starlight
A swarm of insects,
Fly in circling bounds…
Ready to plunge into
Human flesh on the ground.

Mom and Dad Starlight followed Danny's gaze to the stage rafters. The stage darkened. Charlie and the mosquito chorus circled closer behind the oblivious Starlight family.

Chorus
Dreams and visions.
Beyond compare.
Will our thirst for their blood
Change their Land
To despair?

Rudolph Starlight
I have a good job in my company,
Helping young couples find homes.
For their families.

Maria Starlight
And our benefits support our
Children who seek stardom.

Chelsee Starlight
I've studied acting, voice and dance,
Since I was four.
I have faith I'll reach my dream – to
Shine like a star.

Juan Esperanza, the handsome undocumented immigrant hero, played by TV action star Eric Gomez looks past bushes he clips with shears, sees the beautiful Chelsee Starlight.

Juan Esperanza
I see an angel, a shining star.
Who is near, yet she lives
In a world I am apart from -
I see an angel whose dream
I want to share and provide for.

Charlie took a deep breath, flexed his chest muscles around his diaphragm, resonated his full-throated baritone voice into the "buzz" harmony.

Chorus
There's only one end for those
Who reject their fate,
And, like Icarus,
Want to be second to none.

Charlie shuffles across the stage, flaps his scaly brown mosquito arms, buzzes.

Chelsee Starlight
And if I can't reach the stars,
I know I won't forget,
I reached for my dreams,
And will not live with regret.

Stage hands shift the guy wires to lower the stunt insects to land on the Starlight's shoulders. The Starlights feeling the itch, swat at claws that curl onto their shoulders.

The tuba and bass section crescendo as the gross creatures land and extend their proboscises into their human victims' arms. Maria Starlight repeatedly slaps at her shoulder. Stage lights turn blood red, as the insects drink their fill of human blood.

Charlie and the chorus of insects undulate their arms in a flowery choreography that precedes and foreshadows the end of Act 1. Charlie, exhausted from the physical exertion, the heat, and stress freezes into his final position. The stage lights dim as the curtain falls.

"That's it. End of 'Act One.' Great job," Gerry claps as he shoos the chorus off-stage. Charlie hears applause from the scattered well-wishers. The stunt mosquitoes are lowered onto the stage. One stunt mosquito screams as a guy wire snaps, and he plummets the final descent. Several stage assistants rush, and right the stunt player as his backside hits the stage floor with a thud. He pulls his head mask off.

"My back. My back."

Gerry runs over. "Get the nurse. The cables crossed. You blind dicks!" Charlie and the other chorus members, exhausted, clamber offstage, ignoring the newest setback.

"That's it. Two Tuesday nights from tonight, dress rehearsal for Act Two." Gerry runs back to the dressing room. "Be in costume and on stage by seven p.m. No exceptions." Charlie lifts his mask, hops towards the dressing room. Desmond Thornhill hops alongside.

"When can we get together?"

"I don't do legal work on my own."

"How about lunch this Saturday, here downstairs at 'Le Pinot?' Oscar and I would be grateful."

Charlie slipped out of his costume. "Is Oscar okay? I heard he had a bad fall."

"Oscar needs your help, Charlie. Please help us."

Desmond Thornhill's insistence was even more troubling to Charlie than his own fatigue. Charlie was not oblivious to his debt to Oscar for referring him to the L.A. Lyric Opera job. Without Oscar's recommendation, Charlie would still be volunteering in the Bellflower Community Chorus on weekends, or the artistic stage of his life would be only a dim memory.

"Okay."

CHAPTER 50
A VERY PRIVATE PERSON

Ever since the two interviews with that nice police investigator, Charlie's neighbor, Carrie Baxter was scared. If it hadn't been for that McCormack lady interrupting her rose pruning, she would not even be aware of the murder a few doors north of her modest Spanish bungalow home. The sleeping pill cocktail her doctor prescribed a few months back for insomnia must be very effective. Carrie rarely woke at night, and must have slept through the police sirens and the medics arrival on the night of the murder.

Let the police deal with grizzly deaths. Tracking down murderers might put her in harm's way, she rationalized. That would not do at all. She was already exhausted, dealing with escalating neighborhood nuisances.

The infernal rave parties popped up more and more frequently in the stately homes whose desperate or greedy owners shuttled paying crazed Hollywood wannabes to drug and alcohol fueled debauches. At first, it had been a neighborhood parking issue, but when the drunk and stoned teen-age partygoer overdosed on the front lawn of the Doheny Camden home deep in the canyon, and over two hundred teen-agers were arrested, Carrie became the self-appointed savior of the Farmdell and walked incessantly up and down its historic streets, with the "Hollywood" iconic sign ever a backdrop, looking for signs of parties she reported to the police.

At first, she had no luck getting L.A.P.D. cooperation, but as her persistence became an ongoing nuisance at the Hollywood Precinct Police Station on Wilcox Avenue, she was assigned a well-meaning Hollywood Division veteran, Officer Nixon Tracker, who followed up her leads, knocked on doors and informed homeowners in his ex-Marine

Commander's convincing drawl, that drunken rave parties would be shut down immediately, and the police vice squad would cart away everyone on the premises, including the owner.

Carrie had less luck shutting down filming going on in some of the canyon's larger estates. With the proliferation of TV reality shows, the production companies needed upscale bargain sets and nothing served better than the opulent canyon villas which the owners would gratefully rent out for a hefty fee. Despite her neighborhood association's letter writing campaign to City Council, the invasion of noise, grime, crowds, and annoyance escalated.

And now, a murder on her block?

Thinking back on it, Carrie realized she had her first alert to the murder several weeks after it happened when she was clipping back the hydrangea bushes in the gated front yard, and a tie-clad young man knocked on her gate and asked to come in and talk to her. She declined to open the gate, thinking he was a salesman or Scientology recruiter, but the young man talked anyway over the nice Spanish stucco fence that protected her home, but was unfortunately not high enough to blot out the heads of the sidewalk passersby. He asked about the attorney Charlie Tobias who kept renting the tiny bungalow further up the block where Charlie's mother lived till she passed away some six years ago.

Carrie confirmed she knew who Charlie was. When she ignored further questions from the young man, he identified himself as Travis Smith, a Paralegal from Jones Sharke, a law firm working with Charlie Tobias on a case.

Carrie relented and answered a few of the young man's questions, including confirming that Charlie had a visitor who stayed with him a few weeks back for three or four days. The Paralegal scribbled all this down, thanked her, and left.

Carrie didn't think anything more about this interaction, until that nice, earnest young woman in the well-pressed blouse and skirt came by a few weeks later. Unfortunately, when Carrie saw that her visitor was a woman, she opened the protective wood gate. At first, the friendly woman with well-combed short hair didn't quite say who she was, only that her name was Tammy McCormack. She asked questions about Charlie Tobias, as well as Carrie's other neighbors. She then blindsided Carrie by telling her about the murder some four weeks earlier, and confirmed she was an L.A.P.D. Investigator.

Carrie was in a state of shock hearing that someone's life had been deliberately ended so close to her home.

The first time that Tammy McCormack mentioned the murder, Carrie froze, ended the interview, shut the gate and refused to take the woman's business card.

But that Tammy woman kept coming back. Tammy McCormack gained Carrie's trust, talking over the stucco fence, while Carrie, on her knees, cleaned her rose-beds, pretending not to hear. Tammy revealed she had no father, and her mother had given Tammy up to an orphanage in Austin, Texas when she was five years old and only came back for her six years later, with a new boyfriend, who alas, became an abusive stepfather. Tammy McCormack confided she ran away from home when she was twelve to live with a distant aging cousin in nearby Tujunga Canyon whom she cared for until he died shortly after Tammy finished high school. Tammy McCormack inherited the home of the relative in Tujunga Canyon, much as Carrie inherited her mother's home in Farmdell Canyon. Carrie's heart softened as she heard Tammy's hard-luck story. Tammy got a job as a teacher's aide at the age of nineteen and eventually became an investigator for the public defender's office, trying to help those who like Tammy and Carrie were abused, neglected, and abandoned.

At some point, not at the first meeting, but maybe at the second or third time Tammy came around, Carrie gave in, and told Tammy about the street confrontation she witnessed on the day of the murder. She immediately regretted her indiscretion. However, it was too late.

At the next visit, Tammy confided she conveyed the information about the street argument between the actors and the poor handsome man who was found dead in Charlie Tobias's bungalow to her superior, a Homicide Detective Phillip Oswilla, and asked Carrie to come downtown to Police Center and make a full statement about the incident.

Carrie nodded, closed the creaking wooden gate on Tammy, without saying a word, leaned against the backside of the gate to keep from fainting. Carrie panicked at what she was becoming involved in. Danger with a capital "D."

Carrie had nightmares that ended with her demise. She'd wake up, drenched in sweat. She recalled a horrifying nightmare in which she inadvertently stepped into a fountain as she maneuvered past drunken rave partygoers, and was attacked by thousands of bulging-eyed crocodiles coming at her from all directions with horrible open mouths that closed on her flesh and chomped and pulled in frenzy, eating her and inflicting horrendous pain as the equally ugly and cruel rave party goers around the fountain laughed and jeered as she died a horrible death.

In the final nightmare, Carrie was trying to stop one of the rave parties. The confrontation got out of hand, a brawl erupted on the front lawn as Carrie tried to find the home's owner. Then, she saw two figures, the stout bald headed pig-man, and the craggy faced ostrich man walk towards her, with spiked clubs in their hands, menacing and dangerous. It was quite dark, and someone bashed Carrie's skull in with a pointed sharp object. The blunt hurt beneath her wet hair became excruciating as blood streamed out of her cranium down her head, but the crazed partygoers ignored her pain and the inflicted damage, until she staggered through the home's front door and fell down on the steps in a pool of blood amidst the laughing revelers.

Carrie bolted upright from the nightmare. She realized she had replayed that terrifying night of the murder, and the nightmare was a warning from her sub-conscious brain. She sweated as she came to the real-life realization: Those two attackers weren't just in her mind. Pig Man and Ostrich Man were the two shadowy forms she had seen out of her second story window when she had gotten up at night to go pee. They walked up the driveway to Charlie Tobias's place the night of the murder. She had watched their street-lit figures disappear behind the Italian Cypress trees that set off Charlie Tobias's cottage from the south side neighbors. The two men reappeared with a valise some ten minutes later and drove off in their big black car. Carrie was terrified to make the connection that she was awake that night, looking out at the full moon and witnessed the two silhouetted murderers, and heard the victim's screams. She had taken more sleeping pills, and gone back to sleep, hoping she would forget what she saw and heard.

Carrie vowed she would never speak to Tammy McCormack or any other police official about the murder again.

CHAPTER 51
DEAD ENDS

Investigator Tammy McCormack returned to Carrie Baxter's house several times, and was pleased to see the red and orange flowered bougainvillea bushes blossom as March slipped into April, but Tammy received no further co-operation. Tammy knew she could only ask Carrie so often without alienating whatever reservoir of good will existed between the two women.

The murder scene bungalow had been returned to its owner, Charlie Tobias, the week after the crime back in September. The L.A.P.D. forensics team had run its tests without finding fingerprints, nor D.N.A. samples other than those of Charlie Tobias and David Alex. That happened almost seven months ago.

Tammy drove to the Coroner's Forensics Laboratory in Highland Park and reviewed the David Alex autopsy with the staff. The photos of Alex's body showed deep indentations on his larynx. The Assistant Forensics Medical Examiner's theory was that the loss of oxygen in the carotid vein sent a blood clot to the brain, causing a quick loss of consciousness and death, perhaps in less than one minute. Dr. Janet Juibank, the white-uniformed Assistant Medical Examiner had seen few asphyxiations this precisely carried out. Her opinion was that whoever strangled Alex must be very strong. Tammy asked how strong the assailant had to be. Dr. Juibank and her two assistants conferred and gave their opinion that the assailant was "...not your average Joe. The assailant was a trained martial arts expert, possibly a combat veteran."

Tammy wrote her notes, got Dr. Juibank and her two assistants to sign off, thanked the Forensic staff and left to a fitful sleep in her bucolic

Tujunga Canyon home in the North San Fernando Valley which she had reinforced with bars on the windows and doors.

After she submitted her second report to Detective Oswilla, Tammy didn't hear anything for a week.

During that time, she returned to the Farmdell neighborhood to interview the actors. Sandy Tryale was working in his manicured garden, barely distinguishable from the Hispanic gardener who wore a similar wide-brimmed straw hat to ward off the sun. The infant, Darlene was in a multi-colored crib nearby. The little girl lay down in her stroller, protected by a parasol from the sun. In reply to Tammy's forensic report update Sandy volunteered that he was no athlete, nor ever engaged in martial arts. The round-faced cherubic man wouldn't offer any further cooperation. When she suggested he voluntarily submit to a DNA test he recoiled.

"In the little interaction we had with that egotistic jerk, who knows what DNA might have been transferred?" Sandy picked up Darlene, hurried into the house and slammed the door.

Tammy knew it was a waste of time to knock on the door. She left.

Several days later, Tammy called the home number and reached Benton Wayne. Benton, in his thin raspy voice, that reeked of umbrage, was curt, gave her the name of an attorney the actors had hired, and asked her to contact Becket Lance, Attorney at Law, from now on. Tammy knew she could no longer talk to the adoptive parents directly, as they were represented by counsel.

Detective Oswilla chuckled when he read her third report. Tammy had only charged a minimum amount for her update as she had no new leads. He called Tammy on his speed dial and reviewed the report with her. Tammy learned from Detective Oswilla that Sandy and Benton's new attorney, Becket Lance, was one of the top progressive attorneys in town. Oswilla had even read that the two actors were part of a major lawsuit that was winding its way to the California Supreme Court, allowing same-sex parents to marry. Oswilla informed Tammy that the L.A.P.D. would never get that attorney Lance to co-operate without a search warrant. Oswilla had already called Mike Frawn, an Assistant City Attorney to see if Oswilla had enough legal grounds for "probable cause" based on the sidewalk confrontation to obtain the two parents' DNA.

The Assistant City Attorney was acerbic. "Is this witch hunt because they're gay and they are not afraid to press for their legal rights?" Later that afternoon, Detective Oswilla got a call from his supervisor, Captain Jim Abraham. Oswilla knew a call from the Supervising Homicide Officer was not a good sign.

"Hey, Phil. How's it going?"

"Okay, what's up?"

"Swell, say got a minute? I'm on my way over. How 'bout them Cougars?"

"Yeah, sure. Always great."

Oswilla popped a stick of gum, and waited for the scolding. He didn't need Abraham to come give him the guidelines to understand, that as far as the well-connected adoptive parents were concerned, he had to proceed cautiously.

CHAPTER 52
THE THIRD TIME'S NOT THE CHARM

In December, 2007, when Charlie was escorted out of the Law Offices for his second lay-off, Earl was more easy-going about the formalities, certain that Charlie would not put up a fuss. Charlie filled up his cardboard box with personal items without Earl standing over him. Charlie left his office, followed by Earl at a decent distance, said quick good-byes to Amanda and Aki. Jamie looked at Charlie with conspiratorial understanding as she mumbled "Take care, Charlie," as he walked out of the office, holding his desk lamp and box of personal possessions. Charlie could even drive out of the parking lot, with a validated parking ticket which Earl provided to Charlie along with a "Happy Holidays" greeting card for Charlie and Tina.

By now, Charlie gained the karmic wisdom to understand that the reason Earl Guarder laid him off twice had to do with non-paying clients, not with any legal mistake Charlie made. He repeated to himself as he descended in the elevator: *I still have my part-time singing job at the Opera, so things are not dire.*

In fact, after his second lay-off, Charlie was happy to have some time to deal with his own life, instead of clients' woes. Charlie enjoyed walking with Tina on the Ventura beach boardwalk on weekends. The global financial universe had collapsed as the new U.S. President was sworn in, but Charlie was confident of the future.

Then, in February, 2008, the rehearsals for the premiere of *West Nile* were put on hold and Tina was not rehired for her teaching position as the School District enacted major cutbacks.

Charlie was completely out of work. Tina scrambled for an occasional Substitute Teaching job.

Charlie tried to tell himself that *I am better off without my stressful job with Earl Guarder, and if the opera season won't happen, I can look for a new full-time attorney job.*

By the spring of 2008, Charlie's stress level spiked as the lack of freeway traffic mirrored the huge unemployment rise. Unlike several years ago, when commuting was a nightmare, you could get anywhere, even downtown or down the San Diego freeway to the west side without a struggle. Charlie recognized that in a few months he would have to give up on the Farmdell bungalow. Despite his mental preparation to start a new chapter in his working life, Charlie wanted to finish the Beneshan case.

Not being a part of the Law Offices anymore, Charlie was out of the picture, as he had no further legal role to play. Charlie missed Angel's self-confidence and revolutionary righteous wrath at the injustices and pettiness of the California probate court system and at the moral limitations she saw in the legal profession with her ongoing lawyer jokes, put-downs, and apologies that Charlie was the "exception." Charlie knew whatever relationship he and Angel had developed wouldn't be transferred by Angel to another Law Office Associate. Charlie became morose about his separation from the Law Offices of Earl S. Guarder.

While he was laid off, Charlie received several phone calls from Detective Oswilla asking about any developments. Charlie referred Detective Oswilla back to the Law Offices, but Oswilla still called every other week. This made Charlie nervous. In one conversation, Charlie asked point blank if Oswilla thought Charlie and Tina were in danger.

Detective Oswilla's acerbic reply: "Well, I don't have a crystal ball."

In another phone conversation, Detective Oswilla informed Charlie that Candace Rollins' body had been buried by her sister Edwina Graber in Riverdale Cemetery, a small cemetery in the San Gabriel Valley's working-class Toledo neighborhood.

Detective Oswilla concluded that Candace Rollins died of a drug and alcohol-induced overdose and either jumped or was thrown into the L.A. River after she was already dead. He deduced that conclusion from the pathologist's toxicology report which found traces of phenobarbital in Rollins' urine sample, and an enlarged liver. The lacerations in her neck were the result of the trauma from the fall. Detective Oswilla also deduced from which overpass she had been thrown into the L.A. River. Detective Oswilla was certain she was thrown off the Third Street Bridge.

Charlie was impressed with the detective's deduction.

"Well, it is one of two bridges that haven't been under construction and blocked off at either end for the last year or so. Of the two, it's the bridge with the low side indented concrete barriers. It's not that easy to lift a full grown woman over a barrier – even if they're limp or dead."

Charlie was surprised by the detective's follow-up statement:

"She had an okay funeral for a junkie."

"I'm surprised you went."

"Good place to scout out leads."

"Any mourners of interest?"

"That contractor you had your eye on, Eric Dart. Oh, and your client, the Sedona woman."

Charlie wasn't surprised by Eric Dart's mourning his Clean Co. protégé's passing, but pondered why Angel would attend Candace Rollins' funeral.

"Graber and Sedona exchanged some words. Ms. Sedona stalked off," Oswilla said in a smirky tone that irritated Charlie with its condescending attitude about what the correct etiquette should be at a funeral.

Charlie forgot about the conversation after he hung up. This wasn't his problem anymore.

Several days later, Angel called Charlie and asked how he was doing. It was an awkward call. Charlie reminded Angel she had to deal with Earl Guarder, or the re-hired Law Office Associate, Terry Ketchum assigned to her case.

"I'm sorry, Angel. There's nothing I can do about it."

"Wish you could, Charlie."

"Listen, Angel? That acid-throwing Rollins woman? I identified her body back in December. She was found in the L.A. River."

Charlie waited for a reaction, but Angel had hung up the phone and all Charlie heard was the dial tone. Charlie fretted, but had nothing definite to warn her against. His anxiety and wish to jump back in on the case subsided over the following days.

Then, Charlie received a call from Mark Ashland while Charlie was updating his resume. Ashland sounded panicked. Ashland reminded

Charlie about the upcoming Estate of Beneshan Accounting Hearing. Ashland reiterated what Charlie knew: that the hearing would review the creditors' payments Charlie and Angel completed prior to Charlie being laid off. The documents confirming proof of the payments had not been filed in court and could open Charlie and Angel up for sanctions.

All Charlie could tell Ashland was to call Earl and work it out with him.

Charlie was very upset about the call. Charlie had no control over what the Law Offices did or did not do. However, he might be held liable for the Law Offices' inactions.

At worst, Charlie would be able to appear *in pro per* to represent himself at any sanction hearing, pleading his dismissal from the firm as the reason for not having filed the Notice that the Estate of Beneshan checks had been sent out to the creditors as the court ordered.

The very next day, Charlie received the call from Earl that he expected and dreaded. Earl was effusive, friendly, might as well have invited Charlie for a fully-paid safari tour to photograph endangered elephants in Africa. He wanted Charlie back in the office – immediately. Earl was brilliant at dangling carrots. He made coming back to the office sound bucolic, exciting, full of perks and benefits.

On that same day, Charlie received a call from Gerry. Opera rehearsals were back on.

When Charlie told Tina about the call from Earl, she thought he was nuts not to say "no." Although, he protested that with their own tight finances, any work was better than none, Charlie knew there was only one reason he was going back: Angel Sedona and the Barry Beneshan case.

Whether it was Angel's case Charlie was attracted to, or Angel, Charlie didn't know, but by returning to his day job, he'd find out.

CHAPTER 53
FAMILIAR FILES

The reality of returning to The Law Offices of Earl S. Guarder in the spring of 2008 was a far cry from the upbeat word picture Earl painted to lure Charlie back. The challenges that awaited were more like the one General Custer faced at Little Big Horn.

The Law Offices on the 4th floor had contracted by several office desks. The five story historic white brick building with the delicate colonnades set back from Ferndale Avenue was mostly deserted. Even the long-established Hannah Ashley, Tannenbaum Law Firm was bereft of action. Most of its hundreds of cell-block offices were vacant as its private clients finished filing for bankruptcy.

Jamie was happy to see Charlie return and offered an approving laugh when Charlie brought his desk lamp and box filled with a few office supplies through the front reception area.

"Welcome back, stranger."

"It's good to see you. Things okay?"

"We're still here."

"I saw the coffee shop downstairs closed."

"The 'Howdy Do Da' stopped spinning its friendly 'do-dahs' after new year."

"Well, at least our own wheel's not completely fallen off the axle."

"Glad to see you, too, Charlie."

And Charlie knew he was back for a while.

Charlie, upon his return to the Law Offices, recalled the nauseating feeling on his night in the downtown police headquarters cold room, recoiling at the sight of Candace Rollins' squalid dead body. Heading down the empty halls towards his old office, he was reminded by the sticky air and undefined musty office smells, that the air conditioning in the police headquarter cold room worked just fine.

Charlie passed Aki's cubicle and rested his box on the ledge that separated her workspace from the the open hallway. Aki wasn't there, but a white-shirt and thin tie clean-cut substitute, in his mid '20's, introduced himself as Dmitri Smith, a U.C.L.A. second year Law School intern and the new part-time receptionist.

"What happened to Aki?"

"Oh, she's here part-time. I cover the desk on Monday and Wednesday mornings and Thursday afternoon. She's here the other days. Great to meet you."

"Likewise."

Dmitri directed Charlie to his old office.

"Earl is on his way in."

Charlie looked at the familiar space. He grabbed his box, and walked through the office door.

Charlie discovered he now shared the office he used to call his own, not just with Amanda, but with revolving law interns, who came and left at odd-ball times that worked into their law school schedules. Charlie found his computer much as he had left it – slow.

"The copying machine is busted," Amanda called out to him while on the phone.

Amanda got off the phone and gave Charlie a welcoming wave. She was glamorous as ever, her style and confidence not diminished by the onset of financial panic around her, and she seemed genuinely pleased to see Charlie return to the Law Offices. When Charlie asked about Terry Ketchum's whereabouts Amanda shrugged. "Yesterday was his last day." Terry Ketchum had been re-hired when Charlie had been laid off the previous December.

So much for Earl Guarder's promises of Terry Ketchum's willingness to work with Charlie upon Charlie's return, as well as the promises of new-hired colleagues and professional paralegal assistance.

He sighed, responding to Amanda's cheery welcome. "I'm glad to be back."

The truth was, Charlie was glad to be back, even as he tried to access his computer to make sure his previous work files were still intact.

The electronic files were there. That was a good sign.

Charlie perused the file folders on his desk. The file directory tab names were familiar, from the past, the numerous probate cases, conservator cases, a few construction defect cases, contract dispute cases, all waiting for him to return to keep him awake at night.

Charlie's attention shifted behind him to a long-haired blonde third year U.S.C. law student, who introduced herself as Karen Johnson, one of the law office interns. She was dressed in a nondescript polyester black business suit and open-necked white blouse. She had her desk squeezed into the tiny section of the room by the doorway, catty-corner across from Charlie and Amanda's stations. Karen Johnson proceeded to interview a middle-aged couple whose backs arched away from Charlie's own wood chair. Karen's clients, Hector and Melissa Mendoza, were not well dressed. Hector's plaid multi-colored shirt and Melissa's sport vest warded off the cold air, and they hoped Karen was warding off the financial disaster of Hector's layoff from the warehouse job that provided bread for their table for seventeen years. They were filing for bankruptcy, crying their eyes out.

Karen, sitting at her computer on the small metal desk, input information the Mendoza family provided into the computer's "bankruptcy" software.

To Charlie's right, Amanda was at her desk, on the phone, nonstop, calling and cajoling clients to send in overdue payments.

"Do you have a credit card? Let's use it. You're three months overdue. Don't worry, it won't get charged to your card till next month. How about half the balance? Two thousand dollars? We must have the payment made now to keep helping you."

Charlie tried to tune out the cacophony of financial desperation, and concentrated on his piles of files on his desk.

Earl, in a new gray silk suit, ran in for a moment, shook hands with Hector and Melissa Mendoza, charmingly asked Amanda had she swiped the Mendoza credit card (she had), nodded approvingly at everyone, stepped next to Charlie to greet him.

"Those are the most important files for now. The main thing is, get us out of the cases where clients aren't paying."

Charlie nodded, ready to take notes on his yellow legal pad.

"File a Motion to Withdraw Representation from the Freedom Hardware Company and the 'Home Cooking with a Smile' Restaurant. Sign them up for bankruptcy filing if you can. Oh, and there's an accounting hearing on Angel's case. Make sure the Beneshan Accounting is up to date and filed in time with the court for the hearing."

Charlie accepted Earl's hierarchy of assignments, but couldn't fail to notice how the most important major task that had brought him back to the job was left for last.

"Get Judge Bittenkopf to approve us another payment."

Earl turned back to Amanda. "How much is owed us in the Beneshan case?"

Amanda looked up. "About $40,000."

Earl was inches from Charlie's head, intense, stressed.

"Get the money. All of it."

"I got the payment check in before I left."

"These are new charges in the last months. Amanda will give you the billings. Lots of creditors came out of the woodwork once you cut the checks for Jones, Sharke, Blue Orchid and us. We spent a huge amount of time fighting off the jackals."

Charlie's heart leapt. His racing pulse told him he was back on the Beneshan case. Charlie knew he'd have late nights at the office to get the Accounting filed in time.

Images of David Alex's death-stare at the plaster ceiling, Boohau Cyclops' missing- finger handshakes, Will Wonder's extended arm jutting from the concrete, the blast at the Louisiana mansion, Devlin D'Alessio's charred face and arms, plus the visit to the morgue to identify Candace Rollin's corpse, flashed through his electrified nerves. Charlie tried to wipe out the images of death from the past, and was eager to take on the future.

"Right."

"Oh, and see what you can do about the Sly Clemens case. He took the moneys due the Law Offices, and hasn't paid his bills."

Charlie was astounded this was the only reference to the exhausting trial and for the hard toil he put in to get the winning judgment in the construction defect case preceding Charlie's first Christmas lay off a year and four months ago.

Earl raced out, "Oh, and Alice Mobley? She got the home loan, but the funds got placed in Dancy Rock's trust account. Get the money back. Close the case. Close it and get our final fees."

Charlie pulse shifted into turbo-drive. He was back on the job.

"Welcome back," Earl called over his shoulder.

The phone rang. He picked up the receiver. Jamie informed Charlie the next bankruptcy clients, Phil and Mary Swanson, were there for their appointment.

Charlie pressed the "hold" button and passed the message to Amanda. She grabbed her notepad and hurried out to the reception area to bring in the Swansons.

Karen was still inputting the Mendoza family's information into the bankruptcy software as Charlie took notes for a "must do" list.

Amanda came back, sat the Swansons to the right of Charlie's desk, their backs squeezed against the front of the copy machine on the side wall. Their depressed demeanor was a clone of the Mendoza's distress. Apparently, Amanda was adding "Bankruptcy Paralegal" to her accounting and collecting responsibilities for the law firm.

The new law-intern receptionist in the cubicle outside the office door called in.

"Charlie, pick up line two. Outside call."

"Thanks, Dmitri," Charlie punched line two trying to flash on Dmitri's last name "Charlie Tobias here," he said into the phone.

"Desmond Thornhill from the Opera, Charlie. How are you?"

Charlie responded with minimal salutation. "Fine, Desmond. What's up?"

"We talked about a guardianship or trust to help Oscar deal with his infirmity?"

Charlie recalled the conversation four months ago and also recalled the guardianship was not just for Oscar's benefit, but for Desmond's. Charlie had been relieved the meeting with Desmond never happened.

Charlie hadn't seen Desmond for months. Since then, Charlie had read in the newspaper, that *West Nile* rehearsals had been sidetracked after the holidays, not by the crashed economy, but by Italian artistic director Tantonini's depression.

West Nile rehearsals had been re-scheduled.

"Are you free this Saturday for brunch?"

Charlie wasn't sure how to respond. He had been too immersed in his work to give any thought to Desmond Thornhill.

"Please. Oscar trusts you. This Saturday? Lunch at 'Le Pinot?'"

Charlie wasn't sure why he heard his own voice reply: "What time?"

CHAPTER 54
A PRIVATE TRUST

Le Pinot's elegant hostess stepped from behind her post. "This way, please."

"Thanks." Charlie followed the hostess, whose perfect figure, dark blue business suit and Beverly Hills salon coiffure could be a practice run for a film audition for a remake of a classic Hollywood Alfred Hitchcock film.

"The Thornhill family table is under the sky light," she said as she made a perfect turn, bent her head, halted to the side, and gestured to indicate Charlie should walk ahead.

Charlie moved towards a white embroidered tablecloth covered square table illuminated by a crisp shaft of light falling through the milk glass skylight. The light shone on the flower display in the Verona blown glass vase in the middle of the table's three place settings. Thin-stemmed blooms arched gracefully from the vase towards each full-size Wedgewood bone china plate, but one bloom caught Charlie's attention: delicate blue orchids with yellow and white accented petals bent outwards from a saturated deep green stem, towards each of the two seated guests.

Desmond Thornhill shared the table with a silver-haired matron wearing a strand of pearls around her neck and a linen white suit on her delicate body. Desmond, in a dark blue blazer, and perfectly knotted diagonal red and blue and yellow striped tie, much like the old-fashioned style of tie his brother wore, got up, shook Charlie's hand.

"Thank you for coming. Let me introduce you to Gertrude, my mother.

Gertrude Thornhill reached her gloved hand towards Charlie. Charlie, not quite sure of the protocol, shook hands, and was pleased he wore his freshly pressed light gray dark pin-striped suit. Charlie glanced around and knew that in Le Pinot his best might barely get a pass.

"Pleased to meet you."

"Likewise. Desmond told me about your wonderful baritone voice. He said you have a dramatic vocal flair."

"Well, thank you. I try to follow Oscar's lead. His Italian diction is flawless. Mine, alas, isn't."

Desmond pulled a chair for Charlie and Charlie sat.

"Oscar spent five years in Italy. He sang with La Scala."

"I was with Turin Opera myself, in the chorus for three years."

"How long ago?"

"In the 1980's, before there was an L.A. Lyric Opera Company. When I returned, I used to sing in the chorus of my Dad's opera company, The Opera Arts Company of Los Angeles."

Desmond and Gertrude exchanged impressed looks. "The Opera Arts? Your father was Maestro Frank Tobias, its founder?"

"That's right. Our family name was 'Tobiovsky.' But everyone always called us 'Tobias,' so I guess he changed it. Tobiovsky was too – "

"Polish? You're Polish aren't you?"

"Slovak. My family's from Bratislava. My father conducted the Bratislava State Opera before immigrating to the U.S."

"We attended his concerts, at Sacred Heart College, at the War Memorial Auditorium and the Wilshire Ebell. They were memorable. We may have even seen you sing?"

"It's possible. I was in the chorus whenever I could fit in the time." Charlie appreciated the acknowledgment, pleasantly surprised by the connection, adjusted himself in the chair.

Charlie glanced at the leather bound menu the hostess had left on his place setting, and saw no recognizable dish. Desmond caught his out of sorts look.

"We usually get the daily special."

"Sounds fine."

The waiter approached, dutifully waited to be addressed.

"Three specials, please," Desmond said, handing Charlie's menu across.

The waiter poured ice water for Charlie. "Very good. They'll be right out." The waiter took the menu and left.

Charlie lifted his Bohemian Lace Design crystal goblet and sipped the ice water to hide his awkward silence.

Desmond waited until Charlie placed his stem goblet down to make his plea. "I'll get to the point, Charlie. Oscar's in a bit of a jam."

A shiver travelled up from Charlie's fingers cradling the icy glass. "From the injuries?"

Desmond whispered: "He is in rehab. But he may not make it."

"I'm so sorry. I know it's been months. When did he go in for physical therapy?"

There was no immediate answer. Charlie heard that if people are truthful, they answer right away.

Gertrude sighed. "It's not the accident." She wiped a tear with an embroidered handkerchief and clutched it, ready for additional use.

Desmond took the lead.

"Oscar's in a rehab in Malibu, Malibu Healing Meadows. They're excellent and – discreet."

Should Charlie believe Desmond? Potential clients often prevaricate, fearing the attorney won't take a case if they tell the truth. Charlie also knew he was going to be asked to do something that was most likely illegal.

The tiny vegetable sculptures that passed for salads were placed in front of Gertrude, Desmond, and Charlie by the red-jacketed waiter.

"Oh dear, they never bring any dressing but that poppy seed muck. Get me some ranch dressing, dear."

"Of course, mother."

Charlie focused on the fact these clients were very rich as Desmond mouthed "ranch" to the waiter.

Charlie contemplated his options. Working at Earl's gave him experience dealing with the dispossessed. He had no clue how to deal with the wealthy and privileged.

Gertrude caught Desmond's eyes, nodded for him to proceed.

"Oscar is the Trustee for the Gertrude Thornhill Family Trust. The trust includes all the family assets which are extensive. He's not able to function. I must be appointed as the successor. The appointment must be bullet-proof!"

Charlie sipped the ice water which sparkled from the sky-light's light beams, while he thought of his role in the transfer of Thornhill power. *He wasn't sure he liked the term 'bullet-proof.'*

"I can prepare an Amended Family Trust document, making you the successor Trustee, but Oscar must sign it and sign his resignation. Trusts must be signed by the settlors, those who set them up - if the Trust is amended."

Gertrude responded to Charlie. "Oscar is lucid some of the time. He can't do the job. He needs dialysis because his kidneys stopped working after…after…"

Desmond blurted out: "He tried to kill himself. He took a vial of valium, and was unconscious – long enough to severely damage his organs."

Gertrude offered a hopeful point of view: "They wouldn't keep Oscar in Malibu Meadows if he weren't getting better."

"Is he conscious?"

"The medications interfere with his lucidity."

"I see."

Charlie knew the Trustee had to be lucid to run a Trust or to sign away his rights. However, unless a doctor pronounced Oscar completely incompetent, there could be lucid interludes when Oscar's signature could be obtained within "legal" rules. The legal guide books covered every contingency. Oscar's condition didn't appear to be unique.

Other than if anyone would file a complaint against Charlie with the California State Bar.

"Oscar was in extreme pain from the accident at the opera."

"He fell twelve feet onto the stage floor."

Gertrude was defensive. "He was one of the flying mosquitoes. It didn't seem like it would be dangerous."

Gertrude dabbed a tear before it smeared her make-up. "It's my fault. I brought it up at the Opera board meeting and got them to approve. Oscar always wanted to do a stunt."

Desmond offered her his handkerchief. "My dear brother dislocated discs when he fell, broke his hip and needed both hips replaced. He was on morphine for the pain, despondent, and took enough opioid pills to kill a horse."

The ice water trickled over Charlie's tongue.

Desmond leaned forward and spoke in muffled tones. "Oscar is in so much pain. The Malibu Meadows nurses specialize at keeping patients from – hurting themselves."

Gertrude cried. "You must amend the Trust immediately."

Desmond whispered over the water glasses. "We'll get the document signed."

Gertrude dried her tears. "You'll be a wonderful Trustee, sweetheart."

"How much is the *res* to be transferred into the Amended Trust?" Charlie decided to use *res* as a term of art to show his professionalism.

"Oscar is the Trustee for the entire Thornhill family holdings."

"Why did the opera company hide the extent of his injury?"

Gertrude reached into her maroon purse, pulled out a letter, unfolded it on the table in front of Charlie.

"We got this in the mail after the accident. It was addressed to Oscar. The letter had no return address." Desmond handed the handwritten note across.

Charlie read the brief note. The handwriting was printed in a scrawled blue ink with forward leaning letters. The "p" was the only letter with a curlicue accent.

You pulled one too many stunts, Oscar. You don't double-cross me!

Charlie was reasonably certain he had seen the block-printed handwriting. He handed back the letter.

Gertrude teared: "Everyone loved Oscar."

"Well, not everyone."

"Whoever did this may come back."

"Did you report this incident to the police?"

"We're afraid to."

Charlie accessed his memory. Where had he seen the printed forward leaning blocky letters? Not on the left-slanting lettering in the note to David Alex threatening him if he didn't resign. Nor on the waterlogged list found on Candace Rollins' slogged body. His memory jogged back to the drafts of the "Global Settlement Agreement." On many of the drafts faxed back from Attorney du Chevalier, there had been hand-printed insertions with specific new demands.

In a telephone conversation, with Louisiana Beneshan Co-Counsel, Attorney St. Pierre, in which Charlie expressed exasperation with the neat, printed additional handwritten note demands, she speculated the additional demands on the estate were from du Chevalier's adamant, rigid client. The handwriting was Jack Wonder's!

A chill dribbled down Charlie's spine as he deduced the connection to Jack Wonder's role in Oscar's injury, and the implications for his own health!

"Our talk is protected by 'attorney-client confidentiality,' isn't it?"

Charlie flashed on the Rules of Professional Conduct, Rule 3-100. While Desmond and Gertrude weren't technically the clients, and the real client would be Oscar Thornhill, they were confiding confidences to Charlie as an attorney to obtain representation for Oscar.

"Yes, it's covered."

Desmond reached into his attaché case, pulled out two envelopes and handed them across to Charlie.

"This is a list of assets to transfer into the Amended Trust and a copy of the current Trust."

Charlie took the typed sheaf of papers out of the thick manila envelope. His eyes glazed over the list of securities. Charlie flipped to the last page and saw the total. There were a lot of zeros. The "Gertrude Thornhill Family Living Trust" seemed to be blessed with assets.

Charlie's hands were clammy. Charlie took the second envelope from Desmond.

Gertrude did the honors. "I'm sure you'll find your fee adequate."

"Thank you."

"Mr. Tobias, let me be blunt. For the past two years, I have seen our family's wealth dwindle, day by day as the economy crashes into depression." She leaned forward, stared. "We don't know how to be poor. We would die."

Charlie retreated behind the ice water in front of his face.

"Our family's survival is in your hands."

Charlie nodded. "I'll do this for you, your family, and for Oscar."

Gertrude looked at Desmond for reassurance. The waiter approached with the main course – shrimp scampi, accented with arched fennel stalk. Charlie's mental focus was not on the fishy delicacy, but on California Rules of Professional Conduct 3-110 which requires an Attorney must act competently.

I have never written a Trust.

CHAPTER 55
CARROTS OR RAT TRAP?

Desmond and Gertrude were trying to decide on desert, but Charlie made it clear, he had to dash. He shook hands with Gertrude and Desmond reminding them he had to work on the trust document immediately to have it ready by the following afternoon for Oscar to sign. Charlie got up, turned and walked out. Charlie nodded politely to the Hostess as she offered him a pleasant "good-bye."

Clutching his valise with the two manila envelopes, one containing his retainer fee check in a standard ivory colored letter envelope, and the other the mass of Trust and accounting documents, Charlie stood on Grand Avenue in front of the Music Center and across the street from the downtown Central Courthouse. Each of these major Los Angeles landmarks had become part of his routine.

Charlie headed for the underground parking garage entrance, fixating on why Jack Wonder would want Oscar out of the picture. Charlie couldn't be certain the note Desmond showed Charlie was written by Jack Wonder, but the identical "p" curlicue to the note insertions on the Beneshan "Settlement Agreement" was a tip-off.

Charlie understood he was entering representation that had to be kept from the ex-Navy Captain. Whatever rage Captain Wonder had against Oscar would transfer to Charlie's physical well-being if Wonder discovered Charlie also represented the Thornhills.

He took the elevator to the underground parking lot, reached his sedan and threw his valise onto the seat. He was tempted to open the second envelope, very tempted, but didn't.

He started the car, wound through the labyrinth and made it to the exit. It was $20 to park. Charlie didn't have twenty dollars, and handed his credit card across.

While the attendant ran the card, Charlie couldn't help himself. He took the second envelope from his valise, and was about to open it.

"Here's your receipt. Say, your car. It's vintage." The craggy attendant's face was inches from Charlie's as the attendant peered inside the car. "Haven't seen one of these in years."

Charlie's concentration broken, he placed the second envelope back inside his valise, took the parking receipt and his credit card. He tried to look nonchalant, but his heart raced as he dropped the valise back onto the duct-taped naugahyde bucket seat.

The temptation to unseal the second envelope and find out the size of the carrot he was risking his life for, passed.

The inquisitive face moved back from the car window as the parking gate lifted.

"Thanks."

Charlie revved the motor, pulled into traffic, headed to the nearby Los Angeles County Law Library to do homework for his risky assignment.

■   ■   ■   ■   ■

He got up early and spent Sunday morning at home drafting the "Thornhill Family Amended Trust" document. Charlie had checked out the "Trust Practice" guide books from the County Law Library the previous day. It was a matter of adapting the guide book "templates" and inserting the assets listed on Desmond's separate accounting document.

Tina was unhappy with this new distraction until he showed her the monogrammed envelope containing the check. She wanted Charlie to open it immediately.

Charlie balked. Without knowing the check amount, Charlie had a carrot. Once he knew he could have a large fee, the carrot would become a rat trap set to spring.

Luckily they didn't get into a fight. He promised he'd open the envelope as soon as he came back from delivering the document to the Thornhills that afternoon.

Charlie's mind leap-frogged ahead as he adjusted the template into a professional Trust document for the Thornhills. Oscar would have to approve the arrangement. A retainer agreement was an additional essential chore. He downloaded the retainer form from the California State Bar Web-site and filled in Oscar Thornhill's name as well as his own.

Attorneys charge for their time. That's all they had. *Maybe I am for real. Not just a guy with a bar card working a day job. Charlie Tobias, a real Attorney at Law! Fighting for justice. Well, at least, fighting for my client's best interests.*

The content of the Amended Trust was the long laundry list Desmond provided from the Trust's Accountant, Century City based "Sally Warsawitz & Sons, Certified Public Accountants." The list of assets was out of date, ending December, 31, 2007 and prepared three or more months ago, in early 2008.

Charlie made a mental note to call the accountant and have her do a 2008 update called a "Pour-over Will."

Charlie scanned the wealthy family's holdings. Many assets were stocks and bonds invested through Lehman Brothers Private Bank. Charlie's heart skipped a beat. *Panicked stories in the newspapers and on the TV Evening News claimed the huge bank may be insolvent.*

There was no time to review the assets. In the next few hours he had to copy the pages of holdings in the Thornhill Family Trust into the new "Amended Trust" document.

One large entry "clicked" a moment of shock. "Blue Orchid Real Estate Holdings, L.L.P."

Charlie came to a daunting insight: *Oscar was the mysterious backer who financed Barry Beneshan's business ventures after Barry returned from Southeast Asia!* Furthermore, Desmond turned to Charlie because Blue Orchid's attorney, Leon Lambert, had been put out of commission by Candace Rollins.

Charlie wrote fast. He knew he should think through the implications of this connection. *Oscar, as an interested creditor can not be privy to the Estate of Beneshan's negotiations with Jack Wonder.* "Work product" confidentiality was as sacred as "attorney-client privilege."

Ironically, Jack Wonder's debilitating attack on Oscar, if indeed the Navy SEAL Captain was the assailant, was not a legal problem for Charlie, but working for a Beneshan creditor like the Thornhills and their Blue Orchid Financial Company would be if such a conflict of interest became known. He'd have to put in place a Chinese wall, legally acceptable procedures to keep information from two cases with conflicting goals, separate.

Right now, Charlie had a deadline.

Charlie kept glancing at the second envelope as he copied the listed Thornhill Trust assets over to the new document. *Why had I fallen into this quagmire?*

He had to meet the Thornhills with the "Amended Trust" document that afternoon.

Charlie finished copying the list of assets. The total value as of January 1, 2007 of the Thornhill assets was over $200,000,000. Charlie's eyes glazed over.

The "current value" of the assets as of January 1, 2008 was less than $4,000,000. Charlie's heart raced. If this list was accurate, the Thornhills, by now in May, 2008, may very well be broke. Charlie thought about the check he had placed in his desk drawer. *I hope the check won't bounce.*

Charlie finished the "Amended Trust" document just after one p.m., threw on his dark blue pin-stripe suit. He printed the twelve page "Amended Thornhill Family Trust" document three times, proofed it, printed out the corrections, and raced out from the house.

Charlie stomped on the gas pedal until the engine came alive and headed onto the freeway towards the Sunday afternoon 3 p.m. meeting with the Thornhills in Santa Monica.

In his freeway slow lane headed uphill on the San Diego Freeway, Charlie saw a huge SUV bear down from behind. Charlie pushed on the accelerator desperately and rocked back and forth as if the car were a horse needing a "giddy-up" to accelerate. Nothing happened. Charlie closed his eyes, expecting a crash.

The giant black SUV screeched a few inches short of flicking Charlie's tiny sedan into the trash-strewn roadside ivy that passed for freeway landscaping. Charlie opened his eyes in time to avoid drifting into the freeway shoulder.

Charlie coasted downhill and headed for the "Queen's Head British Pub" meeting place on 3rd Street. Charlie also had gained a new insight: *When big moneys are at stake, anything can and will happen. Death is the supreme arbiter of ownership, no matter what the law.*

CHAPTER 56
A SUNDAY DRIVE

Desmond displayed a brusque, confrontational demeanor when Charlie arrived at the tourist-filled Santa Monica British pub. He didn't even bother to excuse Gertrude's absence. As for Desmond, Charlie's work was done. Even the invitation for lunch was an unnecessary nicety.

After ordering the requisite fish and chips and looking over the unsigned Trust document, Desmond insisted Charlie sign the Amended Trust document immediately and leave after the late lunch.

Charlie had expected this moment, took out the monogrammed Crane envelope with the retainer check and placed it on the white linen tablecloth – a poker strategy upping the stakes. Charlie made it clear he could only sign the Amended Trust document after he met with Oscar, and Oscar okayed the transfer of the Thornhill Trust to Desmond's control.

"I have to make sure Oscar has testamentary capacity. I have to see him in person and talk to him. He's the client. You're merely his agent."

Desmond formed a thin smile on his face and deflected his anger in a sharp bark at the waiter to bring the check. Desmond's eyes conveyed an angry respect. Desmond couldn't see Charlie's trembling hands.

"All right. Let's go see Oscar. I want to get back before it gets dark."

Desmond didn't say another word. They left the parking lot in Desmond's cream-colored Bentley, and drove up towards Oscar's hospice in the far end of the Malibu coast. As they drove along Pacific Coast Highway Charlie knew he was going into the uncharted celebrity-scandal strewn world of Malibu.

I wonder what it would be like to live out here by the most famous beach in the world? It was hard for Charlie to gauge the answer to his thought because everything Malibu was famous for was hidden. Malibu was the sun-shade hiding the lives of the rich and famous, and the filter made the residents more desirable and newsworthy.

"The assets your accountant provided are out of date. We're almost in the middle of 2008."

"Aren't the new assets covered?"

"Not until I prepare an Addendum. It's called a Pour-over Will."

"Damn."

Charlie tried to ignore the tense scowl on Desmond's face as Desmond acquiesced. "I'll call the C.P.A. tomorrow. Have her do the update immediately."

"Thanks."

Being an attorney meant not only doing as the client demanded, but taking charge and doing whatever was necessary for the client to reach his or her goal.

CHAPTER 57
A SUNDAY JOG

Earlier the same sunny Sunday Charlie was headed to meet with Desmond Thornhill, Tammy McCormack got out of bed in her sparsely furnished Spanish bungalow that overlooked the tiny lake in Tujunga around which trim joggers ran in cadence under Brazilian pepper tree shaded pathways.

Tammy was torn – between going to the beach and going back to Farmdell to the attorney's bungalow to see what she could see. Her curiosity outweighed her desire for a walk on the beach. She put on her jogging clothes, got in her sedan, and headed for the Hollywood Hills.

Tammy stopped her car about a block down from the attorney's bungalow, got out and jogged up the street joining other Hollywood Farmdell joggers, dog-walkers, and those just simply walking. She jogged past the stucco wall hidden house on the corner, hoping to see Carrie Baxter in her garden, but was disappointed the well-trimmed garden was empty.

Tammy knew knocking on the gate was a waste of time.

Tammy had stopped by the garden, called Carrie a number of times, but the lady in the ever-changing straw hats was no longer forthcoming. Tammy had even called the local Hollywood Division cop on the beat assigned to the case, Officer Nixon Tracker.

He begged off, stating Carrie was a "nice lady." Tammy knew Officer Tracker depended on Carrie's telephone calls to keep the Farmdell neighborhood under surveillance. Officer Tracker was not about to lose his personal "eyes and ears."

Tammy passed Charlie's bungalow. It was quiet. It must be nice to afford a *pied-a-terre.* She thought about her own situation. Luckily, she had inherited the residence in Tujunga, and income from renting out the main house kept her afloat. The P.I. assignments were sporadic. She hoped she wouldn't have to look for a staff job in some far off suburban police department. She wished for something more, but realized that despite her good looks, trim body, if it didn't happen by now, she wouldn't find a man who loved her, and wanted to share her life. Maybe it was the hardness she projected from her years struggling for survival, or her current tough girl attitude that communicated: "don't mess with me" to any man who gave her a passing glance. Maybe, maybe, it was something else, maybe those two same-sex comedy actors had something figured out she should give thought to, namely that she had eliminated half the potential mates, never daring to think her significant other might be anything but a man.

Tammy's personal thoughts gave her no time to react to avoid running into a stroller.

"Watch it, lady."

Tammy maneuvered her legs around, but was no longer incognito.

"What the hell are you doing here?"

Tammy, shocked at the shrill screams coming out of Sandy Trayle's mouth, turned.

"Sorry, I didn't see you."

Tammy heard the crying coming from the stroller. Benton Wayne leaned in, lifted Darlene and bounced her to soothe the complaining sounds. Sandy hurried back and confronted Tammy.

"You think you can spy on us, you little cunt?"

"I'm just out jogging. What's your problem?"

"You don't live here. You're interfering with our parental rights. I will see you fired, you homophobic bitch. You just lost your job!"

Benton had just about quieted Darlene. "Come on, honey. Let's go. Darlene, sweetie, sh…sh."

Tammy couldn't control herself. "Is this your private sidewalk?"

Sandy thought better of continuing the confrontation, turned away from Tammy.

Tammy tried deep breathing to vent the stress. She looked at the two dads push away with their infant in the stroller.

Tammy felt conflicting feelings, urges, and even a bit of envy.

CHAPTER 58
MALIBU MEADOWS

Desmond's Bentley pulled into the inconspicuous driveway just a few winding turns above Pacific Coast Highway and Desmond led Charlie inside. Malibu Meadows was one of many rehabilitation hospitals that blossomed in the Malibu hills to deal with ailments of the rich and infamous. The hillside residents protested the proliferation of addicts and crazed egomaniacs who moved into the rehabs and made ever-changing and amusing subjects for evening TV news flashes, and entertainment TV show segments, but there was little locals could do about these mega-money generating rest homes.

If you had the money, why not look over the beautiful sunset from the pale green sagebrush covered Malibu hills and come to terms with the meaning of your life, lack thereof, or its end?

Desmond checked in at the front desk and walked next to Charlie through the hallway towards a bedroom door.

A burly Security Guard, whose bronze name-plate identified him as "Scotty," and whose tattered shoulder patch identified his employer as "Sam's Security," crossed his arms, "Mr. T" style. Scotty sported a Gluck side-arm holstered in thick leather.

Scotty recognized Desmond, grunted politely and stepped aside. Charlie looked at Desmond with a quizzical look. Desmond knew he had to explain the need for Scotty's presence.

"With the hateful note Oscar got, it seemed prudent to hire a bodyguard."

Charlie fidgeted and sweated. *Do I need a bodyguard? Should I have included that condition in the retainer agreement?*

Desmond led Charlie into the private bedroom. It was clean, understated with off-white walls, a full length window facing the ocean.

Charlie's eyes were drawn to the overweight middle aged prim, white-clad nurse, sitting at the side of the hospital bed in which Oscar was propped halfway to a forced vertical position. Poly-tube IV's and beeping monitors were attached to Oscar's every extremity.

"Hello, dear Oscar, it's Desmond, your brother."

Oscar opened his eyes. There was a hint of recognition. Desmond touched Oscar's shoulder.

"Remember Charlie Tobias? The attorney? Your buddy from the opera chorus? You asked me to get him? He's here. He has the Amended Trust document ready. We need your signature."

"Hello Oscar." Charlie reached his hand and shook Oscar's frail, IV tube connected right hand. Oscar appeared to recognize Charlie, or at least appeared to be pleased to make human contact.

"How's he doing, Jenny?"

The nurse shrugged. "I increased the morphine drip, Mr. Thornhill. He was having problems earlier. "

"Thanks, Jenny."

"Can I go, Mr. Thornhill? My shift is done."

"Well, if you could wait a minute. We might need you to witness something. This is Charlie Tobias. He's the family's attorney." Charlie shuddered hearing his new professional status announced, shook Jenny's hand.

Desmond took the twelve page Amended Trust document, placed it in front of Oscar, and wiggled it under the IV tubes curving on top of Oscar's reading tray.

Oscar's blank look offered no positive response or hint of understanding. Desmond took out a pen, placed it in Oscar's right hand, and folded Oscar's fingers around it.

"Just sign your name, Oscar. Sign your name here."

Oscar looked blankly from Desmond to Charlie, as Desmond's fingers guided Oscar's hand to keep it from loosening around the pen.

Charlie knew he had to intervene, whatever the size of the check in his valise.

"Wait, Desmond."

Desmond turned to Charlie.

"Let me do this," Charlie commanded.

Desmond thought for a moment, then stepped aside.

"Oscar, do you remember me? Nod if you do."

After a blank stare and a brief moment, Oscar nodded.

"Who am I?"

Charlie saw Oscar try to make the sound of "Char-lie's" name.

"Did you want to change your Trust?"

Oscar very emphatically formed the word "yes."

Charlie's heart raced. He wasn't sure how far he had to go. *One more question.*

"Do you understand you are signing away all your rights as Trustee of the Gertrude Thornhill Family Living Trust to your brother, Desmond?" Desmond's eyes locked on Oscar's.

There was a long moment in which Oscar looked at Desmond, looked back at Charlie. Charlie looked at Jenny, the nurse, to make sure she witnessed Oscar's response.

"Yes." Oscar stated clearly.

"Thank you, Oscar. We sure miss you at rehearsals."

Oscar's smile widened.

Charlie placed the retainer agreement in front of Oscar. "Sign this, please. It says, you give me permission to represent you to change the trust. That's all it says."

Oscar looked into Charlie's eyes. Charlie sensed Oscar trusted him. Oscar took the pen, slowly scrawled his name. The tiny pen movements took forever, but when Charlie glanced down at the two page document, he saw the signature was there. Charlie placed the agreement into his valise.

"Thank you, Oscar. Now, to the Trust document. I prepared it for you to sign." Charlie nodded for Scotty, the Security Guard to come in. Charlie gave the pen back to Desmond.

Desmond ever so gently placed the pen back into Oscar's frail IV tube covered hand, and guided the pen onto the paper. Oscar understood what was expected of him, as Desmond released Oscar's hand. Oscar concentrated, moved the pen across the signature line, and finished signing the document. Desmond took the pen from Oscar.

"Thank you, Oscar."

Charlie looked at his friend and looked at the brilliant sunset over the ocean, dramatically framed by storm clouds above the setting sun. Charlie took the signed document, placed his own signature on it and signed the two other originals of the document. He handed each of the two duplicate documents to Oscar to sign. Oscar seemed to gain strength from signing his name a second time, then a third time.

Charlie placed each Amended Trust document in front of Jenny and Scotty in turn and watched them sign on the witness line as instructed.

Charlie looked directly into Oscar's eyes as Oscar finished signing all three documents.

"I'm coming back one more time, Oscar, with an update for the Amended Trust. Do you understand?"

Oscar smiled a pained smile. "Yes, come back, Charlie. Please come back."

Charlie nodded.

"How are rehearsals going?"

"They're not the same without you."

"Wish I could be there."

"I do, too, Oscar."

CHAPTER 59
SPONTANEOUS ACCOUNTINGS

Knowing how difficult it was to get any client to come to the office when they owed the Law Offices a substantial payment, Earl acceded to Charlie's request to leave the Law Offices early to review the Estate of Beneshan documents at Angel's house and have Angel sign them in time to file with the court.

"Bill your time. All of it. Travel time, too, from here to her house."

Charlie nodded, confirmed the meeting with Angel and ran to get a dolly to wheel the three boxes of Estate of Beneshan files to his car. As he took down the boxes in the elevator and wheeled them to his tiny car in the parking garage, Amanda pulled in next to his car in her expensive sports sedan and exited, looking glamorous in a sparkling sheen green evening gown, pulling her street clothes over her shoulders.

"I got the job. I got the job," she crowed as Charlie loaded his Beneshan file boxes into his car's back seat.

Charlie turned to face her. "What's the good news, Amanda?"

"I'll be the Invitational Hostess for this year's Auto Show in November. Two weeks of top pay. That'll make up for a lot of short weeks at this job."

"I'll have to come see you, Amanda. The Auto Show?"

"Yes, in the Sports Arena. My agent has sent me there before, but this time, they hired me. Oh, don't tell anyone. Earl wants me to keep my other life hush-hush. Okay?"

"Absolutely."

Charlie got in his car, waved at her as he headed out and she headed in. *Isn't that great? I'm not the only guy with a side job in the office.*

.   .   .   .   .

The ivy-covered security gate in front of Angel's two story craftsman house in a modest San Fernando Valley neighborhood swung open as Angel stepped out of the front door onto the covered porch, walked up to Charlie, exchanged "hellos," and gave him a quick hug.

"I keep the gate locked. You understand."

"Wise plan." He looked at her smiling face. She looked less cocky than he remembered her. Perhaps it was because she felt more at ease in her home environment than in a law office or in court. He handed her the summary accounting sheets of the updated Estate Accounting document from atop the three boxes of files on his dolly.

The accounting document had to be signed and filed with the court by the following day to meet the deadline.

Charlie followed Angel's gesture and followed Angel, pushing his dolly of boxes up the stairs onto the porch and through the entryway.

"It's so good to see you Charlie."

Charlie nodded. "It's good to see you. I'm glad I'm back."

Angel's smile was genuine, unfiltered. "Let me help."

"No, I've got it. Thanks,"

Inside the small house, Charlie wheeled the dolly into her living room, and unloaded the boxes, as she pulled a chair next to her tiny wood desk in the corner, sat and glanced through the proposed final accounting document. "It looks fine." She stopped, looked up, and blurted out her latest news.

"Devlin and I – he's back in town. We broke up."

Charlie nodded. "How is he?"

"I – didn't want to see him. He isn't the same."

Charlie couldn't quite blame her reticence. Aside from the danger Devlin had placed both of them in when he broke into the *La Reve du Monde* property, Devlin was no longer the glamorous leading man stand-in.

Charlie didn't want to say "I'm sorry" despite hearing the remorse in her voice for the break-up.

"At least, the acid-throwing bitch can't hurt us."

"Detective Oswilla said whoever put her up to taking out attorneys is still out there."

"Oh. I should have known." Her confident tone turned to resignation realizing she and Charlie faced additional danger. "We'll get through all this."

"Yes. We will, but we must be careful. Detective Oswilla showed me the handwritten list found in Rollins' wallet. The list was water-logged, but you could make out the names on the list. We're on the list. Both of us."

Angel's face turned pale. "I've got to get my daughter out of this."

Charlie nodded. "The list's handwriting looked like Jack Wonder's."

"Jack? Jack doesn't delegate. He does what he has to."

"You sure?"

"He's too smart to work with that loser junkie."

Charlie pondered. "Then, it's got to be someone else's handwriting. I don't think Jack Wonder has it in for either of us."

"Did Oswilla track down the license plate?"

"The SUV license plate didn't pan out."

"Any new leads on Mr. Alex's murder?"

"Oswilla said it may be over a dispute about an adoption matter."

"That's creepy, but good news for our health, isn't it?"

"Oswilla's got an investigator working it. He also said he'd re-open Barry's case, do an autopsy."

"I tried to tell him Barry was killed for the cash. That detective never followed up. You want some coffee?"

"Sure."

Angel poured two cups, placed Charlie's coffee on the cocktail table in front of the couch.

"Thank you, for coming back to work."

Charlie wasn't displeased. "I want to finish this."

"We will."

"Both of us, alive and in one piece. Gabriella needs her mother."

"And happy. No?"

"Absolutely."

Angel looked into Charlie's eyes. Charlie knew there was a connection there as he sipped his coffee. Angel dropped her eyes, focused on continuing to glance through the thick accounting document.

Jones, Sharke had started to prepare the estate's Accounting, a few months after Barry Beneshan's death in 2006. They were relieved of their position before the documents were finished and turned in.

Now, almost two years later, in May, 2008, Charlie and Angel were finalizing the First Accounting document, doing the best they could without an accountant's guidance. Charlie had begged Earl for at least an accountant intern.

"When she pays, then, we'll hire someone. Just get it in. File the damn accounting. And get these boxes out of your office. Take them back to her. It's her crap."

Earl was losing his professional polish as he had to confront all the clients who couldn't or wouldn't pay bills. Charlie didn't dispute the concern for keeping the Law Offices solvent in the worst downturn since the Great Depression.

Angel stopped at one section of the document. "What about the problems in Louisiana? You haven't mentioned what happened to us?"

"We'll let Jack Wonder bring up the problems. It's been months and he hasn't contacted us or filed a complaint."

"Maybe Jack Wonder's dead?"

Charlie considered. "I can't call du Chevalier, since he filed a law suit against the estate in the New Orleans court."

"Have you talked to St. Pierre?"

"She no longer represents the estate. She substituted out shortly after I left the Law Offices last December."

Charlie wouldn't have any reason to call her up.

"I left out the fate of the *La Reve du Monde* property in the Accounting."

She sighed. "Colette saw what happened to du Chevalier. She wanted to move on."

Charlie accepted the fact he'd never see Colette St. Pierre again.

"I don't blame her."

"She's a good kid. Cute, huh?"

Charlie thought back. Colette was beautiful. He was distracted by her image in his mind, but only momentarily.

"I also omitted mention of Lambert's injury. If he wants to go after anyone, it should be Candace Rollins's estate, not us."

Angel blurted back, "That *prissy* prick. Screw him."

Charlie thought of the fact, it was only a quirk of fate he represented Angel. He hadn't known Leon Lambert III represented Oscar Thornhill's "Blue Orchid." Now, Charlie also represented Oscar Thornhill at least in resigning from his Trust responsibilities.

They were done with the review. Angel beamed.

"You're the coolest."

"I think we did it."

Charlie, feeling a heart tug, pulled back. Angel noticed.

"So, where do I sign?"

Charlie pointed to the line at the bottom of the last page. Angel finished her flourished signature. Charlie took the document. "I'll make copies, serve and file tomorrow."

"Thanks for coming. It's tough for me to get over to the office."

"Yes, I thought it might be."

As Charlie got up, started to leave, he had a sudden impulse: "Does the name Oscar Thornhill ring a bell?"

Angel's eyes became moon-sized orbs. "What about Oscar?"

Charlie knew he hit a sensitive spot. He looked at her and didn't drop his eyes. She knew she had given away a secret she had not talked about to Charlie or anyone involved with the Estate of Beneshan court case.

"Many years ago. Barry disappeared from my life for a long time over his problems with the business. My girl-friend, Dana Bassett moved in society circles. We went to one of Oscar's parties in Malibu. I didn't know if and when Barry would ever return. Oscar asked me for my phone number. I gave it to him, thinking he will not call. Anyway, he did call me. We dated for a good while. I wasn't exactly a prize for his family. It ended after several years."

"Did you keep in contact?"

Angel spoke haltingly. "Barry returned and wanted to pick up where we left off. I went along because Gabriella, well, I went along. Barry was back on the scene, and Oscar suddenly showed up. He would come over for dinners. I never figured out how Barry and Oscar knew each other, but they were tight. Gabriella was about to start school. Oscar loved playing with her, reading books, teaching the alphabet to her. She loved him. I didn't object. How could I? But Oscar stopped coming over about two and a half years ago – about the time everything fell apart right before Barry's death."

"Did Oscar invest in Barry's business?"

Angel was genuinely shocked.

"It wasn't about money. It was something else. Something special Oscar and I had. Why would you even think I know him?"

Charlie knew he couldn't let on he knew Oscar's investment company, "Blue Orchid" was one of the estate's biggest creditors, since Charlie had gained that knowledge from working on Oscar's trust.

Charlie thought it was better to let her know of his connection with Oscar through the opera.

"I have another part-time job."

"Who doesn't?" She pointed at the piles of boxes. "Lots of product. No sales."

"I sing in the L.A. Lyric opera choir downtown."

"No way. And you never told me?"

"It didn't seem relevant. But, it is. Oscar sang in the choir with me."

"Oscar used to sing Italian lullabies and ballads to us. Eventually, I believed him, when he said he was going off to a rehearsal. So?"

"He – " Charlie thought about whether he could tell Angel about Oscar's ownership interest in "Blue Orchid." He couldn't.

"Oscar had a terrible accident on the stage last December."

Angel sat down, was very upset.

"Is he all right?"

Charlie shook his head. "No."

"Did he mention me or Gabriella?"

Charlie shook his head, "No."

"Desmond, his brother hired me to draw up a legal document. This job is not through Earl Guarder."

"Where is Oscar?"

"At a fancy rehab up in Malibu."

"Can you take me there?"

"I'll have to ask Desmond."

"Tell Desmond Gabriella wants to see Oscar, too. He'll understand."

Charlie nodded, put away the signed document. "I'd better leave."

"I'll come see you perform. Bring Gabriella. What's the next show?"

"It's called *West Nile*. It's a modern story about everything in L.A. falling apart and ending in death."

"I like happy endings."

Charlie shrugged. "So do I."

Angel bit her fingers. "Do you have a little more time? Come with me to the old Clean Co. warehouse. Help me pick up the files."

"I'm not representing Clean Co. Earl would never go for it."

"Understood."

Charlie shrugged.

"Okay. Let's check the warehouse."

CHAPTER 60
MATTRESS OVERSTOCKS

Angel parked next to a corrugated metal warehouse in an industrial park near the Burbank Amtrak train line. She led Charlie through the low-water usage succulent garden that softened the industrial building for commercial retail use. She unlocked the metal warehouse door, turned on the light switch. The fluorescent overheads flickered on with an unsteady buzz.

She gestured for Charlie to walk in. "This used to be the Clean Co. warehouse. Devlin tried to turn Barry's abandoned offices into a wholesale mattress outlet. A bad idea as you can see."

Charlie took in the countless piled up mattresses filling the hanger sized space.

Angel led the way through the mattress mountain maze. "Let's check the files."

Charlie navigated behind Angel, past a grand canyon of piled, plastic-wrapped mattresses.

Angel opened the office door, flipped on lights and walked to the metal file drawers. "All the old Clean Co. files are here before Barry moved off to New Orleans."

Charlie opened a file drawer and glanced through files.

Angel moved next to him. "Should we bring these files? Review them?"

Charlie was getting tired. *Lost properties? Wholesale mattress outlets? What did it matter?* Charlie had been beaten down and thought he had come up with a solid accounting for the court by staying late every night during the first week he was back on the job. *Now, it turns out, there was an entire new set of documents to review and account.* If anyone in court objected, Charlie would deal with the objections then. *You can only use up so much of your life serving the dead, even if you're a probate attorney.*

"We don't need to list this business in the Accounting document."

"Okay, I just wanted you to know. This was Devlin's 'day job.' Checks were still coming from Oscar to support the business until last December."

Charlie blurted out: "That's when Oscar's accident happened."

Angel nodded, shook off a tear.

She ran to the small bathroom. Charlie saw her hand reach to switch the light on. He heard her scream an anguished sound of despair.

"Char-lie! Help!"

Charlie raced to the bathroom entrance.

The unisex bathroom door was open. Fluorescent lights gave the old fashioned white Parisian subway tile a greenish tint. Charlie moved into the doorway.

Angel kneeled next to the body lying face down, with outstretched arms on the bathroom tile floor. The face was twisted sideways, pockmarked from deep lacerations and burns. Blood oozed out of a grand canyon sized gash coming from the skull. All exposed portions of the two arms and hands were covered with boils. Devlin had discolored skin from the burns that never healed.

Charlie was flustered, woozy. *Too many bodies were turning up on bathroom floors.*

Angel kneeled and draped across Devlin's body, shaking him.

"Get up, you sweet thing. Don't just lie there! Get up!"

Charlie took out his cell and dialed "911."

In reply to the voice on the other end of the line, he condensed his message to a shaken blurt. "We need an ambulance."

CHAPTER 61
WALKING WITH THE DEAD

The tasteful art-work on the walls of Santa Monica Hospital's E.R. waiting area did not mask the reality of life and death events taking place behind the automatic double-swung hospital doors through which the orderlies had pushed Devlin's gurney almost an hour earlier.

Angel, distraught, shaking, called her mother, who was still baby-sitting Gabriella. Charlie wished he had never agreed to go to the warehouse. He watched Angel shake, cry and unburden about Devlin's life-threatening injuries, wishing instead for a life altering swim in a forever blue lagoon.

"I have to go back home. Mom can't take care of Gabriella all night. She's got dad to deal with."

Charlie didn't want to pry, nodded, just as the doctor pranced towards Charlie and Angel from behind the double doors.

"I'm Doctor Danielle Ortega, the lead trauma doctor on duty. Are any of you related to Mr. Devlin D'Alessio?

"He's – my ex-boyfriend."

"He wants to see you." The doctor turned to face Charlie. "And you are?"

"I'm her attorney," Charlie replied, looking the doctor in the eye, causing Dr. Ortega to nod a curt acknowledgment punctuated with twitchy eyelids.

"How is he?" Angel whispered the critical question.

"He is reacting to an overdose of a drug cocktail." The doctor looked at Angel kindly, and continued with the bad news. "His body functions including his liver were compromised from his burns. He has a very low immune white blood cell count."

"Damn." Angel instinctively put her head on Charlie's shoulder, faced away.

"You can both come see him," she offered. Her jumpy eyelids calmed, her voice offered hope and reassurance to Angel.

Angel bit her wrist, turned and faced the doctor. "We both will come, won't we, Charlie?" Charlie nodded, unable to fathom Angel's pain.

They followed Dr. Ortega, and entered the E.R. holding room, with its octagonal nurse's stations, battle-hardened for any emergency. The doctor pulled back the white curtain that provided privacy, and stepped back to allow Angel and Charlie to approach the bed.

Angel ran up to Devlin and gawked at his pockmarked face under all the tubes, monitors, and the breathing device. Charlie was too shocked to react as he saw Devlin atop the high-tech bed.

Devlin had more tubes coming in and out of him than an astronaut captaining a lunar-bound space ship. Angel leaned and touched him on a small swat of bare skin.

"Oh baby. I love you, you beautiful, handsome jerk."

Devlin's look was despondent. "The doc told me 'it's over.'" Charlie stepped next to Angel, shocked at Devlin's pockmarked, burned, and caved form.

Angel leaned over him, embraced him gently. "You're a fighter. We'll fight past all this crap."

Devlin reached and took Angel's hand as best as he could, dangling tubes leading in all directions, as the monitor vital signs read-out turned from green to red, indicating he was cutting off some needed IV supply of medicine or nutrients with the move of his hand.

"I've got to tell you something."

"Hang in there, honey. Hang in. I love you." She adjusted his grasp to free the IV tubes.

"Listen, baby, I have to tell you," Devlin turned his pockmarked burned face towards her and looked into her soul through his craggy eye socket sunken eyes showing deep remorse. "I found Barry on the bathroom floor, like me, on the night of his birthday."

Devlin forced himself to tell about the crucial night two years ago. He whispered as Angel leaned over him and tried to keep from an actual embrace, steadying herself on the hospital bed's rails above Devlin.

"I smothered the son of a bitch."

Angel recoiled.

"I heard you talk to him on the phone about jetting away to some island. I was high, baby. I thought he had a stash. I'm fucking sorry."

Charlie, standing back at what he considered a respectful distance from their intimate communication, heard the whispers, but understood from Angel's sudden rigid upright bolt, even if he couldn't decipher Devlin's blurted words, that Devlin was confessing to Barry Beneshan's murder!

Angel recoiled. "How could you?" Angel became energized, furious, grabbed a pillow. Charlie saw what was happening, knew he had to intervene, grabbed Angel as she pushed the bed rail down, climbed atop the hospital bed and pushed the pillow onto Devlin's mouth.

"No, Angel."

Angel expended her fury, pushing at Charlie's restraining arms keeping her from completing her revengeful goal. She lost her rabid energy, trembled, cried, and went limp.

Charlie managed to pull her off the bed.

Angel sobbed, screamed: "You murdering, vile human being. You killed Barry."

Angel's face turned hard as she threw the pillow at Devlin with all her might and even before the pillow found its mark above Devlin's chest and neck, she had turned without looking back, left.

Charlie caught the bouncing pillow, left it on Devlin's gaunt covered torso, rushed after Angel.

In the hall, the doctor saw how upset Angel was, and moved alongside.

Charlie let out his breath in cadence as Angel hyperventilated.

"The son of a bitch deserves to die."

"Is there a problem?" The doctor was solicitous. Charlie interceded, and stepped between the doctor and Angel.

Charlie shook his head, side to side, to indicate "no problem."

The doctor nodded. "It's an extreme case."

Charlie pulled Angel away, thinking there was no problem other than the patsy who confessed to Barry's murder was on his own death bed. Devlin, whether under the influence of morphine or a volcanic burst of guilt had confessed to killing Barry in a most gruesome way. Charlie had his doubts about Devlin's culpability. Charlie couldn't help blurt out: "The poor jerk."

Angel was less charitable. "He did it to himself."

There had been a time in his life, not long ago, when Charlie never knew anyone who died. *Now, everywhere I turn, I'm walking with the dead.*

CHAPTER 62
SIGNED, SEALED

As Charlie drove Angel back home, Angel's mood oscillated from bitter anger to cold withdrawal. She was isolated in her emotions, trying to come to terms, eager to believe Devlin double-crossed her at the point when Barry reappeared in her crumbling life, and was on the verge of swooping in and saving her and Gabriella from undeserved threats, and Oscar's rejections.

Charlie clenched his teeth, to keep from offering solace. He was cut off from her pain, and unable to abate her self-pity with the truth he gleaned about Oscar's role in the Beneshan estate's financial life. His unease grew as he avoided interfering with her demons.

At one point, Angel repeated her strong desire to see Oscar. When Charlie didn't divulge Oscar's whereabouts, she seethed.

Charlie gripped the steering wheel to reinforce his determination to maintain his professional distance. Angel calmed, and asked Charlie to tell Oscar she and Gabriella were well.

"Promise, you'll tell him."

Charlie loosened, acquiesced and knew he meant it. "I promise."

Charlie dropped her off in front of her home. She dialed the house on her cell.

"You heard what he said, didn't you? He killed Barry. How can you be so uncaring?"

Charlie couldn't believe he defended his former tormentor. "I wouldn't believe anything someone shot up with morphine blurted out in a hospital room."

"You don't believe him?"

"I don't know."

Angel couldn't see Charlie's eyes on the dark street, but could hear the hesitation in Charlie's voice that communicated his doubt.

"I was an idiot to fall for him."

Angel wiped a tear away. "Stupid me gave up on Barry when he moved to New Orleans." She cried some more for her lost love, for her lost boy friend, for her daughter, for herself.

Charlie stood, feeling helpless, but knew there was nothing more he could do.

"Thanks for coming." She turned abruptly and headed into the house.

Charlie made sure Angel was safely inside. The gate swung shut and locked.

He headed back to the curb, made sure the finalized Accounting documents to file were in his valise in the car, got back in, and drove off.

Charlie in his own way had accomplished the goal Earl needed: making the numbers in the Accounting Report match up according to probate rules, preparing the documents to file, and getting Angel's okay and her signature.

When he signed up to become a Probate Associate, he would never guess scurrying through a maze to avoid the Minotaur, avoiding dead bodies, and emotional entanglements was the nature of the job, but, it apparently was.

Pushed to the limit, he left Angel's side street, merged into traffic, headed home.

CHAPTER 63
LEGAL MANEUVERS

The next morning, Charlie struggled through traffic headed to downtown Los Angeles instead of to Fairtown and hurried to Los Angeles Central Court to file the Beneshan "Accounting Report" on the final day it was due.

As Charlie reached the front of the Clerk's probate line, holding his hefty tomes in triplicate, Clerk Allhan, a fixture for almost as long as the scales of blind justice and the three chiseled marble wise men, Moses, King John and Thomas Jefferson looked down on the court entrance, recognized Charlie as he took the three documents Charlie placed on the counter.

"That Beneshan case, huh? I knew you'd be back on it, Charlie."

"Thanks, I guess." Charlie took the two stamped copies of the document to prove he had filed it, turned, and was face to face with Henry Gilliam.

"Mr. Tobias, do you still work at Earl Guarder's?"

"Just signed back on. Let's lay the Beneshan case to rest. I'll see you at the Accounting Hearing."

"It'll be sooner. I'm here to file an emergency petition. Might as well hand you a courtesy copy of my Motion to Compel."

"What's the beef?"

"We're missing $50,000 of the moneys you were ordered to pay."

A jolt spread through Charlie's spine. He remembered the copy of the certified check sent to Jones, Sharke attached to the Accounting, did seem on the low side, but had not thought to look back to his notes to confirm the amount the judge ordered.

"Look, I just got back on the case. They made a mistake. I'll check my notes from the hearing."

"I called your law office several times. I sent Mr. Guarder a demand letter a month ago, which he never answered. Filing this petition? At the least, I'm asking for the due moneys, costs and attorney fees for an unnecessary hearing."

"If the amounts are wrong, you'll get your moneys." Charlie's mind crashed into overdrive. Earl may have decided to hold some moneys back to ensure The Law Offices would get paid before all the Louisiana moneys disappeared.

"Now that you're back, there may be another motion I might want to file."

Charlie knew he was potential rodent meat for the hungry Jones, Sharke python.

"One of our paralegals was checking on David Alex's death. He found out Alex was hiding out in your place at the time you swore to the court he was murdered in his office."

Charlie's stomach sank.

"I thought he was dead. He was, two days later."

"I might not get you disqualified from the case, but I doubt Judge Bittenkopf will ever believe you about anything again – for any client."

"Try it, and I'll answer in kind with a Motion for Accounting. I've reviewed your bullshit billing practices. I'll subpoena your idiot administrator Finkenhoff and see how much he authorized in your astronomical bill."

Henry Gilliam was intrigued by Charlie's new assertiveness.

"Get us the moneys ordered paid. That's all I'm after."

"I'll see what I can do."

"I'll hold off filing this Motion for a week."

Charlie and Gilliam left the probate line, headed into the court hall turning opposite ways.

"Let's wrap this up, counselor." Henry Gilliam called out. Charlie nodded.

■   ■   ■   ■   ■

Charlie drove through traffic headed to Fairtown. Now that the Estate of Beneshan Accounting was filed, Charlie could turn to other pressing matters. Foremost was an unpleasant preparation for a "Motion to Enforce the Settlement Agreement" hearing on the Alice Mobley matter.

During the months Charlie was laid off, Alice Mobley had suffered a second stroke from the stress of administering her estate when one of the previous attorneys, Clyvester Kurtz reneged on his agreement with Charlie to hold off collecting his court ordered fees only from Alice's loan. Kurtz proceeded to file the old, signed Court Order with a new Motion to Compel.

The Law Offices had not opposed the Motion to Compel nor showed up in court. Kurtz got his order and judgment, not just for the ordered $20,000 attorney fees, but for a penalty of some $6,000 Kurtz swore was the cost of preparing and enforcing the unopposed Motion to Compel.

While Charlie was laid off, Derrick Stanton, Alice's bulldog and one of the concerned relatives, had called Charlie in a state of panic about the clerk issued "Writ of Possession" personally served on Alice at her Leimert Park home by an apologetic rookie Deputy Sheriff, informing Alice she had thirty days to pay the debt or the Sheriffs would vacate her from her home and sell it at a court auction.

At the time, some months ago, all Charlie could do was feel outrage and tell Derrick to deal with The Law Offices as Charlie no longer worked there.

Derrick fumed "I expected more from you, Charlie," and hung up.

After that angry call from Derrick, Charlie was left with an unsettled concern about what would happen to Alice Mobley.

When Charlie returned to the Law Offices for the third time, and Terry Ketchum took his turn to be laid off, Aki filled Charlie in on the upshot of Derrick's disturbing call some months back: Some twenty eight days after Charlie received Derrick's call, two grim khaki clad deputy Sheriffs (one male, one female) showed up at Alice's door. They forced her to get dressed, and led her, Denise and Alfie, the scraggly terrier, out of the home, moved some of Alice's personal boxes, and her desk with important Ozzie Mobley documents. They also moved Alice's insulin injector and oxygen tank, which the female sheriff acknowledged were essential personal property not subject to seizure.

However, the sheriffs refused to allow Alice to keep Ozzie's record masters and framed Platinum Record Star awards or allow Denise to take her manuscripts and diaries, noting the record masters, framed awards, and manuscripts in their itemization of the personal properties they were turning over to Kurtz and his probate auctioneer specialist, Sammy Snarr.

Denise, crying, hysterical, called Derrick before she was evicted. Derrick raced to the house just as the sheriffs changed the locks, but he could not get the proceedings stopped. In the middle of the "lock-out" legal process, Derrick was pushed aside, threatened with arrest for "interference." Alice suffered her second stroke and had to be taken to E.R. at Los Angeles County Hospital.

Derrick then raced to the Law Offices, in a volcanic state, accusing Earl Guarder and Terry Ketchum of gross negligence which would not go unpunished by the State Bar. Earl, mustering his dramatic TV commentator skills, screamed at Terry for missing the Motion to Compel hearing.

Ketchum took the brunt, and only muttered under his breath so Derrick could hear "you told me to ignore it" as he filled out the new Petition to Vacate the Judgment that Earl assured Derrick would set matters right.

Earl personally rushed to court that afternoon to file emergency papers petitioning to revoke the seizure of Alice's home.

Judge Jennifer Whitsett, a new judge, who presided over Central Court's Writ and Judgment division in Department 96, was shocked to hear about Attorney Kurtz's sneaky maneuver. She issued a Citation for Attorney Kurtz' mandatory appearance the following morning. When he appeared, Judge Whitsett browbeat Attorney Kurtz to withdraw his Claim of Possession.

Alice, Denise, and Alfie were able to reclaim their home and personal possessions. However, Alice was in County Hospital intensive care. Two weeks later, when she was released, her family drove her back to her reclaimed home

■   ■   ■   ■   ■

It had taken months for Alice to regain the use of her faculties, and be able to walk.

Attorney Kurtz had not even been apologetic when Charlie returned to the Law Offices and touched bases with the chastised claimant attorney.

"I didn't even charge interest on that judgment. Aren't I owed?"

"You were supposed to wait to get paid from the loan."

"Well, she got the loan, but I never got paid."

Therein was the rub, and why Charlie was now faced with the unpleasant task of filing a "Motion to Enforce the Settlement Agreement" as Earl instructed him.

During Charlie's absence from the Law Offices, opposing Attorney Dancy Rock, with whom Charlie had reached the Settlement Agreement, had insisted that all the loan proceeds be wired to his Law Offices of Dancy Rock trust account directly. The moneys, funded by Probate E-Z Loans, were sitting in Dancy Rock's Trust Account ever since.

After fending off Judge Whitsett's wrath, Dancy had paid off Kurtz and Field, but the remainder of the moneys, earmarked for The Law Offices and for Alice to fix her house, still sat in Dancy's Trust Account.

Charlie finished drafting his Motion. With this type of Motion, there was a mandatory attorney fee provision. Immense stress weighed on Charlie. Whatever the righteousness of Alice's cause, there was always the chance Alice could lose, and be stuck paying the opposing side's attorney fees.

Earl raced in from his court hearing. "Did you file the Beneshan Accounting?"

"Yes. I ran into Henry Gilliam in probate line. He claims he's short-changed $50,000. He was on the verge of filing a Motion to Compel, but is holding off for a week."

"How can you screw that up? Get a check over to him if the Order called for it."

Charlie knew it was pointless to point out he had not worked at the Law Offices when the checks were disbursed. *Being blamed was part of the job description for any law firm Associate.* He was glad the matter would be resolved.

"I'll get it out in the next few days."

"You've been doing lots of overtime to get the Beneshan Accounting in. Did you bill for taking the boxes to Angel."

"Right. I included travel time."

Charlie didn't mention anything about the warehouse and the E.R.

Earl, satisfied, raced off.

Charlie turned his attention back to finish writing up the Mobley Motion to Enforce the Settlement Agreement and knew he had to get Alice's original signature. He thought about the intriguing "Dart" files in the Hannah, Ashley cabinet. He'd look at them later. Right now, the Mobley matter superseded everything and required a trip to Alice Mobley's endangered home to get her immediate signature on a document to be filed.

CHAPTER 64
CLEAN-UP MAN

Charlie looked forward to see Alice again. He passed through downtown Los Angeles and maneuvered into the right hand freeway lanes. Charlie had grown up surrounded by classical music, nevertheless, Charlie appreciated lighter pop tunes and rock and roll songs. Today, feeling upbeat, having accomplished what he had set out to accomplish, the catchy lyrics of Ozzie Mobley's best known pop hit, *Clean-Up Man* looped through Charlie's head: "Ruba-ruba, ruba, squish squish wipe; I'm going to be your clean-up man tonight;" *Charlie wished he had gone to El Monte dances when he was a teen-ager.*

Ozzie Mobley continued to sing his catchy hits *Clean-Up Man* and *Ticky-Tacky Tock* for adoring Chacoshan Casino crowds right to the very end. Upon Ozzie's passing, Alice Mobley received a huge bill from the Palm Desert Resort Homes.

Palm Desert Resort Homes was Ozzie Mobley's "home away from home" for the last thirteen months of his life since the resort was near the casino.

Since Alice couldn't pay the huge bill, the Palm Desert Resort Homes filed a civil law suit in downtown Los Angeles Central Court against Ozzie's estate for the balance due. So did the Chacoshan Casino and Hotel, in which Ozzie's third floor suite ran up quite a bill for "room service." The total debts ran to some $253,000. That had been more than Ozzie earned in his years performing at the Chacoshan Casino with his vocal group, "The Castaways."

Alice came to the Law Offices introduced by her cousin, Derrick Stanton, who met fellow jogger, Earl Guarder, at a charity triathlon for the

Children's' Diabetes Special Olympics, sponsored by Derrick's boss, County Supervisor Gary Saskatovitch. That was almost two and a half years ago.

Charlie made it clear to the Casino's counsel, Demetronis Kaposaik, Charlie would inform the press how the Casino took advantage of its iconic headliner in his declining years.

The Casino and the Palm Desert didn't want to be seen hounding the widow of a Los Angeles pop legend who was a respected Leimert Park community leader. The lawsuits were dropped and the agreed-upon nominal settlement amounts were paid by Alice's supportive family.

Charlie also negotiated Sonny Field, Esq., the Mobley's previous attorney's fees in half, and obtained court approval for the reduced amount.

However, Attorney Clyvester Kurtz, who represented Ozzie Mobley during the conservatorship's eight years, had always been adamant about getting his owed fees.

The only concession Charlie managed to extract from Attorney Clyvester Kurtz, was a willingness to drop interest charges on the outstanding bill Attorney Kurtz claimed was owed for supervising Ozzie on his jaunts to perform in Las Vegas, Palm Springs, as well as supervising Ozzie's living arrangements.

Attorney Kurtz included four trips on his bill to Las Vegas to check out Ozzie's "New Castaway" parlor show at the Silver Spurs Casino in 2001-2002, and four trips to check on Ozzie Mobley's show at the Chacoshan Indian Casino and Hotel from 2003 to 2005.

After Ozzie got his performing contract at the Chacoshan Casino outside Palm Springs, Attorney Kurtz also inspected the Palm Desert Resort Homes.

Attorney Kurtz wrote a report for the court after each trip, confirming Ozzie was well enough to perform.

At the court hearing where Charlie protested the huge bills, Judge Eva Takim repeatedly commended Attorney Kurtz on his thoroughness and dedication.

Alas, Attorney Kurtz missed inspecting the third floor Chacoshan Hotel Penthouse Suite where Ozzie and Dixie May would engage in passionate preparation for Ozzie's lounge performances before every show. Despite

Charlie's and Alice's protests that this showed gross negligence, and therefore, Kurtz's request for attorney fees should be denied, Kurtz countered vehemently.

Judge Takim denied Charlie's objections, and approved Attorney Kurtz's fees in their entirety.

Charlie hoped if he won on his Motion to Enforce the Settlement Agreement and retrieved the owed moneys from Dancy Rock, Alice could pay the Law Offices the owed bill, file a Final Accounting, and put the Estate of Ozzie Mobley to rest. Charlie deeply hoped Alice would be able to get past the estate's problems and lead a peaceful life.

The downtown landmarks passed by and Charlie exited to the Santa Monica Freeway, headed west. Soon, Charlie saw the Crenshaw Blvd. freeway exit. Charlie put his turn signal on.

"Ruba-duba duba, squish, squish, wipe.

Hold me baby, close and tight."

CHAPTER 65
VERIFICATION

Charlie pulled up at Alice's modest house on a shady side street off historic Leimert Park Square. Whining at Charlie from behind the metal security door and wagging his tail, Alfie the scruffy brown terrier recognized Charlie from previous visits. The dog seemed more insecure than ever, but Charlie couldn't blame Alfie, as he had temporarily lost his home.

Charlie handed Alfie a milk-bone as Denise opened the door.

"Where's my treat?" Charlie wasn't sure if Denise was joking.

"It's great to see you, Denise. Where's your mom?"

"Mom, the attorney is here" Denise looked at Charlie with mock suspicion, backed away, let Charlie in.

"I heard about your ordeal. I'm so sorry."

"Those policemen tried to steal my book. Mom needs this house. I can write anywhere. Did you read my book?"

Denise could be engaging, but time was fleeting.

"I'll read your story as soon as I can."

"Better be soon. 'Cause the end is near. And I don't mean for the story. I mean the *end* as the Bible prophets say."

"Right. I better deal with your mom."

Denise stepped aside, let Charlie into the living room with a comfortable couch, plush easy chairs and carved side tables, and walls decorated with Ozzie Mobley's two platinum records, *Clean-up Man* and *Ticky-Tacky Tock*, and pictures of Denise and other family members. Charlie opened his valise, and placed the Mobley Motion to Enforce court documents on the living room table.

"Alice, you're looking real good."

"Thanks." Alice appreciated Charlie's observation.

"Good thing you didn't see her couple a months ago," Denise interjected.

"I heard. I'm so glad you're better."

"Yes, I am fine."

Denise added, "Glad you're back, Charlie."

"Thanks."

Alice asked, "You think Dancy Rock will give us our money?"

"I think this will do it, Alice."

"I pray every day this court business will end."

"It will, momma, you'll see."

Charlie spread the document on the table.

Charlie, in reviewing the Mobley file, learned that The Law Offices sending the moneys to Dancy Rock's trust account wasn't a mistake. The loan and escrow company knew of the dispute between Alice and the claimants, and demanded Dancy Rock, who was a well-thought-of attorney in Leimert Park, sign off on the loan and hold the money in trust for all parties.

Charlie had been dismayed by Dancy Rock not sending out due checks to The Law Offices and to Alice Mobley. He was also shocked to learn, upon returning to the Law Offices, that the Probate E-Z Lender's house loan was signed by Jones, Sharke attorney Henry Gilliam for the loan broker. The interest rate on the loan was exorbitant.

Henry Gilliam was a python who slithered in the darkest swamps of law practice. However, Charlie had no alternative loan to offer Alice.

The refund due Alice from the moneys in Dancy Rock's account was considerable.

"Right there, Alice. Sign right there."

Alice put on her spectacles.

Charlie thought it best to clarify one more time. "You understand what this document is? We're trying to get a refund of the moneys owed you."

"Ozzie was stupid. The ladies were only after his money."

Denise chimed in: "Daddy was a star, momma."

Alice sighed, rolled her eyes, unconvinced of Denise's defense of Ozzie Mobley's ways.

"Are you able to give me the check for the filing fee?"

"Right here. Thanks to my cousin Ruth Ann."

"Thanks." Charlie placed the court filing fee check into the Mobley file on top of his documents.

"You think you will be able to come to court?"

"Wouldn't miss it."

Charlie watched as Alice painstakingly signed her name providing her verification that everything in the document was true as far as she knew. *Alice's family stuck together. That's what had gotten Alice this far.*

CHAPTER 66
MOTION TO ENFORCE

Charlie raced across Temple Street with his valise, entered the north-side courthouse entrance under the heroic friezes of Moses, King John and Thomas Jefferson who stood watch on all who passed underneath their lofty perches above the swinging court doors. Each of the marble lawgivers held onto their law codes, - The Ten Commandments, the Magna Carta and the Declaration of Independence - to impress upon attorneys and laity, the gravity of the quest for justice.

Charlie emptied his pockets as he got in line to enter through security. Like most attorneys, Charlie had a Court I.D. that made entry easier, but the courts were strict about making sure everyone was scanned.

Charlie raced down the football-length hall to the probate office.

The probate clerks behind the counter on the 4th floor of Central Court, for the most part, tried to help. But there was only so much they could do. If they bent rules too much, the behind the scenes court probate attorney, known only through e-mails initialed by "AG," or DB," or "DF," the monikers of anonymous legal sages, who reviewed each document prior to the hearing, would balk and issue notes to kick the document out and re-file when the corrections had been made.

"How you doing Allhan?"

"Fine, Charlie. Looks like you're real busy."

"Trying to catch up."

Allhan laughed, took the "Motion" documents, reviewed them.

Charlie leaned on the counter. "Just give me a date, so I can wrap up this Mobley matter."

"The crooner case? Hey, I heard Ozzie's getting a star on Hollywood Blvd. Too bad he can't be there. Is it true his girl-friend is going to do the honors?

Charlie had heard the rumors, but dismissed them. He certainly hadn't heard the part about Dixie May. He hoped it was not true for Alice's sake.

"You're reading the tabloids Allhan. It's garbage."

"You've got all the good ones, Charlie. Tell you what. How about Tuesday, June 17th for your hearing at 8:30 a.m.? That's only five weeks out."

Charlie took out his cell phone and speed dialed The Law Offices. The phone rang several times before Aki answered. Today, she was back in her part-time position as there were no law school interns available.

"Hi, Aki. Charlie checking in." The phone screeched with static in the Court. Charlie turned sideways and got a clearer signal. Aki finally understood it was Charlie calling.

"Hi, Charlie. What's up?"

"Did a check come in this afternoon from Dancy Rock on the Mobley matter?"

The clerk took this interruption in stride. Attorneys always checked on hearing dates at the last moment. Charlie shifted his body as he waited, knowing he was holding up the line. Somehow, if he engaged in nervous physical movement, it would let those behind him know he was not just wasting time. He wanted to confirm Dancy Rock had not sent the overdue check, nor filed the original Settlement Agreement in the last few hours. Otherwise, filing the Motion to Enforce would have to be scrapped or the client would be very angry, losing the costly filing fee.

"Charlie? Nothing in the afternoon mail."

"Thanks, Aki." Charlie hung up, slipped the cell phone into his pocket.

"I'll take that day."

Charlie focused on the wall clock as the Clerk wrote the June 17th hearing date on the original document and on the copies he stamped and gave back to Charlie, along with taking Charlie's filing fee. It was seven minutes to four p.m.

Charlie nodded "thanks," hurried out, looked around, did not see any pythons lurking in the court's recesses.

Charlie exited the court, didn't see Rose, hoped she was okay.

The street light on Temple turned green, the three statuary legal eminences gazed down at him with approval and the "walk" sign flashed. Charlie made it back to his on-street parked car with minutes to spare before the tow trucks showed up at 4:00 p.m.

CHAPTER 67
AT THE LAST MINUTE

It was past five p.m. and The Law Offices were closed when Charlie raced in with his stamped copies of the filed Mobley Motion.

Aki had left, so Charlie took on the paralegal task of preparing envelopes to serve notice on all interested parties. Amanda raced past him, headed for the hallway door.

"We got the check for Alice Mobley. We just got served by a messenger before the office shut. They filed the Settlement Agreement in court just before it closed."

Charlie froze, uncertain what to do. There had been several messengers behind him in line at court. What terrible luck. He arrived less than 10 minutes before the clerks had locked the door. Charlie hadn't counted on the last messengers being from Dancy Rock's office.

Earl hurried out of his office. "Did you get that Mobley Motion filed?"

"I am about to serve the documents. But if we got the check?"

"Go ahead. The judge will see they dicked around for months. You sent them a warning letter?"

"Of course"

"When?"

"A few days after I returned to the office. I gave them a week to file. I sent another letter about ten days ago. I kept a log of all my unreturned calls."

"We're fine. Put in our Motion for Attorney Fees."

Charlie had come so close to avoiding a major legal battle.

"Shouldn't we withdraw the Motion. Drop it? Eat the filing fee?"

"Serve the Motion. Go ahead with the hearing. Add up all the phone calls, and other time you've wasted because of their intransigence. Get our costs."

Charlie knew the drill. He couldn't argue with the need to get money to cover the Law Office's overhead.

"Serve it. We'll win."

Amanda ran back in, out of breath. "Look. I saw him on TV in the conference room. Come here!"

Charlie and Earl ran after Amanda as she changed directions, leading Earl and Charlie down the hall to the conference room. She pointed at the news station, where excited newscasters were pushing their microphones into a beaming man's face.

Earl looked bewildered recognizing the smiling face. "Isn't he our client?"

It took Charlie a minute to recognize the subject of the interview. It was the cowboy shirt more than his facial features that clicked in Charlie's mind and brought Jimmy Moon back into his consciousness. Jimmy looked exuberant, full of life, and perfectly at ease with the bevy of reporters who threw the same question at him:

"What are you going to do with all the money from your Powerball winnings?"

Amanda was aghast. "He won the $453,000,000 jackpot. He owes us over $50,000. We must collect."

Earl turned to Charlie. "Call Jimmy Moon in. Get him to pay what he owes. He's our best client."

Charlie thought it best to nod, and go with the flow of positive energy, and not mention Jimmy Moon had been thrown off the client list months ago, and would be an unlikely candidate to pick up the phone call from The Law Offices.

"And take care of Dancy Rock. We'll win!"

With that, Earl Guarder, in his azure silk suit and elegant pomegranate red silk tie was headed to the elevator, on his way to some Fairtown cocktail party that might land a new Law Offices client.

Amanda faced Charlie. "I thought I hit the jackpot with my two-week Auto Show hostess assignment. My modeling career peaked when I was sixteen."

"Well, if it's any consolation, I get occasional appearances in the chorus at the L.A. Opera. That's off the record, too, just as your gigs," admitted Charlie. "My singing career peaked when I was twenty-three. I sang Figaro in Mozart's *Marriage of Figaro* with the Bolognese Opera Company."

"Of course, it would be Jimmy Moon who hits the jackpot," Amanda laughed. She turned the TV off and headed out of the conference room. "You never know, do you?"

"You never do," answered Charlie. "Good night."

Amanda was already in the reception area, closing the front door behind her, leaving Charlie to wrap up.

Charlie headed back to his office, amazed at the turn of events. *There was something righteous about the dispossessed Jimmy Moon becoming the family's newest millionaire. Then, again, money seemed to flow to money.*

Charlie attached his copies of the Mobley court stamped document with his signed proof of service, and dropped the attorney service form into the "out" box.

The phone rang. Charlie ignored the phone.

He hurried to the law library, perused the bookshelf for "Trusts," and impetuously, threw the legal practice guides into his valise. Charlie had a long weekend ahead.

Charlie had received the supplemental Thornhill accounting ledger via certified mail a few days ago at home with updated Thornhill income and expenses. The biggest recent investment at the end of the previous year was no pocket change and came as a shock.

Oscar Thornhill had invested millions in Vision Associates for the Isis Development.

Charlie couldn't fathom the nature of the relationship between David Alex and Oscar Thornhill, but knew he had to keep his new knowledge under wraps.

Charlie headed out of the office as his eye caught the metal file cabinet, where he had seen the Dart Construction files.

The office hallway appeared deserted. He flipped up the cabinet cover.

Charlie pulled the two Dart Construction boxes out and carried them to his office. He dropped them on his desk, opened each box and noted the files were for Dart construction projects, from Los Angeles city agencies.

The files weren't part of the Beneshan boxes. They had been stored by Hannah, Ashley, and mixed with Beneshan file boxes.

Charlie had to discover if there were clues to David Alex's murder.

Charlie pulled out the Correspondence File documents and saw the outraged letters from Dart to Alex threatening legal action. The letters in the file confirmed Charlie's suspicions: Dart Construction and Vision Associates were bitter rivals.

Dart Construction's bid on the massive Golasetti park-like residential complex named after City Councilman Leon Golasetti, which was the gem of the City's whirl at affordable housing in the newly revitalized downtown, was the subject of many nasty letters back and forth. Alas, the project's namesake, Leon Golasetti was no longer a councilman, able to walk the streams and byways of his Shangri-la landscaped low-cost housing legacy.

In fact, the ex-councilman was living on free room and board provided by taxpayers at the San Pedro Federal Prison convicted of taking bribes in return for his vote on construction bids, including the Golasetti Low Cost Apartment Complex. Vision Associates prevailed getting the contract. Eric Dart, judging from his furious letters did not forgive this below-the-belt blow.

Dart's letter to Hannah, Ashley accused Vision Associates of paying Golasetti off with a Caribbean vacation and demanded Hannah, Ashley play hardball. The reply letter promised Dart's account would be handled from now on by outside Senior Counsel Jack Smith, who would ensure Dart's success and satisfaction.

Charlie saw the follow-up letter from Eric Dart to Attorney Jack Smith, complaining about David Alex's tactics to obtain a condominium complex contract over the Sunset Blvd. and Wiltern Avenue Metro subway stop. Charlie flipped to the reply letter written only a few weeks after David Alex's murder, signed by Senior Partner Jack Smith, congratulating client Eric Dart on getting the contract after the law firm hired a consulting firm that specialized in dirty tricks to ensure Alex would lose out on the bid. The letter was stapled to a copy of a wire transfer for a princely sum.

Eric Dart had every reason to eliminate David Alex as a competitor and the six figure "consulting fee" wire transferred to a Cayman Islands bank was serios evidence of murderous wrongdoing.

Charlie made copies of the crucial correspondence, slipped the copies into his valise, and placed the originals of the letters in their reverse chronological order, back in the Dart Correspondence file, closed the boxes, looked into the hallway.

Charlie scurried with the two boxes back down the hall. The custodian was vacuuming several offices away. Charlie pushed the first file box back into the deep recesses of the cabinet.

"Watch yourself."

Charlie froze with terror, looked behind him, as the scolding custodian maneuvered his vacuum cleaner behind Charlie's crouched body.

"Right." Charlie tried to look nonchalant, pushed the second box back to its hold.

"Want your office cleaned?"

"Yes, thanks. I'm out of here."

■   ■   ■   ■   ■

Racing downtown to make it to rehearsal, Charlie knew he made a connection of interest to Detective Oswilla, but he wasn't sure how to pass on the information about Attorney Jack Smith's connection to the Alex case without admitting to acts that at the least, couldn't be used to pursue criminal justice under the widely accepted "fruit of the poisonous tree" doctrine, and at worst, could get Charlie a hearing before the State Bar's Ethics Court.

Charlie's cell phone rang. He pressed the ear-piece "on."

"Hello?"

"I tried to get you at the office."

It was Angel.

"How is Devlin?"

"They called me from St. John's. Devlin died this morning. It's crazy for me to cry over that screw-up, but I decided to have a service for him this Saturday."

Charlie steered the car onto the on-ramp, tried to sound neutral.

"Closure's good."

"Devlin didn't kill Barry."

Charlie couldn't quite concentrate as he pushed into traffic.

"Why would Devlin lie to you?"

"Devlin truly loved me."

Charlie maneuvered onto the freeway, and couldn't concentrate on Angel's logic that true love could be explained by falsely confessing to a capital crime.

"I booked a service for Devlin on Saturday afternoon. Will you come?"

Charlie had to finalize the Thornhill Pour-over Will over the week-end and return to Malibu Meadows on Sunday to get Oscar's signature.

The downtown skyline appeared around the Arroyo-Seco freeway bend.

"Where?"

"Old North Church at Forest Park Cemetery. One o'clock. Please?"

Charlie knew he couldn't deny the request. "Okay."

CHAPTER 68
POUR-OVERS

Inside the Opera Company's men's dressing room, Charlie recognized the multi-colored exo-skeletoned insect that stepped next to him at the costume rack. Desmond, his head cushioned by the costume's foam neck piece, looked gaunt and hollow-cheeked. He held his menacing insect headpiece in the crook of his arm, almost pushing it into Charlie's chest.

"You both look splendid – for bugs." Veronica, in a green and white peasant skirt accentuating her full figure, ran up between them, helped Charlie slip into his insect costume, took pictures with her pocket camera of each. "For my portfolio," she quipped. Desmond crinkled his taut lips.

"You need to smile, my friend," she teased eliciting the hint of a smile in return and another click of her camera.

She ruffled Desmond's costume and succeeded in getting Desmond to loosen his wrinkled face even more. She snapped a few more pictures of Desmond, said "thanks," and turned to Charlie. "You're my masterpiece, Charlie." She snapped a few pictures as Charlie posed in his perfectly fitted earth-toned mosquito costume.

"Thanks to your Vermeer touch."

"I have an art book – famous paintings to use as costume templates. But I don't think Vermeer painted any bugs in costume."

Desmond adjusted his headpiece over his head and dropped it in place. "Hieronymus Bosch, I believe would be a better template for my ghoulish persona."

Charlie recalled the apocalyptic Hieronymus Bosch paintings he had seen in far off museums in Vienna featuring rapacious devils chasing plump, peasant maidens with lascivious abandon, as they speared the human paramours with devilish three-pronged spears. His far-off fantasy was brought back to the present as Veronica made her final adjustment on his costume and looked into Charlie's eyes.

"You're a funny bug."

She dropped a coquettish curtsy and raced on to make final adjustments to other flailing extras.

Desmond clawed Charlie's shoulder in greeting.

"Thought I was some horror film villain, didn't you?"

Charlie was intimidated by Desmond's menacing persona. He laughed off the acerbic comment. "How's Oscar?"

"Not well. Did you finish the Pour-over Will?"

"I'll finish it this weekend."

"Good. We'll go see Oscar this Sunday."

Charlie hesitated. He promised Tina a day just for the two of them.

"This Sunday afternoon at 3:00 p.m. We'll meet and have him sign the document. He's fading."

Charlie knew he had to go along. "Okay. I'll meet you at Malibu Meadows." Charlie wished he could be strong enough to say "no," but he could point out to Tina he was paid a large sum. He had opened the monogrammed envelope he had been given at the brunch and savored the five figure certified check payable to "Cash."

"I've got to include the 'Vision Associates' stock shares in the 'Pour-Over.' The value of that land development is considerable."

"It's the critical asset. Why the hell didn't you check on that?"

"I just got the updated statement from your accountant. Oscar wasn't the general partner until your investment exceeded fifty percent of the total moneys at the end of last year."

"Oscar is the general partner now. He has the final say in Isis. We must control that property."

Charlie recalled hearing about "Isis" the first time he was in David Alex's office. At one point Alex led Charlie to a work-table on which a balsa wood miniature model of the Isis development spread over a green crepe paper landscape.

Alex showed off the Vision Associates project with childish enthusiasm and professional pride. The dome-like residential structures were laid out in concentric circles around public buildings in the center of the community being built in the Greenland western tundra. The entire development was encircled by a solar panel covered wall, which Alex bragged, was modeled after the Great Wall of China.

The domed residences were terraced with open spaces on each level for individual sustainable gardens mimicking the fertile foundations of the hidden Inca cities of Vilcabamba and Machu Picchu.

Alex was raptured by his futuristic colony. The roof panels of the geodesic dome to enclose the community were fabricated out of an advanced metallic solar panel chameleon-like skin. Much like the fleeing Incas, the residents of Isis could camouflage their lives from those who would pry – or invade.

"I've got to control the partnership before Isis falls into some court-appointed receiver's clutches."

"I'll have the Pour-over document done by Sunday."

Desmond seemed satisfied with Charlie's assurance. "At the time he wanted to buy into this deal, the rest of the family thought Oscar was crazy. Now? Face to face with another great depression, moving there is our hope to survive."

"Wasn't the Isis development for future generations?"

Desmond was surprised Charlie knew about Isis.

"How'd you know about Isis?"

"David Alex was my administrator on an estate case."

Desmond looked Charlie in the eye. "I heard he's dead."

"Something like that." Charlie thought it best to leave out the detail that Alex was murdered in his bungalow.

"That makes your work even more crucial. I've got to be the new general partner."

"Unless David Alex's heirs object."

"Make sure I am – the general partner!"

Charlie knew this wasn't the time to remind Desmond, Charlie wasn't omnipotent. "Of course."

"Our investment's worth shit unless I'm the general partner and we're free of any nosy court!"

Charlie recalled at the first meeting with David Alex, Alex listened to someone on the other end of the telephone line for close to an hour while Charlie sat waiting his turn to conference about the Barry Beneshan case.

Charlie could hear parts of the obscenity-laced references on the other end of the line objecting to delays with the Isis deal.

The echo of that conversation reverberated in Charlie's ears as Desmond barked at Charlie: "I'm the fucking general partner. You work for the Thornhills now. Understand?"

Charlie knew he was in over his head. Charlie considered whether Desmond had David Alex murdered? Or was it the revengeful Eric Dart? Vision Associates empire's ruthless competitors and investors were benefitting from Alex's death, not the least of them Desmond Thornhill.

"I'll complete my job and file the documents with the court as required."

"You're our family attorney, now. You see we lost everything other than the last investment Oscar made."

Charlie bit his lip, placed the paper mache insect headpiece over his costume to hide his unhappy reaction.

Desmond's piercing eyes might as well have been a death threat.

The two costumed extras faced off. Charlie looked back at the threatening insect, wondering: *Was signing up for an attorney day job a good idea, or was it the dumbest decision I ever made?*

"All extras on stage." Gerry, grasping his walkie-talkie, ran in, clapped his hands to drive home the rehearsal countdown.

CHAPTER 69
PAYING RESPECTS

Near the front of Forest Park Cemetery's Old North Church. Charlie squeezed into a parking space with his tiny car and joined the groups of mourners headed to the chapel entrance for Devlin D'Alessio's Saturday Memorial Service.

Charlie entered the Hollywood Hills Cemetery's replica of Boston's famed Old North Church. He saw Angel, and Gabriella, dressed in muted dark formal clothes, and he walked towards their reserved place of honor in the front pew. Angel thanked him for coming, accepted Charlie's floral bouquet, and placed the tall curved, glistening vase in front of the chapel's nave.

Angel and Gabriella were happy to see Charlie.

Charlie looked around and saw the back of the stark chapel fill with mourners. Many entering the chapel were Polynesian families.

"Looks like an impressive turn-out," Charlie observed.

"Devlin helped many Cham families."

"They came all the way down from Woodfall?"

"Devlin gave them hope. The tenants grew to like him and saw Devlin cared about their welfare. Devlin visited the Cham to help them just like Barry had done."

Charlie nodded, touched her shoulder politely, smiled at Gabriella, and took his place in the pew behind Angel. Charlie, between other mourners on both sides of the pew, faced the faux-ivory cream-colored velvet-lined casket that was the centerpiece of the service in the apse of the chapel. Light streamed in through the tall, gothic shaped, stained glass windows to highlight the laid out Devlin d'Allesio, who had been fitted to look his best for the celebration of the occasion of his passing from life to death.

Charlie had doubts his own "send-off" would be this memorable. A few mourners stood out. An athletic middle-aged man in a shiny, reflective black suit and dark tie, and a shapely, well-groomed woman, also in a black business suit, with her blonde hair pulled back into a pony tail, stood in rigid poses behind the back row. Each sported aviator sunglasses. Their prissy attire and standoffish demeanor might as well have advertised they were government agents.

Several rows in front of the two "suits," another duo seemed equally out of place in the packed pews. One of the odd-ball duo was a tall thin man with grizzled cheeks, whose eyes were on the side of his crunched, thin bird-like face, or maybe his head had been pressed in a compactor, that stopped at the last moment before all the innards of the cranium flattened. His companion was paunchy, almost as wide around his girth as his torso was tall, with pudgy arms, fat-cushioned ears, and deep-set eyes. The two men glanced discreetly, trying to see who entered the chapel. Their ostentatious clothes – a badly knotted yellow tie for the short sport, whose stomach was hemmed in by the pew in front, and an open polyester short sleeve sport shirt with a gold chain for the tall hairy-armed bird-like dude - didn't offer either man much chance to blend in. Charlie wondered if they were loan sharks looking to score owed moneys.

Charlie leaned forward next to Angel's ear. "Does Devlin have immediate family?"

"His sister Danielle is in New York City. I e-mailed her about the services. I was hoping she would chip in for all this," she whispered half turning to him.

Charlie nodded, acknowledging this was not an inexpensive send-off.

The white haired, white jacketed minister, a perfect central casting choice, walked out from a side doorway, and faced the mourners. Charlie looked at the engraved program and surmised this was Reverend Thomas Denes. Reverend Denes was the avant-garde pastor at Hollywood Second Presbyterian Church. Charlie glanced at his watch just as the digital bell tower clanged a crystalline 1:00 p.m.

Charlie knew these services were booked by the hour, assembly line, non-denominational, impressive cherished memories. Devlin D'Alessio's service would be over in forty minutes. Then, mourners would usher the casket, following the pallbearers towards the hillside burial site, or the mourners could leave, if they chose. This was Forest Park's approach to death. *Deal with it quickly. "We'll make it memorable as well as comfortable and convenient."*

Some memorial service attendees, waiting outside, could be seen through the open side doors, already lining up along the side of the Chapel for the two o'clock services.

Minister Thomas Denes raised his hands in salutation.

A loud "pop" echoed behind Charlie. Then, another "pop" and screams. Charlie turned his head to the side of the chapel and saw a well-dressed dark skinned man flinch and fall in the pew a few rows back – across the center aisle.

Charlie instinctively grabbed Gabriella from behind and pushed her to the floor as Angel dropped, held Gabriella down. All three flattened into their pews onto the cold marble floor.

"Drop your weapons. Now! F.B.I."

There were louder, zinging "pops" amidst screams.

The shooting stopped.

Charlie peeked and saw the bodies of the yellow-tied fat man and the open-shirted, bird man with their hand guns fallen into the aisle, blood streaming from blown holes in cheeks and mouths, falling to the floor in slow motion as their grips loosened from pews. Blood surged over the bald pate of the short gunman, and through the frizzy mop page-boy hair cut of his tall buddy's head. The blood dripped into the two twitching faces. It seeped into the recessed eyes of the short stricken man who screamed as he fell into the center aisle, next to his bloody, collapsing companion.

Mourners screamed, got up, ran away on all four points of the compass, out the side doors.

Minister Denes was confused by the shock of new deaths in his service, as the two shot men lay in death throes in the back of the center aisle, half cushioning each other. Minister Denes walked slowly up the center aisle with raised arms to bless the victims of whatever calamity was occurring, but had no off-the-cuff spiritual uplift to administer other than to clasp his hands in a gesture of prayer.

"This is a house of peace. Stay calm." Minister Denes implored.

The Cham families ignored the minister's plea, pushed to escape through the side exits. The two sun-glassed "suits" moved forward cautiously.

"We're F.B.I. agents. You're safe," they blurted as loud as they could in overlapping cadence.

One of the F.B.I. agents leaned over the two shooters whose blood seeped from the center aisle around the wooden pew pedestals.

The button-down F.B.I. agent pulled out a "walkie-talkie."

"Agent Thomas Long. I'm in the Chapel. Send ambulance. Barracuda One wounded. Larry and Moe are down and out for the count. Check, over."

There were wails and screams in the back aisles in front of the dying shooters. A bloody wire-rim eye-glassed, pill-hatted Cham woman's torso raised above the top of the wooden pew, where the first shooting victim fell.

Her scream echoed the chapel and curdled Charlie's heart.

The victim, the wounded dreadlock-haired, well-dressed Cham man, grabbed the top of the pew and raised himself, holding onto his right shoulder with his left hand, pressing the wound where the bullet entered.

Charlie looked up to see the man's missing fingers on his hand, just as the man turned and disappeared from sight amidst the huddle.

The male F.B.I. agent pushed past Reverend Denes, angled through a pew to the escaping victim, but was thwarted by Cham mourners who blocked his path.

The agent holstered his sidearm.

Charlie raised himself slowly.

He could see the bloody burly man with the glass eye and missing fingers on his left hand race out of the chapel's side door onto the landscaped grass, holding his shot shoulder.

It was Boohau Cyclops!

Sirens of limousines echoed outside. The second F.B.I. agent, the slick woman with the aviator glasses, hurried down the side of the chapel to Charlie and Angel's pews.

"Miss Angel Sedona, I'm agent Denise Trenton, F.B.I. Please come with us."

Charlie, uncertain what to do, helped Angel and Gabriella stand. Mother and daughter were dazed.

Charlie flustered, spoke up. "I'm Attorney Charlie Tobias. What's the charge?"

"You, too. Both of you. Come with me. The kid can stay. "

Angel grabbed Gabriella. Charlie stepped protectively in front.

The agent took off her sunglasses. She was sexy, rude.

"You," she barked, pointed at a well-dressed man in the pew behind Angel near Charlie. "Who are you?"

"I'm Angel's roommate, Gary Frank."

Angel nodded. "He came with us in my car."

Gabriella huddled behind Angel. The agent slipped her gun into her jacket holster.

"Mr. Frank, please take the young lady home."

Angel reached for her car keys, slowly, conscious of the hyped up agent facing her. "Please, Gary. Take her home, now."

Gary nodded, took the keys, nodded for Gabriella to follow him. Gabriella bawled as she looked for reassurance from Angel.

"Go, honey. Go. Momma will be home as soon as she can." Gabriella moved towards Gary.

"I am an attorney. Are you charging Ms. Sedona?"

The F.B.I. agent scanned Angel and Charlie. "We have questions for you. Come with us downtown."

Angel nodded for Gabriella to leave. "Honey, go with Gary. Call Nanna to come. I'll be back as soon as I can."

"Yes, ma'am." Gabriella wiped away a tear and moved out of the pew.

The well-coiffed blonde agent replaced her sunglasses on her model's face, pointed a long index finger at Gary. "Move out, mister!"

Gary retreated with Gabriella.

Charlie moved forward, handed his business card to agent Trenton. She ignored the offering. Charlie mustered his courage.

"Can I see your I.D.?" Agent Trenton flashed a badge at Charlie too quick for him to see whether it was real or a toy knock off.

"Move out. Now!"

Her walkie-talkie blurted through loud static: "Barracuda One out of sight! Outside perimeter emergency."

Trenton clicked the talk button. "Barracuda Two secure inside. Over."

Charlie's attention was sidetracked as orange-uniformed paramedics rushed through the main entrance and knelt over the two shot assailants, followed by swarming agents wearing yellow and black bulletproof vests with oversized emblazoned "F.B.I." logos.

Agent Long pushed through the Cham mourners and raced out the other side of the Chapel after Boohau Cyclops.

Charlie could make out the barked orders outside: "He's bleeding. Three point alert. Catch him and take him in! Twenty four hour lockdown in secure hospital!"

Agent Long's orders intimidated the paramedics. They placed their portable metal IV units next to the shot goons, got up, and raced outside with their emergency kits after the fleeing Boohau Cyclops who was a distant speck on the grassy knoll.

The chapel cleared out except for Minister Thomas Denes, who kneeled over the two shot assailants, rocked back and forth, pondering the deadly turn of events in this house of reflection on life's end.

The minister recited a prayer, a progressive version of *Our Father*.

"Lord, have mercy. There is too much hate. We must love each other and understand and accept our differences whatever our gender, ethnic background or sexual preference, for we are all your children, and need your acceptance and love."

Agent Trenton grabbed her radio-phone. "Trenton, bringing out Barracuda Two. She's got an attorney. Should I bring him in? Over?"

Charlie exchanged worried glances with Angel. The 'Barracuda' moniker was not reassuring.

Agent Trenton listened in on her earpiece to unheard commands.

Charlie looked into agent Trenton's sunglass covered eyes. Charlie had seen TV F.B.I. Agents who didn't look half as good.

Agent Trenton clicked off the radio phone. "Okay, Lawyer. Let's go. Both of you!"

Charlie caught a final glimpse past Trenton's shapely body. Several agents still had guns drawn, just in case.

"Move. Now!" Charlie followed Angel. Agent Trenton coolly adjusted her sunglasses as she surveyed her chaotic domain.

CHAPTER 70
DEMARCATIONS

Outside the chapel, entire families, including crying children were handcuffed and pulled, screaming, along the expansive manicured cemetery grounds. The distraught Cham families rounded up, were photographed and pushed into the ICE paddy wagons, pleading their cases in native tongue whose entreaties could be understood by any deaf-mute listener with a soul.

Six ambulances filled with the wounded, mourners who sat too close to Boohau Cyclops and were caught in the cross-fires. The dead assailants had wounded three of the mourners including a teen-ager, as they took aim at their fleeing target, Boohau Cyclops. A med-vac helicopter landed on the knoll some ways from the chapel. Charlie took in the spectacle. The Los Angeles County Coroner's station wagon pulled up.

Charlie tried to talk to agent Trenton: "Who were the shooters?"

She was not only professional, she was cold. "It's government business," agent Trenton replied tersely and looked away.

Angel wiped away tears, screamed. "What have I done to deserve this horrible treatment? You're supposed to be on my side!"

Agent Trenton's response was crisp: "Get in the back seat, ma'am."

Charlie had no clue about criminal law, nor had the agent accused his client of misdeeds. He could demand to leave. Then, again, he wasn't sure that was a good idea.

"Get in, Angel. I'm coming with you."

Agent Trenton opened the black SUV's rear passenger door. Agent Long came around from the driver's side. "Is he a boy friend?"

"It's her attorney."

"Another ambulance chasing whore." Agent Long sneered.

Charlie winced, fantasized about agent Long's turn at getting handcuffs thrown on him. Then, agent Long would scream for a legal representative as the Constitution guaranteed.

"H.Q. confirmed we bring him in," agent Long confirmed to agent Trenton.

The paddy wagons filled with the Cham mourners who had the bad luck to get caught.

A black, unmarked L.A.P.D. police cruiser, sirens blaring, screeched to a stop next to the F.B.I. SUV just as Charlie was about to step into the rear cabin. Behind the somber lead police cruiser, a dozen L.A.P.D. black-and-whites with shrill sirens, raced up. Charlie stopped, looked at the arriving squad car and recognized the driver's thoughtful bronze face.

Detective Oswilla opened the driver's side of the squad car, reached behind the driver's seat, and pulled a folded wheelchair onto the ground. He placed his folded wheelchair next to the driver's seat, and deftly pulled himself into it, immune to the laws of gravity. Detective Oswilla, face erect, wheeled himself up to agent Trenton, deliberately blocking the SUV.

"What the hell's going on here, agent?"

"And you are – sir?"

"Detective Phillip Oswilla, L.A.P.D. Robbery and Homicide Senior Investigator."

Agent Trenton was flustered, adjusted her shades. Oswilla didn't let up. "My radio's crackling about a couple of dead chapel-goers. What's going on with the gun-play?"

"This is a joint F.B.I., Bureau of FAT, and ICE sweep. I'm lead agent Denise Trenton, F.B.I., Los Angeles Bureau."

"You're in my local jurisdiction, agent Trenton. Why wasn't my office pulled in?"

"Our target has been under surveillance for months. He arrived in town an hour ago to attend this memorial. We followed him, pulled in a back-up from our task force, just in case."

Oswilla popped a gum. Agent Trenton understood more was expected.

"Two suspects, 'Larry' and 'Moe' of the Kalishnikov Mob pulled out firearms and shot at our target, 'Barracuda One,' a person of national security interest."

"'Kalishnikov Mob hit-men?' You should make a simple courtesy call."

"My orders were to shadow and intercede if necessary. We weren't planning a take-down operation."

"Those two gentlemen were persons of interest in a homicide up in Woodfall and a body we fished out of the L.A. River a few months ago. Now, what do I do?"

"Our orders are to protect our target, whose alias is 'Boohau Cyclops.' It's a national security directive. We had to terminate the two shooters after they opened fire."

Angel leapt out from behind the SUV. "I didn't ask for protection. Neither did my tenants who came for a memorial."

"Ma'am, get in the SUV." Agent Trenton's index finger pointed at Angel's chest.

"Ma'am, get back in the SUV, before you're charged as an accessory," Agent Long echoed his partner.

"'Accessory?' What am I a fashionista 'handbag?'" Angel stood her ground.

"Those sardines filling up our paddy wagons aren't innocent. They're hard-core drug smugglers," Agent Long added.

Angel looked at Charlie, uncertain what to do.

Charlie waved and motioned to Angel. For once, Angel didn't resist, even as she flaunted her feelings while stepping back into the SUV.

"They're refugees, not criminals." She looked above the SUV's roofline at Agent Trenton.

"Angel!" Charlie pulled Angel inside the SUV's rear cabin.

The L.A.P.D. officers swarmed the chapel, but Detective Oswilla knew the L.A.P.D. had missed the action.

"Where are you taking her?"

"Downtown for a quick interview."

Detective Oswilla nodded, neutral, but firm. "I want to have the report."

Agent Trenton handed her card across. "Are you cleared for Patriot Act, Level A-5 Top Secret?"

Detective Oswilla took the card, glanced at it, looked up past agent Trenton. "My beat is homicide. You've just added two reams of paperwork to my overflow pile. I'm cleared to decide if your agents' shooting was justified, or to recommend charges be brought against you by the city attorney."

Agent Trenton adjusted her shades while she took in the possible repercussions of Detective Oswilla's threat.

"We'll cooperate, Sir. We saved a lot of people's lives."

Detective Oswilla noticed Charlie sitting in the SUV's back seat.

"Well, Attorney Charlie Tobias. How you doing?"

"Surviving. How 'bout you, Detective Oswilla?"

Agent Trenton glared at Detective Oswilla, stepped sideways to block Oswilla's view of Charlie and stop the verbal interaction. Her point made, agent Trenton walked to the front of the SUV, got in the passenger seat.

"Goodbye, Sir. Sorry about the misunderstanding."

Detective Oswilla focused on Charlie looking out through the window.

"Charlie, call me if you need something."

"Thanks, Detective."

Oswilla wheeled his wheelchair towards the chapel. The SUV pulled out as L.A.P.D. officers set up a perimeter around the chapel with yellow-plastic "do not cross" banners draped from tree to tree.

Charlie could tell Angel hadn't finished saying her peace as the SUV pulled out and they passed the Cham families being processed and escorted to the benches of their taxpayer hired paddy wagon limo seats by the Immigration and Customs Enforcement agents.

Agent Long inched the SUV onto the road towards the cemetery exit.

"What the hell is 'Barracuda?' I'm just a single mom trying to protect my kid."

Agent Trenton stared ahead, didn't respond. Charlie knew Angel was gutsy, but with a squeeze on her arm reminded her not to push their luck.

Charlie looked through the F.B.I. vehicle's tinted glass. Charlie saw the blue "Channel 7" News van pull up. Charlie was glad to leave incognito, and not make the "Six O'Clock 'Breaking Story.'"

Charlie tried to focus beyond his immediate fear.

The first images that came to his mind were his parents' faces. They were buried at Forest Park Cemetery. The memorial for his father had been an eloquent ceremony and the first time Charlie confronted death up close.

Seven years later, when his mother's funeral was held, the arrangements were up to Charlie. The funeral was not as grand as for his father, but it was poignant, memorable.

Before these end-of-life demarcations in Charlie's life, Charlie considered the ceremony and pomp and expense of a funeral as frivolous.

After he got through the two ceremonial funerals for his parents, and reflected on the echoes of the churning emotional experience of those two days for years, Charlie realized how important such memorial services were.

Death must have a demarcation – a finality that stays in the memory of the living. Without an acknowledgment of the finality of death, life is far less precious.

. . . . .

The SUV exited the cemetery's entrance and turned left onto Forest Park Drive. The SUV drove alongside the iconic Walker Brothers Film Studios sound stages to the right, the cemetery hills to the left, got on the freeway headed to the west side, not to downtown. Charlie realized they were headed the wrong way. He wondered if they'd ever be released from some basement holding pen in an obscure building.

Charlie's turned to Angel.

"Should we have a private conference? I'll demand it."

"I've got nothing to hide."

Charlie reflected on the fact he was acting as Angel's attorney.

Charlie spoke up to agent Trenton. "I thought we were going downtown?"

Trenton turned her head briefly. "We're going to F.B.I. Headquarters. I wanted to ensure your security, in case someone overheard us."

Charlie and Angel exchanged glances. Charlie knew however long the interview would take, it wasn't time he'd bill.

CHAPTER 71
DIRTY LAUNDRY

Taciturn agent Long drove the SUV over the Santa Monica Mountains, got off the San Diego Freeway, headed east, turned into the Federal Building's protected driveway, and parked in a secure parking lot underneath the totemic federal building in Westwood, got out, opened the rear door of the oversized SUV and escorted Charlie and Angel to the elevator.

Agent Trenton didn't say a word as she stepped into the parking garage elevator, faced Charlie and Angel. Agent Long stepped beside them and pushed the 14th floor button.

Neither Trenton, nor Long said a word as the elevator breezed up, faster than a balloon on a windy day. As the doors opened to a neutral chime and non-descript voice cautioning the passengers to watch their step, Agent Long motioned for Charlie and Angel to accompany him, led them to a conference room and motioned for them to enter. Charlie and Angel complied and noticed agent Trenton moved on.

Agent Long followed, closed the door of the conference room with a clean slam, walked past Charlie and Angel without saying anything and exited through an interior door and pulled it behind him. He returned within a few minutes, moved to the white-laminated conference table, holding a sheaf of large glossy black and white photographs, and indicated for Charlie and Angel to sit. They complied. He leaned above Charlie and Angel, and glanced into each of their eyes.

"I'm agent Thomas Long, F.B.I. Racketeer Influenced and Corrupt Organization Act Task Force Special Agent, otherwise known as 'RICO Agent.' We're glad you're safe." Charlie was jolted the silent agent spoke.

The agent's considerate words seemed out of character to his previous uncaring stare.

"Charlie Tobias, Attorney at Law. Angel Sedona is the administrator of Barry Beneshan's estate. She's my client."

"Yes, we know."

"Thanks for being at the memorial."

"Those two slick-suits with pop guns weren't after you." Agent Long was matter-of-fact. "They were after your Woodfall manager. He's damn lucky to be alive."

Angel let out a sigh of relief.

Charlie held back commenting on his recollection of Boohau Cyclops in Woodfall chasing the cast-off hookah pipe with his extended three-fingered hand.

"Why did they try to kill him?"

Agent Long looked Angel in the eye.

"You don't know?"

"Why would I?"

Agent Long talked slowly. "Ms. Sedona, did Mr. Barry Beneshan ever discuss 'Jetstream' with you?"

"Hold on. Before we go on, I want to put it on the record: There's nothing she knows about the shooting. I'm objecting to your interrogation."

Agent Long's distant demeanor didn't change, but he took a minute to reflect the proper response: "Do you represent Ms. Sedona in criminal matters?"

Charlie spoke with force and authority.

"Our law office represents Ms. Sedona as administrator of the estate of Barry Beneshan, which includes the Woodfall properties Mr. Boohau Cyclops managed. So, by extension, since this interrogation relates to a shooting of an estate manager? Yes, I represent her."

Agent Long took the cue, twisted his mouth tighter in reply.

"We have been investigating Mr. Barry Beneshan and his partner, Captain Jack Wonder for a long time for 'RICO' violations."

"Who is 'Rico?'" Angel, as usual, was outspoken. Charlie was also unsure what a RICO violation was. He recalled something from a gangster film about a Chicago mobster who came to a bad end in an alleyway shoot-out, cradled in the arms of his sobbing mother, who cried "Rico was always such a good son. Rico, Rico, such a good boy."

"Money laundering. There are a lot of other allegations, but that's the rap. Barry Beneshan launders money, even though he's dead. Who's carrying on the family business?"

"My kid and I barely have clothes to launder, much less 'money.'"

Agent Long was cool, nonplussed. "Let me give you a bit of background Mr. Beneshan may not have shared. Barry Beneshan ran afoul of Federal Securities and Exchange regulations some years ago for wheeling and dealing with other folks' moneys to build Clean Co. He was looking at a potential long-term stay in federal prison, but made a deal approved by Central U.S. District Court Judge Howard Hack."

Angel interrupted. "It was a bullshit indictment. He was a young talented businessman trying to take his mold-remediation company public."

"Nevertheless, he was looking at serious prison time. Instead of risking a trial, Mr. Beneshan cut a deal, volunteered for a dangerous assignment in Southeast Asia with Navy military intelligence officer, Captain Jack Wonder's platoon: the so-called 'Wonder Boys Mission.'"

Agent Long spread the photos in front of Angel. The photos showed a smiling Corporal Beneshan, military weapon in hand, in camouflage green Navy uniform posing with Captain Jack Wonder next to a very happy and regal looking Trengh Dao.

"Barry told me. They smuggled Lao friendlies to the United States, where the government helped the refugees start new lives."

"The refugees were Cham. Cham live throughout Southeast Asia including south India. The Cham sided with the U.S. during the Vietnam War."

Agent Long looked up at agent Trenton who came in, leaned against the door she closed behind her. She nodded an "okay" for agent Long to continue.

"Corporal Beneshan and Captain Wonder operated an underground railroad with a local operative and ally, Boohau Cyclops – or as he was then known: Trengh Dao. Trengh Dao was a revered descendent of Cham kings of the once mighty Cham empire, possibly even a blood relative of French royalty."

Agent Long let this sink in.

Agent Trenton, moved forward, sat across from Charlie and Angel, and added to the story: "Because he persuaded the Cham to support the U.S. in the Vietnam War era, Trengh Dao was hunted by the communist Khmer Rouge when they took control of much of Southeast Asia from Bangladesh and Sri Lanka to Vietnam in the early 1980's and exterminated some four million people."

Charlie's memory of the "Khmer Rouge" rise to power was hazy. "Weren't the Khmer Rouge a radical Cambodia communist group?"

"They were not just in Cambodia. They were killing throughout Southeast Asia," Agent Trenton folded her hands, stared at Charlie from behind her sunglasses.

Agent Long was not surprised at Charlie's ignorance.

"The extent of the slaughter was kept hush-hush. The U.S. top-brass worried that if the magnitude of the Khmer Rouge's spread became public, we'd have another Asian land war. It took over a decade, but special operatives like Corporal Beneshan and Captain Wonder ended the Khmer Rouge's reign of terror not long ago. After the Khmer Rouge leaders were eliminated or bought off, the radical movement imploded."

"Barry told me he worked for Navy Special Forces."

"Well, Ms. Sedona, Corporal Beneshan and Captain Wonder, instead of just smuggling Cham refugees out of Southeast Asia, also went 'solo' and ran a vast criminal syndicate, importing and distributing drugs throughout the United States."

Agent Trenton added: "They bribed U.S. officials to look the other way or throw government contracts their way. The name of the syndicate is 'Jetstream.' The two dead gun men in the memorial were part of the rival Kazakhstan-based Kalishnikov heroin mafia. Your police detective is on the right track. The two assassins snuffed Will Wonder up in Woodfall to send a message to Will's father, Jack Wonder to retire from the business."

Angel was aghast. "They killed that young boy because of Jack?"

Agent Long sat next to agent Trenton and answered. "The concrete burial is their execution style. Their leader, Mandy Chavez is an exiled Spanish communist who was a big fan of Salvador Dali's austere landscape painting style. He inculcated the aesthetic of news-worthy hits of victims into his assassins."

Charlie's mind raced. How had he become mixed into the periphery of an international criminal enterprise?

"If we wouldn't have staked out the memorial, you – or your daughter, may have been harmed." Agent Trenton folded her arms, and let this sink in.

Angel bit her nails.

The pieces fit together in Charlie's mind: Loyal Cham tribesmen from Southeast Asia living in Woodfall and other central California communities? It was a perfect home base from which to smuggle drugs back east and distribute the contraband in exchange for Clean Co.'s New Orleans government contracts.

Charlie knew he and Angel had fallen into a big-stakes money game played for keeps.

"My client knows nothing about this. She's simply trying to administer Mr. Beneshan's estate."

"Even if we believe her, others out there don't."

"What do you propose?"

"Protective custody. Your client escaped today, but it won't be the last kill-trap. We know about the Clean Co junkie's acid attack downtown."

Agent Long leaned close: "We saw the two goons we terminated today strangle Candace Rollins behind the homeless shelter, put her body into their car, and dump her into the Los Angeles River."

Angel was shocked. "You watched them execute her? You didn't try to stop it?"

"Our orders didn't include protecting junkie patsies."

Charlie interjected his skeptical question. "Why didn't you call in Detective Oswilla?"

Agent Long's look became intense. "This is a national security matter, not a garden-variety local homicide."

He looked at agent Trenton's grimace. Charlie felt shivers, saw Angel's terrified look.

"The directives come straight from the highest authority."

There was momentary silence.

Agent Trenton realized she needed to provide more information to be persuasive. "Candace Rollins got junkie fixes from several sources including the two goons. The two Kazakhstan Kalishnikovs tracked her to

New Orleans and used her as a pit-bull until they had no further use for her."

"So, the bitch is dead. Let us go!"

"There are other double-crossers out there, determined to make their mark. You and your daughter may become targets. The moneys at stake are huge. Do you know what amphetamines are Ms. Sedona?"

Charlie interjected. "I'm instructing my client not to answer."

"Shut up, Charlie. Everyone knows what they are. They're in all the over-the-counter medications."

"And the major drug scourge of our time," added agent Trenton. "As Ms. Sedona states, the base amphetamine ingredient is produced in legal factories around the world, especially Cham-run factories in south India from where the drug is smuggled into the United States. Your Cham tenants set up their distribution network. Those drugs are destroying America!"

"Barry loved Gabriella. He would never place her in danger."

"Well, Ms. Sedona, Captain Jack Wonder loved his son. That didn't save Will from execution and a burial in concrete. Our sources say your Woodfall funeral was fake."

Angel was terrified. "Don't let Jack know. Please?"

Agent Long shrugged. "Look, Ms. Sedona, your lucky streak will end. Frankly, with Mr. Beneshan dead, we are only willing to pull so many resources to keep you alive."

"Who murdered Barry?"

"We don't know. Frankly, we don't care."

Angel shook her head. "Barry loved me. He loved Gabriella."

"He's dead, ma'am. So, you want in?"

"What about my daughter?"

"We'd relocate both of you to another state, under another name. You'd also get immunity from any issues relating to using dirty money."

Angel looked at Charlie imploringly.

"I'd like a word with my client."

The two agents exchanged looks. Agent Trenton reached for a blue file at the end of the table, stapled her business card to it and handed it across to Charlie.

"Please give this to your client. It's the terms of the Protective Custody as well as a summary of her new identity, and the daughter's identity."

Charlie took the file, handed it to Angel. She opened it and scanned the document.

"Cindy McCoy? Brittney McCoy?' I'm a hair-dresser? I can't do my own hair. Those are puke-cutesy names."

"You'll be trained, ma'am. Plus, you'll have a state cosmetology license and a monthly stipend. Your daughter will be enrolled in a small Montessori school in Tulsa, with other similarly situated children."

"Tulsa, Oklahoma? I don't know anyone in Oklahoma."

"That's the whole idea, ma'am."

"And my mother? My dad?"

"I'm sorry. You can't contact them, or tell them anything. Paragraph fourteen of the Agreement."

Charlie could see the horror on Angel's face – the thought of being completely cut off from her parents.

Steely jawed agent Long stood and looked down at Angel. "The deadline to get back to us on this offer is tomorrow, five p.m. After that, you won't hear from us."

Angel looked bravely up into the faces of the two agents.

"Who's going to drive us back?"

Agent Trenton got up, walked across the room, opened the conference room door.

"Let's go."

CHAPTER 72
THERE'S ALWAYS RIO

The streets of Los Angeles can be emotionally ice cold especially on a sweltering summer night when the heated breeze from the canyons sweeps across the suburbs. Charlie looked past the empty front passenger seat through the SUV's windshield. He saw no human presence on the narrow unwelcoming sidewalks of the Wilshire high-rise corridor, only a lava flow of glaring approaching white headlights, receding red tail lights, and fluorescent street overheads highlighting the boulevard's emptiness and immense scale.

Agent Trenton's SUV glided north onto the San Diego Freeway. Angel's hand gripped Charlie's on the rear passenger seat. Huge reflective white lights spotlighted the car's interior, icons of the ever-present blindingly lit night construction that was an unvarying part of the trip back over the hills into the San Fernando Valley. Charlie could see agent Trenton's eyes meet his as she looked into the car's rear-view mirror.

Agent Trenton wasn't about to lose the eye contact opportunity to press her case. "We called the two slain Russ-kies, the 'Kazak-khans.' They gave Candace Rollins orders to take both of you out like she did with Lambert."

Charlie thought back on the soggy list with Angel's and his names on its tail end, recalled his brief phone talk with Candace the night before she was found dead. He shivered, realizing how close he had come to being blinded. He realized he had persuaded Candace to hold off, give him a chance to deal with her perceived wrong. When Charlie took "Oral Persuasion" in law school, the class instructor was a fabled criminal defense attorney, Paul Granagos, who emphasized the importance of every nuance in interpersonal communication. Above all, he taught the art of being an observant listener and graded down for any arguing or confrontation. Charlie was grateful he had taken that class seriously. Listening to Candace's grievance may have saved Angel's and his eyesights.

Angel focused on the reality of Candace's death and her own vulnerability. "What could I possibly have they want?"

Agent Trenton responded without glancing back at Angel. "Taking you out of the picture would disrupt the Cham meth distribution network."

"I can't pay my utilities and I'm supposed to be a drug queen?"

"The Kazak-khans were hit-men for the New Orleans' headquartered Kalishnikov mob. New Orleans has been the port of entry for heroin distribution to the East Coast for decades. Once 'Jetstream' amphetamine reached the east coast, the Kalishnikov mob had serious competition."

"My tenants are no meth dealers."

"Mr. Beneshan and Captain Wonder ran 'Jetstream.' Captain Wonder is the remaining godfather. If they eliminate you? The Woodfall based distribution network collapses when the property is foreclosed and the new owners kick out the Cham mules."

Agent Trenton looked into her rear-view mirror, caught Charlie's uncertain look. Charlie listened carefully to the agent. He had no explanation to counter the agent's theory, but had new insight as to why Jack Wonder always lay low.

"Protective custody and immunity. It's your only hope. Think fast. Give us your decision by tomorrow night."

Charlie looked sideways at Angel. Her brown eyes reflected the rhythmic passing headlights of oncoming traffic in the southbound freeway lanes slowed to a stop to skirt a giant twenty-story erector-set crane which pounded the San Diego Freeway center-divide with Valhalla-sized wrecking balls dropped in spurts of earthquake shaking destruction, eerily illuminated by the immense glaring work floodlights stationed on either side of the shut-down diamond lanes.

"My daughter deserves to grow up and have something. Whatever Barry did was for us."

"Your call, ma'am. I've been to Tulsa. I served there for two years after the Oklahoma City bombings. It's a nice, quiet place."

Charlie recalled the death and mayhem of babies and mothers who had been slit by shrapnel or crushed by falling tile in the Tulsa Federal Building's explosion engineered by anti-government terrorists. He didn't want to pass on negative thoughts to Angel. Home-grown terrorists, or vengeful drug cartel hit-men? Neither was a good pick, as far as his legal analysis saw it.

The SUV sped over the top of the Santa Monica Mountains, descended into the San Fernando Valley.

Agent Trenton glided east on the freeway intersection without any hitch, exited the Ventura freeway and headed north towards Angel's home. Charlie was conscious of how well Trenton knew the route.

Trenton pulled in front of Angel's house. Angel got out. Charlie followed.

"I can take you home, Mr. Tobias. It's on my way back. Or I can take you back to Forest Park to pick up your car."

Charlie was also conscious Agent Trenton knew his own whereabouts.

"I have to talk to my client right now."

"You've got my card, Mr. Tobias. Good night."

The SUV took off. Charlie and Angel stood outside the gated entry. Angel held the F.B.I. file, not sure what to do with it.

Charlie tried to sound neutral and matter of fact. "With the Feds? There's no room to negotiate. It's your call."

Angel held onto the F.B.I. file. "I'm undecided, unsure, unsteady about everything."

Before Charlie could offer any opinion, the door to Angel's house opened as lights came on. Gabriella ran out, raced to Angel and hugged her tight while Angel's mother watched from the porch.

"You okay?" Angel asked as Gabriella clutched her mother.

"Sweetheart," Angel assured her daughter, "we'll be fine. Right, Charlie?"

"You'll be fine. I'll make sure."

Angel unclasped Gabriella's grasp. "Did you do your homework?"

Gabriella nodded. "Yes, ma'am." She let go of Angel and turned to face Charlie.

"Charlie, will you come to my birthday party?"

"I'd like to."

"Sweetheart, go inside with Nanna. I'll be right in."

"Yes, ma'am. Bye, Charlie."

"Bye, Gabriella."

Charlie knew he had to deal with Angel's danger. "Angel, as your attorney, I think you and Gabriella should enter protective custody. You're too vulnerable here – with her."

Angel considered. "Is this what my life has come to? Scurrying down a rabbit hole?"

Charlie looked into her eyes.

"You've got your daughter to think of."

"I'm thinking of how she'd miss her friends."

Charlie thought of the F.B.I.'s theory, that Candace lost her life in a turf battle among drug distribution rivals. He thought back on the Dart Construction files he copied. He'd have to pick up his car from Forest Park the following day. That was the least of his problems. Whether the Khazak-khans bowed to some megalomaniac enraged builder who had gone over the edge, or got their marching orders from an East Coast heroin mafia cartel was not important. Survival was.

Whoever sent them to finish off Candace Rollins had Charlie and Angel's name on the scribbled list.

"She'll make new friends – wherever you're safe. Should I call Trenton tomorrow? Work out the deal?" Angel's eyes looked directly into his.

"If I move on, it'll be on my terms. I'm not crawling into some hole in Tulsa. And I'm not going to leave my parents. They'd be vulnerable."

Charlie knew he wouldn't be able to look into Angel's beautiful eyes for long.

"What do you think? Want to come away with us? Rio? I've always wanted to live in Rio. The sun, the sand, the soft jazz?"

Charlie laughed self-consciously, not quite sure how to respond.

"Rio de Janeiro would be a lot of fun."

"How do you know?"

"We could find out."

Charlie was flustered. It was too dark on the street for Angel to see him blush, but silent enough for Angel to catch his self-conscious hint of an awkward laugh.

Angel understood his conflict, sighed.

Charlie knew this was a make-or-break moment with Angel. Angel's flirty offer was all too real. Charlie had other cards to play to help her get through this danger. His new role as the Thornhill family attorney might pave the way to safety for Angel and her family.

"I'll talk to Oscar. He may offer a way out of this."

"I'd be grateful, Charlie." Angel came very close. "Forever."

She gave him a hug, a very warm hug, a hug he disengaged from as he got into her car.

"Okay, Charlie. I'll drive you home."

CHAPTER 73
OSCAR'S DARK HEART

The diminutive white uniform clad Malaysian nurse, who introduced herself as "Teresse," led Charlie past the over-sized artwork hanging on each side of Malibu Meadows's muted-green hallways displaying cheerful blue-red-yellow swirls of art. Even Charlie could tell these were signed lithographs, not Art Emporium knockoffs. Charlie liked the *Bubble Times* lithographs for their cheery blue background and well-proportioned fields of bubbles. *These champagne bubbles celebrate life and happiness, or at least provide hope life would continue for patients.*

Charlie followed Teresse, entered Oscar's room and faced Oscar propped half-way up on the high-tech bed. Red and orange digital read-outs on a portable monitor displayed Oscar's every heart-beat. Several vials of vital liquids and medicines snaked through yellowed plastic tubes into taped receptacles sculpted onto Oscar's arms.

Desmond Thornhill intercepted Charlie's entrance into the room, shook Charlie's hand and thanked him for coming. Charlie looked around at the assembled relatives. There were at least eight adults gathered for the family pow-wow. Gertrude Thornhill, sat in the only arm-chair, presiding over her family.

Desmond led Charlie around the semi-circle of family members, introducing Charlie to the Thornhills' cousins, spouses, and an uncle, Fidelio Thornhill, who appeared to be the eldest in the room. Charlie thought he recognized the faces of several cousins.

"Charlie, this is Orville Sanders, first cousin on Oscar's father's side."

"Hi, Charlie. You're in the opera chorus, aren't you?"

"I'm a high baritone. Pleasure to meet you."

"Yes, I'm the tenor."

Charlie moved to the curly headed mustached middle aged man in the Hawaii style polo shirt.

"George Tamarind."

"Charlie Tobias. You're in the chorus, too, aren't you?"

"I'm a baritone, just like you. We sang together in *Pagliacci,* and also in *Faust.*"

Charlie realized aside from Oscar, four family members in the room were extras in the L.A. Opera chorus. He sang with them for several years, yet never met them socially.

"We're a musical family," Desmond added after finishing the introductions. Charlie may have forgotten most names he was just given, but he understood the purpose of the family get-together. The extended family members wanted the assets passed into Desmond Thornhill's control, so they could benefit from the Thornhill Amended Family Trust.

Charlie turned his attention to Oscar. Oscar's eyes were open, his stare was vacant.

"Hello, Oscar. How are you?"

There was no response. Oscar was sedated, or his consciousness was gone. Desmond got to the point of the meeting.

"Did you prepare the Pour-over?"

"Yes. I brought the document."

"Well, as you see, we have plenty of witnesses."

"Witnesses can't have an interest in the assets."

Desmond looked crestfallen, but regained his composure. "Bring in the staff."

George Tamarind stepped outside and returned with Scotty, the security guard, and Jenny, the nurse both of whom witnessed the main document signing during Charlie's first visit.

Charlie shook hands, thanked Scotty and Jenny for agreeing to witness the signature, and approached Oscar. It was unclear if Oscar's unmoving eyes recognized Charlie.

"Is he conscious?"

"Of course. He asked about you earlier."

Charlie had doubts Oscar was in a state to ask for anything except a stronger drip of morphine.

"Oscar? This is Charlie Tobias. Remember? From the opera?"

Oscar's face twisted into pained acknowledgment.

"I prepared the updated Trust Pour-over Will for you to sign. Is that what you want to do, Oscar?"

Oscar nodded feebly. Charlie was somewhat reassured as Oscar's eyes blinked approval. At least, Oscar seemed to have use of his faculties.

"This Pour-over Will includes all assets that weren't in the Amended Family Trust when you first became Trustee. Do you understand?"

Oscar nodded his head, added nervous eye blinks.

"You will have no further responsibility to administer the family trust. Signing the Pour-over also means you will have no income from the trust unless Desmond specifically authorizes it. Is that okay?"

Oscar winced from pain, but nodded again. "I won't go to Isis."

Charlie glanced out the picture window into the Pacific Ocean. The dark grey clouds overhanging the ocean lifted, leaving a corridor of bright low-lying sunshine. It would be a beautiful afternoon when the sun would break through as it descended into the sea.

Charlie motioned for Scotty and Jenny to step next to him to the side of the bed.

Oscar grasped Charlie's hand. Oscar's hand was bony, cold, but strong. Oscar's eyes lit up in recognition. Charlie pondered whether to go through each page of the Pour-over and have Oscar initial each page.

Charlie stood over Oscar. Oscar's eyes looked up at Charlie, the eyes pleaded with Charlie to end the ordeal.

Charlie considered whether Oscar may not be truly in a state to sign the document. Charlie turned to Desmond.

"I'm not sure Oscar can sign these documents. He can barely move."

"I want to." Oscar's eyes met Charlie's. "Please, Charlie."

Gertrude cried. Other family members sat silent.

Charlie considered his legal obligations. All these witnesses would attest to Oscar's desire to sign the document. On the other hand, they could also be intimidating, forming a chain around Oscar's bed, and overbearing his feeble body.

"Could you step outside?"

"We are his closest relatives."

"It will be just me, and the two witnesses. Please?"

Gertrude made the first move. "We'll wait outside."

The other Thornhills followed her solemn exit. Desmond's eyes pierced Charlie.

"Don't you need me?"

"I'll be fine with Oscar."

Charlie looked at Oscar's bony face. "Right?" Oscar formed the vestige of a smile in response, nodded.

Desmond turned and left the room after the others. Charlie recalled the Trustee had to assign plots of land and homes in the far off Greenland tundra to beneficiaries. Otherwise, if the Trustee died, the ownership of the properties reverted to David Alex's Vision Associates Company and the development would be controlled by whomever was Alex's heir. The Thornhills would lose out. Who knows who had acceded to the crown throne running Vision Associates after David Alex's death?

Charlie recalled Desmond emphasized the urgency of taking control of the properties before the development would be completed, so the deeds to the Isis homes could be signed by the Trustee.

"Thanks, Scotty, Jennie. You'll be the only witnesses. Right?

"Yes, sir." Scotty was no-nonsense. Jenny nodded assent.

"Shut the door, will you please?"

Jennie complied, came back to the bed.

"Oscar, please sign this Pour-over Will giving up your rights to all recent assets."

Charlie placed a pen into Oscar's right hand. Oscar took it with great difficulty. The fingers held on to the pen and scrawled across the signature line: "Oscar J. Thornhill."

"Please date it, next to your signature."

Oscar's fingers complied.

Charlie took the signed Pour-Over document, placed it on his clipboard in front of each witness. Scotty signed first in a scrambled scrawl. Charlie asked Scotty to print his name and address under his signature. Jenny's signature was legible. Each witness dated the document. Charlie signed over the line underneath which he had printed: "Charlie Tobias, Attorney at Law."

Charlie looked into his friend's eyes, squeezed Oscar's bony hand pockmarked from all the IV drip insertions. Charlie knew this would be the last time he'd see Oscar alive.

Oscar's grip became strong and pulled Charlie's entire body next to Oscar's face. Charlie's ear was next to Oscar's mouth. When Charlie heard the pained hoarse whisper "Charlie, I must tell you something very important..." Charlie moved his ear closer.

Jenny and Scotty acknowledged the request for privacy, stepped back. Jenny was about to leave the room.

"No. Just take a seat," Charlie instructed them. He knew once the hospital room door opened, the relatives would stream in like an unstoppable ice-laden mountain spring brook, and Oscar could never pass on the confidence.

His ear was next to Oscar's mouth. Charlie's hand was in Oscar's vise grip. Charlie concentrated on Oscar's unburdening.

Charlie understood Oscar was telling Charlie everything that happened so Oscar could leave the world as he had come into it, without false pretense or untruth.

Charlie nodded, indicating he understood Oscar's fragmented statements about meeting Barry, about his partnership, and about Barry Beneshan's final moments of life.

Charlie pieced together the disjointed words into a chronicle. Oscar had met Barry at Los Angeles airport on Barry's thirty-third birthday in the summer of 2006, drove him back to Barry's Venice cottage. He had patiently tried to get Barry to agree to a pay-back plan for all his owed moneys from Blue Orchid's loan to Clean Co. Oscar was in a bind, unable to make the final payment due Vision Associates, and was in danger of default. It hadn't been part of the plan to hurt Barry.

"I did things I deeply regret. I took the moneys he had on him to pay off the payment due for Isis." Charlie took in Oscar's confession. *So, that's what happened in that Venice hideaway on Barry's birthday.* Unlike when Devlin confessed, Charlie believed Oscar did end Barry Beneshan's life.

Charlie knew he was not invested with religious power to dispense forgiveness with instruction to recite a certain number of prayers, and petition for absolution, but he had to give Oscar something, to bring peace to the dying man.

Charlie whispered to Oscar, what Angel asked him to pass on, and about the danger she and her daughter were in.

Charlie also confided she had wanted to come see Oscar, and wanted him to know about Gabriella. Oscar smiled. He understood Charlie wasn't condemning him for his murderous act, ending Barry Beneshan's life to steal the $200,000 cash in his vest.

Oscar was also relieved to hear about Gabriella doing well.

"She's my daughter, Charlie. My child with Angel."

In this moment of Oscar's candor, Charlie couldn't straighten up. He nodded as best as he could, leaning inches from Oscar's face, not certain he heard correctly.

"I was a coward." Oscar whispered. "I should have married Angel after the baby was born."

"You took care of your daughter."

"I should have stood up to Gertrude."

"She is a very powerful woman."

"I paid Barry to adopt Gabriella when she was an infant. I became Barry's silent investor. Gabriella didn't know. Angel promised never to tell and she never did."

Charlie squeezed Oscar's hand in reassurance. Oscar relaxed his vice grip and Charlie pulled away, bit by bit, as gently as he could.

"The family will take care of Angel and my child." As Oscar's whispered words exploded into Charlie's ear with weak breaths of gasping air, and finally halted, Charlie lifted himself slightly and his eyes locked with Oscar's. Oscar's face distorted from pain. The grip on Charlie's hand loosened, and Charlie pulled back slowly.

"Good-bye, Charlie." Oscar's eyes closed, his lips formed a hint of a smile as his unburdening transferred the moral pain of his heinous acts to Charlie.

CHAPTER 74
GOT TO WATCH YOUR BACK

It was dress rehearsal time, two weeks before opening night. The other extras were suited up. Fidelio Thornhill, nodded to Charlie across the costume rack as the swarthy Thornhill cousin was about to disappear inside his mosquito face mask. Charlie nodded back as he scooted his costume off the rack.

"Oscar died last night."

"At least his suffering has ended."

"Thank you for doing your assignment promptly."

Orville Sanders, half-costumed, walked over, shook Charlie's hand.

"Oscar told us to take care of you."

"It was an honor to be Oscar's friend."

Gerry flew by. "Five minutes to curtain time."

Charlie zipped up his costume. He thought back on Oscar's last moments on earth. Angel's intuition about Devlin had been spot-on. Barry was already dead when Devlin, furious and desperate, raced to Barry's cottage, saw Barry's body on the bathroom floor, smothered it, thinking Barry had injured himself from a drug induced fall, and taken the jacket, having overheard Angel talk to Barry about some two hundred thousand dollars in cash sewn into the lining.

Oscar had already left with the moneys sewn into the vest's inner lining. Devlin never found out why he missed out, but lived with the guilt of believing he was Barry's executioner.

A firm hand from behind caused Charlie to turn and face Desmond. "Oscar passed away last night. He told me about Oscar's child. Gertrude has agreed we'll take care of her, and her mother."

Veronica came by to adjust each singer's costume, cutting the conversation short.

"So, how's it going, Charlie?"

"I'm here, Flora. Glad to be here. Real glad."

"Me, too. Getting through is the name of the game. I did get some promising news."

"From – ?"

"The San Francisco Opera Company. They like my portfolio."

"You're so talented. Congratulations."

"We'll see. I'd miss you, Charlie."

Charlie thought for a moment. "I'd miss you, Flora."

Veronica, pleased to hear the feeling was mutual, adjusted Charlie's headpiece, making sure the curled proboscis uncurled easily when Charlie clenched his fist with the electronic switch.

"You're my favorite bug."

Charlie acknowledged her compliment with a self-conscious laugh. Veronica returned the laugh good naturedly, and moved on.

Charlie ambled between Desmond and Fidelio towards back stage.

"Thank you. Your work has made it possible for the family to survive. In Isis, we'll live in harmony with nature. Our homes are self-sufficient and don't spew deadly fumes and dangerous toxins. Oscar was a visionary."

Charlie never knew about Oscar's bent for utopian social engineering. Charlie knew Oscar loved singing in the choir. Oscar gave no hint the weight of being responsible for hundreds of millions of dollars rested on his shoulders, nor did he give any hint, even when playing the most despicable theatrical villain, that he was capable of murder!

As the extras stopped behind the curtain, Desmond, flanked by Fidelio, faced Charlie.

"Charlie, Gertrude has invited your family to join us."

Charlie was puzzled. "Join you?"

"In Isis. You see what's happening everywhere. The oceans are vengeful because of spewing human filth. Tempests and tsunamis already unleash revenge on man. None of us, those who oppose man's base instincts, – will survive. We're no match for desperate yahoos with AK-47's and rage in their hearts."

Charlie thought back on what he already witnessed in his weekend trip to New Orleans: the downtrodden and the weak succumbed quietly in post-Katrina New Orleans.

"Now that Oscar has passed, there is an extra home in Isis. It would be for your family."

"That's very generous."

"Oscar wanted you to come."

"Quit buzzing! Two minutes to curtain time." Gerry pushed the three extras into their final single-line stage position. "And put your head-piece on," he barked at Desmond.

"Charlie, don't you understand, *West Nile* is about our own death?"

"It's a musical play, Desmond."

"It's a final warning."

As Desmond placed his paper mache head-piece over his costume's cushioned collar, Charlie glanced at the spectacular stage set.

The backyard pool was blood red. Rudolph Starlight, was on his patio lounge death bed, under the patio, surrounded by his hapless family.

Gerry, stressed, pulling at his rumpled hair, adjusted his intercom. This was the final rehearsal.

"All right, on the fourth chord, onto the stage."

Maestro Nandor Picollini, raised his baton and counted out the beats. "Now. Go."

Charlie and the other chorus members hopped on stage.

Chorus
We feast on your blood,
We suck on your skin.
We're messengers of death
Who spread plague to your kin -

Charlie, mimicked the mosquitoes' "buzz" as the chorus circled Rudolph Starlight's family.

The trumpets' staccato heralded a full size helicopter that appeared overhead. The ominous flying machine was anchored by unseen pulleys above the stage. Charlie heard there had been a major dispute about the helicopter. Gerry privately counseled mosquitoes not to spend time underneath the flying prop, just in case.

The helicopter edged across the top of the stage proscenium, emitting puffs of grey smoke that swirled down, enveloping the players.

Charlie heard the Assistant Director's voice off-stage shout directions for each insect to fall and die. He saw Gerry's gestures.

Charlie remembered he was "number six" and fell onto the stage, on cue. Charlie and the other mosquitoes lay on stage, sang a vibrato death "buzz." Charlie wished he could sleep. He was so tired. Charlie lay on the painted stage floor, trying not to inhale the helicopter's enveloping fog pushed onto the stage by four stage fog machines.

As he lay, Charlie recalled Angel recount how she met Barry Beneshan. It had been during the last outbreak of the actual West Nile pestilence that moved across Los Angeles some twelve years ago in the mid 1990's with deadly results. Angelenos died in neighborhoods all over the city without knowing what they were dying from, before the health authorities found the common link: *flaviviridae* or "the West Nile virus."

Government health department helicopter fly-overs multiplied as the death toll passed into panic, whipped by alarming newspaper headlines. Helicopters flew over suburban homes and apartment buildings at all night hours, spewing toxic sprays. The nocturnal bombing runs lasted for months.

Angel confided to Charlie that, at the time, she was an assistant at a film commercial house in Hollywood. She overheard customers mention Barry's Clean Co. in the San Fernando Valley was hiring. She was tired of the high-stress commercial film business, had gumption, showed up to the Clean Co. office in Canoga Park and clicked with wunderkind entrepreneur Barry Beneshan. He was her junior but already a local legend featured in the "Business" section of the city's two major newspapers with his cleaning company empire. She worked as an Account Representative for Clean Co. Business boomed while the West Nile pestilence peaked. There was talk of Barry taking Clean Co. to the New York Stock Exchange and going national.

Then, the pestilence faded and Clean Co.'s business faltered. Barry Beneshan lost his first fortune when he was only twenty-three years old and was no longer on the scene. Angel fell for Oscar Thornhill who courted her after meeting her at an exclusive Thornhill affair she crashed with her girl-friend.

Several years of on-and-off dating and a daughter between them, Angel ended the relationship after Oscar clarified he would never marry her.

Angel had an infant to support. The Thornhill family cut off aid. She didn't have the means to go after Oscar for child support.

Angel returned to work as an account executive for throw-away newspapers' advertising clients. She was personable, learned the business, signed up local pizza parlors, dry cleaners and auto repair shops, and was able to make a living, but was unhappy at having been ejected by Oscar and the Thornhills from a better life for her and for her daughter. Barry, on the rebound, came courting and she was willing. He was good with Gabriella and she soon came to accept Barry as her dad. Angel never told Gabriella otherwise. It was a shock when Oscar re-entered the scene as Barry's friend and business partner in Barry's new business ventures. Angel had lost her love and admiration for Oscar but acceded to his visits to her home for the sake of Gabriella. She knew instinctively, Oscar could and did make a difference.

Angel had no idea Barry disappeared from her life because he ran afoul of the feds and traded his federal fraud indictment by a secret grand jury for a dangerous four year stint with the Navy Special Operations Unit.

When Barry reappeared, some four and a half years later, he made a winning play to re-unite with Angel. He loved Gabriella and loved her. Barry and his partner, military buddy Jack Wonder had some business in Woodfall involving Cham refugees.

Barry was in Woodfall most of the time. When Barry showed up to be with Angel and Gabriella, he would unload bundles of cash on Angel's kitchen table, tell her to take care of herself and Gabriella. Life was too much of a struggle for Angel to worry about the "why?" and "how?"

Then, in 2005, Barry moved Clean Co. to New Orleans. There, government response to Hurricane Katrina's ravages changed from anemic to spending billions of dollars into rebuilding flooded parishes. Business boomed for Clean Co. just as Barry Beneshan died in June, 2006 at the age of thirty-three.

Charlie awoke from his half-doze as the crescendo of orchestra horns announced the score's cacophonic finale that foreshadowed the show's apocalyptic end. Rudolph Starlight expired on his patio lounge chair, overlooking the swimming pool. Swirls of the aerial spray obscured the stage. Maria Starlight threw herself across her husband's lifeless body, wailing her final aria, *I Loved Everything About You.* The helicopter disappeared behind thick swirling smoke.

A forklift rumbled behind the prostrate mosquitoes. The first mosquito extra rolled onto the forklift's giant scoop.

The forklift ambled behind the deceased Starlight family and the swimming pool.

The audience would never see the chorus mosquitoes rolled into the floor opening just under the stage line, behind the swimming pool, not into the pool itself.

Charlie saw Desmond fall into the stage floor opening.

Charlie's turn was next. Charlie rolled over the opening, fell onto the hidden air mattress. Once he was under the eye-line of the stage floor, Charlie rolled off the air mattress end, tried to stand up.

Two cold claws grabbed his neck and squeezed.

The paper mache headpiece crumbled. He felt the pressure on his throat, gasped for breath.

Charlie tried to reach behind to push away the unseen assailant, but Charlie coughed and grew dizzy. His claws couldn't push open the brutal suffocating arms of his unseen assailant. Charlie was being pulled backwards into oblivion.

There was a scuffle behind him. Charlie tottered, gasped for breath, righted himself, couldn't see behind but took the moment to pull away from the fray as the assailant's claws loosened around his throat and Charlie regained his equilibrium.

He stood upright, grabbed the tentacle claws and pushed apart with all his strength.

The scuffle in the darkness became more agitated. He heard a muffled gasp.

Charlie broke free. Adrenalin pumped through his body as he scurried towards the dressing room. He hopped fast and pulled his head covering off.

Charlie made it to the dressing room, and threw off his costume, gasped for breath.

"You okay, Charlie?" Fidelio Thornhill hung his folded costume onto the hanger, adjusted his street clothes.

Charlie threw on his street-clothes, gasped, nodded.

"I guess." He coughed from the pressure on his neck.

"Hey, relax. It's just the rehearsal."

Charlie knew Fidelio had been in front of him, looked around, didn't see Desmond. Charlie's breathing calmed.

"Where's Desmond?"

"He just left. I'll see you Charlie." Fidelio walked away. "Come with us to Isis."

Charlie looked warily as other mosquitoes came in from the rehearsal. He saw no Thornhills. Charlie tried to stay out of the extras' way, folded his costume across the hangers, jumped into his shirt and slacks, signed out and headed for the elevator, still glancing over his shoulder.

It could have been his imagination from sheer exhaustion, an accidental mélange of groping hands in the dark trying to hold onto something to avoid a fall, but Charlie still shaking, could swear: *Someone just tried to kill me!*

CHAPTER 75
FREEWAY PONDERINGS

Charlie drove out from the Music Center parking garage, gasping, shaking his bruised neck to minimize the pain, but calmed as his car headed home without passing Hollywood night-life traffic bottlenecks. As the car slipped by the Hollywood Bowl, Charlie's mind and breathing cleared, and his fear of the backstage incident momentarily erased from his mind as a lightning flash of exuberance from years ago coursed through his consciousness, sparked by the well-lit "Hollywood Bowl Exit" traffic sign he passed.

Charlie's feelings recaptured the happiness of his only singing role in the Hollywood Bowl Master Choir performance about fifteen years ago – a stunning performance of Mozart's *Requiem in D minor, K 626*. He had been a substitute for a choir regular, walking out on stage under the art-deco Bowl shell near the front row, just off-center from the solo singers. Facing the audience of some twenty thousand in the Bowl's majestic setting on a late autumn evening in 1993, was exhilarating, a community music celebration on a grand scale.

Charlie had not been asked to return for another Bowl performance. There was no point calling to ask to be considered or sending a resume. As in many professions, if you wanted to sing in a chorus, people had to know your reputation, and instinctively conjure up your name in their consciousness when opportunity arose.

The car raced along the Hollywood freeway over the Cahuenga Pass Charlie rubbed his neck with his free left hand. He seemed to be okay. Charlie repeated the mantra: it was just one of the extras, grabbing onto something solid to raise himself from the deflating air mattress.

As Charlie's car descended into the San Fernando Valley, the grid of suburban lights spread for miles. A rim of darkness cast by the encircling San Gabriel Mountains was protective and also ominous. The mountains were dark as Charlie's heart. Too many concerns weighed on Charlie.

Charlie thought through his options. He had chosen a second calling as an attorney, a servant of justice, part of the fabric of what makes society function. Within that ordered framework, being an attorney at law, he also had to decide: how to carry out what he knew was right, and how to survive.

On the one hand, he represented Angel, and had a duty to act in her best interest, but he was also an Officer of the Court. She had inadvertently been placed in a position of danger but the government proposed an out: disappear, start life over in Tulsa, Oklahoma under another identity. Charlie couldn't see Angel as a hairdresser, yet that was a real option for her – and for her daughter. The government proposal was likely a wise choice, even if it would leave an open wound in Charlie's heart. It would also create a major problem in the form of the unfinished business left for the estate. Charlie knew Earl would be furious, fearing the Law Offices would not get paid.

Charlie also represented Oscar Thornhill and learned about the darkness at the center of Oscar's heart through a legal confidence.

Oscar, on his deathbed, when only Charlie was next to him, confessed the details of how he killed Barry Beneshan. The details were convincing to Charlie.

Oscar picked up Barry from Los Angeles International Airport. He drove Barry to the Venice cottage on Barry's thirty-third birthday. Oscar, wary of Barry's broken promises to repay the moneys Oscar desperately needed to pay off the Isis contract owed to David Alex, had brought a bottle of *Paris Perignon* champagne with him, two flute glasses to celebrate, and a strong sedative to knock Barry out, if Barry wasn't forthcoming. That night, Barry wasn't just unwilling to pay the debt he had repeatedly promised to pay, he even laughed in Oscar's face, and told him Barry was scooping Angel and Oscar's daughter, his own flesh and blood, off to some Mediterranean island to a new life.

Barry laughed without shame at Oscar, opened the offered *Paris Perignon* and poured the champagne in a show of complete contempt.

Oscar saw his chance when Barry turned to open his luggage. Oscar poured the sedative into Barry's glass.

As the two men lifted their glasses, toasted, and drank the champagne, Barry's eyes gloated in the near-dark, savoring his triumph over his rival for Angel's love. Oscar's eyes responded with a neutral sad gaze, blinking often, to hide his murderous feelings of loathing. Barry started to feel woozy, and excused himself to go to the bathroom. Oscar put away the incriminating glasses and bottle into his recyclable bag, stretched yellow latex gloves over both hands, followed Barry into the bathroom, watched as Barry swooned from the sedative, and fell prone onto the tiles near the toilet. Oscar turned Barry over, looked at the circle of wetness on Barry's pants, reached down to Barry's face, shut off Barry's over-sized nostrils and unevenly formed pedestrian mouth, and proceeded to push on Barry's larynx for several minutes in controlled rage, until Oscar was sure there was no life in the prone body.

At one point, Barry's eyes bulged open. He looked up at Oscar. Oscar confessed to Charlie he was uncertain if Barry recognized Oscar as his messenger of death.

Oscar had done this, not so much out of any personal animus Barry was the pretend father of his daughter with Angel, but because Oscar was desperate to get cash to pay off Alex and retain control of Isis.

While Charlie listened to the confession, he hid his own disgust at the recital of the greatest of Moses' Old Testament ten commandment sins, *Thou shalt not murder.* Oscar whispered he gave Barry every chance to make things right. Previous to the final Venice cottage confrontation, Oscar had implored Barry on the phone: "We need the cash, for the family. You've got to pay me back!"

"Don't worry. The moneys are in the Clean Co. safe. Once I'm out of here, you get the cash." Barry had given Oscar the New Orleans safe combination which he assured Oscar no one else had.

That last lie pushed Oscar's anger over the edge and made him bring the sedative and prepare the contingency plan. How stupid did Barry think Oscar was?

Barry, clever as he was, made one mistake, which proved to be fatal.

The small monthly stipend Oscar paid Candace Rollins for some two years to keep track of what was going on, ever since she moved to New Orleans with Clean Co., paid off. She called Oscar with the news just before Barry was to arrive back at Los Angeles International Airport.

"Barry has two X-ray-proof lead liners inside his vest, each with an accessible, hidden zipper," Rollins confided to Oscar in a hastily placed telephone call. Candace Rollins was anxious about Barry's assurance he would leave Clean Co.'s cash to her. She needed the cash in the *La Reve du Monde* safe to keep Clean Co. afloat, and she had no access. Her hunch that Barry would steal the moneys was accurate, and Oscar got his hands on the money in the vest liner – the money needed to make the final payment to David Alex for Isis.

Charlie considered the legal rules: If Oscar had told the truth and suffocated Barry, then, Oscar's murderous act was a past event, and didn't threaten any future death. So, Charlie had no legal obligation to turn his dead client in. Charlie recalled that in California, "attorney-client" privilege survived death.

As far as David Alex's death? Considering Eric Dart's rivalry to Oscar, Dart was a far more likely suspect to snuff Alex than Oscar, especially as Oscar had made a point of describing the final payment he made to David Alex with Barry's stolen cash.

Detective Oswilla had not arrested his two TV actor suspects for Alex's murder. Only if the comedy stars were arrested, only then would Charlie have to reveal what he knew in the interests of justice – no matter what the risk to his welfare. As Charlie veered right to head onto the Ventura Freeway, Charlie wondered if the Feds would offer him a protective custody alternative in Tulsa to take him away from Eric Dart's revenge.

The comedy actors and Eric Dart weren't the only Alex murder suspects. The F.B.I. believed the two "Khazak-khan" goons murdered the debt collector in Alex's office who they mistook for David Alex, as well as finished off Candace Rollins and executed Will Wonder. To Charlie, the F.B.I.'s suspicions about the two dead goons made sense. The goons were David Alex's likely murderers. At least the goons were no longer able to come harm Charlie.

Why tip the boat?

To Charlie, being a probate attorney started as a day job to get some needed income. How had it come to this?

Charlie recalled his intimate dinner with Colette St. Pierre at "Antoine's" in New Orleans. He had been enamored with her physical beauty, but also attracted by the internal harmony she exuded which made him rethink why he had taken an Oath to uphold the U.S. Constitution some eight years ago.

Colette was passionate about her profession, not as a day job, but because she believed in the sacred pledge attorneys take – to promote justice and the law.

Charlie shook off the memories of the night in New Orleans, the sensual gaze of Colette's dark, passionate eyes, reflecting the single dining table candle between them, making him want to reach out to her in forbidden ways.

He couldn't deal with all the implications of what justice was about in his dangerous circumstance.

Charlie's breathing was uneven, as he passed the eastern San Fernando Valley communities, Studio City, Valley Village, Sherman Oaks. Charlie calmed, helped by the empty freeway's hypnotic painted white lane lines disappearing underneath his hurtling car.

Charlie pondered his deepest feelings about the law and what his role was to play.

As Charlie passed the intersection of the Ventura and San Diego Freeways, the most congested traffic nightmare in the United States, Charlie saw the talisman for his own legal nightmare take shape, and concluded he had no professional duty to inform the court of Oscar's death-bed confession, but did have a professional duty to keep mum about Angel's decision to vanish into federal protective custody, even if it would violate the Rules of Professional Conduct and subject him to attorney discipline, or worse.

Angel's right to life trumped all.

As Charlie exited the freeway off the Haskell Avenue off-ramp, his cell phone rang. Charlie knew better than to pick it up, but did anyway.

Angel's voice was hysterical: "Charlie, please come help."

Charlie curved along the winding dark street, his heart beat. "What's going on?"

"They broke the window! Someone's coming in. Help!"

Charlie grabbed the grimy steering wheel hard as he passed Oxnard Street, luckily while the traffic light was yellow. The next street was Shadow Lane Drive. He turned on his blinkers to indicate the left-hand turn he planned to make to go home.

"Charlie. I'm getting Gabriella. Please, help."

Charlie's heart sank.

"I'm coming."

CHAPTER 76
ANGEL HAS VANISHED

The sliding metal gate in front of Angel's home was open. Charlie raced to the dimly lit front entrance and pushed the jarred front door in.

"Angel?"

Sirens down the street and noises inside the house accompanied Charlie's burst into the house in stereo cacophony. A prone disheveled crew-cut, middle-aged man, in T-shirt and jeans, and barefoot lay on the couch, cell phone in hand, crying.

Charlie ran up to him.

"Where's Angel?"

"She's gone – Gabriella, too."

Charlie recognized the hoarse voice even though he couldn't recognize the banged up crying face. "You – are Gary?"

"Yeah. Gary Frank." He looked up. "Who are you?"

"Charlie Tobias. You called me about David Alex's death? Remember I was at Devlin's memorial?" The bruised man sat up, held his scarred cheek, bloodied eye, and looked closely at Charlie.

"I live in the attic. I remember you."

"Good start."

"I came in to the living room, tried to stop the abductors. They burst in and surrounded Angel."

Charlie recalled Gary Frank's hysterical call about the dead body in Alex's office started the chain of events that led to Alex's suffocation in Charlie's studio. Charlie was wary of all mortgage brokers, especially after having been duped into misleading the court by Gary Frank's phone call.

Gary Frank's very black left eye and a bruised left cheek softened Charlie's suspicion.

Charlie pulled out his cell phone.

Gary blurted: "I've called '911.'"

The police sirens screamed closer, suddenly became silent. "I fought, but they grabbed Angel and forced her to get her daughter."

"Who are 'they'?"

"Two over-age Dick Dale stoned surfers. One sported a slick-backed hair-do I haven't seen since the '70's."

Charlie heard a shouted command behind him: "Freeze. Hands in the air."

Charlie complied instantly.

Gary looked over Charlie's head. "Officers. I called '911'. He's our attorney."

Charlie felt the pat-down from behind him. "Let's see your bar card?"

"Can I lower my arms?"

"Easy. Turn around slowly."

If you learned nothing else in law school, you learned to follow directions to the "t." For the moment, this was a good skill to have. Charlie faced a towering police officer, a copycat of a movie android.

Charlie slowly reached into his pocket, pulled out his wallet, scrambled for his bar card and handed it across.

The police android clone took Charlie's bar card, scanned it suspiciously. Other L.A.P.D. officers swarmed into the house, guns drawn, scattered to the back and went up the stairs.

"All clear." One officer from the bedroom called to the Sergeant who faced Charlie. The voice from upstairs echoed, "all clear upstairs."

Agents with "F.B.I." logos on their high-tech membrane bullet proof vests, raced in, and paired opposite the L.A.P.D. officers who staked out the small house.

Two paramedics pushing a "Medic-sav" cart bee-lined to Gary Frank who appeared to be the only civilian needing rescue. One medic swung a flashlight into Gary's face and instructed him to follow the light beam with his eyes. The second medic attached electrodes to Gary's left arm and checked the "Medic-sav" dials and digital call-outs.

The L.A.P.D. Sergeant returned Charlie's bar card, satisfied Charlie was who he said he was.

Detective Philip Oswilla wheeled himself past the narrow doorway.

"Nice to see you, Charlie."

"Glad to see you, Detective."

"Talk to me, Charlie." Before Charlie could answer, F.B.I. agent Long stepped through the front door. "Hold it everyone, this is a federal matter."

Charlie sat down slowly on the couch next to the injured lodger. Detective Oswilla whirled his wheelchair around, pinching agent Long's shiny black left shoe.

"Sorry." Oswilla backed off, couldn't help suppress a sneer as Long hobbled backwards.

"Oswilla, I have a grand jury fraud indictment to support my case. You've got zip."

"This is an abduction in the city of Los Angeles. It's my jurisdiction."

"The New Orleans grand jury found probable cause to investigate this house as a link in a 'drugs for money for pay-off indictment.' It's a secret grand jury indictment. If you go public and tip the suspects with headlines, I'll make sure you lose your power scooter!"

"If you withheld evidence from my case, I may have a chat with your superiors about your failure to prevent two homicides where you were present."

Agent Long calmed. "Look, I ask the questions. Your turn comes later."

Detective Oswilla turned to Charlie. "Talk to him, Charlie."

"So, Mr. Tobias, why'd you turn up here?"

"I'm Angel's attorney. Angel called me for help."

"What do you say, Mr. black-eyed pea?"

"I live in the attic. The dudes burst in, took Angel and her daughter. I tried to stop them."

"Who's this witness?"

"I'm Gary Frank. I called '911.'"

"New boyfriend?"

"Friend. I rent the attic. Remember? I took Angel's daughter home from the North Church memorial."

"Smart man. You saw what happened to that Devlin guy."

"Angel's been good to me."

"Who took them away?"

Gary shook his head. "Two older surfer dudes and a middle-age chick in a bikini and tank top burst in, argued with Angel. I heard them from upstairs. They pushed Angel to the bedroom to get her daughter packed."

"Ever see them before?"

Gary shook his head side to side. "I heard more arguing. I came down, just as the dudes and chick forced them out of the house. I tried to stop the dudes, got a black eye for my troubles. They were stoned."

Detective Oswilla concluded. "It's an abduction, officer." F.B.I. Agent Long shifted from foot to foot, unable to disagree.

Oswilla turned to Charlie: "Any ideas, counselor?"

Charlie shook his head.

"Let's put out an A.P.B." Detective Oswilla was matter-of-fact.

"Did you see the surfer dudes' woody?" Detective Oswilla had his note-pad out. Gary's left eye was being swabbed by the medic's q-tip.

"A Porsche SUV – silver gray."

Oswilla jotted the information. "Figures." Oswilla finished writing. "Take him in to E.R. at West Hills. Have him checked out."

"I'm okay."

"You could have a concussion."

"I don't have health insurance. Why do you think I rent?" Gary Frank pushed the paramedics away.

Detective Oswilla took charge: "It's up to the vic."

Charlie patted Gary's arm. "Need anything?"

Gary shook his head, cried.

"Let's go everybody. A.P.B. – put it out right now. Amber alert. Notify regional airports. LAX, Ontario, Burbank. Private airports, too, especially nearby Van Nuys Airport. They could fly out of the country on a private plane."

Charlie recalled Angel's talk about flying off to Rio. Oswilla looked into Charlie's eyes.

Charlie backed away. "I've got to get some sleep."

"Call if something develops."

"You, too. She's my client."

Oswilla pushed his wheelchair to the back. Long, surrounded by his F.B.I. agents, wrote a report. Gary Frank lay back down on the couch as one officer got out his report form and wrote the formal witness report.

Charlie wandered into the front yard. He looked at the moon. It was full. Its valleys and indentations were clearly visible above the dark tree-lined suburban street. The moon seemed so close, yet, Charlie couldn't reach the far off world as he wished to do at the moment. Charlie was angry at himself. While he was pondering the subtleties of the justice system and his role as a probate attorney, something shattering had happened. Not only had he lost a client, he lost Angel!

It wasn't the same thing. Sick at heart, he headed back to his car.

CHAPTER 77
IT'S ABOUT THE MONEY

The next morning, Charlie forced himself to stay on automatic pilot, not think about the dreadful events during the previous night as he crawled out of bed, showered, threw on his suit pants and tie, grabbed his suit jacket, left the house with Tina still asleep, and raced to work early. He knew he had to get letters out for other cases and file court documents for deadlines in the Mobley case, before he had to face Earl Guarder's volcanic blow.

Charlie prepared to tell Earl about the abduction. Earl would have a fit. Charlie pondered what scumbags dared break in and take a court administrator and a minor against their will. Or was it her way to escape the witness protection plan? He wasn't sure.

Charlie reached the Law Offices, hurried through his assignments on autopilot. He kept hearing Angel's voice replay "Charlie, come help" in his mind. He was about to call Angel's house, see if Gary received a call from Angel or her abductors when Earl sauntered in to the office about 10:30 a.m. Earl was in a flashy, perfectly tailored silver business suit, polka-dot splashed blue silk tie, and was in a good mood. Charlie took a deep breath, walked into Earl Guarder's office and was blunt and direct.

"Angel and her daughter were kidnapped last night!"

Charlie might as well have socked Earl with a fight-ending right upper-cut directly to the jaw. Earl fell back into his squeaky leather chair and stared at Charlie.

"Why didn't you stop it?"

"I got there too late." Charlie silently kicked himself for his reply. Was saving clients from abductors part of his job? Maybe not, but was saving Angel his job?

Earl Guarder opened his mouth repeatedly, formed words, but no words came out.

"She called me for help Sunday around midnight. I got there just as the cops stormed her house. Detective Oswilla, the detective in charge of the David Alex homicide showed up. So did Thomas Long, the F.B.I. lead agent."

"The F.B.I.? What? Why the F.B.I.?"

"They had Barry Beneshan on their radar in New Orleans for some big RICO violation before he died."

"Why didn't you tell me this before?"

"I found out two days ago, Saturday, I attended the Forest Park funeral service for Angel's friend, Devlin D'Alessio. There was a shoot-out. The F.B.I. ordered Angel to the Federal building for an interview. I went with Angel. At the interview on Saturday afternoon they told us about their Beneshan investigation."

"I saw something on the news. Yes, a shoot-out at some Forest Park service. Two ugly mugs, dead. You should have called me."

"I left you a text."

"Yes, I was in a golf tournament for the Juvenile Diabetes Fundraiser over at the Brandywine Country Club."

"You never texted back."

"What was the gun play?"

Charlie thought it best not to go into details. "I'm not sure. But at their headquarters, the F.B.I. ordered Angel take herself and her daughter into protective custody. She bristled. You know Angel."

"Spunky woman. Did she ask you for legal advice?"

Charlie considered. She hadn't asked Charlie what she should do.

He shook his head "no."

"We're fine. She'll show up. We need our administrator." Charlie thought best to stay silent. Earl's relief was momentary. "What about the money in the blocked account?"

"The abduction happened last night!"

"Call the bank. Make sure no one can access the money. We need to get our fees."

"It's a blocked account."

"Make sure. Get over there!"

Charlie nodded.

"Do it! Is this office a never-ending ATM? The ATM's got to be filled."

Charlie retreated. He wasn't sure what to make of Angel's abduction. Kidnappers don't drive fancy sport cars, wear Hawaiian shirts, and bring along their surfer bunnies. He grabbed his valise and was about to head out the door. Earl ran after him.

"Don't tell anyone. Put down your time. The memorial, the F.B.I. meeting, the abduction. All the time. Call it a "conference with administrator and jurisdictional authorities."

Charlie nodded. He wasn't sure the abduction would be a secret the Law Firm could keep for long. If anything happened to Angel and her daughter? He'd never forgive himself. In the meantime, there was nothing he could think of doing to track her down, so he'd follow Earl's instructions.

CHAPTER 78
"HOW'S YOUR DAY GOING?"

The meeting with the Greater First Bank of Trust officers was bound to take longer than the fifteen minutes the Bank's parking lot validated, and Earl was unlikely to reimburse the additional $15 for parking. Charlie recalled that Greek guy, Sisyphus who kept rolling the rock uphill, but continually fell further into the chasm.

Charlie circled the block, and pulled his sedan into an open street parking spot.

Charlie grabbed his valise into which he dumped his "Order" to open the blocked account, from the car seat.

Charlie hurried into the Greater First Bank of Trust's lobby and met Amir, the bank concierge, who asked how the bank could help Charlie. Ever since the 2008 big bank failures, bank employees appeared to be more helpful.

Charlie told Amir he needed to talk to an officer about the security of a blocked account.

Amir introduced him to an anorexic bank officer, with blonde hair falling around her face, smiling up at Charlie from her cubicle seat. "How's your day going so far?"

He knew Heather didn't want to know. He reached into his valise, pulled out his file and placed the signed Order from Judge Bittenkopf on the curved desk facing the trim employee in the recycled airline-stewardess polyester suit with the shiny "Heather" name badge.

"We opened a blocked account a short time ago."

Heather scanned the Order. "Yes, I remember, Angel Sedona is the estate administrator. She's allowed to write on the account up to $10,000."

"That's right." Charlie hesitated: "Block the account completely. We have an emergency."

Heather accessed the account on the computer. "Well, I guess we could do that without a court Order, although we'd prefer you get one."

"Please do it, *now*."

Heather scanned the computer more closely. "I'm not sure it would make any difference. There's no money in the account. It's all been withdrawn."

Heather's look at Charlie was neutral. Charlie tried to suppress his panic, but couldn't.

"How could that much be withdrawn?"

"It was in $5,000 amounts, one withdrawal each day for the last five weeks. A total of $100,000. I guess it was twenty withdrawals at the bank counter. In small bills."

Charlie's heart raced as if he were a two year colt spurting in the Kentucky Derby. He shuddered, reminded he had sent out the $50,000 check to Jones, Sharke a few days ago, and it would bounce.

"Who withdrew the moneys?"

The woman looked at him, puzzled. "What is your name?"

"I'm Attorney Charlie Tobias."

"You did, Mr. Tobias."

Air escaped his lungs in a slow "whoosh." The blood from his body suspended a vacuum of terrified circulating void. He grabbed the edge of the pressboard and laminate desk to keep from collapsing to the ground. Images of criminal charges, prison whirled in his head. Charlie tried to calm. If he said anything now, it would start a chain of events with the bank investigation that could devastate his world.

Charlie shook off concern for legal niceties. He didn't care about the bar responsibility rules anymore. Strength returned and the void in his bloodstream ended.

"No, I didn't. I haven't been here."

The woman's eyes froze on Charlie. "I have to bring in my supervisor."

Charlie's pulse galloped, and the laminated plastic desk crumbled between his clenched fingers.

"Oh, I'm so sorry."

"Don't worry about it. It's fake wood."

Heather dialed the inter-office phone.

"Mr. Mengers, this is Heather at Station Two. We have a problem."

CHAPTER 79
AN UNEXPECTED RUN-IN

Charlie barely recalled driving back to Earl Guarder's office. The bank supervisor interviewed Charlie for a half hour about the vanished moneys. Manager Bob Mengers, with his combed-over thinning brown hair and bushy arched eyebrows, was courteous, professional and non-accusatory and threw in the aside "one or more checks may have been returned from their payee." He smiled. "We'll waive the overdraft charge."

Charlie groaned at the news of the overdraft, but was more concerned about his own hide than to worry about any bounced $50,000 check to Jones, Sharke.

Luckily, Mengers called over several tellers who recalled the $5,000 transactions and thought back on the customers who signed for the withdrawn moneys.

Both sweet-faced Alina, an Iranian teller, with large beautiful brown eyes, and Katrina, a tall, beautiful, voluptuous Russian, who spoke English with a sexy Slavic accent, verified that whoever took the moneys did not resemble Charlie in the slightest. Alina recalled it had been an attractive woman with a designer handbag who stuffed the check into it, turned and left. Charlie hid his reaction, hearing the description of Angel. The Russian teller disagreed, recalled a distinguished elderly gentleman, sharply dressed. Charlie's hopes were raised. Surely, it wasn't Angel. The two women commenced to argue. Mengers was satisfied, it was time to call the police. While Charlie's fear of being accused of criminal fraud abated, he knew the police investigation could point a finger at him for negligence. Yet, even worse than the consequence of having sent a bum check to Jones,

Sharke, he knew Earl had only one thing in mind – getting paid. Once Earl Guarder found out there was no money, it would get ugly.

The electronic camera light flashed on the Ferndale Avenue corner as Charlie completed his left turn onto Junipero Serra Street after the last car raced south through the changing signal light. Charlie groaned as he realized he was flash photoed in the left-turn lane street camera and would get a traffic ticket in the mail for some five hundred bucks.

Charlie steeled himself. He chanted the inner mantra that he was just the Associate. Ultimately, it was Earl S. Guarder's Law Office, not Charlie's problem. Even with Earl Guarder, Charlie knew there was nothing the California State Bar could do. Charlie followed proper procedures. If Judge Bittenkopf allowed Angel the right to withdraw $10,000 at a time, without limiting the number of times she could make withdrawals, there was nothing Charlie or Earl could do to stop her.

Charlie dismissed Henry Gilliam and Earl's anger at the loss of the funds. Charlie shook these petty legal niceties out of his consciousness. Angel, with or without the absconded funds, was gone. He was heartsick.

Charlie pulled into the Law Office's building's parking lot and squealed the circular parking descent to the fourth level underground. He maneuvered into the only remaining space between a thick round building column post on the left and an SUV on the right.

Charlie stomped on the brake as his headlight focused on the phantom, oversized figure racing towards his car. Charlie pulled the steering wheel left to avoid hitting a seething Jack Wonder. The metal fender crunched as the left front car panel collapsed against the concrete post.

Jack Wonder stomped around to the driver's side. Charlie grabbed his valise, opened the bashed front door and greeted his adversary.

"Nice to see you, Jack."

"You burned down my chateau!"

"I did not burn down your chateau."

Jack Wonder grabbed Charlie by the throat.

"One of the dogs you work for did. Who was it?"

Jack shook Charlie. More important than the difficulty Charlie had taking a breath, was the humiliation. The California Rules of Professional Conduct did not allow you to reveal what your client did unless a future fraud was involved. Here, there was none. Even if it wasn't Angel who was responsible for the mansion's demise, D'Alessio acted on Angel's behalf. Charlie couldn't reveal what happened. Of course, in Louisiana, the American Bar Association rules applied rather than the California State Bar rules, and Charlie was also uncertain if dead D'Alessio's estate had the same rights as the previously living D'Alessio had under the U.S. Constitution privacy protection rulings, but having no chance to research the minute subtleties of professional responsibility, Charlie was going to keep his lips zipped.

Jack's right arm released Charlie's throat, dropped into his waistband and pulled out a small barrel Glock pistol he pushed into Charlie's chest. The metal barrel pushed near his heart, tickling his skin. Charlie had never seen a gun up close, and in fact always had grave doubts about the Constitution's intent in its Second Amendment's protection of a person's right to bear arms, especially those with large re-loadable ammunition packs. However, Charlie, as a member of the Bar swore to uphold the U.S. Constitution the day he took his oath, and thus, had to place his own qualms about guns and automatic ammunition packs on the back burner.

For Jack Wonder, a Navy Special Services Captain and U.S. Secret Agent, involved in clandestine assassinations, drug trading, smuggling illegals, and other schemes, Charlie knew in the existential moment that locked Charlie and Jack into a life-threatening event, it wasn't the Second Amendment that controlled the outcome, but Jack Wonder's rage!

Charlie thought back on his own life, realizing it might end any moment. As long as he could remember, Charlie recalled bending to please others who accused him of misdeeds, and who wanted whatever they wanted from Charlie at any cost.

Charlie tried to get along, fit in, make a living, and get by without making waves. He tried to launch a second career in his forties, whose ostensible purpose was to promote justice, and he accepted that he would always be an "extra in the choir." Charlie's fear of being shot turned to depression and self-loathing for his compromises. He gasped a deep breath and filled his lungs with the putrid garage air.

"Shoot me you assassin Neanderthal! Go ahead, you dope-smuggling pig. Shoot!"

Charlie couldn't believe he had the guts to utter those words of defiance with the gun tickling his ribs. Apparently, Jack Wonder was equally shocked, glared at Charlie for a moment, and re-holstered his side-arm.

"Come on. We're taking a ride."

Charlie knew this wasn't an invitation.

He looked at his sedan's crunched left panel and got back into the driver's seat while Jack moved around and fell into the passenger seat. Charlie started the car. It seemed to run.

"First Trust Bank on Ferndale and Portola. Now! At least I'll get my money back from your thieving client and her arsonist boyfriend."

For a minute, Charlie thought of telling Jack Wonder about the money, but decided against such a reckless move. Let the bank officers do the honors – in public.

Charlie backed the car out of the stall without further damage. "D'Alessio's dead."

"I know."

"Did you do it?"

"He called me from the Lafayette voodoo doctor. He begged me to bring him some shit for his pain. That weak-sphincter ass-hole. He's the one who broke in to my chateau, wasn't he?"

Charlie reached street level, ignored the question.

"Wasn't he? He broke into my chateau?"

Wonder's demanding insistence echoed in Charlie's brain.

"I'm trying to fuckin' drive!"

Charlie gave Jack Wonder a quick in your face "big dog" look he had seen in a rapper documentary.

Jack Wonder reached down for his handgun, but the physical threat no longer mattered. Despite being at the point in his life where he was prepared to die, Charlie realized nothing changed in his subservient manners.

"Yes."

"That cockroach looked like Al Jolson in blackface when I drove out and picked him up. I gave him the vials of shit. He grabbed them and said I was 'paying forward' just as he had for Barry."

Charlie tried to concentrate on driving.

"I was ready to kill Beneshan myself. Slimy scumbag! Back in 2006, Barry emptied out our New Orleans account and stole the moneys from our safe. He double-crossed me twice. A million dollars, gone!"

"Barry told Angel he had two hundred grand when he landed in L.A." Charlie couldn't believe he contradicted Jack Wonder. Jack Wonder was furious.

"He emptied out our Clean Co. account just before he left. What the hell did he do with all the dough?"

Charlie flashed back to what Oscar Thornhill whispered on his deathbed. Aside from confessing to doping and smothering Barry in his Venice cottage and stealing the $200,000 cash, Oscar also confided he set up a Totten Trust for Gabriella – a trust that had to be funded after Oscar died, but which would be a bonanza for her future. Charlie recalled the ledger entry in the Pour-over Will. The Totten Trust was set up two years ago in a New Orleans courtroom by a major New Orleans law firm, Pierre, Smollett, and Reeves.

Charlie had researched the 2006 New Orleans court hearing and ordered the transcripts from New Orleans to make sure the New Orleans court approved The Gabriella Beneshan Trust he listed in the Oscar Thornhill Pour-over Trust and that the daughter's trust was legitimate and accessible to her when she reached majority age.

When he got the transcript back from the New Orleans court reporter, he found the Totten Trust was one of those legal instruments that only activates when the money is deposited. The moneys for Gabriella Beneshan were brought in to the court trustee by Barry Beneshan. Charlie thought it best not to confirm Jack Wonder's suspicion that Barry had moved $800,000 out of the New Orleans Clean Co. business account right before he left New Orleans for Los Angeles. Candace Rollins knew about the withdrawal of the company's cash but kept mum, relying on Barry's promise that the remaining $200,000 in the *La Reve du Monde* safe was hers.

Barry Beneshan withdrew the remaining $200,000 and flew off to L.A. He had left Candace high and dry after he double-crossed Jack with her help.

Jack Wonder silenced into a Buddha-like stance, held his gun with both palms, pointing it at Charlie, then turned it 180 degrees, pointed it at himself, and turned it again, aimed the barrel directly at Charlie's heart.

Charlie understood anything could happen, depending on Jack Wonder's specific moment of despondency or rage.

He turned right, headed for Greater First Trust Bank.

"What the hell is this junk piece of shit?"

"It's a Renault."

"What's the point of my being a warrior if I have to ride around in this pile of garbage?"

"It'll get us there."

Jack Wonder loosened up. "When I found the eight hundred grand gone from Clean Co two years ago, I wanted to hurt Barry bad, but I couldn't. The moneys were in the Court in a fucking Trust for his daughter. I would have screwed myself, if I touched Barry. All I could do was fight the Trust. Then, Barry panicked, stole the remaining two hundred grand from the safe and skipped town. Warriors don't hurt fellow warriors. I contacted Devlin. I promised him shit for life if he got me the money back. He called me the next day said someone had already gotten to the cash and Barry was dead. What a loser hand I got dealt."

Charlie kept silent about Devlin's screw-up getting the $200,000 back, and about Devlin's jealousy and re-snuffing an already dead Barry Beneshan.

"Well, you kept your end of the bargain. You gave Devlin all the drugs he wanted for life."

Charlie thought it was better not to mention Oscar's confession to Barry's murder, and clue Wonder that Candace Rollins worked for Oscar Thornhill for years and had her own designs on the missing $200,000.

Charlie now understood what happened: in 2006, Oscar killed Barry before the injured Devlin could fulfill his end of the bargain with Jack Wonder and get the $200,000 back. Devlin's confession to Angel was right on the mark, in all but two respects: Devlin smothered Barry in the Venice cottage when Barry was already dead, and Oscar had already unzipped the secret lining and stolen the two hundred grand in the vest. Charlie wished he had someone to share his insight with. He knew it wasn't going to be Jack Wonder.

"I'm getting whatever cash is left in the bank. It's my cash!"

Charlie's mind raced but wasn't coming up with any plan to save himself. It was pointless to tell Jack Wonder the reason Barry double-crossed Jack and deposited $800,000 of the stolen moneys into the New Orleans trust account was to fulfill Barry's debt to Oscar and Blue Orchid. Jack Wonder would never believe Charlie.

Charlie decided to test a hunch. "Angel and Gabriella were abducted last night."

"Angel? Someone wants to get his hands on the eight hundred grand. Shit!"

So much for that hunch that Jack Wonder engineered Angel and Gabriella's kidnap!

Jack Wonder looked away from Charlie – out the car window. "She's not Barry's child – you know, don't you?"

Charlie's mind raced. He suspected as much but hadn't quite been sure if Oscar told him the truth.

"She's Oscar Thornhill's biological daughter?"

Jack nodded. "Back when Barry got out of the armed forces, and needed cash flow, Oscar Thornhill supplied it, in return for Barry adopting his daughter."

"Blue Orchid?"

Jack Wonder nodded.

Charlie's fear was overcome with fascination. "And Angel?"

Jack Wonder laughed a wounded laugh. "You never know where you stand with Angel."

Charlie turned left onto Portola Street, moved over to grab a parking space.

Jack placed his gun in his waist. "I saved your hide the other night. Some mosquitoes backstage wanted to sting you bad."

Charlie felt the vestige of pain memory in his neck, swallowed hard. 'Thanks."

"If you're going to die? I'll see to it personally!"

Charlie, while grateful, wished the bank had installed metal detectors.

CHAPTER 80
WITHDRAWAL SLIPS

Heather, the anorexic, peroxide blonde bank officer was nonplussed when Charlie and Jack approached her curved mangled desk. She politely asked the two to take a seat, and inquired if this was about the "blocked account."

Charlie replied with a quick "yes," looking directly into her eyes as he tapped on the mangled pressboard edge of the laminated vinyl desk. She turned her friendly look at Jack Wonder who did not smile back. Charlie assumed she thought Jack Wonder was Earl Guarder.

Charlie thought he should let her hear Jack Wonder's demand and hope she was smart enough to deduce this was not Charlie's supervising attorney and act accordingly.

"We need to withdraw all the moneys left in the Beneshan blocked account. All the remaining $100,000."

"But Mr. Tobias, we…"

Charlie cut her off and reached into his valise and pulled out the Order.

"This is an emergency. We need all the money, now."

Luckily, Jack, focused on Heather and echoed Charlie's demand with undertones of physical threat.

"Yes, all of it – in cash. Now. It's my money!"

Heather looked at Charlie, looked at Jack Wonder and back to Charlie again. Charlie tried to keep his face neutral, while locking his eyes to her quizzical gaze, to communicate gravitas.

Heather's face stayed tight, and after a moment she replied: "Yes, Mr. Tobias. Of course, I have to get my supervisor's okay."

Jack Wonder was suddenly suspicious. "Call him over, on the phone. We don't have time to waste."

"Yes, sir. I understand attorney's time is valuable. How's your day been going so far?"

Before Jack Wonder could respond, Charlie saw Heather's eye move above Charlie's head.

A familiar gravelly baritone commanded "Freeze. Raise your hands slowly. Now!"

Charlie prayed the voice belonged to whom he thought it did as he complied. From the corner of his eyes, he saw Jack Wonder's face grow steely, Jack's eyes twitch.

"So long, Charlie."

Jack reached for his Glock hand gun, dropped and rolled to the ground aiming at Charlie's chest, but before Jack could pull the trigger, a barrage of bullets hit him in the chest and in the neck. Blood splattered.

Charlie dove away.

Charlie rolled away from Jack Wonder's collapsing body.

Heather shrieked and dove next to Charlie away from her desk. Officers ran in.

Jack gasped for breath through a punctured neck wound from which blood gushed as if from a Bakersfield oil well. A bullet must have severed Jack Wonder's aorta. For a moment Charlie was mesmerized by the color of Jack Wonder's blood spurting out of his neck in all directions. It was jet black.

Charlie looked at the well-shined shoes next to him, looked up into Detective Philip Oswilla's taut face as Oswilla's left hand maneuvered his wheelchair past Jack Wonder's twitching, spurting, bloody body and he still pointed his service revolver at Jack.

"Charlie, you're becoming my best customer. All I have to do is follow you around and business is good."

"Thanks. You saved my life."

"We were waiting hoping Angel or whoever abducted her would show."

Charlie got up slowly, helped Heather to her feet.

Heather sobbed, hysterical. From a back area, Mr. Mengers gazed, open jawed, and did not approach to supervise.

Charlie found himself surprisingly calm. Detective Oswilla wheeled back and motioned for the two police officers behind him to step aside and make room. Two paramedics raced over, carrying a gurney which they placed on the floor next to Jack's prone body. One paramedic took Jack Wonder's vitals and called in over his radio phone while the second paramedic zapped the gush of blood from the aorta, and succeeded in slowing it.

"I need to suture." A third paramedic rolled over a portable red-colored robot electric zapper. The second paramedic applied two foam-covered electrical handles to Jack Wonder's aorta. After repeated zaps of electrical energy, the blood gushing stopped just as Heather threw up.

The first medic threw up a bag of blood onto a hook. "Type A-O? Check?"

The second medic checked the chart, gave thumbs up as he handed Heather twinkle-wipes to clean herself off. The first medic inserted blood transfusions into Jack Wonder's left arm.

"Move him out."

Charlie looked down, saw dark fluid creep around his shoes, across the marble floor. Charlie was mesmerized. This was Jack Wonder's blood, covering the floor, not Charlie's.

Charlie's mouth smiled despite himself. *He was glad to be alive. Everything else was secondary.* Charlie viewed events from the existential perspective – surviving the shoot-out. The flood of emotion left Charlie shaky but full of gratitude to Detective Oswilla, to the L.A.P.D. for being there when it counted and to Heather for being cool under pressure.

"Thank you, thank you. Detective. Officers." Charlie wiped away a tear. Heather cried quietly as she cleaned herself, gave Charlie a hug, and calmed down in the war zone.

The paramedics lifted Jack Wonder's limp body onto the gurney. The first medic called in on his radio. Jack Wonder's body no longer twitched.

"We need a med-Evac helicopter. Vic critical. Schedule immediate surgery at Harry Harrington Trauma Center. Time estimate 15 minutes land on E.R. helipad. Over."

Charlie looked into Jack Wonder's eyes. They were still open, bloody.

"I'm sorry, Jack. I'm so sorry."

Jack's eyes focused on Charlie's emotional empathy. "Fuckin' lousy day."

Heather broke down, her shrieks grew louder. A police officer raced to calm her. Mr. Mengers, straightened his tie, hurried over to take charge of his flock of geese.

The F.B.I. swarmed in as Jack was raced out on the gurney.

Agent Long took his sunglasses off, assessed the damage, fixated on Jack Wonder's horizontal departure, clenched his fist, walked up to Detective Oswilla and stood over Detective Oswilla's wheelchair.

"You shot my guy. If he dies, you're scrubbing latrines for the rest of your pitiful career."

"I never shoot a U.S. warrior to kill."

"Pray he lives!" Agent Long turned. His team raced out to provide the gurney with unofficial bearers as Jack Wonder's med-evacs scooted his prone body out the bank's front door.

Charlie heard the whir of the helicopter land on Ferndale Avenue. Bull horns and police sirens echoed from outside the bank.

"Evacuate. This is an order! Bank robbery in progress. Everyone inside evacuate!" Charlie heard the helicopter land.

"So, Charlie, anything you want to tell me?" Detective Oswilla was suddenly solicitous.

Charlie pulled himself together and recalled he had wanted to tell someone about his insights into how and why Oscar murdered Barry. He focused back on his role as a probate attorney – for Oscar Thornhill. At the moment, there was only one thing he could say.

"We've got to find Angel."

CHAPTER 81
EVERYONE HAS A LAST STAND

As Charlie drove back up Ferndale Avenue to the Law Offices, his left hand gripping the steering wheel trembled, his eyes twitched, and his forehead and armpits drenched sweat, but he judged oncoming traffic and yellow lights. He made the left turn before the traffic light turned red, and the Junipero Serra Street camera photo flashed him a second ticket. Charlie knew he must confront Earl about the vanished moneys. There would be a huge fight. Well, at least a one-sided fight, as Charlie would retreat from such encounters, defeated, stressed, depressed.

This time, he didn't care. He had two guns pointed at him, and a shoot-out in which he dove for cover to save himself. He had smashed his car, got a $450 dollar left-turn ticket, not counting the cost of traffic school.

Whatever fight he'd get into with Earl Guarder would be nothing compared to what had already happened.

Charlie flicked on the radio. The national news was the same as ever: foreclosures, Wall Street bail-outs, plant shut-downs. The radio announcer interrupted with the breaking news that the Greater First Trust Bank at the corner of Ferndale and Portola in Fairtown was on lock-down because of a bank robbery by armed masked men holed up inside who had taken a manager and teller hostage. Charlie couldn't help but laugh.

Charlie twisted down into the parking garage's fourth level, moved to its deepest bowels in the "annex" where he parked his car in the very same spot he had encountered Jack Wonder. He edged in to the parking spot gingerly, especially as part of his fender stuck out.

Charlie took a deep breath, got out, surveyed the crushed bumper and side panel of his car.

The car could be fixed.

CHAPTER 82
IT ALL COMES DOWN TO -

Jamie was behind her fourth floor reception desk answering phones, her clear blue eyes just visible over the desk's counter.

"Hi, Charlie. How are you doing?"

Charlie didn't know why he said he felt "fine." Maybe, because he realized he could survive anything thrown at him.

"Oh, Charlie?"

"Yes?"

"I need to get your parking pass. Do you have it?"

"Yes, what's up?"

"Well, I was just told to get it." Jamie's embarrassed shake of the shoulders said it all. The Law Offices must be delinquent paying its parking bill.

Charlie reached into his wallet, pulled out his plastic parking permit, and passed it across the side of the desk. "It is okay." Charlie suddenly thought about how he would get out of the building. If you didn't have a permit, the maximum $22 daily parking fee applied.

"What about leaving the building?"

"Can you get some validation coupons from Earl?"

Charlie knew this request for the parking permit wasn't Jamie's idea. Nor Earl's idea, either. Charlie knew there were no more validations left in the office drawer. Clients had been upset when Charlie apologized, shrugged and told broke clients, who had just cried their troubles out in a free introductory consultation, they had to pay the $22 building parking fee to leave. Charlie reached into his valise and fumbled for the plastic parking permit, found it.

"Here you go."

Charlie handed over the parking permit and leaned forward.

"Jamie, can I ask you something?"

"Sure, Charlie. What is it?"

"How long have you worked here?"

"Oh, about eleven years. A long time, huh? I always think I'll find something better, but I never have time to look. I have two kids."

"They're almost out of high school."

"Graduation will be a blessing."

"Jamie, in all the years, have you ever met Jack Smith, one of the senior partners?"

Jamie thought for a moment. "No."

"Isn't that odd?"

Jamie looked momentarily uncomfortable, but the calm look and manner returned.

"Charlie, this job has made it possible for me to raise my two kids on my own. Don't you understand?"

"You're right, Jamie. That's what matters. Thanks." Charlie backed away as Jamie's focus turned to an incoming call.

Charlie made his way past the long corridor of empty office space and mountains of archived file boxes from past Hannah, Ashley major clients to the tiny island of current legal operations, the beleaguered Law Offices, still holding on in its remaining three cubicles and three offices.

Earl Guarder wasn't in his office. Aki waved from her end cubicle, while she handled phone chores and let Charlie know Earl was on his way back from his Kiwanis luncheon. Charlie nodded "thanks," reminded this was a Monday, one of the few days when Aki was still working, and the receptionist job hadn't been given to some unpaid law school intern to save the Law Offices cash flow.

Charlie walked straight into Earl's office, sat down facing the carved mahogany desk, looked through the tinted glass-sheathed windows over Fairtown. Charlie became perfectly calm.

Earl Guarder, in a different suit from what he wore to court, a flashy, new, subtle ice-purple silk suit and bright orange tie, ran in. He was in a good mood. The luncheon must have gone well.

"Charlie, you should come to these luncheons with me. Lots of interesting people. Some are influential in politics. They want me to run for congressman. I may even do it. Serve the people in whatever way I can."

"Sounds great, Earl." Charlie was about to tell Earl about the bank shoot-out.

"So? Did you get the money from Greater First Trust whatever Bank?" Earl, like Charlie, wasn't sure of the name of any bank anymore as the banks had gone bust and been absorbed by other banks and renamed every few months or so.

"Earl, there's no money." Earl continued to unload documents from his valise uncertain if he heard Charlie correctly.

Earl Guarder fell into the handcrafted English country club style high-backed leather chair behind the desk, facing Charlie.

"What do you mean, 'there's no money?' Did Angel take it?"

"I told you Angel's been kidnapped. The bank officers are investigating what happened."

Earl lost his easy going demeanor.

"How do you think I can keep this law office going? This is not a charity. Get the money. Now! Call her. Call her, now!"

Earl jumped up behind the desk, bore down on Charlie with the desk phone receiver.

"Earl, I don't know where she is."

"Call her, *now*."

"Listen to me. She's gone. I've just about been shot!"

"I need the money. I'm running for congress."

Charlie thought of all the times Earl Guarder lost his composure. It always concerned money - demanding Charlie or some other Associate get money for a screaming client or for the Law Offices. As Earl Guarder tried to push the cheap plastic multi-line phone receiver into Charlie's hands, Charlie thought of the purpose of being a probate attorney. He saw his function. *Yes, the job concerned distributing assets of the deceased in a way the deceased had willed or wished, but it concerned more than money. Being a probate attorney was akin to being a funeral director at a mortuary. It meant providing closure to all loved ones, a feeling the community would be there to make sure whatever a deceased had requested would be acknowledged, dealt with fairly, and carried out.* Charlie looked up into Earl's tight face, pulled flat from tension, as if in preparation for a surgery.

Charlie focused past Earl through the full-length window on the Fairtown skyline as Earl bent over Charlie, pushed the phone receiver into Charlie's hand.

Charlie saw past the Serrano mountain range that bounded Fairtown from the south. Charlie could see the Music Center downtown which was where Charlie had wanted to make his calling as an opera singer, and which was still a minute reality as his part-time "extra" job.

Charlie saw past the City of the Angels in which millions of people, every day, went about their business, tried to make ends meet, tried to keep dreams alive. He thought he could see the glimmer of the Pacific Ocean past the beach towns south-west of the metropolis.

It was one of those rare picture-perfect days when the low-lying clouds framed the City of the Angels with the panoramic beauty that regularly returns on the first Sunday of January of each year, to make the Garden of Flowers Bowl Parade a national metaphor for beauty, and entice yet more dreamers to come to the City of the Angels to reach for their dreams.

Charlie realized he never gave up on his original dream, but if he continued to stay at Earl's, he might not make it to a spiritual blessing in the afterlife under whatever universal religious order he might accept.

Charlie, for the first time in years saw things clearly. After all, this was just his job.

"I quit, Earl."

"Call her. Now! Get the money."

"Good bye."

Charlie got up, put the phone cradle down on the desk, grabbed his empty valise.

"Oh, and Jamie has my parking permit."

Charlie felt nothing as he walked out of Earl's office, past Aki's cubicle. She was still on the phone, talking a mile-a-minute to some anxious client.

Earl threw the phone receiver back on the desk, raced, caught up with Charlie. Earl shouted, implored, cajoled.

Charlie walked into the reception area. Earl stopped at the foyer edge, yelled for Charlie to come back.

Charlie exchanged a secretive look with Jamie.

He heard Jamie from behind the reception desk, without seeing her eyes move above the counter. "Take care, Charlie, and break a leg."

"Thanks."

The elevator arrived, opened. Charlie stepped in, *Only I have the power to break the chains that held me down, and I just did!*

CHAPTER 83
EMOTIONAL VOLCANOES

During the next few weeks Charlie vacillated between anxiety and elation and plunged into depression. He ignored the phone calls his cell phone display showed were from "The Law Offices." At first those calls snaked into angry voice mails and Earl's demands for Charlie to return immediately to the Law Offices. After a few days, the calls and voice mails became kinder. Those were harder to deal with, but Charlie stayed resolute. By now, Charlie knew Earl had learned of the shoot-out with Jack Wonder. Charlie wondered whether Angel was all right, but he rationalized it was best not to dwell on her and get sucked back in.

Little by little, the Law Office's calls subsided, and Charlie's internal volcano calmed. One call, however, put him into a tailspin. Aki's voice quivered as she told the distressing news to his voice-mail.

"Charlie, please call back. Alice Mobley died. I thought you'd want to know."

Charlie's heart sank, but he called back anyway and reached Aki who recounted what happened.

"She died in court this morning at the Motion to Enforce the Settlement Hearing." Aki choked back tears as she told Charlie about the good-natured Alice Mobley's final moments on earth in front of Judge Bittenkopf.

"Earl went to the hearing with Alice Mobley. I was his assistant. Dancy Rock protested he had sent the moneys over to us and demanded sanctions against Alice Mobley for pursuing the petition."

Charlie fell back onto the chair he sat on and listened to Aki's halting replay of what happened that morning in court. He held the phone pressed to his ears as he heard that Judge Bittenkopf denied Dancy Rock's demand for sanctions and was about to dismiss both attorneys when Henry Gilliam came in and informed Judge Bittenkopf that Jones, Sharke represented Probate E-Z Loans, LLC. Attorney Gilliam informed the court he had placed a lien on Alice Mobley's home because of the non-payment of additional interest charges that had accumulated to the Mobley estate since the last court hearing.

Earl Guarder, Dancy Rock and Henry Gilliam engaged in a shouting match, in which Henry Gilliam brought up the Law Offices' bounced $50,000 check in the Beneshan estate matter over Earl's loud objections, while Judge Bittenkopf pounded his gavel, and only managed to quiet the attorneys after he threatened each with sanctions. The commotion was so intense no one noticed Alice slumped over her seat on to the bench. By the time paramedics arrived, she was dead.

"She died of diabetic shock."

Charlie groaned.

"No one knew how to give her an insulin injection. I'm sorry, Charlie."

Charlie's body froze. He wiped away a tear. "Give my condolences to Denise, will you?"

"I'm sorry, Charlie. I can't. Today's my last day. I can't do this job anymore. I have no health plan, hardly any moneys coming in. Earl gives me fewer and fewer hours. We're moving back to Croatia."

"Croatia?'

"Yes, Zagreb is a beautiful city. My family is still there and at least my baby will have the health care she needs."

Charlie was silent for a minute as he heard her blow her sadness into her handkerchief.

"Good luck to you, Aki and to your baby. What's her name? I don't think you ever told me her name?"

"'Theodora,' like the Byzantine Empire's Empress."

"'Theodora.' Good luck to you and Theodora."

"Thanks, Charlie. Good luck to you, too."

Charlie answered the phone when the display showed Desmond Thornhill called. Desmond informed Charlie that Oscar's remains had been cremated and his ashes would be scattered into the sea off Santa Catalina Island on the leeward side, as Oscar wished. Charlie, recalling the unknown assailant's claws around his neck beneath the stage, declined the invitation to join in the ocean ceremony to scatter Oscar's ashes.

Charlie wanted to stay away from anything having to do with death. He wanted to focus on living.

It was awkward being with Tina most of the time, when previously he hardly saw her. Each of them tried to adapt to the other's daily presence. It was a nice feeling that grew.

Charlie still had his chorus singing job even though it was not exactly enough of an income to pay the bills. Tina was getting more Substitute teaching jobs, so things were not dire. Charlie, cashed the Thornhill check, waited nervously for another few days and the check cleared. He shared the news with Tina. She was elated and she agreed he should concentrate on the upcoming opera productions for the rest of the current L.A. Opera season, before proceeding to look for another attorney "day job." Charlie wasn't even sure his attorney work was a "day job" anymore. He recalled the dinner with Colette St. Pierre. Being an attorney meant you were committed to justice. Charlie was, and had no way to cut off his newly integrated persona.

For now, opening night for *West Nile* was just days away – the following Saturday.

Charlie could now do what he couldn't do before, take his modest "extra" role seriously, and give it all he had. At least, he would get pleasure out of doing what he loved to do most – sing. He pulled out old librettos from the closet and perused their faded pages. There was the Mozart *Requiem,* from the Hollywood Bowl evening, the Palestrina *Missa Papae Marcelli* from his graduate U.C.L.A. Master's performance in Royce Hall, the magnificent well-thumbed and underlined *Ode to Joy* from Beethoven's 9th *Symphony* he had sung in choirs from Ventura to Palm Desert. He understood why he never chucked those old scores to the thrift store. They were there "just in case." He would look for other opportunities where those scores might be useful again.

At one point Charlie got an unexpected call from a phone number he didn't recognize. He half-expected a phone call from Detective Philip Oswilla asking him for another round of "identifications." He shuddered to think of Angel's disappearance, but was surprised to hear the flat monotone voice on the other end of the line. "Mr. Tobias, this is agent Thomas Long, F.B.I. You recall, our paths crossed?"

"Is this call about Angel? Have you found her?"

"No. But there's been a development. Come down to the Westwood office and I.D. some photos tomorrow morning at 10 a.m. Consider this meeting 'confidential.' Top secret!"

Charlie understood this wasn't a request.

"Right."

CHAPTER 84
PRO HAC VICE

Charlie left a note for Tina the following morning, drove to the F.B.I. office in Westwood crawling in horrible traffic down the San Diego freeway, the one major artery connecting the San Fernando Valley's bedroom communities to Los Angeles' glamorous west side. The exhausting trip on the most congested freeway commute in America reinforced Charlie's dread. He parked in the visitor section of the outdoor parking lot, entered the imposing federal building, took the elevator to the 14th floor and was let in to the offices he remembered from the previous visit by freshly pressed dark-suited and neatly coiffed secretaries.

Aside from Agent Long, taciturn, drab, and well-groomed, Charlie was not surprised to find Agent Trenton, well-coiffed, and sun-shaded, presumably to avoid the piercing rays of the morning sun that glared through the tinted windows into the Federal building's offices.

Charlie was shocked to see Attorney Colette St. Pierre present in a trim tan business suit, as beautiful as ever, very ill at ease.

"Hello, Charlie."

"Hello, Colette. Not your usual beat. Doing a *pro hac vice* in California?"

Charlie's reference was to an attorney's privilege to appear once in front of a judge in a different state, without admission to that state's bar. Charlie had made use of the *pro hac vice* legal courtesy when he appeared in New Orleans in front of Judge Aurora d'Arcy.

"I'm here to protect my client, Jack Wonder's rights."

Charlie was pleased to hear there was still a client to protect.

"How is he?"

Agent Trenton interrupted harshly. "We've taken Captain Wonder into federal custody, and placed him in solitary confinement prior to a military court trial."

Colette was livid.

"I flew out here and met with him at Harrington Hospital. Then, he disappeared. They won't let me see him."

"Miss St. Pierre. That will be all."

"I filed a *Writ of Habeas Corpus* petition in Central District Court downtown. I was denied! Can you help me, Charlie?"

Agent Trenton slammed the table. "You're not a licensed California attorney."

Charlie was perplexed and turned to the government agents. "Jack Wonder has rights."

Colette blurted out before the two F.B.I. agents could stop her: "Charlie, they're charging him with treason. He's on his way to Gitmo."

Agent Trenton was icy to St. Pierre: "You want to follow him to a solitary cell?"

Charlie calmed Colette and faced the two agents.

"What's going on?"

Agent Long spread large glossy photos across the round conference table. The photos showed Boohau Cyclops, distinguished in a dark suit, enter the chapel with his wife and several elderly Cham at the Forest Park memorial.

"Do you recognize the man with the dreadlocks in this picture, Mr. Tobias?"

Charlie looked at the series of eight-by-ten inch black and white photos set in front of him with the braided brown ropelike strands of hair framing a heroic face whose gaze was as terrifying as Medusa's.

"That's the Woodfall apartment manager, Boohau Cyclops. He was wounded at the service. You were headed to lasso him as I recall."

Agent Long took a deep, embarrassed breath, spread additional photos. The photos showed Cham worshipers fleeing through the side doors.

The sequence of photos showed the paramedics race towards the fallen Cyclops. The paramedics then looked confused in additional photos and Boohau Cyclops wasn't to be seen. The final photos showed Charlie and Angel led away by Agent Trenton.

Nowhere was Boohau Cyclops seen leaving.

"Didn't you chase Mr. Cyclops down, on the lawn?"

Agent Trenton's face turned crimson. "He escaped."

Agent Trenton leaned over Charlie.

"Is Boohau Cyclops aka Trengh Dao your client?"

Charlie thought for a minute. Boohau Cyclops worked for Angel and the Estate. Charlie wished he had access to *Witkin* or another dispositive legal tome, but he was sure whatever the legal scholars cited, it was best to not give information.

"I no longer work for the Law Offices. You'll have to contact Mr. Guarder."

"Has Cyclops contacted you since the shoot-out?"

Charlie was increasingly annoyed. He had stood up to Earl. He wasn't going to back down.

"Have you found Angel Sedona?"

Charlie got his answer as he caught agent Trenton's perturbed side glance at Agent Long. Charlie stepped up his defiance.

"Find Angel and her daughter. Then, we'll talk!"

Charlie got up to leave. Agent Long seethed. Trenton nodded for Long to calm. "Tell him what the New Orleans secret grand jury found."

"Sit down, Mr. Tobias. Listen, please." Long returned to his neutral inflection.

Charlie, curious, looked at Colette. Her eyes asked Charlie to 'listen.'

Agent Trenton's face was icy. "We're deadly serious. I emphasize 'deadly.' Have you heard of an organization called *La Reve du Monde*?"

Charlie shrugged to be taken either as a "yes," or "no." Charlie looked at Colette for help.

Colette responded: "The secret French society we talked about in New Orleans?"

"We talked about my childhood memories in French class."

"I told them you know nothing."

Agent Trenton interrupted: "They're a terrorist cell with revolutionary goals to overthrow the government of the United States."

Charlie suppressed the urge to laugh in the agents' faces. He looked at Colette, saw she wasn't laughing.

Charlie locked eyes with agent Trenton, but couldn't see past her sunglasses. He turned to respond directly to agent Long.

"That's a joke, isn't it?"

"We have good reason to believe Captain Wonder is in a conspiracy with the Cham leader, Boohau Cyclops, who is the bastard great-grandson of a linear descendent of Emperor Napoleon Bonaparte, the Third, of France."

"Last time we met, you claimed they were meth smugglers."

"That's part of their scheme. As you may recall from your history, the first Napoleon Bonaparte sold the Louisiana Purchase territories to the U.S."

"So?"

"We have reason to believe *La Reve du Monde* is a revolutionary conspiracy to retake part of those territories."

"Nonsense."

"We placed a mole who fed us the progress of their conspiracy. Unfortunately, he died in a blast, while trying to get further information."

Charlie's neural connections made the shocking connection. "Devlin D'Alessio?"

The two agents looked at each other. They weren't certain they should share their top secret intelligence.

Charlie was furious. "Devlin was a scheming guy, who took you on a wild joy ride."

Agent Long appeared to be personally insulted. "He stopped the Woodfall Cham refugees from a new Cambodia invasion. The Cham were on the verge of restarting a new Southeast Asia war!"

Agent Trenton took off her sunglasses and looked directly into Charlie's eyes. "Mr. D'Alessio was a true patriot who gave his life for our country."

Colette blurted out: "The agents claim Jack, after he recovered from his third surgery at Harrington Hospital, gave the U.S. government an ultimatum to withdraw all U.S. forces from Louisiana by next month or face deadly consequences."

Charlie noticed neither agent contradicted Colette. Agent Trenton bit her lips. Agent Long looked away.

"What was Jack's threat?"

Agent Long looked into Charlie's eyes. "Captain Wonder claims there are two Hiroshima-sized armed nuclear weapons in the United States under the command of Trengh Dao and his Cham followers. Captain Wonder threatened one bomb will detonate in the Gulf of Mexico as a warning if the first demand isn't met four Sundays from today for all United States officials to vacate New Orleans' government offices. The second bomb is timed to go off in four months at an unspecified location if all demands are not met! Those demands include the withdrawal of all American sovereign forces in the ancient French areas of America south of the Missouri River and West of the Mississippi River."

Charlie looked from agent to agent. Agent Trenton's face twisted into nervous silence as she replaced her sunglasses. "It is insane, but Wonder's threat is real."

Colette nodded. "Charlie. They won't let me see my client."

"Who's going to set off the bomb? Cyclops? Wonder?"

Agent Long leaned over the conference table, responded to Charlie's doubts with alacrity.

"Two members of the Southeast Asia Wonder Boys team, Dylan Vincent and Coombs Kroft have the know-how in ordinance detonation and computer hacking. We can't track them."

Charlie recalled the picture of the clandestine group of Wonder's three Wonder Boys including the two claimed terrorists and Barry Beneshan. He looked at Colette. She nodded.

Long paused to let the enormity of the danger sink in to Charlie's consciousness. Agent Long moved closer to Charlie's face, as if the short distance would drive the truth of his accusation home.

"Last fall, when the Libyan civil war threatened to turn hot because of the rebel commander's capture in Chad, we learned from our on-ground sources that the Libyan dictator had received shipments on two unregistered cargo ships that satellite images showed could be nuclear weapons. Our Navy Special Ops went into Tripoli. Navy Intelligence had correctly identified six armed nuclear bombs set to be detonated if the conflict escalated into a full-scale civil war. Our operatives parachuted in, stormed and secured the bunkers, and de-activated the nuclear weapons. The ruling junta was apprised of the mission's success, and we pulled out."

Agent Trenton's twisted inward anger exploded into continuing the details of the F.B.I.'s perceived life-and-death threat.

"In dealing with this operation, the Pentagon brass brushed aside concerns about Captain Wonder's questionable drug connections because of his extraordinary skills and distinguished past service. Captain Wonder was the commander of the clandestine Tripoli interdiction operation. He took two operatives, Corporals Vincent and Kroft in his squad. They parachuted into Tripoli on the mission, penetrated the weapon's compounds when the Libyan guards ran away during the raid. The commando unit defused the nukes and programmed their controls to self-destruct. The backup troops parachuted in the next day, took over the compounds. They didn't find Captain Wonder and his Wonder Boys. All three disappeared."

Charlie looked from agent to agent. The timeframe of the supposed commando raid in Libya matched the time-frame of Jack's absence from communications about the estate.

"My client, Captain Wonder is an American citizen with rights to speak to an attorney."

The agents didn't even respond to St. Pierre. Charlie wasn't convinced of the agents' theory, but he couldn't say for sure it wasn't true.

Agent Trenton added: "Two nuclear weapons are missing."

Agent Long pushed two additional photos in front of Charlie. "See these two trucks?"

Charlie looked at the two military trucks leaving some desert rat-hole. He looked at the close-up satellite pictures of the American drivers. The two scruffy men looked like the men he had seen from the Southeast Asia photo of Jack Wonder and his Wonder Boys. One of the drivers appeared to be Coombs. The other truck driver was a definite look-a-like for Corporal Vincent Kroft.

"The two missing nukes fit into these trucks easy," agent Long paused, then continued. "The trucks drove down into Namibia, and were later found by local military in Tunisia at the Mediterranean port of Tunis. They were empty. We've lost them. Do you understand?"

CHAPTER 85
AN ALPHABET SOUP OF FEDS

Charlie's interview progressed, and agents from other Federal Agencies joined the meeting. There was the National Security Agency, Navy Special Intelligence, Navy Military Special Operations, and even a White House Defense Liaison.

Charlie wasn't sure he got any name in his memory, nor was he sure he was supposed to, but he understood the government officials considered this matter grave. One silver-suited crew-cut agent was in direct contact with the National Security Council in Washington, D.C., briefing the U.S. President on an hourly basis on the White House red telephone hot line.

After perfunctory explanations by the two F.B.I. agents to the alarmed government officials, there was complete silence. No alphabet-soup representative had anything to add. Each looked grim.

Agents Long and Trenton had gotten all the information they could get from Charlie. Agent Long nodded to the other government officers, who picked up their writing pads, brief cases, iPads, and left the room without so much as a "good-bye."

Agent Trenton, her deep-red rouged lips off kilter, exuding tension and spite, stared into Charlie's eyes.

"Everything you heard today is 'Level One Top Secret.' Under the Patriot Act, I'm authorized to arrest you if you disclose anything. I don't need a warrant. You would be charged as an Accessory after the Fact to the Treason, conspiracy, or – ?" She let this sink in. "I'm not a prosecutor, but I think you get the point. You can't tell anyone – your wife, clients, – no-one. Do you understand?"

Charlie did not want to debate the niceties of due process or U.S. constitutional law.

"Yes."

"You can leave."

"What are you doing about Angel Sedona?"

"We always get our man – or woman."

"You want my help? You find her and get her back – safe."

Charlie got up, noted the squared off pistols at the agents' belts. Charlie caught Colette's eyes.

Colette got up. "May I leave?"

The agents exchanged looks, nodded in her direction, very unfriendly. Trenton gave the final instructions.

"Same thing, ma'am. If you are contacted by Mr. Wonder's associates, friends, anyone? Call me, immediately. Here's my direct line."

Agent Trenton handed her card across to Colette, and gave a second card to Charlie.

"You, too, Mr. Tobias. It's a matter of the highest national security. You understand the gravity. Nuclear terrorists! The sanctity of American sovereignty!"

"Let's go, Charlie."

Charlie took the card, followed Colette out of the conference room and muttered to no-one.

"Let's bust out, while we can."

■　　　■　　　■　　　■　　　■

The elevator was high-speed, yet endless in its descent. Charlie looked at Colette's beautiful eyes. Colette self-consciously looked back at Charlie. Neither said a word. Charlie was about to ask about Boohau Cyclops, when she squeezed his arm so it hurt. He instinctively understood not to talk. The elevator plunged from the upper floor to the ground floor, where the shiny aluminum doors opened to the Federal Building's nondescript government architecture lobby.

They walked out swiftly, headed for the row of glass entrances - exits through which those with government business passed, oblivious that in

WALKING WITH THE DEAD

addition to passports and a large post-office, the building also housed the might of the U.S. intelligence community in Los Angeles.

Colette put her hand through Charlie's arm as they walked out into the daylight.

"I'm staying at the Le Verdain Hotel. It's over on Rexford Avenue in Beverly Hills. They have a lovely courtyard. We could talk there. Do you want to come over?"

Charlie looked into Colette's beautiful eyes, into her beautiful face. There was something odd about the way she framed the invitation, something incongruous since she didn't look him in the eyes.

Charlie was distracted by Colette's trim body, by her perfectly coiffed hair, and her unwrinkled, elegant business suit. Yet, she kept looking away as she squeezed his arm. The squeezing was hard. It hurt.

Charlie recalled she squeezed his arm as they entered Judge Aurora d'Arc's New Orleans courtroom. She had whispered she'd press Charlie's arm if he needed to stay silent.

Charlie suddenly understood – she was communicating to him – something important for his own protection. There was something terribly wrong. She was warning him.

"Some other time."

Colette's looked into his quizzical face. The tension in her eyes eased. She dropped her vise-grip of his arm, leaned forward, kissed him French-style on both cheeks.

Colette's eyes flinched back to the federal building up to the floor from which they came.

Charlie understood her warning.

Colette and the hotel she was staying in were wired!

As Charlie headed one way and Colette headed in the opposite direction to the outdoor parking lot, just south of the monolithic Federal building, Charlie felt a piece of paper in the palm of his hand. He knew better than to look down, or open the note she had palmed him when they exchanged "good-bye."

Charlie walked to his car without looking back, got in, and exited the vast parking lot surrounding the Federal building. Only when he was several blocks away, as he turned onto the freeway on-ramp to head back home, did he unfold the paper, and read "Meet at 'Louisiana Café', 2 p. m. tomorrow. Fondly, C."

Charlie's heart raced as he maneuvered north onto the San Diego Freeway. His head calmed his trembling hands. *He was an attorney, in the service of justice. He had nothing to fear even if he had everything to lose.*

CHAPTER 86
COLETTE'S RIGHTEOUS WRATH

At precisely two o'clock the following afternoon, Charlie stood outside the Louisiana Café in West Hollywood's night-club district which expanded in all directions from Santa Monica Blvd. and Crescent Heights. He perused over the café's ornate metal grill fenced patio for Colette, but only saw amorous couples of indeterminate gender having various levels of sensual romantic interactions in the warm afternoon sun. Charlie took a deep breath, crossed the Rubicon to find Colette.

Inside the café, Charlie winced and dropped his eyes as he saw the nude male dancers with perfect butts, sporting a "g string" fig-leaf in front, cavorting and slow-dancing with each other on the slightly raised spotlighted stage in the far dim corner of the club to a piano, bass and drums jazz combo's erotic riffs. His eyes searched for Colette amidst the mascaraed and rouged café crowd, but saw no one who could be his elegant New Orleans colleague. Charlie's eyes moved to a beautiful sailor in striped navy dark blue-and-whites with a kerchief around the neck, exiting the rest-room, holding an oversized designer bag. As the sailor approached Charlie, he saw the distinctive eyes, one slightly larger than the other, the model thin, gaunt, flawless cheeks, and recognized the sailor as Colette.

Charlie relaxed as the sailor approached, but was not prepared for the sailor coming ever closer, and her mouth moving towards his in a full kiss. This was no polite peck-on-the-cheek kiss, but a full, warm, open-lipped envelopment of his emotions. Charlie's entire body shuddered as he closed his eyes, become dizzy, and responded. The kiss did not stop. He forced himself to slowly release and moved backwards to take in her full face.

"Mmmm. You don't like my kiss?"

"You are alluring. We are also a spectacle, not exactly blending in."

"Well, let's sit, no?"

Charlie nodded, pulled a chair for Colette at a nearby empty table, sat opposite, continued to look into her beautiful, angular face, and hailed a server, whose exposed chest, complete with pasties over his tits and black-ribbon tied bow tie, could easily compete with skimpy-clad bunnies and well-endowed female servers at rival jazz clubs up and down Santa Monica Blvd.

"I didn't recognize you."

"That's the idea." She lifted her oversized bag just a bit to drive home the point. "My street clothes are in here. I just changed."

"Why are you of such interest to the F.B.I.?"

"They mistakenly believe I can lead them to the missing Wonder Boys."

"And you can't?"

"No, Monsieur Charlie. I don't have a clue. I fight in court to have Jack Wonder released from solitary confinement. Will you help me?"

Charlie thought for a moment. "I can appear here in court in California for you."

"Thank you, Charlie. I'm counting on you."

Charlie thought for a moment. "We are servants of justice, aren't we?"

"Yes, Charlie. And for whatever it's worth, we also have a common client, aside from the Beneshan estate matter."

Charlie was puzzled for a moment. "Angel Sedona and Gabriella Beneshan. You are the tutor's representative in the Louisiana courts where Gabriella has a sizeable trust."

"Yes. I represent Angel and Angel's daughter. Will you help bring them to New Orleans to claim their future?"

"Angel has vanished, with her daughter."

"I expect she'll appear."

"I hope so. Of course I will work with you."

"Thank you, Mister Charlie."

Charlie looked around the café. The jazz combo next to the stage was taking a break. Charlie looked at the upright piano and watched the musicians disperse. His mind recalled one of his favorite piano pieces, a simple, haunting melody by the French composer Georges Delerue in the classic film, *Shoot the Piano Player*. That piano player in that Parisian bar was also named *Charlie*. He snapped back to the matter at hand.

"How will I contact you?"

Colette reached under the table into her bag, handed Charlie a cell phone. "I have one, too. It's a throwaway, so they can't trace it. If I get a new one, I'll call and leave a number on your throwaway phone, so you can call me."

Charlie grabbed the flimsy cell phone under the tablecloth, out of her warm hand, held it with his other hand for a moment too long. Colette gently disengaged.

"It's time for this sailor to head out onto the streets, go into another club's rest-room, and Attorney St. Pierre can go back to her hotel."

Colette rose. "I'll be in touch in the service of justice." She turned and left.

Charlie couldn't take his eyes off her as she walked out of the club. He was elated. Was it the kiss? The meeting? Justice? Or a possible connection to Angel and Gabriella? Charlie couldn't be sure as he paid the bill, headed out of the club as the mostly nude dancers returned to their gyrations, this time to an undulating provocative sexual position that earned a few approving laughs, hoots, and applause.

CHAPTER 87
M.I.A.

Several weeks passed since Jack Wonder was whisked away from the Bank shoot-out. Detective Oswilla's requests to interrogate the wounded warrior about the botched bank robbery kept being denied, supposedly due to Wonder's bullet caused grave health. Recurring phone calls from local news reporters eager to get the homicide detective's take on the bloody robbery irritated the detective. Oswilla was savvy enough to refer all media inquiries to his supervisor, Captain Jim Abraham, and pleased to let Abraham take the incoming glory, or more likely, the incoming fusillades.

The only follow-up snippet in the TV media relating to the shoot-out Detective Oswilla caught was a brief interview on Channel Six one evening, about a week after the actual attempted robbery with a beaming Attorney Earl Guarder introduced by Diane Fernwood, the Channel Six bleach-blond reporter as the hero in the Greater First Trust Bank shoot-out, and also introduced to the viewing audience by the dynamic anchor duo, Carter Daniels and Casey Freeman as the returning legal commentator with the local news channel. Oswilla had a vague recollection "Earl's Law" segments used to cover local criminal law capers, and noticed that Earl's hairdo and demeanor were more polished than Oswilla recalled.

■　　■　　■　　■　　■

Tammy McCormack kept tabs on Wonder's recovery, but several days ago, Harrington Hospital stopped updates. Tammy dealt with the special hospital secured section for criminal patients, but could no longer get through. Puzzled, she called the hospital general line using an alias, but the hospital's telephone operator denied Jack Wonder had been admitted to Harrington Memorial.

Detective Oswilla was not surprised, told Tammy to investigate further.

Tammy returned to the beautifully landscaped hospital grounds, and made it as far as the "Information" desk, but received a negative shake of the head after the receptionist looked up the names of patients and found no record of "Jack Wonder."

Tammy told the receptionist she was a police investigator, working for the L.A.P.D. The receptionist apologized, sent her to the Administration offices, where a middle-level hospital manager instructed Tammy to leave the premises immediately.

·　　　·　　　·　　　·　　　·

Detective Oswilla, getting the wash-out report from Tammy, considered getting a warrant from a Fairtown judge to enter the secured Hospital premises and copy the records for Jack Wonder's care. However, without at least evidence of Jack Wonder having been admitted to the hospital, it would be difficult to get such a search warrant approved. The judge would listen, but since bank robberies were always investigated by the F.B.I., the judge would tell Oswilla to call the feds for help. Detective Oswilla knew calling the local F.B.I. office for access to its files was a waste of time.

Tammy McCormack thought an informal investigation during the hospital's night shift might produce results. Oswilla went deaf and before he hung up his office phone, blurted in to the receiver: "Can't hear you, Tammy. Your line's gone bad. Call me back later." Oswilla wasn't taking any chances. He could always deny hearing about her beyond-the-rules plan.

A few nights later, Tammy returned to the hospital about 9:00 p.m., dressed somewhat provocatively for any night visitor, much less for a police investigator. She met and chatted up a butch blond-streaked short haired security guard at the main entrance, whose nameplate on her buxomly chest said "Mary," and whose job was to guard against homeless junkies raiding the night nurse's prescription cabinets.

Tammy was a clever chameleon and sweetly asked Mary how a beautiful woman like Mary had come to this mundane line of work. Mary Megy, for that was the guard's name, must have been in her late thirties, but camouflaged in mascara and rouge to hide wrinkles. She responded to Tammy's flattery, and confided she was on this assignment after being laid off from one of the glamorous Burbank film studios where she had been too friendly in the parking lot with an aspiring starlet in the back seat of her car.

Tammy cozied up to her more. Mary, hoping for the best, gave Tammy the once-over, answered her question, confirming Jack Wonder had been a patient, and told Tammy about the hot, flashy New Orleans attorney who visited Jack Wonder, night after night. Tammy asked the name of the attorney. The Security Guard thought and mouthed "'Pierre,' or some fuck French name."

Oswilla received an e-mail report from Tammy about the potential "go-between" who had accessed Jack Wonder's secured hospital area for a week or so.

Detective Oswilla e-mailed Tammy back to get contact info on the identity of the flashy visitor. He didn't say anything more. Oswilla had worked long enough for the L.A.P.D. to understand all e-mails were read. Oswilla was just asking her to follow up a lead.

Tammy complied, dressed in her frilly outfit, returned to the hospital, cozied up to Mary in ways Oswilla would never learn, and was able to look over the "Visitor Sign In Log" for the previous two weeks, making sure whatever pleasure she was giving Mary was done underneath the reception desk, where any security camera's intrusion would not capture the not-too-subtle reach by Tammy with her warm fingers up Mary's legs, thigh, and beyond. Mary just kept looking at Tammy, forming the slightest smile, nothing more. Tammy looked down on the sign-in sheet, as Mary flipped back slowly through the calendar days, so Tammy could see the names of the visitors. Even if that interaction was captured by the video security cameras, it was a perfectly normal thing to do and wouldn't get Mary a reprimand. Tammy saw the sign in sheet for Jack Wonder's flashy visitor and the attorney's full name, "Attorney Colette St. Pierre," but no phone or e-mail contact information. She felt Mary reach with her right hand touching Tammy's arm beneath the desk, move over her fingers, and help her give Mary additional flirtatious pleasure. Tammy, at last, learning the visitor's full name, slowly moved her hand away from Mary and placed it on the counter. The two women exchanged intimate looks.

Mary loosened up to Tammy, and confided Mary was on the point of turning the visitor, that classy "St. Pierre" chick, but then things went south, the woman was so upset by the patient's disappearance. Mary confided that the last day Attorney St. Pierre came, Jack Wonder had been whisked away by two well-dressed dark-suited officers following orders from a stacked blonde woman in business suit and pony tail who wore dark shades and caught Mary's fancy.

CHAPTER 88
SOMETHING'S UP

Detective Oswilla reviewed Tammy McCormack's follow-up e-mail report on the identity of Jack Wonder's visitor. Tammy noted Colette St. Pierre's signature listed her as a New Orleans attorney. Now, Oswilla could research the Louisiana attorney rolls and track her down. He made a note to himself to have McCormack do the telephone legwork. It would cost, but it was still better than spending hours on the phone. Being wheelchair-bound and having a serious disability, people assumed you needed help for the slightest chore.

Detective Oswilla also followed up his lead about Barry Beneshan's 2006 death.

Since Oswilla had interviewed Attorney Charlie Tobias about that druggie woman's corpse in the L.A. River, and heard about the Beneshan girlfriend's recent disappearance, the death of Barry Beneshan had returned front and center to Oswilla's consciousness. It was too coincidental everyone involved with that messy Beneshan estate such as that big-shot developer Alex was either dead or, like Angel Sedona, missing. Now, Jack Wonder was the newest M.I.A. Taking the sitcom actors off the table for the moment as suspects, Oswilla pondered. *Exhuming Beneshan's body was a Hail Mary pass, but you never knew till the pass was in the air, if it would be caught.*

He filled out and sent over a Police Department Form 2014 to the Coroner's office in Highland Park to exhume Barry Beneshan's two and a half year old corpse from the Catholic cemetery in the Culver City hills. Luckily, Beneshan's family had gone first-class and bought an above-ground crypt, where the embalmed body would still be in decent shape.

Oswilla called the cemetery, and got an okay from the director of the morgue to open the crypt so the Coroner's office could pull out the body.

Once Barry Beneshan's embalmed body was back in the Coroner's cold room, Detective Oswilla had a hunch the medical examiner would find bruising and lacerations – the sign of a crushed larynx on Beneshan's throat which the original cursory examination missed. Had the killer been careless, the smudge of a fingerprint or DNA evidence might still be lifted from Barry Beneshan's neck.

Detective Oswilla wasn't sure where his case was headed, but he signed the form to exhume Beneshan's corpse without informing his department head, Captain Jim Abraham. Oswilla had placed the document in the interoffice mail without bringing the matter up at the weekly Homicide Department case management meeting. He had placed one copy of the document into the Barry Beneshan file in the "closed cases" cabinet and a second copy into the David Alex "open cases" file. That had been almost a week ago.

. . . . .

Oswilla's phone rang.

He picked up the receiver and punched the speaker phone button.

"Detective Phillip Oswilla."

"Phil, it's Jim. How are you doing?"

"Okay. What's up?"

"Swell. Listen. I think we need to talk about the David Alex case. You got a minute?"

"Sure."

"Swell. I'll come by."

"Okay."

Oswilla was glad he got the interoffice memo to the coroner's office out of his out-box four days ago, before Supervisor Abraham, nervous as ever, paid him a visit and closed the door behind him. The tic on Jim's left cheek indicated this would not be a good meeting.

Jim sprawled into the wooden chair opposite Oswilla's desk.

"So, how 'bout them Cougars?"

Abraham always led with a non-sequitur, but jumped past the sports small talk and dropped his cavalier laid-back mask.

The meeting with Abraham was short and not "swell." Captain Abraham was one smoothie who made you reach for your wallet after he left.

In the short face-to-face, Abraham said something about shifting priorities and the understaffed Venice sub-station where there was increased gang activity interfering with the tourist lookie-loos and panic about the murder of the German couple on the boardwalk who were flashing their cameras at every crazy passerby.

Abraham shrugged, slightly apologetic as he communicated the directive from "top brass" about the transfer. There was nothing Abraham could do to keep Oswilla downtown despite Oswilla's years of exemplary service and spotless record, not to mention Oswilla's almost ninety per cent record of solving the most grizzly homicides in the City of the Angels.

In his mind, Oswilla clicked that his Form 2014 had reached the Coroner's Office the previous day. Apparently, the follow-up reaction had been swift and brutal. Oswilla had expected blowback but not this fast and furious.

"Say, Phil. You ever heard about a contractor around town named Eric Dart?"

"Seems, I've heard the name somewhere. Why?"

"Nothing. A big law firm reps him. They don't want any hassle for him."

"I don't hassle anyone."

"Just in case you have a tail on him drop it. You've been keeping your P.I. going strong on the strangled developer's case. That - "

"The David Alex case?"

"Yeah, him. Eric Dart is a big shot competitor to David Alex's construction company from what the scuttlebutt gives."

"Eric Dart has clear sailing now." Oswilla made a mental note to look further into Eric Dart's background.

"Could be. But I'm told Dart's squeaky clean, at least in the homicide bureau. Might be a shade shady in other ways. All those big-time contractors are."

Oswilla nodded in reply as he thought he'd better pass on the old news Abraham already knew.

"I'm exhuming the guy who started the snowball of bodies in the morgue - that Barry Beneshan stiff from June, 2006. We had a case opened briefly on him. Never developed into a solid homicide. Pulled it back from the cold files."

"Yeah, so I heard. Seems like an extravagance."

"Lot of murders followed Beneshan's death."

"Wasn't it ruled a straight overdose?"

"Yeah, but I'm taking another look. Even the F.B.I. has some task force on it."

"The F.B.I.?"

"Yeah. Some RICO violation surveillance started after his death. Beneshan had a lot of sticky fingers in some very hot pies."

"No shit."

"Is that why I'm being transferred?"

"Phil, no way. I told you, it's tactical, to beef up the Venice beach sub-station. All the homeless crazies on the boardwalk? We had to do it after those Kraut tourists were stabbed. We can't have tourists killed in L.A.'s number one attraction."

"So, can I stay on the David Alex case?"

Jim Abraham saw where things were headed. "Okay, and I'll make sure you get whatever support you need. If you get any hassles? I'll back you up. This move is just a tactical office shift to appease the L.A. Tourist Bureau."

"Thanks."

"Swell."

After that order to move his office, Oswilla called the phone number on the business card that F.B.I. agent Denise Trenton had given him at the Forest Park shoot out. The phone line was disconnected. Nor did the F.B.I. return his direct calls to the two lead agents.

Oswilla looked around the bland office in the Los Angeles Central Police Station that had been his home for eight years. A move may not be a bad idea. It would free his mind to concentrate on important cases such as the victims littering the Beneshan corpse's wake.

Oswilla unwrapped a stick of gum, popped it. Chewing gum always helped him focus.

CHAPTER 89
SHOWTIME!

The following Saturday, Charlie spent the day at home going over the *West Nile* music score, practicing lyrics, arpeggios, scales, and thinking about Angel. He desperately wanted to find Angel. He was also coming up with a plan to point the finger at David Alex's true killer.

Charlie had not talked to Tina about his Westwood F.B.I. interview, nor did he confide to her about his meetings with Colette. He took the F.B.I.'s admonitions to total secrecy to heart.

Charlie wanted to make sure Detective Oswilla would not arrest the two TV stars who Charlie now knew through the Jack Smith correspondence to Eric Dart, were innocent of the murder in his bungalow. Charlie came up with a plan to pass on the necessary exculpating information about the two actors as well as the information linking Eric Dart and David Alex's murder to Detective Oswilla without violating his attorney-client confidentiality rules.

Charlie had kept all his notes and insights about his legal work in a diary including notes on the contents in the Eric Dart correspondence file he had come across in the Hannah, Ashley cabinet. It was a matter of getting the notes to Detective Oswilla without personally passing them on.

Charlie wished there was a way he could let Tina know what he was going to do, but, he couldn't take a chance and put her at risk. Charlie would have to leave the diary for the Detective to find, once Charlie vanished from town. The diary had all the essential information Detective Oswilla would need to exonerate Darlene's adoptive parents, and connect the dots that conclusively pointed to Eric Dart's conspiracy in David Alex's murder.

Charlie had thought this plan through. Since the California Supreme Court had voted to allow same-sex couples to marry in its June 16, 2008 *In re Marriage Cases* ruling, and the two stars of *My Momma* were among the first to wed, Charlie hoped to avoid injustice to the two trailblazing social activist actors who had stepped out and changed the state's laws.

He used his cell phone that Colette had slipped him at the Louisiana Café, met a second time with Colette at Nathan and Hal's noisy Beverly Hills delicatessen, where the din from celebrity patrons was so loud, even a sophisticated eavesdropper would not hear Charlie and Colette's whispered, mouth-covered planning to avoid the F.B.I.'s intrusion. Colette St. Pierre agreed to whisk Charlie out of town after the opening of *West Nile*, on Saturday, September 13, 2008 until things cooled down. She would fly him to New Orleans in her private family jet her brother in New Orleans was sending to pick her up and return her home. Her brother, Henri St. Pierre had agreed to put Charlie up for several weeks before his return to Los Angeles in time to make his next performance two Saturdays out.

Charlie counted on Tina reporting him "missing" to the L.A.P.D. after he had disappeared for several days. Tina had become suspicious of his circumstances, especially as she overheard his phone call where he agreed to go down to the F.B.I. building for the last interview. She had repeatedly demanded he explain what was going on, but Charlie had to keep Tina from knowing the facts, to make his plan work out and for her own safety as the F.B.I. agents demanded.

He wouldn't be "missing" for long, but by the time he would resurface back in Los Angeles, Charlie was confident Tina, panicked about his not returning home from the opening night performance, would find the diary, read its incendiary facts, contact Detective Oswilla, file a missing person report, and hand the diary over to Oswilla, with its open pages recounting the critical events Oswilla could piece together.

Oswilla would read the diary and find the the evidence that implicated the Hannah, Ashley, Tannenbaum Senior Partner Jack Smith as the go-between, who referred Eric Dart to the two dead hit men who had killed David Alex.

Charlie was so nervous about his plan, he paid no attention to the news headlines. Reports of financial collapse had become a cacophony of daily distracting distress. Charlie's focus was on catching David Alex's murderer, and on the thrill of opening in *West Nile* the next night. Charlie was going to be on stage, as he had wanted to be. Tina caught his excitement as he prepared for the big Saturday evening opening. She was happy for him, unaware his nervous energy also came from anxiety about the imminence of his bold plan to pursue justice.

There was going to be an opening night gala after the performance of *West Nile.* Charlie, habitually racing from job to job, never had the chance to attend such a "black-tie" affair. Tina understood attending the party was part of the job, and he had no way to get her a ticket as he was only an extra in the choir. Charlie hugged Tina very tight and told her how much he loved her. He would not see her until after his plan to identify David Alex's killer was carried out.

.　　.　　.　　.　　.

Saturday afternoon, Charlie parked in the Music Center parking lot in the employees' section, near the exit, hurried upstairs into the cavernous stage area.

Desmond saw Charlie enter the men's chorus dressing room and stopped shimmying into his costume.

"Charlie, I have something to share." Desmond reached into his coat pocket on the wardrobe rack, pulled out a package and handed it to Charlie.

"Here are a few photos of Oscar's memorial."

Charlie took the photos of Gertrude, Desmond and other Thornhill family members scattering Oscar's ashes off Santa Catalina's Avalon Bay.

Avalon Bay was a beautiful setting to end one's days, romantic, peaceful, unchanged from the 1930's. Since then it had blossomed into an elegant, isolated principality, barely a part of the United States.

Charlie slipped the photos of the Thornhill family gathered on the oversized yacht into his jacket, hung the jacket onto the crowded wardrobe rack, along with his tuxedo, and prepared to get into costume.

Veronica came by. "Charlie. I've got great news."

"Sure, it's our opening night." Charlie took the freshly pressed "mosquito" costume from the rack, and slipped into the tight leotards.

"I got the job in San Francisco."

"San Francisco Opera? That's huge."

"They want me to start right away on their new *Magic Flute* production. The show opens in three weeks."

"I'll miss you, Flora."

"You don't have to miss me," she said coquettishly. "I've rented a nice houseboat in the San Francisco Marina. There's room for two." She gave him a quick hug, moved on. Charlie wasn't sure where her fluttering eyelashes were leading, but he forgot about Veronica's good fortune as Gerry came by.

"One change, guys, listen up. When you tumble through the stage trap door at the end of Act Two? Roll off immediately and go up to the roof party in costume for the gala!"

"No tuxedos?"

"No tuxedos."

Charlie sighed. He just had his tuxedo pressed for the occasion at a non-discount price. The other semi-costumed mosquitoes nodded approval. "Real champagne?"

"The best."

Charlie was less concerned about the quality of the champagne, than about the claws wrapped around his neck two weeks before.

"Hey, Gerry...?"

"What's up, bud?"

"It was jet-black beneath the stage at rehearsal. Can you place some stage lights around?"

"Sure thing. Thanks, Charlie. Wouldn't want a mishap."

Desmond leaned over to Charlie as Charlie pulled on his arm-length extended talons. "We toasted with 'Ricci's Prosecco' at Oscar's wake."

Charlie felt good hearing of the homage to Oscar's life, adjusted his cushioned tunic over his upper torso. Everyone seemed to have a nice send-off. However, Charlie wasn't prepared to chance his.

"Sure hope we get good reviews."

Gerry chimed in "Amen. Praying we'll extend the play-dates."

Desmond ignored Gerry's hope, placed his head-piece over his head.

Veronica adjusted Desmond's head-piece on top of his costume and closed the latches. She turned her attention and lifted the remaining headpiece over Charlie's head and looked him in the eyes.

"I left my new phone number in your tuxedo jacket. Remember. if you're going to dream? You've got to dream big. Beyond San Francisco – the Met in New York? Wouldn't that be awesome?"

Charlie nodded, not paying attention, moved his line of sight to check his walkie-talkie ear-piece to make sure he'd get Gerry's directions and to avoid Veronica's romantic offer.

"Testing…testing. Veronica, I've got to go. It's great you got the job."

"You're okay, Charlie. I hear you." Gerry adjusted the volume on his belt-strapped walkie-talkie.

Charlie gave a good-bye glance to Veronica. "Good to go. Thanks, Flora."

She backed away, not satisfied with Charlie's response, but hopeful he would think about it and change his mind.

"I'll see you, Charlie."

Charlie nodded to her and turned away as she continued down the line of extras.

Charlie moved alongside Desmond, headed towards the stage. Suddenly, he heard a voice through the earpiece.

"Charlie? Can you hear me?" Charlie wasn't sure who the voice came from. He pressed the toggle switch by squeezing his talons.

"Desmond?"

Charlie saw the huge praying mantis head next to him nod.

"Charlie, this will be the last night here for all the Thornhills. We're going away. Come with us."

"Are you going to Isis?"

"We're going to our new homes. Yes."

Charlie nodded through his headpiece.

Desmond's strident voice in Charlie's ear-piece hurt. "The pestilence is coming, Charlie. Come with us. The pestilence is coming."

They were almost at the side of the stage.

Gerry walked ahead. Charlie shrugged, tried to ignore Desmond's urging in his ears, hopped after the other insects and reached his off-stage launching area on the side of the stage.

Charlie peered through the stage curtain towards the audience and was thrilled to see a packed house. The enormous chandeliers and the house lights dimmed. The musicians, visible from their individual lights in the orchestra pit just in front of the stage proscenium, were in place.

Maestro Picollini stepped onto his raised black apple-box, his head slightly above the orchestra members' heads, turned to face the audience, gestured for the musicians to stand. For a moment they stood in their tuxedos and formal evening dresses holding their classical instruments, violins, violas, flutes, bassoons. The audience clapped politely and the maestro bowed and gestured for the musicians to take their seats.

This was opening night.

Charlie looked past the orchestra and saw the applauding glamorous jewel bedecked society wives and their tuxedo clad husbands. Among the front-row celebrities, Director Michelangelo Tantonini, seated next to his beautiful red-head actress wife, Monica Vitelle, pushed his body into the seat, anxious about the imminent performance.

A silhouetted tuxedo and black dress clad duo sat near the left edge of the front row. Charlie tried to make out the shadowy couple. He wasn't sure in the darkness. Their lack of enthusiastic applause, more than anything they were doing made Charlie suspect: it was F.B.I. agent Trenton and her escort agent Long.

Gerry's hand grasped Charlie's shoulder. "Showtime!"

Charlie moved back into the extra's line.

Maestro Picollini wheeled around to face the stage, raised his sliver-thin baton, brought it down precisely as the orchestra began the lyrical overture.

The magnificent red velvet vertically creased stage curtain raised in cadence to the music revealing the stylized suburban San Fernando Valley backyard main set. There were polite gasps and applause from the audience. The performance was underway – an opening night culmination of months of rehearsals to ensure a perfect performance.

The audience "oohed" and "aah'ed" as the life-sized insects hopped, flew, and buzzed to stage center amidst beautiful multi-colored prosthetic birds plummeting from above the stage to the stage floor in a virus caused death plunge.

Charlie felt proud to be a part of the innovative show, bringing music, melody, visual splendor and an avant-garde mythic story to a large audience. Whatever was going to happen would happen.

Charlie was achieving his dream and would not let go!

CHAPTER 90
ACT BREAK

At the end of Act One, the extras hopped in front of the lowered red velvet curtain, bowed after the principals had taken their bows. The audience loved the hopping, and the bowing of the giant insects and rose to its feet with "Bravos." It would be the chorus's only bow to the audience, as the bug chorus would scoot under the stage at the end of the second act. Things were going well.

Charlie hopped back to the dressing room amidst the other extras and grabbed a folding chair.

Desmond sat next to Charlie with cousins Orville Sanders, Fidelio Thornhill, and George Tamarind. They passed pictures of Oscar's wake, holding the photos with their claws, – silently, reverently.

"Are you coming with us, Charlie?"

"Charlie, didn't Oscar tell you why Gertrude insisted on Gus Gas's opera being included in the repertory? *West Nile* is about the end of Los Angeles."

"It's only a story."

"The story's vision is coming to pass. The financial destruction in this city, and in the entire country is a portend of the environmental disasters to come. Oscar sensed the civilized order as we know it, was dying. We're leaving for Isis. Come with us."

"To Greenland?"

"Yes, the homes are ready to move in. The buildings are magnificent. The dome will close over the city when the oceans roll in. The city will stay safe no matter what happens. It's a new city in the arctic becoming the hope for mankind."

"What would I do there?"

"We need an attorney. You're our family attorney now."

Charlie thought back on his life. For the first time someone offered him something major in scope he hadn't sought.

He shook his head. "My life is here. Tina, my wife, home, whatever I do, it is here."

"The end is coming." Orville Sanders sounded sincere. "Oscar had a vision of the seas rolling in. He said a new flood would come to destroy this town's corrupt civilization."

"You won't be alone if you come." George Tamarind chimed in.

Before Charlie could ask what George Tamarind meant, Gerry came in and herded the group outside. Act Two was about to start.

The extras complied, hopped into the corridor, adjusted their headpieces with Veronica's help. She moved opposite Charlie and closed his headpiece clasp with a harsh snap. She held the face mask for a moment.

"I've got to go, Flora. Please." Charlie tried to reach for her hands with his talons, but she moved away, without a word or a glance.

The orchestra started its dissonant crescendo, the harbinger of the final act's scenes of pestilence and death.

Charlie cleared his throat and made sure his small microphone was taped in place to amplify his voice. For the first time in his life, he had undreamed of choices to make.

CHAPTER 91
FINAL CURTAIN

The curtain rose on Act Two, timed to open as the audience applause subsided. The Starlight family was in its stage set back yard. Everything proceeded as it had for the final dress rehearsal.

As the staged pestilence unfolded, and more birds fell from above the stage onto the stage floor, crows, cardinals, bluejays, finches, all victims of the west nile virus, Rudolph Starlight caught his deadly infection from the buzzing insect that landed on his shoulder. The stage lighting turned bloody red. Charlie and the other extras buzzed into position around the swimming pool where Rudolph lay back on a lounge chair, covered in blankets, surrounded by his family.

Rudolph Starlight
My illness is but a minor cold.
I will get well,
With your support.

Maria Starlight
Of course you will.
We love you.

Danny Starlight
We are a family.

Maria Starlight
Maybe going to the doctor would be best,
Although we lost our health insurance,
I can pay for it and work with no rest.

Rudolph Starlight
There's no need. I'll be fine.
I'll take it easy.
All I need is your love,
Rest, and time.

The whir of the helicopter preceded its appearance above the stage. The giant helicopter was dark, ominous, spread its toxic fumes from the air and enveloped the stage with deadly exhaust.

One by one, each insect danced its death dance into the stage opening and fell into the inflatable mattress below the stage floor as the lights faded on Rudolph's family.

Charlie's turn came. He braced himself. Even an eight foot fall into the opening onto a soft landing gave quite a kick, especially in a clumsy costume, where Charlie couldn't control his fall. He saw the basement area light up with two stage lights with bright bare bulbs. Gerry had followed up Charlie's request.

His toes moved past the edge of the stage floor opening for a free fall into the unknown, but Charlie landed squarely on the inflatable mattress below the stage. He rolled towards the edge of the air mattress, as instructed, and two stage hands pulled him off onto the basement floor and stood him upright.

Overhead, Charlie could hear the muffled blast of music at the opera's climax. Charlie could sense the entire building vibrate as the climax became the finale and a crescendo of applause shook the building. The opera resonated as heard from the crowd's sustained applause. Cries of "bravo" echoed in Charlie's ears as he hopped towards the elevator as instructed – to join other chorus members, still in costumes, riding to the roof pavilion for the gala.

Charlie was tired and sweaty inside his costume, happy to get out of the basement's dangers. He felt a sense of euphoric accomplishment. Desmond, cousins Fidelio, Orville and George stepped next to him, took their headpieces off, didn't say a word as the elevator door closed.

CHAPTER 92
ANGELS TOO CLOSE TO THE GROUND

As the elevator opened on the Music Center's rooftop, Charlie stepped forward with the other extras, holding his headpiece in the crook of his arm and saw a helicopter on the rooftop's far corner, its rotor turning. The massive helicopter had flown over the stage. It was not a prop. The helicopter was real!

"Charlie, this is it. Come with us!"

Charlie looked from the four Thornhill extras to the doorway of the helicopter. Standing in front of the doorway was Angel Sedona, arms around Gabriella.

Charlie stopped, not knowing what to do. Angel looked at him.

"Angel wants to come start a new life with us in Isis."

Charlie looked at Desmond.

Angel, with Gabriella following, raced across the roof to Charlie. "Oh, Charlie. I'm so happy to see you. Charlie, are you coming away with us? Please come."

Charlie, uncertain what to do, reached out and pulled her to him, tight as he could, dropping his headpiece. He was very relieved to see her and her daughter again, very happy.

Gabriella started to cry. "Charlie, we love you."

"I missed you," he replied.

Charlie raised Angel's lovely face, looked directly into her eyes. "Oscar told me about what happened."

"Please come, Charlie." Gabriella tugged at Charlie's talons.

Charlie thought of the promise Angel had given him with her eyes, and he could feel her warmth. Oscar had told Charlie in his final whispers why he kept Barry Beneshan afloat for a decade of schemes and dreams. Oscar confided he was Gabriella's biological father. Charlie had not been sure, but now, looking at Gabriella's upturned face in the arced roof-lights left no doubt in Charlie's mind. Gabriella replicated Oscar's bony, gaunt, elegant features. Oscar had become a parent at an advanced age when he needed Barry as the surrogate father.

It wasn't just a matter of Gertrude Thornhill's disapproval. Oscar Thornhill had been in his early seventies when Gabriella was born. Oscar was too old to be a father to a rambunctious, growing infant.

Charlie looked into Angel's large brown eyes, saw her head move, questioning his intent. She had so much to offer. Charlie thought of the life he led back home. It wasn't perfect, but it was getting better.

He thought back on David Alex's staring eyes, as he lay in the studio, dead – killed on Eric Dart's orders to the hired Kalishnikov hit men. Charlie had little doubt about the truth of Oscar's additional confession to Barry Beneshan's murder. Even if Oscar had been delusional in his deathbed private confession to Charlie about snuffing out the surrogate dad, Barry Beneshan and David Alex's deaths were the foundation for this flight to Isis by the Thornhill family. Charlie could not be a part of it.

"Charlie. Come with us now." Desmond gestured towards the sparkling lights of night-time Los Angeles. "Soon, this city will be under the angry ocean."

Charlie looked over the city lights Desmond pointed to. Charlie had heard the rumors for years, about the coming of "the big one," the final cataclysmic ending to the City of the Angels, in which everyone would die and Los Angeles would fall back into the sea – the ocean from which alluvial primate ancestors slithered ashore millennia ago. In the natural order of things, going back into the sea had always been part of some grand plan by the Grand Creator.

Maybe civilization would end with the two rogue bombs – ready to take Jack Wonder's and Boohau Cyclop's revenge for the loss of French sovereignty in North America some two hundred years ago. More likely, things would continue as before – not perfect, just everyday hassles of dreamers like Charlie, chasing their dreams for something better in the City of the Angels.

Desmond looked at Angel. "We must go."

"To Oscar's dreams for a new world." The Thornhill extras, Orville, Fidelio and George stepped next to Desmond, took off their insect costumes. They stopped for a moment, looked at Charlie and sang in unison – a chorus: "To Oscar's vision!"

Charlie got up his courage, looked directly at Angel. "Angel, don't leave. Oscar's vision of destruction is false."

Angel, confused, looked back at him. "What are you saying, Charlie? What am I going to do? Go to Tulsa?"

"No, Barry is taking care of you. You and your family will be safe. I promise. Stay."

The Thornhill clan surrounded Angel. Gabriella, uncertain, moved in front of her mother.

Charlie knew when helicopters took off, you have to hang on to something bolted, and hold on tight. He also knew he couldn't let Angel leave.

"Angel, come with me. Oscar's vision is a *lie*." Angel trembled, clutched Gabriella in panic. Charlie felt an urge possess him. He grabbed her right hand and pulled. "Trust me." Several of the Thornhills tried to pull her with them towards the helicopter. Gabriella huddled next to Angel, was pulled along.

"Remember Rio? You and Gabriella and your parents will be safe. Barry made sure."

Charlie looked into Angel's eyes. She looked at Charlie's. Angel's eyes asked for assurance and seemed to find it in Charlie's confident return unrelenting gaze.

Orville Sanders leaped forward, swung his fist at Charlie. Charlie ducked, pulled Angel away. Angel froze, saw Charlie's fight for her, looked at the Thornhills' panic, and ever so slowly, then faster, followed Charlie's lead away from the Thornhills. Gabriella shadowed Angel. Orville Sanders saw two figures, a couple in tuxedo and formal dress leave the party on the other side of the roof, head towards them.

"It's the F.B.I. We've got to go."

Angel looked Charlie directly in the eye. "Are you sure, Charlie?"

"I'm your attorney, Angel. It'll work out for you and Gabriella, and your mom and dad. Barry set up a trust fund in New Orleans for Gabriella.

Colette St. Pierre agreed to help you through the rough patch. She's leaving tonight and taking you on a private plane to New Orleans."

He grabbed her hand harder, pulled.

Angel acquiesced, then ran faster, alongside Charlie, pulling and pushing Gabriella ahead of her as Orville retreated with the other Thornhills, backwards to the helicopter bay and made it inside before the bay slammed shut.

The powerful overhead rotor energized, and created a hurricane blowing towards Charlie, Angel, and Gabriella.

The two F.B.I. agents, Long and Trenton, were half-way between Charlie, Angel and the helicopter, as the giant mechanical bird became airborne.

Charlie led Angel and Gabriella behind a concrete column next to the elevator, pushed Angel, and Gabriella down, and held on for dear life.

The helicopter rose slowly from the Music Center's rooftop. The F.B.I. agents on the open rooftop fell, flattened by air burst from the helicopter jets, and were pushed backwards towards the gathered guests at the post-performance gala who grabbed onto flying cocktails, glasses of wine, and bottles of beer.

Charlie watched for a moment as the air vortex provided a moment of protection, grabbed and pushed Gabriella into the open elevator as the helicopter receded into the night above the shining lights of downtown Los Angeles before agents Long and Trenton could get up, regroup and race forwards to block Charlie, Angel, and Gabriella's escape.

Charlie didn't say a word to Angel, as he and Angel followed after Gabriella into the elevator, the door shut behind them, and the elevator descended to the parking garage. Angel looked half afraid, half trusting in his confidence as the elevator hurtled down. Gabriella started to cry. Angel hugged her daughter and tried to soothe her fear.

"You missed my birthday party," Gabriella blurted.

Charlie gave an apologetic shrug as the elevator reached the parking lot and he pulled Angel and Gabriella out of the elevator, pushed the emergency button to keep the elevator from ascending to the roof-top, and pulled Angel and Gabriella towards his car

"I'm sorry. I'll make the next one," he assured her. He hurried them through the parking lot maze. Gabriella spoke as she ran alongside.

"Charlie, will we be okay?"

"Yes," Charlie said as he reached the car. "It's going to be fine."

Charlie pushed mother and daughter into the sedan's passenger side, raced around to the driver's side, shimmied out of his costume, started the car and drove out of the Music Center's opened exit gate, just one of the long line of attendees leaving the opening night performance of *West Nile*. He looked at Angel's hopeful look at him in the dark deserted street, and felt the same euphoria he had felt knowing the opera performance ended.

Charlie wasn't sure what the future would bring. He hoped for the best for Angel and Gabriella. He hoped the opera would have a good review in the Sunday morning Los Angeles newspaper, and especially hoped his diary notes would be useful and direct Detective Oswilla to wrap up the David Alex case.

Charlie turned onto the on-ramp of the Hollywood Freeway, headed to Van Nuys airport in the heart of the San Fernando Valley, where Colette's private plane and Colette waited. He looked beyond the red tail lights of other cars and saw the entire sky fill with stars. It was a clear beautiful night, well lit by the full moon. Somewhere, a better life awaited, at least for Angel and her family. Colette would help them reach it. Charlie, in his heart, knew he had a lot of business to finish, before the City of the Angels would let him go.

ABOUT THE AUTHOR

Charles Domokos has written educational media, PBS documentaries, a Telly Silver Award prizewinning independent feature film *Return to Vietnam* and worked as ghostwriter for feature, and cable TV suspense films. He was a staff writer for *Loyola Law School Alumni Magazine* and is a member of the California State Bar Assn. Charles lives in Los Angeles, and Cocoa Beach, Florida with his wife, Jeanne and his Pomeranian dog, Francis.

Author's Website
www.charlesdomokosauthor.com

NOTE FROM THE AUTHOR

Word-of-mouth is crucial for any author to succeed. If you enjoyed *Walking With The Dead*, please leave a review online—anywhere you are able. Even if it's just a sentence or two. It would make all the difference and would be very much appreciated.

Thanks!
Charles

Thank you so much for reading one of our **Mystery-Thriller** novels.

If you enjoyed our book, please check out our recommendation for your next great read!

A Grave Misunderstanding by Len Boswell

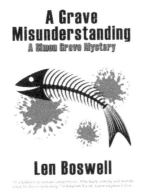

"The Bottom Line: A truly hilarious mystery in the tradition of Janet Evanovich, Thomas Davidson and Rich Leder."

–Best Thrillers

View other Black Rose Writing titles at
www.blackrosewriting.com/books and use promo code
PRINT to receive a **20% discount** when purchasing.

CPSIA information can be obtained
at www.ICGtesting.com
Printed in the USA
FSHW021158070720
71556FS